THIS IS OUR UNDOING

LORRAINE WILSON

Text Copyright 2021 Lorraine Wilson
Cover 2021 © Daniele Serra

First published by Luna Press Publishing, Edinburgh, 2021

A CIP catalogue record is available from the British Library

www.lunapresspublishing.com

ISBN-13: 978-1-913387-65-5

To Granny
For showing me that anything is possible.
I think this would have tickled you pink.

Contents

Chapter One

Some days, Lina Stephenson forgot about her ghosts entirely. She almost believed that the miles between her and her family were choice rather than necessity. Today was one of those days, and the last.

There was a storm spinning in across Western Europe, extinguishing wildfires. There were bomb attacks and migrants drowning, but here in the Rila mountains there was only Lina cycling old roads to Beli Iskar, its red-tiled houses dotted between trees and incandescent in the sun. A cat crossed the track and it was still a surprise to see them, after flu and the culls. Two women in their garden shifting logs were watching her. Here it begins.

'Dobro den,' Lina said, lifting one hand briefly. The younger, darker one gave a curtailed nod with her hands full of wood; the elder murmured, 'Dobro den.' Then, without emotion, 'It was dead.'

'Alright,' Lina said in the Bulgarian she had carefully mastered. 'May I retrieve the tag?' They had known she must come and if she got her tablet out she could localise the signal perfectly, but she made no move to do so. The women glanced at each other, then away, and it was the elder who moved into the road, her hand making a graceful gesture that was somehow both inviting and resigned.

She took Lina to the open barn of the neighbouring house, its irregular walls draped in roses and hops. There was no-one around other than the two women, but as always the ancient walls seemed watchful to Lina, the shadows dense beneath the twisted vines. The dead deer was waiting in the dusty shade, already gutted, hanging from its hocks and skinned neatly, limbs long as if it were still leaping.

'Blagodaria,' she thanked the woman and, as she did so, heard new voices. Three men, the younger woman standing with them in the road, her face turned to the two cows now waiting sleepily beside her, their dark eyes mournful and their bells silent. 'Dobro den,' Lina said again. 'I'm here for the tag.' To collect the tiny data tag either she or Thiago had injected into the thick muscle of the deer's neck three years ago. From it she would learn its last moments, its heart rate, stress level, immune response, reproductive condition. For her research, of course, but first and by the laws of the Environment Security Force who owned this mountain reserve and thus everyone in it, she must distinguish the crime of poaching from a permitted scavenge.

These people would not have dared poach one of the deer, so many of which were tagged. If they took such a risk it was only ever for smaller game, less likely to be missed, but they knew she must check anyway. One of the men, young and corded with muscles and hostility, pushed his way into the garden.

'The tag?' he said, and laughed. At the harsh sound, one of the cows lifted its head, bell singing quietly and the old woman murmured something Lina didn't catch, his name perhaps.

'May I?' Lina said. It was the wrong thing to say, she realised immediately, the request too glaringly empty.

'Will you collect them from us too? When we die? It is not enough that your cameras watch us but you must track us as well, make us animals.' He gestured at the hanging deer, the cavity of its emptied body like an eye and an accusation.

Given the timing, Thiago had offered to run this errand in Lina's place and Lina had said no. Yet now she was hyperaware of her own body, as tall as the men but without their solidity, faster perhaps, not stronger. She had a knife in her bag for dissecting out the tag, but the thought of it skimmed over her mind without traction.

'I know,' she said gently, 'it must feel that way. An insult and an invasion.' The other men shifted but she was watching this one, young enough to still think he could change things. Perhaps he could, she thought, but not like this. And neither could she. 'I am sorry,' she said. 'I cannot...' the defence she had been about to give died in her throat and she sighed. 'I am sorry.'

The old woman spoke again, 'Let it go, Kolev. Let it go now.' Lina looked at her sharply, thinking that the suggestion in her *now* had been instead *for* now.

'And if she says it was poached, to justify this new law?' It was one of the men beside the patient cows, beside the young woman with her head still averted. He spoke as if to no-one, voicing a thought aloud. The young man stared at him and then spun back to Lina.

'I would not,' she raised her hands. 'If it was gathered then that is what I will tell them. I want this no more than you. You know that.'

They didn't, though – she could see that. ESF's new law had obviously made them doubt her. After all, they only knew her as a foreigner scientist come to study their mountains. Isolated from the politics of nation States perhaps, but still belonging to ESF, who were, on their protected lands and in their own way, totalitarian. She met Kolev's eyes and wanted to say to him, *I understand, and if I were you, I'd fight too.* But of course she didn't.

'I carry an ESF tag as well,' she said instead. 'It is nothing like these,' gesturing at the silent carcass. 'Just location, and life, that is all it does.'

His fists tight against his thighs like he was holding them there through sheer will, Kolev opened his mouth. The knife came to Lina's mind again as his brown muscles moved and she wished now that Thiago had come. But the young woman spoke over Kolev, resting a hand lightly on the shoulder of one of the cows.

'But that is for your safety, doctor. And can you say this is also why they wish to tag us?' She tilted her head, catlike.

'Partly,' Lina said slowly, 'Yes. From accident and ... we think there are traffickers using the border here.' Trying not to emphasise the word *traffickers* in case they thought she knew who else moved through the high passes, and why. She wasn't lying; the people who smuggled refugees towards covert slavery in the north were dangerous. But the woman watched her steadily and everyone else, Lina realised, watched the woman. Ah, she thought, so it would be this woman's choice whether she were allowed to leave peacefully. Lina was ESF; they would not dare hurt her, and yet the woman watched her for a long time and Lina wondered if the woman could read her past, whether that would be a good thing.

Eventually, with a shrug and already turning away, the woman said, 'Well then, collect your tag, doctor. The deer needs jointing and it is getting warm.'

Lina nodded. The young man glared at her but then swung away, the cows' hooves whispering in the dust and their bells the only sound other than the river and a thrush scolding them from the roses.

It took less than a minute for Lina to pull the tag from a shallow cut in the deer's neck, and when she turned the old woman was holding a bowl in her peaty hands, filled with water for her to wash. 'Blagodaria,' Lina said again, but the woman was already moving away and by the time she was back at her bicycle, the sound of logs being stacked had already begun.

With the tag safely stored, she rode slowly back towards the station. When her tablet chimed, she reached back to pull it out, freewheeling around potholes and the flowerheads of chamomile rising from broken tarmac, but it was only Thiago checking in, so she pinged back a single symbol confirmation without stopping. He was up on Ibar's west slope today and it might, she thought, not have gone any differently back in the village if it had been him there instead of her. For all his physical presence, the villagers hardly lived soft lives, and she didn't think they saw him any differently to her; provisionally accepted, provisionally safe.

The track wound uphill lazily from meadow to forest to meadow, passing a shepherd with his three huge, matt-coated dogs, the sheep's voices fading behind Lina to be replaced by the early grasshoppers' erratic chirrs. Thiago knew, just as she did, about the people who slipped away from the villages to fight or sabotage or rescue and slipped back again if they did not die.

And where she only deleted their photos, he paid attention to the people using the forests and passes, so perhaps he would have recognised that woman's face. But just as Lina had come here to escape London State's eyes, she suspected he had done similar for Spanish State, or the PeaceKeepers, his old force. She didn't know, but she knew the people here were not in any danger from him.

A nutcracker laughed harshly beside the track and another answered further away. Speeding up over the crest of a rise through canopy-spangled light, Lina stopped thinking about secrets and States, something she had become very adept at, and instead listed the tasks she needed to do. The next small mammal survey was due, and one of last year's young bears had developed a fever, so Lina would go in search of her, unhappy with the clarity of the camera images she had gathered. Two jackals had strayed beyond the reserve boundary and Lina needed to decide whether that mattered enough to the population for her to retrieve them.

She was in the older part of the station, once a farmhouse, now their laboratory, when Thiago returned through a dusk stretching itself out of spring and into summer. She heard him washing his hands at the outdoor tap but didn't turn until he spoke quietly from the doorway.

'The deer?' He held his heavy bag easily in one hand, the other rubbing over the dark stubble of his hair.

She shrugged lightly, 'Natural. TB. And they are within their scavenge quota.'

'The villagers?'

She knew what he meant. 'They were okay.' Then, more honestly and because he was watching her, 'some tension. Understandable though.'

'Hmm.' His black eyes narrowed very slightly, but that was all, and then he sat at his desk, stretching one leg, the false one, out with a slight sigh.

She thought of telling him about the woman, asking how they might manage when ESF tagged them all and ought she and Thiago do something to let them keep their secrets. But, prevaricating, she instead ran a quick scan of all her tag data. Carnivora, Large

Herbivores, Raptors, Owls, Galliformes, Bats; each animal's tag appeared on her maps as a galaxy of lights. Most were apparently motionless but a couple, assuredly eagles or vultures, were swinging vast arcs across the landscape. It was a strangely potent sight, a world of teeth and herbivory, birdsong and night-times, all gathered onto her map like jewels.

In the corner of the map window, an amber alert icon flashed. Lina leaned forward, clicked on the alert report and when the comment read only, *short-term offline alerts at frequency above 2% threshold,* she accessed the time stamp and watched twenty minutes of the afternoon replay itself. Short-term offline, yes. But not anything she had seen before. On her map was something passing peristaltically over a forested mountain flank like the shadow of a cloud, a small space where every single layer of tags darkened until it swept on and the tags re-awoke.

'T?' she said quietly, setting the time window to replay, zooming in. He came to stand behind her and they watched it together. A shadow turning all their tags off then on again, and then vanishing itself.

Tags occasionally failed, their tiny thermal-charged batteries giving out for no reason other than chemical churlishness, lightning sometimes, fire or a particularly determined poacher. Weather or satellite movements might chew at the signals, or an animal's burrow reach so deep that they winked out like blown bulbs. All of these faults Lina knew, but this was different.

'Problem with the satellite link,' Thiago said. 'I'll take a look at the connection logs.'

'But the scale,' Lina said. The lab door was still open and a moth flew in as if summoned to reel bewildered against the ceiling. 'It's too small to be satellites.'

Thiago was already moving back to his own desk. 'Maybe,' he said. 'Let me look. I'll check my layers too.' Trees and water, seismic and weather, which she didn't cover. She left it because he was probably right and was better able to check than her. But still, she watched the time loop again, disconcerted. Things that did not fit always disturbed her; it was an old instinct made usually meaningless, now.

'Leave it,' Thiago said abruptly and without turning. 'Check the news. There's something about London. Nothing bad.'

London. Her family was there, her father and adopted brother. She was already clicking away from her data and onto a news feed where headlines were screaming about assassins and resistance plots and manhunts. A name that she remembered distantly, a position of power he had been aiming for even back then.

'Christopher Wiley,' she read aloud. 'Minister for Internal Security. Found dead in his home late this morning by his teenage son. State Investigators are looking for two suspected resistance terrorists.' It was a relief to hear the steadiness of her voice. When she turned to look at Thiago, he was facing half-away but smiling very slightly.

'One less then,' he said, and it made her laugh.

But *who*, she was also thinking. Surely no-one she had once known. It had been years. And then, not entirely disconnected, *the poor boy.*

'It doesn't say how,' she said. 'I'm going to call Dad to check in.' Thiago turned to look at her, the lines around his eyes a little pronounced but that familiar half-smile still there. He cannot have missed her tension, but he only nodded and she left him there to cross the three-sided courtyard into the new house.

On the third floor, past two floors of unused bedrooms, was their kitchen and lounge. One large, glass-walled space that gathered every inch of the vast landscape around them like a gift, or, she thought some days, like a mirror. She always vidcalled her father from here because he liked to see the mountains and she had never dared ask whether that was because he saw little other than tired streets and the city walls or because he wanted to see for himself how far away she was, and how safe.

Those mountains were nothing more than grey-blue outlines now against a darkening sky, but she sat with her back to them anyway, so that he could see.

'Lina,' he said almost before his image had formed, as if he had been waiting.

'Hey, Dad,' she said, smiling helplessly at his worn face, the half-visible shape of the cat at his elbow. The microphone was just barely picking up Aristotle's purr and Jericho's music pulsing in another room. 'Everything alright?'

'The streets are quiet,' he said. 'There's a curfew and a few more checkpoints. But we're perfectly fine, Lina love. School is open and so is my office. Life continues undaunted.'

Behind him, Jericho slipped into view and Lina waved. He waved back unsmiling, gathered Aristotle up into his arms and moved offscreen with a slow spin, almost a pirouette, the cat cradled against his dark cheek. They barely knew each other, she and her brother, because their father had only adopted him in the short weeks before she left. But she knew these things: he hated blood and moved with rhythm and grace, he rarely sat still; years of their father's love had almost erased the years in the camps. 'You seen any foxes?' she heard him call. This was something else she knew – he loved foxes. Perhaps because they survived the camps too.

'Yes,' she laughed. 'Dad, tell him yes. There should be cubs out soon. I'll send vids.'

Then, when her dad was already talking about neighbours and books and asking quiet questions about her work, she said, 'You will be careful.'

It was unnecessary, but just like he needed to see her mountains, she needed to say this.

He smiled, curled his hand around a mug that she knew would hold tea gone cold, and said gently, 'There's no need, Lina. But yes, of course.'

The first of the night's stars was reflected on her screen, overlaying her father's face. He must be able to see the stars too then, behind her, untouched by light pollution, air pollution, walls. When they cut off the call she could hear Thiago's fractionally irregular footsteps climbing up towards her, and she tilted her head back against the chair, waiting, thinking again, *who had done it*, and, *did she know them.*

Chapter Two

She was sitting below the Seven Lakes peaks in a high clearing where true forest was giving way to dwarf pines and juniper. There were late crocuses in the snowmelt and their colours shone ethereal in the lowering light. Lina had laid honeycomb in the grass below her and the bear's tag was already moving this way along the contour of the slope because there had been honey here last evening and the evening before, drone-dropped by Lina in readiness.

'Come on, sweetie,' Lina whispered to the forest edge where the bear would hopefully emerge. The telescope and the barrel of the rifle were cool beneath her hands and habit made her check the loaded syringe again. A black woodpecker called to her left and its heartbeat flight crossed the clearing in the corner of her eye. Two ravens passed overhead, painted by the sun when they turned their wings, and the dot on Lina's tablet screen paused then moved forward again. The bear appeared between the trees, lifting its delicate muzzle into the air, tasting honey, the coming rain, probably her but hopefully not more than a trace.

She moved slowly, one steady swing so that the bear coming towards the waiting honey did not think to look up. It was favouring its left hind leg heavily, and although she couldn't see it from here the tag had told her plenty. Fever, leucocyte count, hunger. Two things now: she only got one chance at a shot, and if it felt the needle hit it might run towards her. Unlikely, as she was uphill and the slope was strong. But it was a possibility you had to be aware of before you took the shot. Thiago was further behind her, waiting with a rifle that was loaded with a flare instead of antibiotics, and another loaded with neither, but he had never yet needed either.

The dim screen of her tablet lit with a message icon but Lina barely noticed, her hands steady and grass around her shoulders. The bear lifted its head again, turned a little, poised like time itself held still, and Lina fired.

Two partridge exploded from the grass just behind her and them, or the shot, made the bear spin her way, groaning anger and confusion and fear. Lina lay the rifle down, pressing her palms against the earth, aware of Thiago above her so strongly it was as if he had reached out to touch her. The bear came forward, growling again, swung its head and lifted its wounded paw from the ground. Honey, she thought to it, honey. Not sure if it was enticement or endearment. Her tablet flashed again beside her, but the bear when it growled again sounded only sad, its voice low and lonely in the quiet clearing and she knew it would turn before it did so. Knew it would go back to the honeycomb before it did so, the bright flash of the syringe already fallen from its dark fur.

'Nice shot,' Thiago murmured beside her and Lina jumped. The bear had gone only a minute or two ago and, despite listening for him, she had heard nothing until he spoke.

'You bugger,' she said without weight.

He laughed softly. 'Ready?' But she was already coming stiffly to her feet, feeling at last the cold that had crept into her legs. Above them, the mountains were an amber chiaroscuro as the sun slipped away, and it was a long walk back to the truck. But the bear was full of antibiotics now, the balance of anthropogenic harm a little redressed. Besides, it was always wondrous to see such an animal with her own eyes, to be beside it in the wide world. She smiled at Thiago and knew that he knew exactly how she felt.

They were down into the trees when she remembered the message. The ground underfoot was black mulch scattered with ferns and fungi, so she did not slow as she pulled the tablet out.

The message that had come while she waited in the grasses was from her father and only eight words long.

JH arrested. State investigating connections. Be careful, love.

JH? JH.

James Hanslow.

Lina didn't realise she had come to a stop until Thiago's voice reached her, repeating questions from some vast distance. Arrested. Investigating. Christ, she thought. Christ, oh fuck, oh Christ.

His smile, his hand on her thigh, his dark face in the dawn full of fear and courage.

'Lina? Lina, what is it?'

It took an eternity to get the tablet back into her bag, to then look up at her friend without ... without screaming, without crying? She was not sure. She'd known this would happen eventually. She'd *warned* him. Jesus, she thought. Oh James. Jesus.

'Yes,' she said, the muscles of her mouth numb. 'I'm fine. Just ... just my dad checking in.' Shaking her head slowly. 'It's nothing.'

But it wasn't nothing, and those eight words were so vast that it felt impossible to contain them. Thiago was watching her in the coffee-rich dark, and her mouth was opening to tell him, when she froze. *State investigating connections*, her father had said. She shut her mouth and stared at Thiago. She trusted him with everything, her life, her soul.

But you didn't trust, even when you wanted to. That much of Lina's old conditioning remained.

'Lina,' Thiago said, so quietly it was barely more than air.

She wanted to turn and walk into the forest until she was alone. Have time to separate out her father's words from memories of love and from Thiago here, black-eyed and waiting. *State investigating connections*. Oh god, she thought again. Oh James, what have you done?

'It's nothing,' she heard herself repeat, felt herself take one step and then another, felt Thiago follow just behind. He wouldn't ask again, she thought. 'Just my dad. I need to...' to what? Become someone she had been long ago? 'It was just about that assassination.' Taking a breath, pine needles catching in her hair, Thiago steady and silent. 'You know.'

There was movement in the trees downslope and another time Lina or Thiago might have checked their tablets for bear or boar or deer, wolf or jackal or just something smaller made large by the darkness. Neither of them did so.

'Getting nasty, is it?' Thiago said eventually, the forest quiet around them once more. He didn't ask.

Oh James, she thought again, broken doorways and prison walls rearing up behind her eyes. *Where are you from*, she wanted to ask Thiago suddenly. *Really from? Are you from hunger and Statelessness, from war or camp or just the insidious weight of fear? Have you ever had someone you love taken away?*

If I tell you this, will you risk yourself to help me, or will you protect yourself and turn away? Could I bear it either way?

Instead, as if she was tearing herself into two people, she said steadily, 'Just the usual, I guess.'

And then remembering that she *did* know where Thiago was from, some of it. He was from the PeaceKeepers. Keepers of the peace through strategic wars and political threat, who State Investigators turned to when their troubles crossed borders.

Be careful, her father had said and for a moment Lina feared she might be sick. She breathed deeply, an owl called hollowly from the opposite slope and neither of them spoke as the track dipped down to a stream cradled by mosses.

Be careful, he had said. But how? James Hanslow, her brave and stubborn James. Tears she could not shed scalded her lungs.

It was late when they got back to the station, but Iva had left a flask of tea on Lina's desk and a pot of honey beside it. As Lina put the three guns away, secured the darts, flares and bullets and set her tablet to charge, Thiago made tea, holding one out to her when she was finished. Steam coiled over her face as she lifted her drink and she could smell the honey that Thiago had added to hers without needing to ask.

'I love Iva,' she said, thinking, please let us be normal.

Thiago laughed and the muscles of Lina's stomach eased a little. He was massaging absently at the point where flesh met prosthesis on his leg, so it must be aching a little from the steepness of the climb.

James had not been like Thiago. Had never had the hardness

nor the silence that Thiago held, nor, if she was honest, the ability to be so unspeakingly, unquestioningly *there*. He'd been beautiful and restless and sensitive and ... and she was already thinking of him in the past tense.

She held her breath and set her mug down so carefully it made no sound at all. There had been a moment long ago, cornered in an abandoned building awaiting either discovery or deliverance, when he had laid his fingers on her cheek, kissed her and said in a whisper, 'We are unbreakable.' It had been said from fear and fierce belief, but she remembered it now like he was in the room with her. Oh James, she thought.

'Remember to breathe,' someone said and Lina was back again, James far beyond her reach and Thiago not quite watching her, drinking his tea.

'Sorry,' she said meaninglessly.

Thiago gave an abbreviated shrug. 'You go so still sometimes I think you'll stay that way.' He grinned at her. 'Good for darting bears. Not so good for drinking tea while it's hot.'

Good for avoiding detection, bad for escaping it. Of course, she thought, realising what she needed to do. Her pulse pressed against the skin of her wrists, but it was steady and when she lifted her tea again, so were her hands. 'Well then,' she said. 'I'm just going to see where our bear went afterwards, then shower and bed I think.'

Thiago looked at her slantwise but only nodded and pushed to his feet. 'Goodnight then,' he said from the doorway and she was surprised how easy it was to smile at him. How natural it felt to set his deadly past separate from the him, now, in this single moment.

One quick message to an account and a name that might have been abandoned years ago. Just an *Autumn, what's happening?* Three words, but enough to exhume things she'd thought gone for good. Then, after a moment of thought, one more on a site selling salvaged boat parts in Folkestone and a man who owed her and was honourable enough for that to matter. *'Jaco, long time, how's the wife?* Codes and backup plans. Old habits.

There was Helda too for new IDs and travel permits, and Vitaly in Gdansk, if she could find them and if they were still alive. But she needed to hear from Autumn first, and contact head office to ask for permission to leave the reserve. But that would have to wait until tomorrow.

So, finally, her dad. This time the call rang several long seconds before he answered.

Quietly, because Thiago was out of the shower now, moving around his bedroom, 'Dad, listen.' Knowing that ESF's encryption was the best there was, but also knowing that they might be listening, 'I think you two should come visit. I'm–'

'Lina love,' he said, his voice granulated by the connection, 'wait, don't–'

'No, Dad, listen, please. I think it's a really good time, right now. You understand? I'm going to ask ESF for travel permits then meet you en route, okay? I don't know the details yet, but it will be soon, hopefully a few days. Will you be ready?'

'It is that bad?' he said without accusation, but it felt like one regardless. What could she possibly say? Maybe not, maybe not at all; but how could they take that risk?

He watched her steadily but she couldn't speak and finally he said, 'Alright. Alright, if it comes to that, we'll be ready.' And the simple fact that he had acquiesced so easily made her heart skitter. 'But Lina, stay on ESF land. You must. If we can come to you, then ... yes. But stay there. Please. Promise me.'

The call ended and Lina sat in the dark, the house quiet now aside from the subliminal sound of dormant machines and a low wind pressing against the windows. Her father would not go back to sleep immediately. He would rise quietly so as not to wake Jericho, Aristotle would wend around his ankles, and they would sit together to drink tea in the city-lit night. She pulled tangles and heather stems from her hair and sighed. The very best she could hope for James was that if he was not accused of direct involvement in the killing then he might sing them enough betrayals to earn a Stateless life. Exiled into transience or the lawless, unofficial shanty-camps. But at least not dead.

When she had been nine and ten, she'd liked to imagine her mother in one of those camps. Surviving miraculously, waiting for her.

Carefully, as if the memory lay within blown crystal, Lina shut the thought back away.

It might make no difference to her family whether he talked or not. Her name and his would be linked somewhere in old State files, her name would lead to her father's, and neither of theirs would withstand too much scrutiny. And her father and Jericho in London...

She rose and went outside into the meadow clearing surrounding the station that in daylight was a universe of flowers and insects on the wing, but now was a dreaming sea silvered by a waning moon. There was a tree stump twenty paces out where a wagtail often kept watch, and she sat there with grasses whispering around her legs. The breeze tasted of rock and high places, ghosts of the mountains that had been her sanctuary for so long.

She did not know how much her father knew, beyond the simple fact that if James were part of that assassination then she would be suspected simply because they had once loved one another. It only touched at the truth, but he had agreed without arguing. That was good, and it was also terrible.

Chapter Three

Sheer habit got Lina up early despite a night of being hunted through her dreams. She dressed in field clothes stained by mosses and tiny smears of blood, mostly hers, and only standing in a misted dawn-light did she pause, turning from her bike to go up through the main house to the kitchen seeking something to chase half-remembered horrors from her head.

Over the kettle's hiss, she heard the old house door open again and came to the balcony to see Thiago walking to the truck, pausing when he saw her bike. Then, as if feeling her gaze, he turned to look up at her. She raised a hand, said, 'Coffee?' and when he shook his head, added, 'I'm doing the small mammal transects.'

Normality. It always seemed so solid, until it wasn't.

Thiago gave his short, inverted nod. 'I'm off to the east villages. Want a hand after?'

'If they're busy,' she meant the traps, 'I'll let you know.'

He nodded, gave a gentle sort of salute and then was gone, the truck's too-loud engine quickly swallowed by trees and layers of mist. With her coffee in the flask waiting, Lina ought to have gone too but instead sat on the balcony, tipping her head up to an amber and pearlescent sky, listening to the meadow's susurrations and the very first cirl bunting singing from a solitary birch tree. Above her, Iva had recarved the god Perun's circle symbol into the wooden lintel, protecting them, but Iva was not here yet and the house was empty.

There was no reply from Jaco, but there was a ping from Autumn. Simple code to let the sender know when the other person was online. Lina let it activate and waited, pressing the tips of her fingers against the very edge of the tablet until the nailbeds were bloodless.

An app opened on her screen, an unknown account but a familiar call sign.

- *Gemini. Pole Star. You heard then. We'll get your family out now. One hour. Bakerloo to port 2. Use this contact only.*

Scrabbling to type, stunned, Lina replied, *Will do. Is there news of-*

The app deleted itself.

Lina stared at the space it had occupied. Fuck, she thought, running a hand through her hair. She hadn't even needed to ask for help, had been expecting them to say, *A week, maybe two.* Say that there was no danger. Fuck.

The call to her dad went unanswered the first time, and Lina curved over the tablet like someone sheltering a flame. 'Wake up,' she whispered, pressing the call icon again.

'Lina?' The screen lighting his sleep-creased face ghoulishly.

'Dad,' she spoke fast. 'Dad, pay attention. I have friends coming to get you and Jericho out now. Take a small bag with a change of clothes, meds and water. They'll be there in an hour. They'll say Autumn sent them, okay?'

'What?' He was pushing himself up to sitting, blinking, frowning.

'Quickly, Dad.' Her hands were cold, all her blood pooling in her heart. 'They'll keep you both safe. Autumn, remember that.'

'Already? But there's no need–'

'I'm coming to you,' she interrupted. 'I'll meet you further along the line, okay? Dad, you have to go. It might be the only chance we get.'

He looked away from her, then back again. It was happening too fast, she thought. Or was she only out of practice?

'Alright. We'll go. But Lina, stay there.'

'Thank you. Don't worry about me. Go get ready. Be careful.'

'Lina...'

'*Go*, Dad.'

He went and she wanted immediately to call him back.

She sent a meeting request to her line manager in Zurich,

mentioning leave and travel permits, not mentioning her family until she could do so face-to-face. *Use this contact only*, Autumn had said, so she didn't message Helda and instead rose, needing the physical exertion now and the dawning forest.

After she had cycled as far as the old road allowed, she left her bike among the dark, dusty leaves of faded peonies to walk on through the upper margins of the fog, and because it did not do to startle some of the wildlife, she made no effort to be quiet. Humming snatches of song out of habit, allowing her feet to land on brittle branches, her mind drifting between prison cells and the Bakerloo route twisting out through the city walls down to Folkestone. They would move through London in daylight, wait for evening to slip around the barriers, then to a safe house in the drought country of the High Weald. The next night, or the night after, down to the coast where Jaco would be waiting, or his replacement if he was lost. She remembered the route vaguely, although it hadn't been hers and it might have changed.

There was a stream off to her right; a dunnock and a mistle thrush were both singing, a squirrel *chirred* alarm and its claws skittered audibly as it climbed. The air smelled of dawn and water as she reached the point in the valley where a small electronic beacon marked the first trap in her first transect of the morning. The path forked here, and there was a stretch of mud full of last night's footprints. Lina frowned at it. A badger, some small mustelid, men. Two of them passing upslope. And up here they could only be those nationalist rebels leaving home. She would mention it to Thiago, but soon it would not be enough simply to delete the camera captures.

Kneeling in the soft earth, she lifted the first trap, thinking: they would be on the move now. She wouldn't hear from them until they were outside the city, perhaps not until they were with Jaco. Two indignant striped mice stared out at her from their cage, whiskers brushing the metal bars and pale paws wet with dew. The morning's first butterfly wove sleepily past her and Lina slipped one mouse into the bucket and the other into the palm of her gloved hand. 'Hello,' she murmured to it, and the familiarity of data collection, the boneless sinuosity of the warm life within her palm, briefly stopped her counting the miles between here and home.

The fifth trap contained a weasel, caught in pursuit of whichever rodent it was whose blood streaked the floor of the cage. Its tiny, galactic fury would normally have made her laugh but today did not. Something about the metal bars, the blood and the undaunted hate in the weasel's eyes made her hands cold as she lifted the cage from the ground. Although normally she would weigh and measure this creature too, today she only released it, then sat back and pushed hair from her eyes with the heel of one hand. Over her left shoulder, sunlight was sparking fires from remnants of fog and lighting the treetops vermilion. A buzzard screamed. It would be okay, she thought. Perhaps the weasel was her and her father and Jericho. Perhaps even James. *We are unbreakable.*

She rose and went to the next trap, then the next and the next.

Later, moving uphill again towards the last transect, an alarm sounded on her tablet and she paused. It was one she'd coded thinking it was unnecessary but doing it anyway. She opened the map and tag data layers, and watched with something like anger as tags winked out and, after a pause, winked back on. It was not large, perhaps covering as little as thirty metres, but it was also directly upslope and drifting slowly west. Shoving her tablet into a pocket, she cut uphill away from the path.

Thiago had said it was only an upload fault, but she went anyway. Checking her screen every few minutes, her progress against the shadow's, then on again till she was panting, gathering scratches on her arms and shins. But she got there in time.

The base-station was attached to a metal stake and Lina sank to the ground beside it, tablet on her knees, prepping data loggers, cutting access down to local passive only; then there was nothing to do but wait. She could have moved towards it, intercepted it, but that would muddy the data, so she stayed and tried not to let some stone-age instinct make her shiver.

'Two hundred metres,' she whispered. A wren shouted alarm, her tablet sounded another. Fifty metres away and all around her, silently, every single piece of tech failed.

Then restarted. She stared through the trees and down at her rebooting tablet, and when the maps reloaded there was nothing there. Or everything. Because the shadow had stopped moving thirty metres away, then vanished. Unvanished. The tags all running without a flicker.

'What the fuck,' she whispered, already scrambling to her feet, but it wasn't any use. At the point where the shadow had vanished there was only a small sub-storey birch tree, a patch of ferns. After a long moment, she turned back the way she had come and wove downslope to the trail she'd left.

Thiago found her, or she found him, where an old bridge leaned doubtfully across a snowmelt ravine. He was sitting on a boulder and studying his tablet, but when she reached the centre of the bridge, he said without preliminaries, 'You went looking for it.'

'Yes,' she said, 'for all the bloody good it did me.'

'Nothing?' he said, looking upslope the way she had come rather than at her.

'No. It vanished.'

'Damn,' he grinned lopsidedly and pushed himself upright, stepping back down the rock, blade flexing and fitting to the slippery contours. 'I'll check the individual cameras for faults,' he said. 'Now?'

She considered it, but with it moving she couldn't believe there was an issue with individual tech, more the models or the uploading. 'No,' she said. 'We'll do the data checks at home.'

He nodded and moved ahead of her along the track. 'You done with the transects?'

'One left.'

They worked the traps together, one handling the animals, the other the weighing scales and tablet. One trap held a fire salamander, the very last had been prised apart and they took a few minutes repairing it, trying to identify the vandal.

'Fox, then,' Lina said when they had ruled out corvids and anything larger.

'Likely.' Thiago set the mended trap back against its stake and looked up at her with a strange expression on his face.

'What?' she said.

He narrowed his eyes infinitesimally and straightened up. 'You're not going to like it.'

'T?'

'I had a call from Sofia earlier.' He rested his hands on his bag, and she looked at them rather than him, the strength of them. 'They want to send us some ... guests.'

'What?' ESF didn't let *guests* come into their reserves. That was the entire point.

'The family of that dead politico in London.'

Lights danced in the corners of her vision. 'What?' she said again, faintly, staring at him. 'No.'

Thiago grimaced. 'Mother and son, possibly some uncle. Bastard politicos. For a week or two, they said.' He paused, began again. 'I tried, Lina. But ESF must have some motive I can't guess at. They wouldn't listen.'

Robbed of breath because this was a haven, *her* haven, defined by snow-painted peaks and the twin gods of science and ecosystem. 'You said no.' It was the haven she was bringing her father to, and Jericho who surely deserved safety. They would be nearing the walls by now, with luck, already on their way.

Thiago's eyes flickered and she looked away to the fractal cathedral of tree trunks behind his broad shoulder.

'I tried,' he said again. And she heard belatedly his anger. 'I threatened to shoot them on sight.'

She closed her eyes and gave a ghastly little laugh. ESF were brave to call his bluff on that. 'Why?' she said quietly so she did not shriek.

'Apparently they're *at risk* after the assassination. The wife persuaded someone in ESF and...' He ran a hand over his scalp, pine needles falling from the folds in his jacket. 'It's fucked up, Lina. I'm sorry.'

It took her a moment to realise the significance of the apology, saw him become aware of it too, of how much he'd revealed by saying that and how much she'd revealed by being unsurprised. Just as she suspected that he had fled from something, he had to guess she had done the same. Even with their pasts tacitly unspoken, she thought they recognised those parts of themselves in each other. It hardly mattered, only she had always been grateful

they'd set their pasts firmly behind them. But his eyes reflected the
vertical shadows of the noonday forest and he spoke as if nothing
had happened.

'The mother's a state journo. Kid's seventeen. Uncle, if he
comes, some security consultant type.'

'Let's go,' she said, packing her bag and standing, then paused. 'A
journo?' Seeing Thiago grimace again. 'When are they getting here?'

'Don't know. Flying, so depends on the weather. Three days?'

'Okay then.' She'd contact Autumn as soon as they were home,
set a different route. Jaco could take them to Stavanger instead of
Gdansk. Or even just Calais, but god no, not France actually, not
with the riots.

She began to walk back along the transect line, Thiago ahead
of her. 'Watch,' he said, pushing aside a branch for her to pass and
she thanked him reflexively, saw him smile.

'They won't stay long. They won't like it here.'

She came alongside him as they reached the track and smiled.
'Good.'

But when she contacted Autumn again, there was no reply. When
she tried to backtrack along the message app's logs, it ended in
dead addresses. It didn't matter, she told herself. As long as she got
in touch with someone before Jaco put out to sea, there would be
time to change the route. She would still meet them because even
if they were couriered the whole way, she wanted to touch her
father's hand and hold Jericho's restive body against her own. There
was nowhere obvious she could think to take them yet, which was
another reason for needing to be there. People were so easily lost
when they did not belong, so she would be beside them until she
knew they were safe. This place here had promised perfect safety,
but now, with the dead politico's family coming... No. Her father
and Jericho would have to hole up somewhere until they left. Two
weeks. Not in Gdansk; Vitaly drank too much to be good for
anything beyond a flying handover. But Stavanger, perhaps. And
there was an ESF office there.

Her line manager sent a message even as Lina was thinking these things, running the cursor of her tablet over maps of the channel and the Baltic sea, the clock in the corner of her eye like a dwarf star.

- *Can't talk today, I'm afraid. Tomorrow at 4.30 any good? Re: leave, you're due plenty, but depends where to. No travel to Med coast, of course, or the flood regions in France, Belgium etc. We'll need itinerary as you know, and our own security clearance. If you pull that together, I can take it to Group Head in our Monday meeting. Isla.*

'Jesus,' Lina muttered, rereading the message as though the words might become less intractable. Tomorrow was Thursday and Monday was a whole five days away. She looked at the clock again. Four fifteen. Nearly twenty-four hours until she could speak to Isla, and Jericho and her father would be at the walls now, in a nondescript flat in an overcrowded tower block, with perhaps two more hours before they began the most dangerous part.

She put the call through to Isla's office, but it was answered instead by a neat, pretty, clever-looking man.

'Dr MacKenzie's office,' he said, half an eye on her camera, his hands still typing.

'Hi,' Lina frowned. 'I'm Dr Stephenson. Can I speak to her, please.'

He looked at her properly, briefly. 'I'm sorry, Dr Stephenson, she's in meetings. Is it urgent and what does it concern?' His hands busy, eyes flicking over the screen so it looked like he was reading her body. 'Ah, you asked to file a travel permit request?'

Of course he would be able to see that. 'Yes. Can I–'

'Is it urgent?' he asked again, and his hands had stilled. Almost. One finger scrolling slowly.

'No,' she said. She had done nothing noteworthy, she reminded herself, and her voice was calm even though she was not. 'Not urgent. I was just ... I am out all day tomorrow so I hoped to catch her now. Never mind. Thank you anyway.'

He was watching her now, not with suspicion, because she was ESF too, and ESF looked after its own. But because no-one got to have secrets and he was cleverer than his position warranted. 'Alright, Dr Stephenson,' he said. 'Have a good day.'

'Yes,' she said to a screen already gone blank. 'Fuck.'

Chapter Four

They would be through the walls now. The thought rose as she fell from deep sleep to wakefulness. They would be in the second safe house, the dead farmland around them, and if her father was not sleeping then he would be sitting against a wall with Jericho's head on his lap, running his fingers over Jericho's cornrows the way he had once stroked Lina's hair. Sometimes with her weeping, most often with her staring into the dark scarcely breathing in case in doing so she forgot her own name.

There was no message from them, but that was okay. They might be sleeping now.

Iva was still there when Lina returned from another morning of weighing small rodents and waiting for news. She was cooking both lunch and dinner at the same time, as she always did, so that she could return early to her home in the nearest village, Govedartsi. As Lina reached the kitchen Iva gave her a long, frowning look, pushed a chair away from the table and said, 'Sit. I made only salad, but I will cook you eggs too.'

'Oh no,' Lina began. 'You don't–'

'You slept badly? It is the news of these people coming, no?' She made a hissing sound that drew deep lines around her mouth and slapped the palms of her hands together. 'Mr Ferdinando, he told the village and we said keep them here,' pointing at the floor, meaning the station. 'Only here, it is best, yes?'

Iva was speaking English because it pleased her to speak her fourth language and, Lina had always suspected, also because it was a small way of keeping her job here with ESF separate from her home in the village where her family had lived for all of history and ESF had granted them permission to stay.

'I'd much rather not keep them anywhere,' she said.

Iva's eyes were full of glittering understanding and not a little malice. 'So. Perhaps the food here tastes so bad they will go?'

Lina laughed. 'Genius. Perhaps they will find snakes in their rooms too, or...' struggling to imagine what a State person might find disgusting, 'swarms of horseflies?'

'That is better,' Iva said, nodding and pouring tea into a waiting mug. 'Here,' handing it to Lina, 'you have colour in your face now. That is better.'

'Is Thiago here? I didn't check.'

Iva had her back to Lina again so Lina only saw her shoulders move. 'I do not know. But is that the truck?' It was, and unusual for Iva to hear it before her, as if she had been listening. 'There. I must take the milk down to the old house. I will tell Mr Ferdinando that his lunch is waiting. Here, eggs. Eat.'

She filled a shallow bowl with milk and carried it to the stairs balanced gently in both hands, her eyes on that and not on Lina. The milk was for the domovek, the folkloric guardian of the old house, but Iva seemed more urgent than her old ritual deserved. Or perhaps Lina was simply reading urgency into everything. She woke her tablet again.

And at last there was a message. She was already smiling as she opened it.

-Lina love, your friends never came. We're still home safe. Talk later? Dad x

They never came.

Her dad and Jericho were still in London State.

But Autumn had started their message with *'Pole star'* - safe and uncoerced. She could picture them now, a soft-eyed agendered figure who she'd met in abandoned buildings and foul roadside cafes; they had always looked too kind to survive the work but they'd outlasted Lina and she trusted them as much as it was possible to.

They never came.

And Autumn had also said '*use this contact only.*' She hadn't thought about it at the time, but years ago she might have done. Perhaps they *were* compromised and all these messages were a betrayal. *Pole star* for safety, *Orion* for coercion. Paranoia could destroy you just as completely as fear.

She realised she had not truly believed the need for such immediate flight, until now.

Her father answered her call quickly, as if he had been waiting.

'Dad, I don't know what happened, but you need to get yourselves outside the walls. I can get you travel permits,' unless she couldn't trace Helda, but her dad needed certainty, 'but first–'

'Lina–'

She only had a minute alone, her mind moving frantically. 'Go to Stevie's. Can you do that? Or somewhere else away from the house. Wait there till five, then go to the bakery on Old Cambourne Road. Tell them Andromeda sent you. They'll help you. I'll send through the permits. Okay, Dad? Okay?'

His face showed doubts and nightmares, but he said simply, 'Old Cambourne Road, bakery, Andromeda.'

Smiling, touching a finger to the screen. 'That's it. Be careful. I have to go.' Jericho appeared on the screen behind her father, his pupils wide and as reflective as a cat's. Below her, Lina heard the front door open, close again. She said goodbye quickly and closed the window down. Thinking, *oh Jericho*. Dread and sorrow, and the fragility of a child.

Thiago and Iva reached the top floor, but Lina did not look up, her tablet facing away from them.

There was a possibility all of this was for nothing. If the Investigators thought Lina's link to James was too old or was only romantic, then they might never bother looking for her, or for her family, and if so then there was no need at all to tear apart her father's carefully constructed life or undo all the delicate healing that security had given to Jericho. She might be being too paranoid. But was it possible to be *too* careful when the consequences of being careless were so dreadful?

And besides, the couriers had not come. And besides, her father would have refused to do this to Jericho unless he was frightened. Which meant he either knew more about her and James than she had ever told him, or he did not believe in the strength of their own fabricated identities.

She sent a message to the new profile she'd been given. *What happened? Orion?* Then deleted all record of it.

Thiago sat opposite her, Iva beside him. One of them slid a plate in front of her and Lina made herself look up, smile and reach for a fork rather than watch the reflection of mountains in her screen.

No coded reply.

The windows facing her showed the foothills and, beyond, the lowlands. There was a sooty pall towards the northeast, distant farmland burning again and if rains came to extinguish them, then they would come heavy enough to raise the floods. The world knew only extremes now, one death or another, one danger or another. To stay or to flee.

When she was a child, after a frantic, hushed journey in the night, leaving everything they owned behind them, her dad had sat her down in their new house and called her by her old name for the last time.

'Lucia,' he'd said, taking her hand in his. 'Do you see this box?' He'd held up a tin, silver and blue, unfamiliar. He opened it to show three small white capsules, each in their own plastic bubble.

'If they find us, my love, we are going to take these tablets. They will keep us from harm.'

'Are they magic?' she had asked.

He'd laughed a strange, ragged sort of laugh. 'There is no magic, only truth and lies.' A sigh. 'No, they're not magic, love. But they are very special. Only for if there is absolutely no other way. Let's have a secret word, shall we?'

It was like a game, to choose something you wouldn't normally say, but would not forget. Frangipane, she thought, because she'd read it somewhere the day before. Elephant, because she wanted to see one. But they were not secret words, and there was really only one of those.

'Maria,' she said quietly, and her father did not move for a long time, the tin with its tablets in one hand, her fingers curled into the other.

'Maria,' he repeated eventually.

Lina did not think of her very often. Memory meted out in small doses, and today was not a good day to be remembering. But thank god for it, she thought fervently, because she'd forgotten about the tablets. She had to-

'Lina.'

She flinched, cursed herself for doing so, and looked up into Thiago's perceptive gaze. He said only, as if repeating, 'Setting the third block of traps this afternoon?'

While her father waited once more. While Lina waited to hear from ghosts from her past. Ghosts, she thought, and held herself still against another flinch because, aside from her father and mother, there was still James and she had no way of knowing how he was.

'Yes,' she said. 'How about you? Any news on that data shadow?' She saw, without really registering, Iva's face tighten, turn to Thiago's and then quickly away.

'It's with IT in Sofia,' he said, lifting a shoulder fractionally and spearing salad leaves, apparently oblivious to both Iva's reaction and Lina's sense of dislocation, semi-presence. But he would have seen both, she knew that. You did not live the way they did here and not become attuned. Which is why she felt as though both their pasts, so long insignificant, were scratching at the door.

She took a breath. 'Did Iva tell you we are going to give our guests food poisoning?'

There was a hint of a smile in his eyes. 'Chase them away, is it? Better not, regrettably.'

But Iva was not smiling this time, 'They'll get in the way,' she said.

'They won't,' said Thiago, not looking at Iva but speaking to her. 'It will be fine.'

'They'll create a lot more work for Iva,' Lina said, only realising it now.

'We'll get help in. Your niece, Anais?'

Iva pushed to her feet, gathering plates with unnecessary energy. 'Anais will not want to. Neither will anyone else, I think.'

'Oh Iva,' Lina began, but then couldn't think what more to say. *Are they really so angry with us? Do they despise you a little and how do you bear it? Do they really think we here could stop the tagging?* And defensiveness too, because yes, ESF were proposing to beacon tag its residents but it was to protect these last bastions of wilderness, to protect the forests that Iva's people were so much a part of. Not like the States that were doing the same tagging for policing and control. Not like that. Better than that.

As if Thiago had followed every one of Lina's thoughts, he said quietly, 'Reasons don't matter, do they? Only freedom does.'

Iva paused, her tight face softening as she looked down at Thiago. But when she didn't speak, Lina heard herself say just as quietly as Thiago, 'And protecting it.'

It was too much of an admittance, both of herself and of what she knew about the locals. But just then, with these two people and their home about to be invaded, she didn't care.

In the end, Thiago went back to Govedartsi with Iva, hoping to talk them around, show them the data that ESF collected from Thiago and Lina's own tags and how little of it ESF bothered to store. If he recognised faces from the camera network, he might hint at strategies to adapt to the tags. If anyone could think of a way to remain covert whilst being satellite tracked then it would be Thiago, and these mountains had been keeping secrets for millennia. A few more should not be so much to ask.

Lina went north this time, walking through forest rides laden with pollen and a slow confetti of butterflies around teasel heads. A wood warbler's song fell from a birch as Lina passed into the lush low hills below the mountains, the forest slipping from pine and hornbeam into oak, damsons, linden. A hare started from the track ahead and from here Lina could no longer see where forest ended and the climate ravaged plains began. With the sun on her skin warm with promise this should have been peaceful, but her mind was gone helplessly west.

Still no word from Autumn, and she did not dare contact her father again, so she was left suspended, excised from events and yet too familiar with the dangers. Her dreams last night had been filled with her mother's laugh, the touch of a palm cupping her cheek; the sight of overturned chairs and the front door standing open, splintered wood bright against the old paint.

The chat request from her line manager came through when she was halfway through baiting and opening traps ready for the night. She took the tablet with her to sit in a small pool of sunlit track, brushing ladybirds from her legs, wanting to be warm without really understanding why.

- *Isla*, she typed quickly, *thank you for getting back to me, I was wanting to ask you something about those travel permits.*

- *Were you? Well hold that thought. I've got serious news.*

The blood left her face, her skin going clammy and numb. This was why she had sought sunlight, because a part of her had been waiting for this since the beginning.

- *Your name has popped up on a couple of London State lists that we monitor.*

- *Isla...* she hesitated, her mind in freefall. Her manager carried on typing.

- *To do with the assassination of the London Minister. Had you seen that news? Don't worry, it's low level at the moment, and ESF look after our own, so we aren't especially concerned. But we do ask for a report so we are prepared if they approach us.*

If they approach us? Oh James, Lina thought, wanting quietly to weep, because if he had talked, her name would not be on a low-level list, so he had not talked and oh that sweet, brave man. Did he know she didn't expect him to keep her secrets, that she would forgive him anything he might be made to say, even the very worst of it, the secret that he had only learned by piecing together her nightmares?

- *Lina? I am sending through an internal personal security report form and I need you to send that back to me by the end of the day. Is that OK?*

-*Yes,* Lina typed nervelessly. *I'll do that. Isla, if they approach you what happens then?* Still with a part of her weeping, and realising as well that the minutes until five o'clock had become more terrible and endless than ever.

-*They'll either ask for interview access or file an extradition request. Standard practice is to refuse either. Full staff immunity, remember? Whatever it is, we'll look after you, but we need full disclosure. You won't be able to leave ESF land until this is over, of course.*

For a moment, Lina simply stared at the screen. She had promised her father she would stay here, with no intention of doing so. But Isla's words lay in front of her and she wasn't stupid; she knew why ESF would do this. No legal immunity or ESF papers could protect you from a knife on a crowded train, the car behind you on an empty road.

She could leave anyway, but ESF would know because she already carried the tag that the villagers saw as a trap. There was irony in that, somewhere.

A near-dry puddle by her feet held last night's tracks of a deer where it had crossed the road in two effortless bounds. Lina began to type,

-*Of course. I understand. But can I ask are there protocols for family? Can I apply for ESF travel permits for them, perhaps to bring them here?* Even with the murdered man's family coming, she wanted them here, safe from the knife or the empty road. Get them papers to come here, then if the Wileys left quickly they might never even meet.

The wait for Isla's response felt eternal.

-*It is possible, yes. It will depend on your report, I think. The level of urgency and risk. But I can get that application started for you if you like, expedite the process. Your father and brother, yes?*

-*Please.* Please, please, please. *I'll get the report to you tonight then. And thank you, Isla.*

-*All being well, we can get permits issued in 24 hrs. Just FYI, when we get these reports, our Investigators run checks to ground-truth them.*

It was a trap then, in a way, or at least a test. Still mourning, still reeling, her thoughts were all shards of glass in her skull.

Chapter Five

Lina wrote fast, the light fading from white to sepia and then silver as evening swelled around the station. It was gone five now, so they would be on the move, trusting her to keep them safe. Thiago was not here and through the open balcony doors of the lounge, the swifts screamed on long parabolas up into the eaves for the night, bending their sickle-bladed wings unfamiliarly, something fragile and fierce made helpless.

She wrote about the years when she and James had been lovers and in love, when she had found in him a listener for her anger. First it had only been marches and protest banners, signing their names determinedly to banned petitions for the reinstatement of the old Bill of Human Rights, for victims of red water poisoning, against marine mining. Then one day someone had fallen into step with her in a march and murmured that there were other ways to fight, to help, if one were brave enough.

She'd agreed there in the nervous crowd, then she'd persuaded James, and high on passion and the invulnerability of being twenty, they'd become couriers. Secreting refugees, wounded resistance fighters and orphans on their slow passages north to safety in places like Stornoway, Iceland, even Tromsø. Bringing others south to fight. Years of terror and ferocity and heartbreak, losing friends constantly, some in the Bradford Massacre, most simply vanishing overnight. Until one day her father found her weeping for another camp burned as a deterrent, and he placed his hand very, very gently over hers as if she were a bird he did not wish to startle. After a while, and when it was obvious she would not speak, he said, 'I don't know what you are into, Lina love, but please stop. You have to stop.' She'd pulled her hand away and looked up, blazing, but he had not let her speak. 'If they take you in for anything at all, they will find out, Lina. They will find out and we will both be killed.'

She had always known it but to hear him say so, to have him lay his own life in her hands, there was no bracing herself against that.

Then, like the sun setting, he said, 'Find a way out, Lina. Find a safe place and then stay there. If you love me, get out of this.'

The next day, he'd brought a hollow-eyed, malarial child home and held her gaze over their cowed, filthy head. 'Love,' he'd said, 'it might be a drop in the ocean, but it is the greatest thing we can do.'

She had left soon after, despite the endlessness of the task she abandoned, or perhaps because of it. She left because she loved him. But also because each life she saved, and each life she failed to save, had taken a part of her with it, and those parts had become heavier than what was left.

She wrote this, parsing the ache in her chest into dates and facts, all the things she and her dad were not saying. Or most of it. James had not given her name as more than a lover, but if he did, that name would be scrutinised and it would only stand up to so much before it led to a different name, and another name, and an older, far worse crime than hers or James'.

Her dreams last night had been full of an empty doorway, a silver-blue tin and a name made into a code for death. Lina stopped typing, looked up to where the evening star was wakening against a milky sky.

She found Thiago in his workspace within the open barn that made the third side of the courtyard, bent over some unidentifiable mechanism. Glancing up as she entered, he used one foot to push a chair towards her then bent back to his work.

She sat and despite the urgency did nothing, with Thiago's hands busy and the smell of the barn filling her mind with somnolent cattle and slow, pollen-dense sunlight even while the night was gathering. But then finally, and without looking up, Thiago spoke.

'Is it about the Wileys coming?'

Lina shook herself. 'No. Not really.' He raised an eyebrow. 'It's about ESF policies on staff immunity.'

Thiago levelled a long look at her. This was their unspoken pact, that what mattered was who they were here, to each other. But there was no way not to tell him now, and she so desperately needed to talk to him.

'I wondered,' she said slowly, 'how far that really goes.'

'ESF gives us full immunity. You know that. We sign over our citizenship, they protect us.'

Yes, she knew that. Hence the reputation of ESF's militia.

'Yes, but out here...' gesturing with one hand to the mountains and their lonely house that had never felt lonely at all.

Thiago grimaced, but he would never soften truths for her. It was why she had asked. 'I guess if a State were desperate enough, there's always someone who'll take the job.' To find her, even if it meant their own death. 'It would take something massive for a State to risk it though, against ESF.' The way he said it, so simply, told her he thought this was the reassurance she had needed.

Something massive, or something priceless and heartbreaking and old. It was all a matter of perspective.

'How about internally,' she said. 'What do they do with you if you need that immunity?'

Thiago studied her face. 'Mostly, they like it. It gives them control over us.' He paused. She could hear bats beneath the tiles, subliminal voices, the delicate rustling of straw. 'At worst, they'd give a permanent travel ban.'

Confinement here? It was no punishment at all, but that was not what mattered. 'What about protecting families?'

He showed no surprise, only curiosity. 'Bringing them here?'

Cautiously, 'Yes. I think they're in danger.' From London State, or the PeaceKeepers who Thiago once served with. From a silver-blue tin that Lina saw again every time she closed her eyes.

Thiago rubbed a hand over the stubble of his hair, smearing oil above his temple. 'Because of you?'

Lina recoiled. 'No! Yes, I mean...' she took a breath, 'State arrested an old boyfriend. I'm listed as an associate.' A partial truth. Sometimes known associates were arrested, sometimes they were exiled, sometimes they were ignored. Arbitrary justice.

'That assassination?' She could see him piecing together everything she had said and not said in the last few days. They knew each other so well. 'Not much safer here then.'

With the dead man's family on their way? No, it wasn't. She looked away to watch the emerging bats pass beyond the barn's light. At the edge of the meadow, a tawny owl called.

'Fuck, Lina,' Thiago said very calmly and it made Lina laugh a little. 'State never tell the family anything, and won't bother passing this on to the PK,' he added. 'They won't stay interested in an old relationship. Lying low should be enough.'

Lina turned to face him.

Looking at her, he said very slowly, 'Not just an old relationship.'

She couldn't read the emotion that passed over his face; it was so slight anyone else wouldn't have known there had been anything there at all. And she didn't want to ask this next question.

'What *will* they bother passing on to the PK, T? And what will the PK bother with?'

He held her gaze without blinking, and god but she trusted him fathomlessly. 'They will stay away if ESF are involved. I promise you that much.' When she couldn't speak, he leaned forward and touched the back of her hand, callouses on his fingertips, oil from the machines. 'Lina. Get ESF permits for them. Tell Isla whatever it takes to do that.'

It was what she had wanted to know. That ESF could save this, that it was safe to tell them. She smiled at Thiago, the owl called again and its mate answered further away. 'I will,' she said, rising. 'I will.'

As she reached the edge of the light, Thiago called and she turned.

'I don't...' so unlike him to be hesitant, 'If ESF think your family will endanger you, they might cut their losses.'

She didn't understand, wrapping her hands around her ribs. 'What?'

He shifted his leg and in the still evening, she could hear the tiny whirr of its motors. 'Just that. But as long as the risk comes from you, then it's not an issue.'

Breathe, she thought. Breathe. The risk only comes from you so ESF will give them safety. *This risk.* Her and James.

Once she was back at her tablet, with the windows now refracting darkness and the eerie echoes of her own face, she raised her fingers to end the story there. Her and James, their history and the fact that James had carried on after she left him. The older secret she left buried, which was a risk because if ESF knew already then she would have failed the test.

If ESF think your family will endanger you, they might cut their losses.

Her father had never done anything to endanger her; he had spent his every minute keeping her safe. It had only ever been the women he loved endangering him. And yet he had been so willing to leave.

No, Lina thought. She would finish the story there. It would surely be enough, and in a week perhaps, Lina would drive down to the checkpoint at the border of ESF land and she would watch a truck coming along the old road, dust and butterflies spinning in its wake. When it stopped she would shield her eyes against the light and her father would step down, he would turn to help Jericho out and Lina would gather them both up into her arms. Her father would lift her hand and press it to his cheek and she would know without him needing to say that at least some of the tears in his eyes were because she looked so much like her mother.

But the dead man's family would get there sooner. It was inevitable that State could get people here quicker than all of Lina's machinations. And the next day, when she came back to the station beneath a dense white sun, Thiago came to lean in the lab doorway, watching her unload her bike and shake dust and seedheads from her boots.

'You saw the message?'

'This evening.' It was such a relief now that he understood at least some. Enough.

'Helicopter, of course. Fucking politicos.'

'Not the uncle though?'

Thiago stepped aside so she could pass him into the lab, moving to her workbench dazzled by the loss of sunlight. 'No. He's to follow. No timeline on that though.'

'Marvellous.'

Thiago laughed and crossed the room, opening a window to free a bee batting itself against the glass. 'It'll be okay,' he said, and something about the certainty of the way he said it made her glance up at him, eyes narrowing. But when he said nothing else she let it go.

'I'm going to put a camera on that bear's new den,' she said. It was not vital that she do it today, and Thiago knew that very well. 'Just so I can get decent footage of how she's moving now.'

'They're due half six. Weather permitting.'

She had been so focused on how to avoid being here to watch them arrive, she had forgotten about the weather. 'Will it?' she said. 'It's windy up on the tops.'

Iva appeared in the doorway with her domovek's bowl of milk, placing it by the hearth and lifting the old one with its yellow skin like a setting moon. Lina smiled at her, but her mind was on the smell of the breeze coming through the open door, the floral mosaics and hot dust of the meadow and beneath that the cold stone and desiccation from the peaks. It would be dangerous up there today, the sun deceptive, the wind in the shadows deadly. She found herself hoping that no-one tried to cross the border tonight. And that the helicopter perhaps couldn't land.

'They will come,' Iva said, staring down into the bowl she held as if looking there for someone to hold accountable.

'Yes,' Thiago said. 'The foothills are fine.'

Lina nodded and pressed her hands against her stomach, stilling the nausea there, thinking how quickly a life delineated by sunrises, by the bloom and fade of flowers and snow lines on the mountains, could become instead about hours and minutes and digital silence.

As she was prepping the camera and checking the bear's tag data to get a location on her den, Thiago went quietly out, talking to Iva in the courtyard too low to be understood. Then an app opened itself on her tablet and everything around her – the maps, Thiago's voice, the white walls – fell away.

- *Jaco. Meridian. At stage 2. Papers hot & offline. Awaiting alternatives? Gemini feared down.*

Lina sat without moving, the light in the room shifted and then brightened again as a cloud passed across the sun. A pair of swifts tore a bell curve through the courtyard, screaming, and Lina realised she was counting her breaths to hold herself still. They were outside the walls. Past the dogs, the scanners, the checkpoints, through the worst of it because Lina knew too well how many journeys ended there on the line between city and country. Oh dear god, they were out. Her fingers came to press against her mouth, beneath them a smile, a tremor. *Dad*, she wanted to say, *Jericho, you must have been so brave and I hope you are sleeping now. I hope you are holding one another because your bodies are so fragile and so precious. Dad*, she wanted to say, *I've got you. I've got you.*

But they were offline. Jaco or the courier must have destroyed all their IPs, and if they'd had more time they might have got new ones ready, but there had been no time. There never was. So she had only this:

-*Andromeda. Meridian. IDs and permits coming. Hold still. Thank you.*

Then a vidcall, and the too-clever man again, smiling his perfect smile.

'Dr Stephenson, shall I put you through to Dr MacKenzie?'

'Please,' she said, faintly surprised. 'If she's free.'

'She's been expecting your call.' He'd read her report, Lina thought, because the look he gave her was just that bit more speculative than before, a touch sceptical. Perhaps she did not look like his idea of the resistance, but surely that made her perfect for it. She smiled wider than she might have done, her spine straightening just a little, and his eyes skimmed sideways just as the image on her screen changed.

'Lina,' Isla was leaning back in her chair, a window behind

her showing Zurich's pale skyline, a clock tower and a sliver of mountain beyond, scaffolding from a bomb attack and the rain falling like a river.

Lina pressed her fingers against the edge of the lab bench out of view and hard enough to feel the smoothed topography of the grain. 'I was wondering about the visitors coming here...'

Isla smiled. 'Thiago forgiven us for that yet? Do you mean re: the lists? Don't worry, they're higher rated than the wife is.'

Meaning confidentiality clearance. Good, that was good. She was still wrestling with whether her father and Jericho would be safer here with the Wileys or kept away. But if the Wileys knew nothing... 'I see. That's ... is there any news on the travel permits for my family?'

Isla looked out briefly at the rain, then back again. 'Protocol is to issue them only once our internal checks are complete,' she said. 'You understand that, Lina?'

'Yes, of course.'

Isla leaned forward, her face pixelating and then sharpening as the camera adjusted. 'But I've pulled some strings and we are issuing them early.' Lina began to speak but Isla carried on over her. 'Our Investigators gave me some news this morning which might actually have swung it in your favour. A couple of people on the same lists as you were picked up last night. Both died in custody, possibly self-inflicted.'

Autumn. Lina's eyes burned. Even if Isla had let her speak, she didn't think she could have done. Autumn, and a small white tablet, just like the ones in her father's silver-blue tin.

'I managed to persuade the Group Head that if your family were not brought to you, then you would find a way to go to them. I think they felt that you being picked up by London State was more of a diplomatic hassle than simply issuing some travel permits.' Isla laughed, pleased with herself.

A breath as deep as the ocean, 'Isla. I can't thank you enough–'

'Don't thank me yet,' Isla interrupted again. 'We can offer no security en route, and their residence on ESF land will be provisional. But it's a start, isn't it?'

'It is,' Lina whispered, more to herself than Isla. 'It really is.'

Chapter Six

Lina stopped on the track to the station, eyeing the building with her shoulders tensing already. Unfamiliar voices fell from the open balcony doors on the top floor. Where the helicopter had landed, the meadow was swept flat, crushing the colony of butterfly orchids that had almost finished flowering. The air smelled wrong.

Iva emerged from the house, pulling a coat on despite the day's trailing warmth, and paused beside Lina with a small nod.

'They are here then,' Lina said, unease in the muscles of her stomach. It would be fine though, Thiago had said so.

'I cooked them only fermented cabbage,' Iva said. 'That is all we non-State eat, I think.' And although she would never have done such a thing, Lina smiled.

'What are they like?'

Iva shrugged and, in a remarkably good imitation of Thiago, said, 'Bastard politicos.'

Lina laughed, and would have hugged her if Iva's dignity had permitted it. 'I'll see you tomorrow,' she said instead. 'Will Anais come?'

'Yes,' Iva said, hoisting her bag back onto her shoulder and turning towards home. 'Mr Ferdinando agreed it with her.'

'Good,' Lina said, but Iva only nodded again and walked away, her steps heavy and certain even as wood larks exploded from beneath her feet.

It was as she was crossing the courtyard from lab to new house that Lina realised there was someone in the meadow. The wagtail gave it away, piping indignation at something Lina might have otherwise missed. Beneath a lone pine tree was a small tangle of hair so blonde it was almost white, everything attached to it hidden by grasses and a sprawl of vetch. Lina hesitated, then walked towards the tree, orlaya and the stiff stems of pinks brushing against her calves. The child was sitting with too-thin legs crossed, running a grass seedhead back and forth through his hands, and he didn't look up although he must have noticed her coming.

'Hello,' Lina said, made quiet by some strange stillness.

He looked up quickly, eyes the colour of backlit amber, unblinking. 'Hello,' he said. He was about the same age as Jericho, although with camp kids you often didn't know, and this child had that familiar hollow, wise wariness. This child, Lina thought, did not dance.

'I'm Lina,' she said, kneeling down, all her primed hostility gone. 'That's a kind of oat,' pointing at the grass in his hand, 'like the ones we make porridge from.'

He held it still, then touched a finger to one of the long filaments on the seedhead. 'It's like a really thin knife,' he said. 'A claw.'

'Yes, I suppose it is.' Lina looked towards the house, where voices that reeked of *London* were just about audible, and she was beginning to understand. When the news and ESF had referred to 'son', it was because some children counted less than others.

'Do you want to come in with me?' she said. 'It's time to eat, I think.'

The boy looked at her with those strange eyes and smiled almost kindly. 'I am not hungry,' he said. 'I like it here.'

'Okay,' Lina rose, disturbing a small blue butterfly that skipped away like a part of the sky cut free. The true sky above was beginning to shift towards evening, and clouds that threatened a storm were gathering in the west. 'It might rain in a while though,' she said, then added, 'What's your name?'

He was looking at the house now rather than at her. 'Kai,' he said. 'I don't think I'll mind getting wet.'

She found the mother at the top of the stairs as if waiting, also blonde – it had probably been one of her adoption criteria – and perhaps mid-forties, dressed for a soirée, worrying at the pearls around her neck. Everything Lina had expected her to be.

'Hello,' the woman said, stretching out a hand and then letting it fall. People no longer shook hands since the bird flu epidemics became so regular, although in certain circles it was rumoured to persist, power-playing. 'I'm Silene Wiley,' she said, brushing her untouched hand against her dress. 'You must be our resident scientist...' Raising her eyebrows expectantly.

'Lina. Annelina Stephenson.' Be pleasant, she told herself, and uninteresting. 'Nice to meet you.'

'Likewise,' Silene Wiley laughed lightly, all manners and delicacy, moving back to perch on the edge of a sofa. Lina realised her hands were clutching at her tablet too tightly and forced her fingers to relax. There was a teenager standing at the window, his broad back to the room, fingers tapping on the glass.

'Xander, darling,' Silene Wiley said, 'say hello to Dr Stephenson. We can call you Lina, can we? Of course?'

Xander moved his head fractionally and made a noise that might have been greeting. He was the one who had found his father's body. 'Hello, Xander,' she said, but he ignored her.

If only Iva had stayed, and where had Thiago absented himself to? 'Have you met Mr Ferdinando?' she said, cursing him mildly.

The almost-grown boy did turn now. 'He's arranging net access for us, he said.'

Of course, ESF would want non-disclosure agreements and devices scanned and registered before they opened up their net, and god forbid these poor souls be deprived of their access for a moment longer than necessary. Lina smiled noncommittally and moved to the kitchen area, checking the food Iva had prepared, sadly not cabbages, and putting the kettle on to boil.

'Darling, you won't...' Silene's voice had dropped as if Lina were not meant to hear. '*Do* anything, will you? You will wait for official access?'

'Fuck's sake, Mum,' the boy said, sounding younger and smaller than his seventeen years and too-heavy frame.

'Well, darling, you need to be careful, don't you?' Still in that pseudo-whisper that made Lina wonder if she were *meant* to hear, and if so why. She breathed rice water and set glasses on the counter. Was Silene telling her that Xander had the ability to hack through ESF's systems? And if so, why? To suggest that Xander might be able to access other networks – State lists, for example?

No. She was being paranoid. But it was paranoia that kept you alive sometimes, and how were you supposed to tell when it was saving you and when it was crippling you. Jesus, Lina thought, why had they come?

'Is this our meal?' Silene Wiley said from behind her, and Lina felt her hands tighten on the saucepan, consciously relaxed them. 'Gosh, how delightfully rustic.'

Lina smiled. Compared to a guarded house on a gated street, this place must feel wildly isolated, unfathomably basic. What could possibly make them want to stay? It was a comforting thought. She stood in the fading sunlight and smiled at the strangers, 'Dinner is ready.'

Be careful, her dad had said back when this all began.

With enviable timing, Thiago arrived at the exact moment that Lina began serving, touching her lightly on the shoulder as he swung himself into a chair, straightening out his blade with a sigh. He raised one hand to massage knuckles into his temple and said shortly, 'Net access approved.'

Xander Wiley was tapping on his tablet before Thiago had finished talking, angling his screen away from everyone. Secrecy, Lina thought, but that and his hostility were certainly grief or angst or a desire to be anywhere but here. They could not conceivably hold suspicion.

Silene Wiley said something with a laugh and Thiago replied, and Lina made herself pay attention. On a normal day she'd still not have liked them. But now, god, they were *London State*, sitting right here when somewhere inside the city walls a person called Autumn had poisoned themselves rather than talk and a man called James Hanslow was sitting in a cell, or being interrogated, or dying. She looked at Silene Wiley's smile and saw James' face the last time they'd met, when they were both trying so hard to stay whole.

For the sake of seeming present, she asked at random, 'Any news on your ... brother, is it? When he's arriving? Is he coming from London too?'

'Oh, he's not my brother,' Silene's fingers fluttered thinly. She seemed made of porcelain and money, her eldest son of money and too much time indoors. He looked up and then back to his screen, almost a smile on his face. 'He's just a very, very dear friend, so we call him Uncle, don't we, Xander darling? Are you from London, Lina?'

'Long ago,' she said shortly, and Thiago, without looking at her, repeated the question Silene had left unanswered.

'So when's he coming?'

'He's on his way,' Xander said, the suddenness making him sound harsh. 'He's coming from the Drowned State, so the storms held him up.' Shooting glances at Lina and Thiago, 'He'll be here soon.' The fact of this man's arrival was wielded almost like a threat.

Lina lifted her cup of tea, the heat passing into her palms like a touch. It was, she decided, because they were so used to being guarded, and this man, whoever he was, was coming to guard them. Such irony, such poor vulnerable people.

'Who is he?' she said. Thiago did look at her now, a slight narrowing of his eyes as if he thought she ought not have asked.

'Devendra Kapoor.' Silene said. 'You will adore him, everyone does.'

Kapoor. Lina ran the name through her memory and although it rang no bells, that meant little. She'd cut herself away too well. Although if he was from Paris, the State long-drowning but refusing to concede defeat, then she thought he must be little risk to her. It was this politico wife and her angry son who were the danger, not the amber-eyed boy in the meadow or the French 'uncle'.

The lights in the high ceiling flickered and died. Xander looked up frowning, and the room became strangely silent. Lina and Thiago glanced at one another but didn't bother saying anything. The backup power would protect the essentials, and Lina was already rising, reaching for the lamps ready in a low cupboard.

'You haven't lost power?' Silene was watching Lina light the lamps with sharp fascination. 'The great ESF, I thought you were untouchable.'

Lina kept her head bent, her hands busy setting one lamp and then another next to Thiago as he reached to hang them from waiting hooks. This was exactly how she imagined politicos to be, the constant baiting and facsimile manners.

'It's not power failure,' Xander said, turning his screen to face the room, the frown on his face different now. Intelligent rather than mulish. The screen was black.

Thiago tilted his head and the movement made Lina realise that no, in fact the generator had not yet kicked in. 'I'll go,' he said, starting for the stairs. 'Check the other tablets?'

But Silene's and Lina's were both dead too. Lina looked out of the window at clouds blossoming dark against the damson spectral sky. It was the season for storms, although only normal ones here against the mountains, blessedly not the super-storms that mauled the Atlantic States.

'Power surge or something?' Xander said behind her, but it wasn't that, Lina thought, remembering her tag data mapping a shadow and noticing the strange amber-eyed boy below, looking up at them holding something small and red in one pale fist.

'No,' she said. 'It must be something electromagnetic to affect the tablets as well.' Lightning began an intermittent white tracery between the peaks, but this sort of storm would consume itself quickly and leave them alone. 'Maybe from the lightning.' Maybe a mystery travelling across the mountains like an inverse searchlight.

'Oh dear, I hope your Mr Ferdinando can sort it out soon,' Silene said, her reflection in the glass, still seated, lifting her wine to pale painted lips, her fingers unsteady. 'We really are rather cut off here, aren't we? Out on our own. I thought with Dev here, and with it being ESF...' She looked at her son and put her wine glass down, the base of it rattling against the wood. 'Xander, darling, why on earth did we decide to come *here*? We could have gone to Zurich, or gosh, it's not even peak fire season so we could have gone to Italy.'

Lina studied the woman's profile. There were shadows beneath her make-up, although you had to be looking to spot them. *I will not pity you*, she thought to Christopher Wiley's widow. Her sons, perhaps, but not her.

Xander shrugged, still frowning. 'Was your idea. ESF was safe, you said. Whatever, Dev's going to get here and it'll be fine.' He wasn't looking up from his screen, and Lina wondered what he was doing, just how clever those soft fingers were.

'But darling, it really is quite important to know what is happening, don't you think?'

Her son muttered something under his breath, his spine hunching. It ought to have looked like self-protection but did not. Below them her other son, the adopted, tokenist charity one, lifted the hand holding the red object like a salute and Lina gave him a small wave.

'I should go and see if Thiago needs a hand,' she said, wanting to get away, but also ... it was bad enough having rogue data errors across her networks, but here, at the station?

'It's rebooting,' Xander said.

If it had been the shadow, then it had moved on. Lina sighed, turned away from the window, wavering. 'I didn't give you my condolences,' she said eventually. What had Thiago said? *One less.* 'It must be very hard to have to leave home just now.'

Silene had been reaching again for her glass but now she drew back, her eyes moving restlessly between Lina, Xander, the window, the stairs; then she rose, smoothing her perfect, slave-sewn blouse. 'Yes, naturally, but it was necessary.' She touched her son's shoulder, seemingly unaware of his shrugging her away. 'I think I will go to my room. I am rather tired after our journey. Xander darling?' He looked at her, his eyes angry but the contours of his face lax and undefined, making him again very young. 'Xander, darling, will you come down with me?'

It looked like he would refuse, but then they were both gone, and Lina was alone with the lamplight and the dark sky lit with distant flashes like celestial fireflies.

Chapter Seven

Night was fully settled over them by the time Lina and Thiago were done checking and rebooting all their electronics. It was a fair test in a way of exactly what the shadow did and didn't do. Anything mechanical or not actively using electricity while the shadow passed was untouched, but everything else simply turned quietly off. Just a couple of fuses blown from a surge as the power came back on, and even if this issue paled compared to others, it was still an irritant in an evening full of them.

She had been good at reading people once, her life and that of others hanging on her ability to read faces, hands, habits. But there was something between the mother and her eldest boy that did not fit neatly into grief or a relationship foundering on emotional repression. She sighed and pushed the thought away. Neither one wanted to be here, so if they were having second thoughts, then perhaps they would leave once Devendra Kapoor arrived.

'Done?' Thiago said, turning off the barn light, the unlit dark slipping a little closer.

'Yes. Solar panels okay?' Lina tipped her head back against the wall of the old house, watching there-and-gone stars between clouds. Down on the low ground frogs were calling an alto note beneath the crickets and the grass.

'We'll find out tomorrow.' Thiago leaned against the doorframe to her left, facing her but looking up at the new house where one light remained on behind drawn curtains. Xander's, Lina thought.

'Oh, look what the boy gave me,' she said, remembering, pulling a small figure from her pocket and handing it to Thiago. Kai had appeared silently beside her as she was checking the camera on the track and handed it to her without a word, wandering back out into the dark grass before she could think to tell him to get inside, before she could remember that it was nothing to do with her how Silene Wiley chose to parent her children.

'A martenitsa,' Thiago said slowly, tilting it into a sliver of light. It was a figure of a girl made from red and white wool, a simple thing, quickly made. This one looked a little mournful, bedraggled by the months that she must have been hung out in the forest.

'Mmm.' It was strange that neither she nor Thiago had noticed it before, if Kai had found it in the meadow. Perhaps Iva had hung it there in the spring on one of the flowering bushes, the blackthorn or greengages where only a small boy's intent eyes would spot it. Still though... 'He's a little...' fey, lost, familiar.

Thiago hung the martenitsa from an edge of stone in the wall and gave a short, low laugh. 'The mother's worse.'

The frogs in their pond fell silent, frightened by a fox maybe, a deer, something seeking a drink or seeking them. Lina said carefully, 'You won't do anything, will you? To make them leave?'

Thiago's gaze shifted to her face, his attention like a touch. 'Like what?'

'Like ... Oh god, I don't know, T.' She smiled at him, his strong face made subtle by the shadows. 'Like offend them, or look so fierce they fear for their lives.' Those last few words hung in the air and she heard herself make a small sound at which Thiago jerked, then subsided against the wood again.

'Would it be so bad?' he said.

The frogs were still silent, and Lina had no idea what to say. No, if she were thinking only of herself, then no. But it was terrible enough fearing for her father and Jericho; she could not imagine what it had taken to make someone like Thiago hide away, and she couldn't see him lose his sanctuary too.

'Promise me, T,' she said, without answering. 'Don't give them reason to fear you.'

He was still watching her, studying her face as moths wove patterns through the light. 'I won't,' he said quietly. Then perhaps pointedly. 'Where are they now?'

Lina closed her eyes. 'Outside London,' she said.

'You'll keep them away from here.'

Isla's reassurance and Silene Wiley's strange, hooded comment, Xander's pale fingers. 'I don't know,' she said. 'Yes.' The frogs began to call again. One, then another, summoning bravery.

She managed to largely avoid them for the next few days, doubling up on the small mammal transects so that she was out from before dawn and into the evening. But then they were done, all their data needing processing, and although she could have found reason to postpone it, a voice in her head was whispering *be unremarkable*.

Then, finally, there came the message she had been waiting for.

- Jaco. Meridian. Delivered to stage 4 with ESF papers. Good luck.

Her father and Jericho were in Gdansk. Tomorrow they would be on a train crossing Poland towards ... either Lviv or Slovakia. She didn't know which route was safest, but Vitaly would. They had papers and a guide, and Thiago knew someone in Botevgrad who could keep them for a while without residency permits. The risks of staying somewhere unknown weighed against that of raising Silene or Xander's curiosity. It was impossible to be sure, but she had chosen anyway.

So this morning she was in the kitchen helping Iva prepare breakfast and, due to Silene Wiley's presence on the balcony, listening to an English language radio station. Xander was on the sofa, fitted solidly into a corner with a tablet propped on his thighs. Lina had seen Kai only as flashes of movement in the meadow or the edges of doorways, and he wasn't here now, which made her want to say something out of pity and anger but she daren't. She'd forgotten this; the moments of cowardice on which you built survival.

Iva handed her a plate of melon slices, the colours a soft spectrum from ivory to jade, and Lina set it on the table where sunlight cast a shortening line across the wood. Condensation was runnelling down the water jug, Iva brought over sliced bread still warm from the baker in the village, and neither Xander nor Silene had offered to help.

'Breakfast is–' she stopped, Xander's head coming up sharply.

'*The investigation into the assassination of Internal Security Minister Christopher Wiley is said to be progressing well. Several members of the immediate terrorist cell, and their associates, are in custody with further arrests expected. Reports of deaths in custody remain unconfirmed by the police. One government source has suggested that ultimate responsibility for the murder might lie closer to home, but was unwilling to say whether they thought there was a traitor within State.*'

The news moved on to a bomb attack in Manchester and even though no-one had been talking before, and even though there was birdsong spilling in through the open doors, the room was silent.

'I don't understand,' Silene whispered. She had risen and was standing in the balcony doorway, one hand braced against the frame and the other pressing into her cheek, painted nails like pink tears. 'Xander darling, I don't understand.'

'It's the terrorists, Mum,' the boy said, frowning at his screen although Lina suspected he was watching his mother. 'They're just looking for more terrorists.'

'Yes. The resistance. Yes, of course.' Her fingers tightened on the frame briefly before she took a step into the room. 'Do you know, I think I might go and sit in the sun for a little while.'

Iva turned back to the kitchen counter and Lina still hadn't moved. Torn between wanting to say something, anything, and the words, *Reports of deaths in custody*. Silene went down the stairs quickly, unsteadily, and once she had gone Lina forced herself to come forward and perch on a chair facing Xander.

'I'm sorry. We should have turned the radio off. I didn't think.'

He shot a glance at her from beneath the fashionable tangle of his hair, and she wished she could separate out her heartache from her loathing.

'It wouldn't be on the news if they'd just fucking arrest everyone, would it?'

The breeze brought a whisper of ice from the peaks and Lina took a breath although her mind was scattering. 'It sounds like they have everyone they think was actually involved.' She added cautiously. 'Will you have to go back to identify anyone, do you think?'

He laughed like it hurt. 'You think they need anyone to actually check who they arrested?' Lina stared at him, startled, and he added quickly, ducking his head, 'I don't care. As long as people stop spreading lies and they stop going on about it on the fucking news.' But he was scrolling web pages that looked like news sites, as if torn between the need to know, and the need to forget.

'They will soon, I'm sure,' Lina said, although was that not almost as bad? She stood and said softly, remembering pity. 'Will you come and eat something?'

He shrugged, made some noncommittal noise and she didn't push, but as she turned, she saw something else appear on his screen. A window filled with scrolling code. *What are you doing?* she wanted to ask. *Where are you looking? And what for?* He curved over his screen again, the breadth of ribcage like a shield, and Lina left him.

'Lina,' Iva said very quietly as they sat eating melon, watching cloud shadows race the contours of the mountains. The data shadow had reappeared late last night in the valley near Beli Iskar. 'When will they arrive, your family?'

'I don't know,' Lina said, tilting her head a little towards Xander.

'I hope it is soon then,' Iva said, who did not know about James, lining up melon peel on her plate like ribs. They both flinched when Xander spoke.

'Why're your family coming here?'

Lina turned, aware that Iva did not, aware that swallows were alarm calling over the meadow, mobbing a passing sparrowhawk. The teenager was watching her with that same dark frown as earlier. 'Holiday,' she said, smiling, lifting one shoulder. 'ESF agreed they could come, as they've never been.' It was so implausible that her voice came close to wavering. But perhaps because it was the ESF, rather than a State, he would believe her.

'They got permits?'

'Yes.'

Iva picked up the plates; only she and Lina had eaten. Xander looked down at his screen then back up. 'Where from? Not

London?'

Oh god, she thought. 'Yes, London. That's where I grew up.' The swallows had stopped calling, and clouds were gaining traction in the sky. She rose as if the conversation were over, picked up her mug.

'Huh,' she heard Xander say quietly, then a little louder, 'you don't sound it.'

No, she thought, I don't. Or at least not like the Londoners you know. In another time and place she might have said so. Now, here, she only refilled her coffee, murmured about work waiting and slipped away down the stairs. She was on the ground floor, two paces from the door when she spotted the other son in a bedroom. He was curled beside the patio doors, his forehead against the glass, looking as breakable and abandoned as the bones of a bird.

'Oh Kai,' Lina whispered and went to kneel beside him. She hadn't seen his mother even talk to him yet. 'Are you okay, sweetie?' Why did you ask such a thing when it was so obviously untrue? She thought of Jericho cradling the cat and even though she wished Kai's family far away and forgotten, she was suddenly glad to be here, sitting beside a boy who could easily have become her adopted brother if the lists had fallen differently on that day.

Kai turned his head towards her without opening his eyes. His voice was quiet but very calm. 'Is she sleeping? She was taking tablets. Is she sleeping or dying?' Lina watched the curve of his eyelashes.

'Sleeping,' she guessed. 'She's not ill, she is just very sad and tired.'

'She's sad about him? Why?'

Lina saw again Xander's bent back and rested the tips of her fingers on Kai's shoulder. 'I expect you're all feeling sad, aren't you? But you're here now, and you have each other.' The words tasted false and Kai shrugged beneath her touch.

'What will happen to me?'

'What do you mean, sweetie?'

The child looked up at her for the first time, his eyes golden. 'Can I go outside?'

'It's raining,' she said, because it had just begun, softly, 'What did you mean?'

He seemed to take her words as consent because he pushed himself to sitting. 'Nothing,' he said.

Moving the hand that had touched his shoulder to take gentle hold of his fingers, Lina waited. Not stopping him moving, but also still asking. He sighed. 'I thought she would want me afterwards, but she will send me away.'

'No!' Lina said, her whole body recoiling. 'No, she wouldn't. You belong with her.' Kai's expression was strange and yearning, then he walked past her and she let him go, kneeling on the floor with her head bent, motherlessness clamouring for space in her heart.

Chapter Eight

Because the sun had cleared the sky and the very last of the snow was evanescing on the peaks, Lina went up to the kitchen to get coffee then sat on the balcony instead of returning to the lab. When her work was just on the tablet, she often did this, so she made herself do it now too. Besides, none of the Wileys were up here, and the rise and fall of Iva chatting with her niece made a calm songline in the hot air.

A roe deer, a young male, high-stepped delicately out from the trees. Lina touched her tablet with the innate urge to know if a number lay digitised beneath his fur, to see life in heart rate and hormones while she watched him choose between purple clovers and the tall, bright stars of chamomile flowers. But then he froze, one foreleg lifted and his ears forward, then pivoted on his rear legs and was gone, the grasses rippling in his wake. Heart rate elevated, borderline significant increase in adrenaline. Lina watched in the direction the deer had watched and, after a few seconds, saw Silene. She was walking slowly, looking from the tablet in her hand to the path in front of her, the thin material of her dress lifting on the breeze. Perhaps thirty metres from the house she stopped, studying the screen, and even though Lina could not make out her expression, something in the angle of head and arms spoke either outrage or fear.

News reports, perhaps. She had fled from the radio, but like Xander she might be unable to resist. Lina had been too young to do the same for her mother, but she remembered it from later, that compulsion to watch the reprisals on the news, to watch the trials of people she had known by names not their own, of people she had failed to save.

Silene pushed her tablet into the handbag she was, ridiculously, carrying, and took out something small. It must have been medicine because she shook it onto her palm, extracted a water bottle and swallowed whatever she held. Then she pressed the bottle against her cheek and stood there beneath the beating sun for a long moment before coming on towards the house, her steps just as slow as before but less certain. Lina listened to the front door open and close two floor below, sharp-heeled footsteps and then another door closing, the balcony door below Lina opening, silence.

When she came up for lunch, Silene sat gingerly beside Xander, her skin flushed and her eyes unfocused and Lina wondered what it was she was taking. She remembered the constant, quiet presence of her father when she had been young, and had to fight the curl of disgust from showing on her face. Kai was not here, and Silene did not look for him. Lina was about to ask, but then Anais murmured something to Thiago and Lina rose to help serve. Anais took the dish from her hands though, unsmilingly, leaving her redundant. So she turned instead to face the wide windows and the mountains beyond, aware of Thiago's attention on her but watching the climbing flight of a lark against the treeline. There was a spruce in amongst the alders at the meadow's edge, and although the alders were motionless, the spruce was shaking. It would take, Lina thought with excruciating slowness, force to shake a tree that size.

Bear? Climbing just out of sight? Her fingers twitched for the tablet but it was still on the balcony. Bears did not often venture so close though, especially in daylight and with the smell of human in the grasses and the rising air.

Too slowly, thinking too slowly. Human in the grasses. *Kai.* Bear. Kai.

'T,' she said, already running down the stairs, swinging around each turning on the pivot of her hand. The tree was still shaking when she reached the landing, it was still shaking when she flung the door open. It stopped the moment she stepped over the threshold.

'Don't,' Thiago said behind her. 'Lina.' Almost pleading. But she moved into the meadow, aware of her own footfalls, the exact number of paces between her and the half-hidden boy, between the boy and the spruce tree. Three swallows wove flightpaths low over the grass and Kai looked up at Lina, his eyes wary.

'Kai,' she said softly. 'Sweetie, could you go to your mum for me?' He stood unquestioningly. 'Slowly,' she added. The tree still did not move, but that meant nothing and she said without turning, hearing footsteps, 'You got your tablet?' Kai began walking, petals falling from his hands.

Thiago made a noise.

'Bears?' she asked.

There was a pause, and then, 'No.'

Lina threw him a quick look. 'Tags all online?'

Silene was further back, and Lina saw without emotion that she was holding a knife out in front of herself. 'Just there?' Lina pointed to the tree.

'Yes.' Thiago began to add something else, but Lina was moving in a slow arc towards the tree that would bring her through a geum-decked miniature clearing. Thiago followed silently.

There was nothing at the tree, and no claw marks of bears or territorial lynx, no torn bark from a velvet-shedding stag, not that it was the right season. Then the light shifted and something wedged into the trunk glistened like an eye.

'Jesus!' She hesitated, then warily pulled the thing free. Black clots slippery as jellyfish leaving trails across her palm, strands of muscle fibre and the glaucous gleam of fatty tissues. And her mind flooded with the red sucking flesh of a wound, her fingers slick and the bullet slick and James' sweat as he tried not to move. His blood. She couldn't breathe, she couldn't breathe.

'Lina. *Lina!*' Thiago grabbed her shoulder and she stared at him. 'Fur,' he said. 'Look, there's fur.'

She didn't want to look. She didn't want to look at anything, because she had dreamed of blood last night, fresh stains on concrete and silence. And James. And James. But *fur*, she looked and yes, there was fur. Short, grey-brown, clumped by blood and fragments of skin.

'Deer.' She glanced up at Thiago and he nodded once as if she had not reacted oddly at all. Then with one finger he moved the mass on her palm and it wasn't a bullet at all, but a data tag.

Lina did what she would have done with a tag retrieved normally from a predator's leavings, the snowmelt, a village. She bagged it, photographed the site, took it into the lab and checked the cameras on the meadow edge. Iva brought her abandoned lunch but set it down and left before Lina could speak. None of the cameras had a view of the tree, and the tag itself had been damaged beyond salvaging so she couldn't even track that. It had been a matter of seconds though, between her and them, so she sat trawling the cameras until Thiago appeared at her shoulder.

'I can do that,' he said quietly. 'You run the tag.'

She caught the strain in his face and said, 'Did you see anyone?'

Pulling another stool up beside her, he angled her screen towards him. 'No.' He was flicking between camera live feeds as if expecting something to be out there now, but there was only the sun-bleached track, forest floor, meadow, the back of the barn and the old cold store.

'I'll ask the others,' she said. Kai; if anyone had seen anything it would be him. Without analysing why, she added, 'Did Anais say anything to you?'

Thiago shot her a narrow, unfathomable look then went back to tapping on pictures, zooming into patches of bare ground. 'No.' He leaned forward to study a stretch of old leaves and scuffed earth. 'We'll sort it, Lina.'

Not 'Don't worry' or 'It's nothing' because either would be useless, but 'We'll sort it', which was not. Lina smiled and rose to her feet.

'I'm going to speak to Kai,' she said and went out into the courtyard, the sunlight falling onto her like a waterfall.

She found him sitting in the barn, on the floor beside Thiago's workbench, arranging and rearranging a handful of nails into patterns in the dust.

'Did you have some lunch?' she said, lowering herself against the wall, the sun lying short-angled alongside her.

He looked up with his fingers poised above a long, thin nail, rusted red. 'Yes,' he said slowly.

She saw the hesitation on his thin face and said quietly, 'You can get more whenever you want. There's always food in the fridge, and bread and fruit out waiting. It's okay; you don't need to be hungry.' She'd seen this in those short weeks she'd lived with Jericho. The assumption that food was not for him, that taking it might be dangerous. Jericho had hoarded it, bread going hard beneath his pillow, biscuits fallen to crumbs in his pockets; it had taken him months to stop and Lina hoped the journey would not bring it back.

Kai smiled like an unfurling flower. 'Lina.'

'Yes?'

He shifted the nails into some new configuration, the beginnings of a face. 'What was it in the trees?'

This was what she'd come for, but it still made her catch her breath. 'Did you see something?'

The face gained eyes that were crossed nails. 'A monster.'

The mouth was given two short nails as fangs. Lina wanted to reach out and scrub her hand across it all. One of the swallows was perched watchfully on a beam above them, its chicks murmuring. A wall lizard dashed beneath Thiago's bench into a strip of sun, head tilted, also watchful. The boy noticed none of it, drawing his fingertip down each fang, rust marks on his skin.

'A monster?' Lina said eventually. 'What did it look like?'

'Fierce,' Kai sounded thoughtful and not at all afraid. 'Quiet.'

'Was it a man? Did you see?'

He frowned. 'It was a shadow,' he said.

The lizard ran past the boy's knee towards a line of ants, stopped again. The swallow cast itself out into the sky. Lina flexed her fingers carefully. *The* shadow? It had not been though. Not this time. The cameras had all worked, so it was only someone who had known where they were.

'I think,' she said, 'that it was a person who's good at hiding, and wanted to ... play a joke on us.'

Kai lifted the fang nails away, studied the face and put them back.

'Can you stay out of the forest, Kai? When you are on your own?' He looked up. 'You can go further if you're with your mum or Xander, or one of us, but stay in the meadow otherwise, won't you?'

'Why?'

Lina hesitated. 'Your mum might worry if we don't know where you are.'

He lifted the fangs away again, set them aside and turned the mouth into a smile. 'She does worry,' he said, removing one nail from each eye so that they became slits, or asleep. 'But not about someone hurting me.'

There had been the slightest emphasis in his voice. *Someone hurting me.* Lina replayed it again in her mind but couldn't bring herself to ask, because however she looked at it, the words were too sad. 'I think we'll all worry if you get lost or hurt,' she said. 'The meadow is very safe, and the forest is too, most of the time. But still please stay close, is that okay?'

'Yes,' he said, giving her that startling smile again. 'I will stay close.'

Lina nodded, said thank you and rose, dusting her shorts down and hearing the swallow chicks begging again although she had not noticed the adult arrive.

'It's not me the monster wants to hurt, anyway,' Kai said as she was turning, and Lina looked down at his bent head. 'Not this time.'

'It won't hurt any of us,' she said firmly.

Chapter Nine

'I've asked HQ to postpone the tag programme.' Thiago was sitting at his desk, one leg stretched out, one hand holding a mug of coffee half-drunk.

Lina looked up from her screens full of data files. 'Did you tell them about the deer tag?' They had tried arguing against the tagging programme before and no-one had listened. This, presumably a villager's stark protest, hardly seemed likely to convince them.

'No.' Thiago was frowning abstractedly.

'Then you really think we can make the villagers come around?'

'No.'

Lina sighed and Thiago grinned at her.

'Then why ask for the delay?' She was not sure what she wanted to happen about this macabre statement of fury. Nothing perhaps, because she sympathised. But there was the shadow too and although she could see no connection between them, it was something unknown alongside something new, so she wasn't sure.

Thiago studied his coffee. The light in the room shifted and, as quietly as it had begun, the rain stopped. 'It's bad timing.'

Because the Wileys were here? Or because anger from the locals was obviously so high. It was no answer, even by Thiago's minimalist standards. 'How, T?'

He raised an eyebrow. 'The Wileys being here aren't helping ESF look neutral. They aren't happy.'

They had been unhappy before, but it made a kind of sense that London State coming had made it worse. Another mark against them. And yet ... and yet there was something in Thiago's face that

Lina couldn't interpret. 'Will HQ agree?'

'I think so.' His blade was sliding back and forth along the floor, just a few millimetres, but she recognised the tension and thought perhaps she knew what it meant.

'Can we help?' Another unsaid being spoken. 'The locals, I mean.'

'Maybe.' He'd been looking away from her, his eyes narrowed against the rising light, but he met her gaze now and his voice shifted. 'But not now, Lina. You can't do anything right now.'

No. And yet another mark against the Wileys. Cowardice for survival, she thought again. But soon her father and Jericho would be here. Even if Xander or Silene did somehow connect the dots between James and her, this was ESF land, not London State, and that meant everything.

'I'll ask about the tag,' Thiago said when she didn't answer. 'If you like.'

She had run a DNA test overnight and managed to ID the deer it had come from, killed eleven days ago by wolves. Whoever these people were, they had scavenged the tag from the remains and brought it here with the old blood still slick. She might be able to track some of that on the cameras, but would it be better to find out from the villagers or go to them with proof, or just let the deed lie unchallenged? 'It died above Beli Iskar,' she said reluctantly. 'Perhaps ask there.' She thought of the young man who had challenged her, the woman who had let her go.

'I'll do that. Don't bother doing the cameras till then.'

Lina nodded. It would save her time if the villagers talked, but she thought of Kai building a monster's face from iron and wanted to see for herself anyway.

For now, though, she returned to her real work, fitting the data from her latest small mammal surveys into the databases, updating population models, forecasting the season. She had collected blood from a sub-sample because a study in Russia had isolated a genetic mutation causing mass die-offs from a flulike virus. Although the virus had not reached Bulgaria yet, Lina wanted to map the mutation anyway.

She would still check her data for the shadow, and the cameras for the person who had left the tag. But she wanted, irrationally, to do both when Thiago was not there, because he'd told her that he would resolve it and she trusted him and yet would still look herself. Because she had only been annoyed by the shadow materialising on the slopes, harming nothing. But it had come to the station the day the Wileys arrived, and Kai had murmured 'shadow' in the dust of the barn, so it was more than an annoyance now. When Thiago went out to repair a treefall-damaged footbridge then, she looked. Although it did not help.

No equipment failures, no weather or satellite correlates, no geographic correlates other than that the shadows were all close to paths. But the forests were full of old roads, old powerline ridings, tracks from people and deer. She frowned at the screen and almost wished the shadow back again to give her another sample.

She was just beginning to trawl camera images from yesterday when Iva appeared in the doorway. She had her domovek's shallow bowl of milk in her hands which she placed on the hearthstone, picking up the other. Lina smiled at her but Iva did not smile back.

Straightening and studying the bowl, she said, 'Mr Ferdinando is not back?' And Lina was about to say no when they both heard the truck, so they waited silently. Lina shut her camera windows and let her mouse drift aimlessly over data files instead, her inbox. She was waiting for that too, of course, waiting and trying not to imagine the crowded trains, the stop-start of them through stable towns and dangerous ones.

'Mr Ferdinando,' Iva said so heavily that Lina shot Thiago an amused glance. He was brushing rock-dust off his trousers and pretended not to notice her look or Iva's tone.

'Iva?'

'That ... that woman. She wants lunch outside!'

Lina looked up. 'But it's going to rain again,' she said redundantly. From her window, she could see the very edge of a deckchair that Silene had pulled out into the meadow, the tip of a broad sunhat.

'Exactly it is!' Iva declared. 'It is going to rain, but she sits out there sunbathing and waved her hands like,' Iva demonstrated one-handed, 'and tells me it will be lovely. *Lovely?* I am not here to be *servant* to *them*. This is not what we agreed.'

They were not exactly dangerous to Iva, but they were still *State*, and Lina remembered what Thiago had said earlier about that. He was watching Iva steadily.

'She's not, Thiago,' Lina said when it looked like he might not speak, and Iva's gaze jerked to hers as if startled. 'They can't boss her about like that.'

Lifting his hands, Thiago said, 'I know. Stick to what we agreed. You're not on your own. We'll manage.'

'But–'

'Iva,' Thiago said levelly.

Iva hesitated, then gave a small nod and stepped back. 'But lunch…'

Thiago stood. 'I'll help you, and it will be sheltered enough under the barn roof. Hopefully the swallows will crap in their food.'

Iva snorted, a small, sharp smile pulling at her mouth, lines lace-working around her eyes. Lina ought to have offered to help too, but they were already gone and she delayed, setting another data import running on her tablet while a butterfly basked on the windowsill, gathering warmth.

A chat app opened on her tablet; an account and name she didn't recognise but with a greeting that Autumn had taught her. Her lungs ached and she realised it was not just Autumn she had lost, but her link to James, to news of James and hope for James, and the time when they had loved each other entirely.

- *Andromeda, this is Volya. Bad news*, they typed. With a codename like Volya, they must be Polish, might be the guide and her heart was already bruising itself against her ribs. *We're in KSL, father injured not serious but not mobile.* The words deleting themselves automatically, self-devouring.

- *What happened? What about my brother?* She couldn't think where KSL was, needed a map, needed to focus.

- *Mugging. F wants b to continue on direct to you. Can arrange this with f to follow when recovered. Yes?*

She wanted to write 'I'm on my way', or 'bring my dad anyway, whatever it takes', or 'no, no, it's not safe, don't come' but instead typed, *Yes. Bring him. Can I call?* How is he?

- *Not yet. Need new IPs. It's not serious. Will update you once in R.*

Romania, she realised. Which meant the SL was Slovakia. Not the Ukraine, at least. Tallying trains and border crossings and thank god for the ESF permits making those crossings simple. Lina breathed in slowly, carefully.

- *Do you have news from LUK?* They might, more at least than she did. There was a long pause and she thought for a moment that they had gone, but then, slowly,

- *Someone talked. People missing. It's a good thing you got them out.*

She couldn't imagine anyone not talking, there in the cells. And oh James, how much? How much had he said and if only...

- *No-ones claiming it.*

- *Not us?*

- *Not that I've heard.*

- *Are they alive, the first ones picked up?* James, was James alive and was he hoping for rescue or plea bargain or death? Her words consumed themselves and the cursor waited.

- *Some. Time's up. Will be in touch. V.*

The app closed and deleted itself, and a message was waiting that the Tengmalm's Owl productivity model was ready but she opened a map, tracing the lines from Kosice, where her father lay injured, to Deprecen, over the border to Oradea... then where? Across Romania straight to the Bulgarian border, or through Serbia first? She didn't know, and it was terrible not to know the steps her young brother would be taking, alone and so incredibly vulnerable. Her mind tallying itinerant war zones, hostile enclaves and safe ones, disease seasons, floods, storm paths...

Oh Jericho, she thought, and *It's not serious.* But what was serious depended so much on how much you loved. She wished she could call him, both of them, press her fingertips over the pixels of their faces and hear her father's voice so she knew they were both unbroken.

'Lina?' It was Thiago. Lina fished herself slowly out of the depths of her heart and turned, her neck muscles stiff. 'Lunch,' he said, his black eyes studying her face, her still hands.

'Yes,' she said, looking at the map one last time. 'Yes, I'm coming.' *It's a good thing you got them out*, Volya had said.

Silene Wiley's voice chattered unceasingly, Xander loaded food onto a plate then went out into the meadow, purple vetches and ivory bistort brushing water-stains onto his legs. He sat on his mother's deckchair and Lina saw that Kai was beside it, hands weaving figure of eights, his wrists pale and far too thin. Xander did not look at him or offer him any food, but it was strangely reassuring to see them there, together. Kai was holding a flash of red that looked again like a martenitsa. He must have reclaimed it, she thought. What a strange child.

'You will, of course, join us?'

Lina turned and saw that Silene had directed the comment not at her but at Iva and Anais, the condescension so saccharine it was a wonder neither of them walked away. Why do we do it? Lina thought. Why do we let them insult us? Is it really out of fear or is it exhaustion?

Anais looked perhaps fourteen and Lina knew her, but not well. She smiled and Anais returned it reservedly, almost wary, then looked over her shoulder into the meadow, towards the teenage stranger.

Rain was falling softly on the forest above, approaching. 'Why don't they come and eat in the dry?' Lina said. Silene set her glass down, knocking it against her plate, lifting a hand to press fingers over her eyebrows as if smoothing out frown lines.

'Xander?' she laughed tinnily, 'Oh, boys need their space, don't they? I don't think we realised quite how ... remote it is here. How very quiet.' Another of those laughs, Lina tried not to wince. 'Isn't it quite lovely though? Perfect, if only... Dev will adore it here. Just his sort of place.'

The mysterious Dev. 'Oh?' Lina said, watching Iva serve Anais, pass the salad bowl to Thiago and refuse to look at Silene. 'Why is that? Is he a scientist?'

'He was in the military for absolute years, roaming all over the place like they do.'

In the corner of her eye, Lina saw Thiago running a thumb over two near-invisible scars on his other hand, his face expressionless.

'And even now he's out of that, he still can't resist anywhere dangerous, can he darling?' She was speaking over Lina's shoulder to Xander as he returned for more food. There were several spaces where he could have leaned in, and yet he had positioned himself between his mother and Thiago.

'I tried to call him,' Xander said as he straightened. 'He didn't answer. Is that some stupid ESF block, 'cos I need to get through to him.'

'No,' Thiago said.

Xander scowled and put his plate down on the table, closing his fingers over the back of the bench. A swallow fell through the air from sunlight into shade and up towards its nest in the eaves. Xander flinched as it passed and his grip on the bench tightened. 'Well why the fuck can't I trace him then?'

'He's probably busy, darling,' Silene said but Xander ignored her. 'He's just like Christof when he...' her voice trailed away and again one hand pressed against the skin around her eyes, the other smoothing her dress in her lap.

'He flew from the Drowned City to Sofia yesterday,' Xander said.

Thiago was no longer rubbing his scars but instead frowning thoughtfully at nothing. Beside Lina, Anais shifted and Lina could see the muscles of her arms twitching. She might not understand enough English to follow anything other than the tension, so Lina tipped a knee to touch hers and whispered, 'It's okay, it's nothing.'

Anais stopped moving and her arms relaxed, but she didn't acknowledge Lina. Instead she met her aunt's gaze fleetingly across the table and in that glance Lina saw warning, anger, warning.

'Oh good,' Silene said, smiling up into her son's face. 'Then he'll be here soon and it will all be alright. That's wonderful, darling. He will stop it—'

'Mum!' Xander's hand moved clumsily and Silene stopped talking, her eyes widening, smile gone.

Stop what? Lina wondered. Their feeling unsafe, she supposed, but why had they come here if they felt so unprotected? It made no sense. If there were threats against them, wouldn't they be safer in London with their security and gated compounds than here with only this absent friend and the mountains? Why had they

Chapter Ten

'If he has his military tag still, ESF will log him when he crosses the border,' Thiago said. 'I'll let you know.' The words and the offer were kind but he was looking at Iva rather than Silene. Tags, Lina thought wearily.

It was enough to make her want to curl forward and hide her head in her hands. The shadow and the tags, the Wileys and Devendra Kapoor, her father injured and Jericho having to come on alone. She had made Thiago promise not to drive these people away, but perhaps she had been wrong.

'I don't know. I would imagine he had it removed, don't you think, Xander?'

Xander lowered himself onto the bench, looking down at his abandoned plate. 'Nah. Said it was useful for when he's out at sea or whatever.'

'At sea?' Anais half-whispered to Lina. She was watching Xander with quiet fascination.

Lina shrugged but Silene tilted her head and explained, 'He works in anti-piracy. In the Mediterranean mostly. You're all rather sheltered from the horrors of pirates here, you lucky things.'

Offshore piracy, maybe. But Lina would bet that Anais knew more about people trafficking, black market extortion and the human costs of all of it than this woman ever would. She didn't expect Anais to say so.

'I think we do know *why* there are pirates though, yes? Because of States like London.'

Xander lifted his head to stare at her, and Silene stared at her, and Lina felt the whole table give a tiny collective inhale.

'What?' Anais said. Iva said something in quick, harsh Russian that she knew neither Lina nor Thiago would understand.

'What a young anarchist you've got working for you, Mr Ferdinando,' Silene laughed.

Thiago glanced at Anais' flushed, stiff face. 'Honest, I think.'

Silene opened her mouth to speak, or in shock, but her son got there first. 'Support them, do you? The pirates and terrorists and shit? Think they're saints or something and State is, like, evil?'

Oh Christ, Lina thought. She pressed one hand against the table, her fingers so straight the tips curved up away from the wood. 'No-one's claiming sainthood. Of course not. I'm sorry. We aren't used to having State here.'

'Cramping your style?' Xander's chest was pressed into the table, his voice rising. 'Do you think we *wanted* to come to this shithole? Sit out here in the absolute middle of fucking *nowhere* with you fucking morons? Well shocker, we're only here because some of your terrorists decided to *kill my dad*, and I promised to–' He cut off abruptly and pushed upright, the table shuddering. 'Fuck it. Fuck you.'

Lina met Thiago's gaze, her pulse like a voice in her ear and his steadiness steadying her.

As Xander slammed the house door Iva rose, jerking her head at Anais, gathering dishes without speaking. Behind them a high thread of laughter made Lina turn, Kai's thin form chasing through shadowlines at the edge of the meadow. She turned back strangely lightened, enough to say gently to Silene, 'I'm sorry we upset him. Anais does not know about his father's investigation.' Which was almost certainly untrue, but she would try to be kind to this dreadful woman for the sake of her sons.

Silene was as restless as a child, running her hands over her sleeves, her hair, her gaze shifting between Lina and the house door. Then, with visible effort, she focused on Lina and smiled, revealing teeth made sharp by the sweetness of her voice. 'I'm surprised the news has not reached here. I thought all these people,' with a flick of her hand at the meadow, the hills, 'would delight in such a story.'

Thiago reached for the teapot, poured himself a cup gone dark with tannins, did the same for Lina and placed the pot within Silene's reach, although she ignored it.

'Many people here have never had anything to do with the States, Mrs Wiley,' Lina said carefully. Perhaps she should simply apologise until Silene lost interest; it would be the sensible thing. But faced with Anais' courage and her own slow anger, she said only, 'They have no interest in events as far away as London.'

Silene laughed and, like an echo, the boy in the meadow laughed too. Music began to pulse syncopated rage from within the house. 'Perhaps not, Lina. But you must do.'

The rain had stopped. Lina hadn't realised until now, seeing the sun refract through the steamy air. She should have apologised.

'You are safe here, Mrs Wiley,' Thiago said. 'And will be until you wish to go home.' He looked at Lina without waiting for Silene to respond. 'Are you starting the blood tests now?'

Lina shook herself and smiled. 'Yes. Yes, I am.' She rose and was gathering plates when Silene said faintly,

'Where's my boy?'

Lina glanced at her, the muffled music shifting beats. 'In the meadow,' she said. Thiago turned to look and then frowned at Lina very slightly, but Silene didn't look at all, only stepped backward uncertainly. 'No,' she murmured. 'No, no.' Fingers pressing around her throat. 'Gosh, it's so hot,' she said more clearly, dropping her hand. 'I think I shall have a little siesta.'

Lina was lining up eppendorfs and labelling them when Xander knocked on the open lab door. Both his presence and the unlikely courtesy of him knocking made her slow to react, to invite him in. But he didn't seem to notice and came to sit uncomfortably on a stool further along the workbench.

'What's up?' she said because he was studying the equipment along the walls more intently than was perhaps warranted.

'Will you actually tell me if Dev's tag appears on your systems?'

She hadn't known what to expect, but perhaps this would have been the most obvious. 'Yes, of course,' she said.

'Because if you don't I'll–' he stopped, glared at her, 'find out myself.'

One breath to absorb the confession, another to let it go. 'We will. But it might depend on the tag's security. Are you worried for him? It sounds like he's very capable of looking after himself, but I can go through the cameras if you like.' The data processors tagged photos with people in automatically, but the uploads weren't daily and checking every tagged image was still a slow task that she would rather not do. And she honestly didn't care whether this boy was worried for his saviour-uncle ... but he had found his father's body and then come here, almost alone.

'No. Yeah. No.' He looked down at his hands resting on weighty thighs and his face wavered perfectly between bewildered child and angry near-adult. 'Please. Yes.' A pause. 'But don't tell my mum, right? Not till we've found him.'

'Alright.'

As if she had asked, he added, 'I shouldn't've said anything before. I'm supposed to not let her worry, and stop her, like, getting in touch with anyone, you know?'

She didn't, actually. Why did he not want his mother contacting anyone? 'Yes,' she said. 'Is she okay?'

'Of course she is.' Then, as if his own defensiveness surprised him, he added, 'Yeah. Like, people talk, you know? It was all getting fucked up at home.'

Lina made a faint noise that could have been sympathy or agreement, but he barely seemed to notice. He was looking at the rows of tubes on the desk in front of her, half empty and half holding samples of blood dark as wine. As if the sight of them had reminded him, he said, 'Everyone should be tagged, then it would be easy.'

At least, she thought, he had not said that at the lunch table. 'Would it?'

Still staring at the small teardrops of blood, his eyes a furnace, he spat the words as if they burned him. 'Yes. 'Cos then they'd know exactly who did it and they'd have caught them all, and there'd be no more insinuations and fucking veiled accusations, and we could go home.'

Lina didn't speak for a moment, watching him watch the blood from a hundred tiny hearts. His words were a minefield. 'Hopefully you'll be able to go home soon,' she said eventually.

He pushed upright, the stool screeching. 'They just want to get rid of us. Everyone fights. Fuck, *I* fought with Dad all the time and no-one's ... And I know they said not to, but they're my fucking parents, so *I'll* find who did it. And *I'll* destroy them.'

He rose, and she thought he'd leave her alone now to dismantle all the things he'd said, but at the doorway he hesitated and his face, turned back to her, was awash with uncertainty. 'You will tell me though, about Dev?'

Again, she had so many reasons not to help him. Again, she couldn't possibly refuse. 'Yes, I will.' A wasp butted against the window from outside, landed on the frame in search of wood for her nest and Lina added quickly, 'Is your brother alright?'

Xander looked at her blankly. 'I don't have a brother.'

Lina watched him through her window, watched the wasp scrape a dainty line along the wood, and could not see Kai in the meadow at all. She didn't know which was worse – to leave any child at all in the camps and alone, or to put them into a family like this, as uncherished as this. No wonder he absented himself so much, and no wonder he feared. It must have been Christopher Wiley who had chosen to adopt, so Silene and Xander's rejection now might be more an infolding of grief than simple dislike. Unless he had only ever been a performative gesture for all of them, made redundant without cameras.

With a wrench, Lina returned to her work, pulling the eppendorfs towards her to finish labelling them. It was painstaking, mindless work and, seeming busy, she could pretend not to be worrying, or thinking, or loathing; but be doing all three.

Xander had said people were making accusations of his mother. That Silene and her husband had fought, so people thought she might have killed him, or at least wanted to blame her for it. She was sure that had been Xander's fragmented meaning. So that was why they had come away, to remove her from the heat of suspicion. And Volya said no-one had claimed the killing.

And yet... And yet...

Investigators were arresting both suspects and their associates, as if they firmly believed it had been a resistance-led attack.

Lina finished the last tube and pushed the rack away. She ought to begin pipetting chemicals in now, prepping solutions for a proportion of the blood taken from each animal. The rest she would prep as slides to do blood cell counts and look for bacteria, perhaps plasmodium parasites. And then ELISA tests for a couple of diseases.

Instead of doing any of those things, she did what she had been trying not to. She scoured news sites from State-owned to pirate blogs, hunting hints of Xander's suggestion or James' fate. But she could find nothing. Salacious descriptions of Christopher Wiley's body and the way Xander had found him curled into the corner of his office, between bookshelf and window, stabbed and blood-soaked.

It conjured too-vivid memories and an awful quiet satisfaction. He was the Internal Security Minister; he would have devised armed police and military actions in camps, in inner-city communities, universities; he might have recommended tasers and tear gas some days, live ammunition on others. He'd have done it all from his quiet offices in Whitehall, or from the room where he died.

It was honestly not a killing Lina could picture Silene doing, and instead was a killing that suggested the resistance, or at least a citizen driven to desperate acts by desperation, and it would be naive of Lina to think that no-one in her old disparate, spiderwebbed underground community had ever killed for the sake of the killing. But not James. Never James with his gentle smile and wish for children, one day, perhaps. Lina touched a hand to her face, her lips, and couldn't believe he'd been a part of this but even if he had, he did not deserve the hell he was living now.

Even if it was the resistance, and Silene Wiley innocent, it would still be fairer if she were accused. A summary justice for all the other guilts she was a part of.

And then Xander would be parentless, perhaps orphaned, and Kai would be ... returned to the camps or trafficked away by the State childcare system.

Shutting down vague and baseless articles, Lina instead did what she had begun to do before lunch and then forgotten. She went into Thiago's recent photo logs. They did this often, checking the others' data when they needed to, so it felt less illicit than it might and there they were – photos between the dead deer and the tag in the tree. Two men that Lina recognised from Beli Iskar: Kolev, and another who had spoken but remained unnamed. Here they were again, their shadowy faces in yellow-green evening light, their stained jackets and heavy footsteps; no camera on the carcass and they had managed to avoid the ones approaching the station. But it had to be them. Lina studied their faces but could see nothing other than reflected forest and resolution, nothing to let her gauge the anger behind the act.

Perhaps she should ask Iva. There were enough reasons to worry at present without having to watch the woods for locals. The day's humid heat was climbing again and through the open door of the lab came the sound of crickets like a radio silence. That led her to the mysterious Devendra Kapoor travelling silently towards them; and Jericho, of course, always, constantly. Jericho and her father, and the waiting.

Chapter Eleven

She slept badly and rose early, working on lab samples through the morning before being forced to stop by hunger and the sound of Iva's voice in the courtyard. Coming out blinking into the sun, sparks floated at the edges of her vision and it would be a hot day, she thought, the white-limned peaks suspended against an eggshell sky. 'Iva?' she said, seeing her standing at the door to the main house, talking to someone within.

'Lina,' Iva said, turning a little too quickly and stepping forward away from the house. 'You did not have breakfast. You are getting some now, yes?'

'Yes,' Lina said. 'Thank you, I got caught up.' Reaching Iva, the morning shadow slicing angles across the stones, she lowered her voice. 'I wanted to ask about the men who put the tag in the tree. Don't worry, I'm not ... I just wanted to know how–' she faltered, 'whether this is it. This protest. Are they done now?'

It was not quite what she had wanted to ask, but it was close. Iva looked over her shoulder towards the main house, then down the track as if measuring distances.

'I do not know this, Lina.' Lifting her palms to the sky, 'They are just boys, yes? Angry boys meaning no harm.'

Lina nodded, also looking down the track towards the forest and mountains and villages, mountain tracks and the battered road to the outside. 'Okay. That's what I thought,' she said, strangely unreassured. 'I can't say I blame them.'

Iva did not answer and behind them, Anais emerged from the house cradling her palms in front of her.

'These were in a bedroom,' she said in Bulgarian, lifting her hands to show them the small pile of tablets. 'On the floor. What do I do with them?'

'Loose like this?' Lina picked one of the pills up but it was nothing she recognised. 'Was it Silene's bedroom?'

'No, the empty one on the ground floor, there.' Indicating the windows behind them, curtains drawn.

But surely still Silene's. Lina held her own palm out and Anais poured the tablets into them with visible relief. Perhaps it was the potential hazard of them, but Lina thought it was more their cost, the risk of accusations of thievery.

'I'll see if they are Silene's,' she said. 'Thank you.'

'Good,' Iva said. 'Come Anais, we will do the lab now.' Then, already moving away, to Lina. 'Maybe you should not go to Beli Iskar, yes?'

Lina stared at her departing back. 'Right,' she said quietly.

Climbing the stairs to the top floor still blind from the sunlight, she was suspended halfway between Kolev's angry gaze and a wolf's tattered leavings when someone said 'hello' from the top of the stairs, and Lina's whole body flexed. Silene Wiley was looking down at her, one nervous hand on the newel post as she shifted back out of the way.

'Sorry,' Lina said, unsure what she was apologising for, trying to hide the way she had started. 'Morning.'

She reached the other woman and consciously put on a half-forgotten mask. It was, she thought, exhausting. But her father's injury, Jericho's solitude as well as Kai's, and Kolev's rage were all there in the room even if Silene was oblivious.

And James Hanslow ... shying away from the thought of him because he deserved her whole heart and she couldn't give it, and couldn't bear it.

'There is coffee still hot,' Silene said. Even though she had been leaving, now she curled onto the sofa, fingers scraping ceaselessly against the cushion. 'Pour me another, would you? I might go for a walk, I can't... I'm–' She stretched her restless fingers out in front of her and examined them warily. 'Maybe a walk would help.'

Lina held out her hand. 'Are these yours? They were on the floor downstairs. I wondered if they'd fallen out of somewhere.'

Silene leaned forward to look and Lina watched blood leach white from her face, making her older. 'No!' she whispered, standing, '*No!* Where did you get them? They are nothing to do with me.' And yet she scooped them out of Lina's hand, knocking some loose. 'Who gave them to you?' Wrapping her fist around them, knuckle-bones stark.

'Anais found them on one of the bedroom floors when she was cleaning.' Three had fallen loose and Lina wanted to know what they were now, although she hadn't before. There were ways to test tablet contents, even the black market ones without markings or regulated ingredients.

'The girl?' Silene's hand tightened further, pressing into her abdomen. 'That girl gave them to you?'

'Yes.'

'Then she is lying.'

'Why?' Lina said. 'Why would she lie? I can get rid of them for you if you like.' Pausing, 'Perhaps Thiago dropped them.' *Or one of your sons*, she wanted to add, but didn't.

'Yes. No, she is lying. You must watch her.' Silene was shaking her head, stepping past Lina then going down the stairs with her sharp heels skittering.

'Huh,' Lina whispered to the empty room. Luminous light from outside made the shadows pale and stark, and Lina stood still, watching them, before bending quickly to pocket the fallen tablets.

She was sitting at the dining table watching two vultures weave helices in the sky when Xander appeared at the top of the stairs. He gave her a half-nod and went to the counter where the coffee pot still steamed. Lina turned back to the birds and was surprised when he spoke from behind her.

'Where's Mum?'

The vultures turned again, one then the other peeling away from one thermal towards the next. 'She went down a few minutes ago. She mentioned a walk.'

Silence and the high buzz of a fly somewhere in the rafters. 'Right. Not fucking *sleeping* then?'

Lina didn't answer, because she doubted he wanted her to, but she closed her eyes for a moment, seeing her father at their kitchen table, the cat on a pile of papers and tea steeping in his mug. The way he said her name so often, as if he feared forgetting it, as if nameless they might both disappear.

'What d'you do out there?'

She looked at Xander, startled. Was he thinking of his uncle the way she had been of her father? Is that what this man was for him? The person who held you together? His contourless face was hard to read, but she thought that as well as Devendra Kapoor, there was a simple curiosity, almost bafflement. She smiled. 'It depends. Various things to monitor the wildlife and plants, some that help protect them.'

'Like tagging and cameras?' He sat at the table, the furthest end from her.

'Yes,' she said. 'But that's only part of it. Habitat surveys, disease inoculation. Tomorrow I might go that way,' pointing with her mug, her smile full of the forest, mulch-scented and ferruginous. 'To try to get a visual on a jackal. A drone would be too much disturbance, and I wanted to check on her kits.'

Xander didn't speak and Lina studied him, searching the wealthy boy's sated flesh for his mother's porcelain bones. He drank from coffee surely still too hot and propped his tablet on the table, bending over it and beginning to tap at the screen. Lina finished her own coffee and rose, but he lifted his head again, pulled something from his pocket and threw it along the table towards her.

'Oh yeah, what's this?'

A ragged wool doll, a boy this time, red-shirted and white faced.

'It's a martenitsa,' she said, a little mystified. 'The locals hang them out in spring to celebrate new beginnings.' And yet it had also become the symbol of a rebellion.

'In spring? So who hung it on the front door?' Xander said. 'It wasn't there yesterday.'

Observant, for a teen who rarely looked away from his screen.

Lina turned the doll, stained by rainfall, bleached by sun, and thought about angry young men. 'I guess someone picked it up from somewhere. They hang them on blossom trees.' She realised that she had no idea what Thiago had told the Wileys about the deer tag in the tree.

Xander frowned at his screen. 'Martenitsa,' he repeated, 'Says here they're...' he fell silent, reading, and Lina said quickly, 'Someone must have found it. It's nothing.'

The boy met her eyes and Lina realised that she kept underestimating him, judging him on his surliness rather than on the intelligence it so nearly hid.

'Right,' he said. 'Whatever.' Tapping at his screen again as if she were dismissed. Would it be possible, or permissible, to track his online activity? she wondered. Half appalled at herself, but the look in his eye lingered as she left him and went down the stairs. Passing quietly behind Silene's immobile form on the sunbed, she caught a fragment of murmured words. Talking to Kai or on a call.

'You don't understand. I had to get us out, to keep Xander safe.'

How dare you? Lina thought. *How dare you talk about keeping family safe?*

An hour later a call request came through on her tablet, an ID she did not know, but her heart echoing in her lungs. Please, she thought, walking out into the meadow as she answered it, wanting warmth and birdsong and to be able to see anyone approaching.

It was her father. She sank onto the tree stump with grass heads softening the edges of her vision. 'Dad. Oh god, Dad,' pressing her hand to her mouth because she didn't know if she was smiling or crying.

'Lina, my love. I'm okay. I'm okay, I promise. Don't you worry about me.'

Of course I do, she wanted to say. How could you ever not? 'How are you? What happened?' He looked thin, his skin heavy with fatigue.

'It's a cut across my chest and arm,' he said, shaking his head and speaking quickly as if that would lessen the words. 'Nothing serious, but I need to rest and get my strength up.'

Lina watched the flicker-image of his face and said slowly. 'Blood loss or a punctured lung, or what?'

A sigh, a pause either electrical or real. 'Blood loss, mostly. Cracked rib as well, but Lina love–'

'It wasn't a mugging.' Mugging injuries were a slash across the shoulder to release a bag, a threat, perhaps a knife point pressed to side or neck. A wound this violent... 'Did you see them?' Not that it made any difference.

'It makes no difference, love. But no, I did not. It was as we left the train station, it was dark and busy. I'm sorry–'

'Don't be ridiculous, Dad.' But he was not apologising for what had happened, rather for causing her any hurt at all. 'Has Jericho gone?'

The image came perfectly clear in time for Lina to see the heartache and guilt and constant strain of fear on her father's face before he wrestled it back beneath his smile. 'Last night. Reluctantly, but he's ... the people he's with seemed kind.'

That was what he would be worried about, perhaps more than anything else. And it wasn't that he didn't appreciate the danger Jericho was in, but that he trusted Jericho's safety to Lina and her contacts, whereas he trusted no-one else with Jericho's heart.

'They'll look after him,' she said, seeing in her peripheries Kai's figure flitting between shade and sun at the edge of the meadow near where they had found the tag. *Monster*, he had said, and *shadow*. 'He's got new ID?' If their old ones had been tracked then perhaps new ones would give them a headstart on whoever had been hired to ... Lina shied away from finishing the thought. 'Actually coming separately will make you harder to identify too.' And they must come here now. There was no longer any evading that.

'Oh,' her dad's face lightened. 'I hadn't thought of that, but yes, I suppose so.'

'How about your visitors?' he added.

Lina shook her head. 'They're harmless, and will be gone soon.'

Let him think her haven unsullied if it gave him one less worry, and whatever was here, she would protect Jericho from it. They couldn't talk for much longer. ESF encryption was the best, but that didn't protect her father if he was already being watched.

'Rest,' she said. 'Are they getting food?'

'Yes, love. You will take care, and you won't worry.' An order, a question, a hope.

'I might hear from them before you. I'll call this ID, but if you have to ditch it then don't worry, we'll get news to you somehow.' She laid her fingertips on the screen. 'Dad,' she whispered. 'Get better, okay?' An order, a question, a hope.

'Yes, Lina love. Yes.'

With the dormant tablet resting on her thighs, Lina tipped her face up to the sun, letting it sear the darkness and heat her cold skin, trying to burn away images of overturned chairs, splintered wood in a painted doorframe, a woman's voice screaming once then silent.

London State wanted her father enough to put a price on his head, and that made no sense unless he was more to them than just the father of an old lover of a supposedly guilty man.

Chapter Twelve

- Volya. You there?

Lina pushed herself upright in bed, looking at the clock and the faint light through the curtains. *- Andromeda.*

- We're in BG. Handing over to Daria.

Bulgaria already? Sleep tattered her. *- That was fast. All OK? Where?*

- Some pursuit. Vratsa. Handover Kost tomorrow 0800. Church Archangel Michael.

Oh god, Lina thought. Oh thank god. *- Yes. How is he?*

- Coping.

- Thank you, Volya. Safe return home.

- Safe return home.

Repeated like a mantra. It was strange how much latent power words held sometimes. The app window closed and Lina sat in the filtered early dawn, awash with hope. It was Saturday. Tomorrow, at eight in the morning, worshippers would be gathering outside the church and somewhere amongst them Jericho would be standing beside a stranger, a heartbeat away from safety.

As she set the latest batch of blood tests running, Lina was humming softly and when Thiago came in, he paused to watch her, a half-smile on his face.

'Hey,' she said. 'I'm going down to Kostenets tomorrow.'

The smile deepened. 'Your brother.'

'Mmm.' Lina pressed buttons on the machine, then turned to face Thiago fully. They still had twenty-four hours to survive, but she was singing.

'Lina,' Thiago said. 'About the tag and the martenitsas.'

'I know,' she said. 'It was Kolev Asenov down in Beli Iskar. I'll stay away from there. So should you until we can sort something out.'

He crossed the room to his desk, lowered himself into it. 'Like what?'

'Another round of village meetings? Or ... well, meetings with leaders.' Of the resistance, those who fought to rescue trafficked children, to sabotage State both here and across the border in the shattered furnace of Greece.

Thiago crossed one foot over the other knee, absently brushing earth from the blade. 'Or we let it continue,' he said, his eyes on her and black as ink.

Lina studied him, thinking. And perhaps it was because Jericho was so close and she had seen her father's smile yesterday, but suddenly she saw. 'You *want* them to do this. You ... did you *tell* them to?'

Laughing and lifting a hand defensively, 'No,' he said. 'But I think it has potential.'

'To make ESF review it.' Lina turned to the window. The cirl bunting was singing, probably from its favourite perch in the hawthorn. Somewhere further away she heard a kestrel's high, staccato call. 'It's a fine line, T.'

'Yeah,' he said noncommittally, so she turned back to face him.

'If they overplay it, ESF might just send a taskforce in and round them all up.'

'I'm keeping an eye.'

But it was too easy to forget that side of ESF sometimes, its mercilessness. 'T,' she said.

'I promise. Nothing bigger than this.' Then he lifted an eyebrow and smiled again. 'It might serve another purpose.'

Yes, Lina had thought of that. Xander's suspicious face yesterday across the dining table, woollen boy between them. But... 'I don't know,' she said. 'I think they can't go home till the investigation closes.' She'd said something of her garnered thoughts to him already, so he understood.

'She's State,' he said. 'She'll be more frightened of the unknown than the familiar.'

Because even if State were suspicious of her, that was a cesspit she was adept at navigating. Lina remembered the tablets though, and doubted. She had not done anything with them, but perhaps she would after breakfast. Know your enemy, especially when your young brother was nearly here.

'That shadow hasn't reappeared,' she said. It was not quite a non-sequitur and Thiago shot her an unfathomable look before setting his foot on the floor and angling himself towards his desk.

'No. Resolved itself.'

It must have done, yes, but the fact that it had correlated, even if loosely, with paths still niggled at the back of her mind. She wanted to ask Thiago about tech or secrets the villagers might have given away, but then she heard Iva and Anais' voices and the chance was gone.

The tablets were easily identifiable in the end. A black market heavy dose of the sedative Zolpidem with a low concentration of Phencyclidine as well. A sedative known for its hallucinogenic side effect, and a dissociative hallucinogen. Lina was betting Silene did not know about that second cut-in ingredient. It was no wonder she swung between jittery and sleep, and perhaps no wonder she had reacted with such alarm when Lina had shown them to her. The moral thing to do now was offer her a legal, regulated substitute from the station's vastly expensive medical supply. And yet how could that conversation possibly go?

Thiago had said a hint of danger from the forest would drive the Wileys away. This could help. Lina frowned at the remaining tablets in their bag, weighing duty over danger, and went up to lunch still undecided. But Silene was not there, only Xander stretched out along one sofa with music pulsing from his headphones., and Kai curled on the balcony, trailing his fingers over the metal railings. Lina joined him, watching the swifts circumnavigating the house, the light scrabble of their feet as they folded themselves into the eaves.

'They look like knives,' Kai said.

Lina smiled. 'They're pallid swifts. There used to be swifts in England too.'

'They all died?'

'Yes,' Lina said. 'They ran out of places to nest, and food to eat, and too many died migrating until there were none left.'

'They migrate? These ones too?'

'To Africa, yes.' One fell from its nest just above them, carving an inverse parabola down into the courtyard then out over the meadow, up, and up again.

'My mum migrated to England.'

He meant his real mother, not Silene. Lina looked at him, trying to gauge origin from his gold-brown eyes and too pale skin. She failed. 'Really? Where from, do you know?' Inside the house, Xander looked up at her and then back to his screen. He was doing something, she realised, not simply watching it.

'I can't remember.'

Lina wanted to ask when she had died, or vanished, or had him taken from her. Jericho remembered his mother, but most of his memories were of her dying of the drug resistant TB that held the poor in its claws. He used to flinch when someone coughed; she wondered if he still did.

'Mine came from Spain,' she said, shocking herself. But Kai just nodded, as if she had said nothing earth-shattering or dangerous. She laughed softly at herself and heard Thiago drop something in his workshop below, the low murmur of a curse in the molten air. She noticed for the first time Silene's figure on the track where it curved into the trees, walking towards the house, then turning away.

'I want a family,' the small child at her feet said, eyeing his brother warily. 'I want them to let me stay, but I think the monster wants them too.'

Silene turned back towards the house, her head moving as if she was talking to herself, her shoulders tired. Lina touched Kai's ivory hair but he did not move.

'The monster?' She had not thought of this, that allowing the locals to frighten Silene and Xander also meant allowing them to frighten Kai.

'It's angry, I think,' he said. 'It's hungry and angry and sad.'

'Sometimes people are angry and want to scare people,' Lina said slowly. 'But that doesn't mean they would hurt anyone.'

Kai looked up at her now. Xander did too, again fleetingly, frowning.

'The monster will though,' Kai said.

What did you say to that? How could you deny the existence of monsters when he already knew they were real, that they looked like men?

'My brother is coming here tomorrow,' she said instead.

Kai frowned. 'You have a brother?'

'Yes, he's about your age. Perhaps you can be friends. I think he'd like that.' She almost said that he was a camp child too, adopted too, but it felt wrong to set them both apart that way. Besides, it would be obvious.

'I'll find the monster,' Kai said, not to Lina but to himself now. 'I'll stop it from hurting them.'

Lina had no idea what to say that could possibly make Kai's strange imaginings more bearable, but Xander's voice pre-empted her.

'You on a call?'

Lina looked at the tablet dormant on her lap, then at him. He had pulled himself a little more upright, his own screen's light reflected in his eyes. 'No,' she said. 'Just talking to–'

'Your brother's name is Jericho Stephenson, right?'

Lina rose and came into the room, the loss of sunlight like bleeding. 'Yes,' she said, sitting, pressing her hands against her thighs. 'Why? You looked us up?'

Xander shot her a glance, unable to hold her gaze. 'Yeah. So what? I wasn't going to, like, *not*, was I? 'Specially as Dev still isn't here.'

'I see.' Lina did see, and would have done the same. But someone had knifed her father in a Slovak train station, and the same person or someone else had hunted Jericho across three borders. 'And what did you find?' How hard had he looked and just how capable was he?

He smiled just shy of a snarl. 'That he's some camp kid they got out of London without permits and there's a bounty out on your dad.'

Lina breathed out, counting the seconds off, breathed in. If she only breathed slowly enough, her heart would slow. 'I see,' she said again.

'So why'd they run?'

Breathe out, pulse slowing, breathe in. 'Why does anyone run?' she said. 'It's not exactly an idyll, and ESF offered them the chance to get out.' Temporary permits, but he did not know that.

'So what about the tagging programme here, then? That's what the locals are fucked off about, right? Your family safer here?' As if martenitsas and angry villagers could compare to State Investigators, the dogs at the walls, the endless monitoring of money and web activity, opinions and friendships.

'Yes,' she said. 'I believe so.'

'The cook's nephew was killed in Greece,' Xander said. 'He was with some terrorist set up from here.'

Truth or obfuscation. Truth. 'The Balkanite za Budeshte. Yes. I know.' She remembered Xander's age and added softly, 'He was seventeen. He died freeing a containment camp.'

Colour climbed Xander's neck, dotted his cheeks. He looked away from her and she wondered if she had humiliated rather than silenced him. And even if he had already tied the martenitsas to the BB, ought she have mentioned them?

'It was a long time ago,' she said eventually. 'And irrelevant to you.'

'Yeah,' he said, the colour gone again and his eyes drifting back to his tablet. 'Maybe.'

Someone was climbing the stairs, but he said in a rush, 'She's not normally like this, y'know? That's why—'

But Iva was here and the ghost of her nephew was present in the room like a whisper, and Xander fell silent.

Although Silene had vanished from the track, she did not come up for lunch and Kai came to the table but ate nothing, instead trailing his fingertips along the edges of the knives. Once or twice he reached out to touch Xander's arm but so lightly that his brother did not notice, or appeared not to, bent over his food with his tablet propped in front of him and his headphones thrumming. Thiago met Lina's eyes across the table and raised his brows fractionally.

Anais put the radio on, a local station that crackled and hissed, interspersing jagged music with a man talking in a breathless rush. Not a State broadcast, but Silene wasn't here, Xander couldn't hear, and Kai... Kai had folded his arms on the table and laid his chin on top, amber eyes on the window and the forests beyond. Abstracted and yet also intent, and Lina shivered.

'Xander,' Thiago said, nudging his plate to one side and waking his tablet. 'Xander,' louder. The boy looked up, frowning, pushed his headphones down around his neck. Thiago turned his screen so that both Lina and Xander could see. 'This your missing man?'

It was a camera-trap photo of a tall man carrying a military pack. He had tilted his head up as if listening and the sun on his cheekbones had made the dark skin bronze.

'Yes!' Xander leaned forward. 'Fuck, yes. Where is that? When–' already zooming into the time stamp without asking. 'Seven forty-two this morning, what does that mean?' Pointing at the camera ID, 'Where is it?'

She had known he wanted Devendra Kapoor here, and known both he and Silene felt vulnerable without him. But the blinding relief on Xander's face still surprised her. She leaned forward as well. 'That's near Dupnica, isn't it?'

Thiago nodded. 'It's the ESF border cam. He is tagged, it seems.' So ESF HQ would have been alerted – a military tag crossing into their territory.

Xander already had a map up on his tablet, but it was barely helpful. Dupnica was marked, but the ESF zone was a great green blank. 'Why'd he come that way, and why's he on foot for fuck's sake?'

'He must have had to go west around the wildfires.' Lina was studying the camera image again. Then clicked through to a couple more, picking him up as he walked east towards them, noting the times and the speed he was moving. Devendra Kapoor looked capable and wealthy and yes, she could see how he might be someone you depended on. But also, if you had things to hide, he looked like someone who would find them.

'Where is he now?' Xander said.

Thiago lifted a shoulder. 'Not here yet.'

'But where's his tag?'

Lina clicked back to that first camera image, the upturned face. Iva and Anais, who had both been listening silently, began murmuring together in quiet Bulgarian.

'We don't track military tags unless there's a need.' Thiago caught Lina's sideways look but remained expressionless.

'When'll he get here?' Xander was leaning forward, tense and solid.

Thiago shrugged. 'That depends.'

'What?'

Lina sighed and answered. 'It's only about thirty kilometres as the crow flies, but it's hilly, and rough going.; and he won't have an accurate map.' ESF locked out satellite imagery over their territories and did not release maps. The only people meant to be on ESF land were those who belonged to ESF, one way or another. If only that were still true.

'I could send him a proper map.'

'No,' Thiago said without looking up, but finally relented a fraction. 'He'll be fine. He's more than capable.'

And there was no way Xander could argue that, because he clearly believed it. He sat back, pulling up headphones sullenly, staring ferociously at the map on his screen. His frown was deepening, the arc of his shoulders rising as if pressure were building within him, so Lina knew what he was about to do before he did it. Turning the screen so no-one else could see it, he began typing furiously, his large fingers graceful in a way the rest of him had not mastered.

Lina looked at Thiago, but he seemed unaware. 'Xander,' she said carefully. 'Xander.' He glanced up but didn't remove his headphones, so she said simply, 'Don't.'

His face all was mute refusal and challenge. So ESF caught him sneaking into their systems, what could they do to him, a State son of a murdered State politico that they themselves had invited in?

Lina gave in. He was probably right, and besides, if he was chasing Devendra then he was not probing into her family. Kai rose to his feet as she did and drifted down the stairs while she was helping Iva with the last of the dishes.

Chapter Thirteen

Lina waited beneath the white arches of the church, watching old women in black and men with their tattered shirts. There were few children, because faith was difficult for the youth to cling to when no god could justify what the world had become and perhaps only the old still believed in permanence. Perhaps they came seeking forgiveness for their inaction, their complacency.

Jericho would stand out here amongst the gathering figures with their tannin-tinted skin, but still she checked every small face, her heart leaping each time a child wove into sight. No, she kept thinking. Not them, and not them. And, please. Please.

Then a woman moving slantwise towards the church steps so that they would meet as if perchance. Her eyes met Lina's and every muscle in Lina's body flexed with the urge to leap forward. Jericho, she thought, Jericho, Jericho. She couldn't see him yet because the bells were ringing now and the crowd's tide rose. She couldn't see him, and daren't move, and then there he was and her heart was a fire.

His hair had been released from its cornrows and pulled into a bunch on the top of his head. He was wearing a t-shirt with a purple unicorn in threadbare sequins, holding the woman's hand. Only when they were two paces apart did he look up, his eyes holes in the universe and Lina was on her knees without knowing how she got there, her arms reaching for him, and yes, she barely knew this child, and yes, he barely knew her. But she loved him, she loved him and they were both lost without the man who loved them both.

'There's news from London,' the woman who must be Daria said. Lina look up at her. She was perhaps sixty, older maybe, and could have been anyone. Mother, grandmother, teacher, nurse, all those assumedly female roles that reduced wondrousness to the mundane. Perhaps she was all of those things, but she was also this, here.

'What is it?' Lina said. Jericho was motionless within her arms, his head bent but barely touching her shoulder. 'What news?'

Daria looked down at her with the sun haloing the fraying edges of her jumper. 'The man linked to you. He is dead.'

'Oh.'

Some small star was collapsing in on itself in her chest. 'Oh no.'

She heard Daria make a soft sound that was both sympathy and brusqueness, a reminder of where they were and who they were. Lina pulled herself to standing, her hands against Jericho's shoulder blades, her eyes on Daria's seamed face with the entire world just that little bit more broken.

'Thank you,' she said. 'You should go. Thank you. Safe return home.'

James, she thought. She had imagined herself prepared for this. James.

Daria slung a bag off her shoulder that Lina had not even noticed, laid it at Jericho's feet, handed Lina a fold of papers and touched her arm. 'Safe return home,' she said and turned away, slipping into the church like a latecomer, anonymising herself in the crowd.

Lina unfolded the papers, Jericho's ID and travel permits. Someone had altered the ESF permit to match Jericho's false ID name. Genni Mathews. It was surprisingly easy to make anyone into another gender, but especially so with children. 'Jericho,' she said gently. 'Shall we go?'

'They hurt Dad,' he said, and she brushed a hand over his cheek, the dense bound hair. Come back, she told her heart. Come back to me.

'I know,' she said. 'But I spoke to him and he's okay. He'll be here soon and we can look after each other till then, can't we?' He looked up at her and with the sun catching him fully, she could see how grey his skin was, shadows gathered damson beneath his eyes. 'My truck is just around the corner,' she said. 'You're nearly there.'

She thought he might fall asleep in the car, hoped he would so that she could be alone with this raw heartache for a while, but the taut, endless tension had not yet left him because although he leaned his head against the window, his eyes were open. He watched the village fall away and the forest swarm in, a tideline of roses along the road, fractured ruins visible here and there like watchtowers or ghosts. At the ESF barrier, he let her press his fingertip to the print reader after her. The gate flashed green and parted to let them in.

'Are you okay, sweetie?' she said as the truck turned into the first snake-spine bend.

He did not answer, his face averted.

'Jericho?'

They passed into shade and out again before he answered.

'Genni.'

Lina frowned a little, changed down a gear. 'You can go back to Jericho now, love. That was just for the journey.'

He made a strange, awkward movement, shot her a glance she did not catch and looked away again.

'You're safe now,' she said. She would make it so. But he still did not speak, his thin brown fingers fiddling with the hem of the t-shirt, sequins catching the light. It might, she thought, be the fear of the hunted, the need to hold tight to a safer self. Or it might not; it didn't really matter right now.

'You want to stay Genni?'

One shoulder lifted, his face averted.

'You want to be a girl?' Look at me, she thought. The truck slowed as she waited, wrestling with understanding. He, she, turned and met Lina's eyes fleetingly.

'Yeah.' A little defiantly, a little uncertainly.

Another bend and she had to look away. The truck roared and protested. She wanted to ask more, to know whether this was new, whether their father knew, whether this was fear or a hidden

truth, but after a moment, she only said, 'Okay. Genni, then.'
And reached out to take her sister's hand in hers for a moment. It
flexed around her own briefly before pulling away and Lina wished
desperately that their father was here for this.

When a snake wound across the road ahead of them, Lina stopped
the truck so that Genni could see. But she barely looked, her eyes
like burnt-out coals, so Lina waited for the snake to pass and drove
on, all her memories of a good man and all the words she wanted
to say battering like moths in her head.

'Your room is next to mine,' she said, laying Genni's paltry bag
down and pulling the curtains against the heated sunlight. They
were upstairs above the lab in the old house where she and Thiago
lived. There was a larger empty room in the new house, of course,
but Lina had to hope that her proximity would be some comfort
for now. 'Or if you want, we can put a bed up in my room so we're
together?'

Genni shook her head and sat on the bed, dust from her clothes
settling on the cover like ashes.

'Shower then food then sleep? Or just food then sleep?'

Thiago had taken the truck as soon as she got back, and
although he hadn't said, Lina thought he was going to try to
intercept Devendra Kapoor. Not entirely out of kindness, but
rather because neither of them liked the thought of someone so
potentially hostile roaming their mountains unchecked.

'I don't know,' Genni said. Lina wavered, aware once again of
how little they knew each other, and how little reason Genni had
to feel safe with her.

'Tell you what; I'll bring you some food, you lie down. Here's a
tablet you can use if you like. It's safe.' Genni took it as if it might
explode, the dark screen reflecting her dark face like a hollow
mirror. Lina paused at the doorway to look back at the child her
father had entrusted to her. 'Perhaps we could go and find some
foxes in a day or two, when you've rested.'

Genni looked up, her exhausted face expressionless. 'Foxes?'

'Yes. There is a family nearby we could watch.'

'Yeah,' Genni said, and something in Lina unwound. 'I guess.'

She was asleep by the time Lina returned with a plate of food, the tablet fallen and her legs curled up in a tangle of clothes and bedcovers. Lina eased her shoes off and pulled a sheet loosely up to her shoulders. She lay the food down on the bedside table then set something else down beside it. A framed photograph of the three of them, her, her father and Genni when she was still half-starved and just beginning to learn how to be held. She set it here now for the same reason she kept it beside her own bed – so that when Genni woke the first thing she would see was a reminder she was not alone.

Genni slept through lunch and into the afternoon, her brown skin ochred by the light and dust making pale freckles on her hands, her hair. Lina worked in the lab, or tried to, heartbreak in her chest like a held grenade. The need to mourn was held back only by the fear that she might never stop. When she went up again at five o'clock, Genni was awake, lying on her back watching the slow creep of sunlight up the wall. She startled when Lina appeared, but did not look away from the light.

'Hey, love,' Lina said. 'Come and get some supper.'

If Genni had not been a camp kid, Lina suspected she might have denied being hungry. Something in her was holding itself withdrawn despite that first moment at the church when she had stepped mutely into Lina's arms. But because Genni had known real hunger she rose and came to Lina's side, ignoring the hand Lina held out, but following like a shadow.

Xander and Silene and Thiago were already in the top floor room, the meal prepared by Iva in the oven and Thiago's frown leaving his face when he saw Genni. He was sitting at the far end of the table and did not rise, but pushed the chair next to his out with his foot, and said, 'Glad to have you here, Genni.' He poured a glass of water, set it in front of the chair, then looked back to his tablet. Genni hesitated, but Thiago's attention was on his screen and, after a moment, she sat in the chair he had moved and wrapped her fingers around the glass, watching him. Lina had told him about her sibling's new name, new self, and had said something of her worry that it was driven by fear, but he had echoed her conclusion in the truck. It did not really matter. Whatever its roots, if this was what Genni needed, then that was enough. Lina had nodded gratefully at that and gone upstairs to find her sister awake.

'This is your brother?' Silene was sitting on the balcony now, looking over her shoulder to study Genni. Her voice was sharp but her hand, holding a glass of wine, was shaking.

'Sister,' Lina said, directing her answer to both Silene and Xander. Despite the headphones, she thought he was listening. 'Her name is Genni.'

Xander couldn't see Genni from where he was slumped into his favourite corner but he only shifted fractionally and laid a tablet onto the sofa beside him. He had two, Lina realised. The one he had put aside was running something in a black html window, text scrolling up the page. Silene scraped her chair around, high spots of colour appearing on her cheeks.

'But you said it was your brother coming. Xander, darling, wasn't it—'

'I did,' Lina interrupted calmly. 'And now she's my sister. Same person.'

Genni was playing with her glass, turning it and tipping it as if fascinated.

'But he's, but she's...' Silene stopped and Lina realised it was not the gender that she was struggling with after all, it was the skin. Or perhaps what the skin implied. Kai was not here.

'Adopted, yes,' she said, a little less calmly. 'As is obvious. And very, very much my sister.'

Behind her, Thiago opened the oven door and the hum was briefly louder than Lina's heartbeat, the birdsong outside, her memories of James.

Silene came into the room. 'From the *camps*?' she said, her wine tremulous within her glass, her knuckles whitening. Lina did not bother to answer, taking plates down from the shelf and moving to the table.

'Which one? No. Don't. I don't wish to know.'

Lina frowned sideways at her, and saw Thiago doing similar. Genni's head was bent.

'Mum,' Xander said. 'For fuck's sake.' Not cutting so much as weary, or worried.

'Darling.' She dropped down beside him.

'Here,' Lina said to her sister, handing her cutlery, 'help me put these out will you?' Genni did so slowly, carelessly, knives and forks canted at angles across the table.

Xander muttered something that made Silene flinch in a way his swearing at her had not. Above the sounds of metal on wood, the oven and the birdsong, Lina thought he had said, *It's over.* Or perhaps, *Get over it.* And then something that held the word 'Dad' like a fist.

'It was not about that,' Silene said. The tinny pitch perfectly clear. 'It was about... Actually, darling, it was something private between your father and I.'

Xander laughed bitterly and stood. 'Fucking Paul Ellis, was it then? Dad had enough finally? Good thing he's gone then, isn't it?'

'Alexander!' Silene stared up at her son, one hand wrapped around her throat and her eyes wide and pale. Xander laughed again and turned his back. Surprisingly, he came to sit at the table, and it was his mother who said faintly, 'I do apologise, but I'm really not that hungry.' Then she fled downstairs.

Xander hunched over his tablet like a cloud before lightning and Lina wished, fervently, that he had gone too. 'Alright, Genni,' she said into the quiet, spooning food onto a plate, 'Here's yours. There's plenty more though, if you can eat all that. T?' She held her hand out for his plate as well. She realised belatedly that he had been watching her very closely for a while and averted her gaze, thinking, not now, T. Please. Not yet. 'Xander?' She thought he would ignore her, but he did not and, when she returned his plate, even thanked her.

After a while, once he had emptied his plate and refilled it, Xander looked at Thiago. 'Did you go out looking for Dev?'

Thiago raised one eyebrow fractionally. 'I did. No sign yet.'

Which was surprising, given both the tag and the probability of passing at least a handful of their cameras, and Thiago's ability to track.

'You really couldn't find him?' Xander's disbelief might have been more insulting if there had not been an undertone of panic.

'Sorry,' Thiago said, only the slight tightening of his jaw revealing anything at all.

'Fuck it then,' Xander muttered, pushing his plate aside, second helpings forgotten. Genni had eaten more than Lina had hoped, and was tearing a thick slice of bread into bits, eating them slowly. Her attention switched from the food in her hand to the teen. His mother might have stopped him if she had been here, but Lina and Thiago only glanced at each other. If he had the skill, then better they know it. Perhaps this was why Thiago had not asked ESF to track the man's tag.

'His tag's here,' Xander said after a few minutes of silence. Evening was half-fallen now, the windows uncertain mirrors. He turned his screen to face Lina and Thiago, showing a flashing red icon on his featureless map of the mountains. 'It's not moving.'

'He gave you prior access to his tag?' Lina said.

'No. Why would he?' He was watching Thiago, who was studying the coordinates expressionlessly. 'I hacked in.' He said it like that was not a criminal offence, when even possessing the skill was a crime regardless of the act. Either he was so assured of his own privilege he did not care, or he wanted them to know.

'A military tag,' Thiago murmured, impressed and unintimidated. 'Send me the access and I'll find him for you.'

'Why's he not moving?'

Lina looked out at the unblinkered view of mountain and sky, the last traces of sunset a shimmer of orange. 'He'll have stopped to camp,' she said. 'It's not safe walking at night without a good map.'

Genni yawned and Lina smiled at her gently. 'Tired, love?' she said. Xander looked at the girl as if only now remembering she was there, and she saw an echo of his mother's reaction pass over his face very quickly. Not Silene's horror or disgust, but something related and quieter – refusal, denial.

'I'll fetch him at first light,' Thiago said to Xander as Lina rose and Genni followed.

'Shall I take some food down to Kai?' Lina said. 'Or your mother?'

Xander looked up from his screen to Lina, then Thiago, then Lina again, as if surprised she was speaking to him. 'Mum'll be asleep,' he said and then glanced at Genni with that same strange blend of emotions flickering over his face.

'Okay,' Lina said, touching her hand to Genni's shoulder to propel her towards the stairs. 'Goodnight.'

Chapter Fourteen

Once Genni was in bed, drifting obediently anonymous through chat rooms and social media, Lina left her and went back outside into the meadow, scanning the silvery darkness for something paler than silver, frail as silk. 'Kai,' she said, inexplicably hushed. 'Kai, are you here?'

Silene's bedroom door had been closed earlier, but Lina doubted that Kai would be in there with her and sleeping. And she had not been able to forget, helping her sister prepare for sleep, the way Kai's mother had held herself erect with revulsion, a borderline fear. Her saying, *It was not about that*, and Xander's loathing.

Genni had asked to call their father and Lina had tried to explain why that was impossible, aching at the tight hurt on Genni's face, the loneliness. No child should ever feel so alone, she thought, and she could have wept for that as well as everything else.

'Kai?' she called again, but the meadow's crickets sang uninterrupted. Along the edge of the trees, a shadow floated butterfly-like above the grass, calling mournfully, and Lina watched the nightjar until it fell to the track, rose again and drifted beyond view.

'Lina?' His voice was coming from the station, and Lina thought she might have been mistaken, that he was after all curled inside with his mother or brother or alone. But as she came closer and he answered her again, she realised his voice was not coming from any of the open windows in either house. Even with her eyes unblinded by the dark, she only saw him when he materialised out of the barn's black mouth.

'There you are,' she said.

'Yes.' His face was almost luminescent.

'What are you doing out here?'

Kai tilted his head to look past her out at the moonlit meadow, the black forest. 'Keeping watch.'

Lina could not help herself; she turned so that she too could look outwards, trying to see this great dark wilderness as Kai might see it. Something unimaginable, inhuman in a way that was more about being unknown than about cruelty. 'We're very safe here, sweetie. You should go to bed.'

Kai looked at her with wide eyes washed silver, seeming blind. 'The monster is hunting.'

It was only this morning that Lina had gathered her sibling into her arms and known they, she, was safe from the people who had chased her across Europe. Only yesterday that she had seen her father's face made thin by a knife between his ribs. The air was abruptly cold on her bare arms, heavy with the weight of the mountains above.

'They aren't going to come here. I promise.'

'They always come,' Kai said, utterly calm. 'I've seen it.'

Lina shifted to lean against the dusty flank of the truck. The swallows in their nests chittered softly then fell silent again. 'The people here, the ones who left the tag, they aren't like...' she hesitated but could think of nothing but the truth, 'State, or the gangs, or–'

'Christopher Wiley.'

Lina stared at Kai's silver-outlined shadow. 'Christopher ... your dad?'

He made a small noise, blinked his moon-blind eyes. 'He was a monster too. You know that.'

Yes, she knew that. But even with Silene and Xander being so cruel, she had assumed that to Kai Christopher Wiley was a rescuer, the person who had saved him from a broken life. 'How?' she heard herself say and instantly wanted to take the question back.

'He led the monsters, and told them to feed.' Kai was watching the forest again. A roe deer barked in alarm twice, a third time, then was silent; if Lina had looked at her tablet, she might have discovered whether it was being hunted through the black trees. 'I think,' the child said, 'if a monster catches you, you have to choose if you are going to fight, or be a monster too.'

'Yes,' Lina said, wanting to change the conversation but strangely powerless. 'I think that's true. Is that why you want to protect your family, so they don't have to choose?' So they would be kinder to him, love him, keep him. So they would not become the monster their husband and father was.

Far away, too far to be hunting the deer, a wolf howled, then another, a third, blurred by trees and echoes into one fluting, mournful note that made Kai cant his head, smiling, his teeth sharp and white. 'Maybe.'

And because his smile and his quiet made her shiver, she said louder, defying the dark, 'Did you see my sister, Genni? I'll introduce you properly tomorrow.'

'Maybe,' Kai said again, stepping out into the moonlight. 'Goodnight, Lina.'

'Goodnight,' she said, following him. 'Get some sleep. You are safe, I promise.'

She turned when she reached the lab door and saw his narrow shadow slip past the new house out of sight. Above her Genni's bedroom light came on, throwing amber angles down onto the stones as Lina went inside.

Genni found the martenitsa in the morning, hanging from the balcony of the top floor. A girl again, her red hair plaited with black cotton, sodden from the dew. Thiago was banging at something in the undercarriage of the truck and if Lina was avoiding him a little it was only because there were words she could not bear to speak aloud. Not yet. Iva or Anais must have put the martenitsa here, she thought, watching the red wool glow against Genni's skin. She wondered if any of them, even Thiago, fully appreciated the line they were treading.

James murmured in her mind, a gap in her chest that kept catching her unawares and leaving her breathless. *We are unbreakable.* And yet he had broken. Or perhaps he hadn't; perhaps he had won. There were a million ways of dying and not all of them were defeat. But he had left *her* just a little bit broken, and a small, selfish part of her was angry at him for the dominoes of his capture that led to her father wounded and Genni unbearably lost.

'Why's Dev's tag gone offline?' Xander had arrived without her hearing him, which said more about her distractedness than his stealth, and she had to fight memories of James back down into the safety of her heart. Anger and heartbreak and homesickness for nothing so tangible as geography. Before she could turn, he said, 'Another one?'

The martenitsa. 'Mmm,' she said. Genni offered it to him with her eyes flicking from his face to his tablet as if waiting for him to perform miracles.

'Can you find who put it there?' Genni said.

'Genni,' Lina said quickly, then softened. 'It doesn't matter really. It's just a kind of gift.'

Xander was holding the doll up by its loop, the girl twirling slowly, dancerlike if not for the noose from which she hung. 'Yeah, not really,' he said.

Allow him to feel threatened, as she was meant to, or protect Genni from threat. It was no contest. 'It's nothing,' she said firmly. 'More a prank than anything, a ... like claiming a territory.'

Xander looked from her to Genni's intent face, seeing what she was trying to do. 'So not at all like a threat or anything then?'

He wrapped a fist around the doll's body then released it and opened his palm. It was smeared with red two shades darker than the wool. Not much, but enough. Lina grabbed at his hand as if she could stop Genni seeing it, as if that would matter.

'The girl, right?' Xander said, trying to sound laconic, but she heard the waver. 'Anais or whatever?'

Probably. Almost certainly. Jesus. The truck roared to guttural life in the barn.

'Is that *blood*?' Genni said. Lina cursed a long stream in her head.

'Look,' she said to Xander quickly, 'why don't you go with Thiago to pick up your ... Dev, and I'll speak to Iva and Anais?'

He was torn, looking from his stained palm to the open doors and back again, then wiped his hand against his shorts. 'They're fucked,' he said, spinning away. 'You better tell them who they're fucking dealing with.'

Lina went to the balcony and called Thiago, who heard her even over the engine. He cut the ignition, leaning out of the window. When Lina told him Xander was coming, he grimaced at her before pulling his head back in.

'Why's the doll bloody?' Genni said, her voice high, staring at the stains on her own hand that neither of them had noticed. Lina found a tissue and wiped the red away, part of her thinking *how dare they*, and another thinking, *swab and analyse*, because whose blood was it this time?

The truck pulled off and Lina could hear Iva coming up the stairs from the ground floor. Xander had said Devendra Kapoor's tag was offline, but Thiago would find him anyway, and then there would be another politico here, grieving a bad man openly while Lina must hide her grief for a good one.

'Have you seen Kai yet?' she said to Genni, but her sister shook her head. Her topknot looked dry and matted, her hair needing care that Lina had not thought to give.

'Lina.' It was Iva, looking at the martenitsa with something in her eyes that made Lina think she hadn't known. Lina held it up gingerly.

'Anais?' she said. 'It was on the balcony railing.'

Iva switched to Bulgarian. 'Lina, Mr Ferdinando said—'

'I know,' Lina interrupted, in the same language. 'But it has blood on it, Iva. It's too much. My sister has gone through enough. How do I make her believe that this is anything other than a threat?'

'They are...' Iva turned to fill the kettle and coffee pot, put them on, faced Lina again with a sigh. 'It is not just about the tags now. You know who he was, the man who died?'

Someone I loved, Lina thought, abruptly wretched. But said instead, 'A murderer.' Because his death had caused James' just as certainly as his life had caused countless more. *He led the monsters and watched them feed*, Kai had whispered about his own father. She saw burning refugee camps, huddled children beneath bridges and packed into guarded warehouses.

'The...' Iva muttered something that Lina did not catch, a curse she was not familiar with but that sounded ancient and monumental. 'The repatriation, yes? Of the descendants. That was his idea, his job.'

'Oh.'

'People, families, children, who lived in England for all their lives, their parents' lives, even their grandparents'. He kicked them out, saying, *Go back to where you came from; you are Eastern European, not English.* And now where are they?' Iva's movements were violent as she cut bread, pulled plates down from the shelves. 'Where are these people who had never lived anywhere but England?'

'I know,' Lina said quietly.

'Yes, you know. Dumped into boats not fit for use, and how many drowned on the crossing?'

'I know,' Lina repeated.

'Yes, you know.' Iva paused in her bread slicing and leaned over her hands. 'Yes, you know,' she said again, weariness in every angle of her arms, her shoulders. She did not turn to look at Lina, but she fell silent and accepted Lina's hand on her forearm with a tiny nod.

So it was not just about the tags anymore, and she and Thiago were not the targets anymore. It might have been a relief, but she had never been scared for herself, only for the locals and what their protests might bring to their doors.

'He's dead,' she said after a while. 'It won't change anything.'

'No,' Iva said to the stream of pouring coffee catching the light like earthy gold. 'But his family get to pretend innocence, and live protected, and that is not right.' Which Lina had no answer to, because it was true and if she were not worried about Xander's sharp eyes and her family, she might leave bloodstained messages at their windows as well. For James, she might.

She and Iva and Genni ate breakfast quietly, Genni intent on her food and then returning to her tablet and headphones without speaking. She was scrolling a chat room page that Lina did not recognise. 'Remember not to log in, won't you?' Lina said and Genni looked up at her sharply over the rim of the screen.

'I'm not stupid,' she said, and then challengingly, 'When can I call Dad?'

'In a bit,' Lina said, seeing Genni bristle and wanting to touch her but resisting. 'I need to see if we can get a call through to him safely.'

'Why wouldn't it be?'

Lina eyed her sister, not sure whether she was looking for reassurance or a fight, and if the latter then why? 'Safe? If someone could trace it, they could trace him. And if we're not sure then we won't risk it,' she said. 'We're protected here, but we need to keep Dad safe, don't we?'

A flicker of fear, resentment, blame. 'If ESF say they can't make a safe call then they're lying,' Genni said, not looking at her now, her brows drawn. 'I bet Xander could get us through. He hacked that man's tag.'

Iva dropped a glass and swore as it shattered across the floor. Lina rose to help, but Iva waved her away, colour in her face like a banked fire.

'He might,' Lina said. 'But I think he's better at breaking the law than being safe.' Trying for lighthearted and falling short.

'You can do both,' Genni muttered and Lina wondered what her father was doing now. Still sleeping perhaps, or nursing a tea that held herbs and honey instead of milk. She wondered whether he could grow to like it like that.

'Not always,' she said, reaching out to smooth Genni's hair, unsure whether her tolerating the touch was a win or a loss. 'Sometimes being safe means taking big risks, but often it means being quiet and careful.'

'Or running away, which I guess you know all about.'

Lina frowned. 'Genni, why are you angry with me?'

Genni pushed her chair back. 'You made us leave because of your stupid friend and all the stupid things you did. We had to leave *everything* because of you.' She stood and spun away, throwing over her shoulder, 'Dad wouldn't have been stabbed if we'd stayed in London.' Her bare feet picked up speed down the stairs, blowing out through the front door like a storm, and Lina stared at the space where her sister had been for a long time without moving.

Chapter Fifteen

- L. You there?

- Yes. Thiago's message caught her as she was crossing the courtyard, trying to decide between forcing Genni out from behind her bedroom door or calling HQ to ask about her father's travel permits and risk hearing answers she did not want. Or cycling to Beli Iskar to talk to a young man about frightening her sister.

- Kapoor's tag offline and no sign. Free to pull up cameras from last loc and due east?

- Will do. Hold on. No camp?

- Yes but signs of disturbance. Coming back to offload kid.

Ah, yes. It was hardly an environment Xander would be comfortable, or useful, in, and he would be worried now, which would look a lot like anger. It might have amused her but for the image of him finding his father's body cowering and bloody. There was so much she would forgive him because of that. Thiago left the chat and she looked up at the thin drifts of mist still sleeping on the forest canopy. Silene was standing by her sunbed, staring down at the dew in dismay, her fingers tugging at the cushions and a tablet hanging limply in the other hand.

'Ah, Lina, dear,' Silene said, looking up and smiling at her with such false warmth that Lina almost recoiled. 'I had a lovely idea.'

'Oh?' Lina watched the other woman like she might watch a disturbed wasp nest. Anais appeared from the new house, a bundle of clean bedding in her arms.

'I thought I would come out with you tomorrow. I need ... an adventure. Show me what you do in the wilds.' She gestured at the cascading skyline.

Anais paused behind Lina.

'Why?' Lina said. Restlessness driven by drugs and nerves? The missing saviour, or curiosity about her, Lina?

Silene laughed and Anais still had not moved, perhaps as mystified as Lina. 'Oh well, I don't know,' Silene said, patting at the cushions again, wiping the dew off on her dress with a moue of distaste. 'I feel the need to ... to get away from here, you know? And won't it be lovely, just the girls having a chat?'

Anais made a noise somewhere between a growl and a snort, and Lina said as levelly as possible, 'I might not be going out,' although she wanted to so very much. 'But if I do, I have to warn you it's quite arduous work. Cycling and a lot of rough hiking.' She looked at Silene's dress, her delicate heeled sandals, her expectant face and was torn perfectly between repulsion and ridiculous, indoctrinated good manners. 'But if you are happy with that then of course you'd be welcome.' Thinking, god no. Bloody hell, no.

Anais moved away, and the image of Silene covered in old mud, sweating up an incline was so utterly unbelievable that Lina *couldn't* believe it. She would offer a driven tour and a river walk another day, and that would be it.

She settled decisively onto her lab bench, setting up one tablet to start filtering camera images from last night, reaching for another to call her father. Two so nearly ordinary acts.

If she got safely through then she would take the tablet to Genni, but some wary instinct made her start it alone. The call to the last account her father had used buzzed and disconnected. She tried again. Call, disconnect. Again. And finally someone answered it, but with no video, Lina stared at the greyed box and was not surprised when it was not her father who spoke.

'Andromeda?'

'Yes,' she said, cleared her throat. 'Pole star. Is that ... who is that?'

In accented English, 'State pick him up this morning.'

'No.' Her chest caving in. 'Oh god, no.'

'Slovak, no London.' A pause. 'Sorry. Someone tell them, yes?'

Someone tipped them off.

'Was it definitely State? And what charge?' He had still been so weak. Had they been gentle with him? London would not have been, but Slovak State was supposed to be kinder. She had been so close to hopeful.

'It is certain. I saw them. They say no visa.'

'But–' she cut herself off. 'Are you safe?'

A soft laugh. 'Yes. Thank you.' Another hesitation, and then putting into words something already crystallising in Lina's mind. 'It maybe is safest for him. If ... you are ESF, yes? ESF speak to State, then he is safe.'

Maybe. Maybe. 'What if London ask for him?'

'I don't know.'

'What if London have someone inside?' There was always someone bribable, she thought. Always someone who needed the money, or had family to protect. The other person did not speak, which was all the answer Lina needed.

'I have to go,' they said eventually. 'I lose this IP. If I have news I call you, yes?'

'Okay,' she said, perhaps too quietly for them to hear. When the call ended, she stared out of the window, the soft red of the new house, the meadow coruscating, butterflies above the grass like glitter. She could not tell Genni, she realised. Not this, not yet.

She called the Zurich office and Isla's gatekeeper said softly, 'Urgent, is it?' When she nodded mutely, he eyed her for a long minute before putting her call through, his fingers typing unceasingly just out of shot.

'Lina,' Isla was smiling but in a way that spoke of distractions, or lack of time. 'What's up?'

'Sorry to call without warning,' Lina said. 'I ... can we talk about my father, quickly?'

Isla looked down at her desk then back to the screen, some of her distractedness gone. 'I heard he was hurt. Sorry about that. But your brother got to you alright.'

'Sister, now,' Lina said, but ploughed on without letting Isla ask. 'Slovak State are holding him.' Isla's gaze sharpened. She hadn't known. 'Can we do anything? He's travelling on an ESF permit, so shouldn't they release him at the border?'

Isla frowned down at her desk, one hand twirling a pen at the very edge of the screen.

'Or can we apply for extradition or release? Isla?'

'Wait,' Isla said. 'No visa, I assume. But the attack was mercenaries.'

'A London bounty, yes. ESF can ask for his release, can't we?'

Isla made the same movement again, look down at her desk, pause, look up to Lina. There's something there, Lina realised, her file or a report containing something that Isla was undecided on.

'We can extend the travel permit so it does not expire. But, Lina,' steepling her fingers, and she was a good woman, which was why Lina's skin was cooling as if stepping out into frost. 'Lina, we might ... it looks like his situation is somewhat unstable, and there is already some reluctance to involve ourselves.'

The first camera had finished uploading its photos from the night, the second began. Lina wished she had messaged instead of called. To hide her face and the view of Zurich in the rain. 'But you said, as it was part of protecting me, that you would—'

'Please, Lina,' Isla grimaced, looked at her desk again. 'I assume you've heard the news from London, about the...' glance downwards, 'James Hanslow's death?'

'Yes,' Lina whispered.

And she couldn't hide her expression. Isla's face changed. 'Oh Lina, I am sorry, I shouldn't have just... I'm sorry.'

'I know,' Lina said, her voice husky, pressing her fingertips along the edge of the bench until her nails blanched. 'So what does that mean for my dad?'

'Well, it's not straightforward. Possession of our permit means he was entitled to pass through Slovakia, but he stopped and, well, there are clearly other factors at play. London are more interested in him than we anticipated.'

So they may have requested the arrest. Had they, when the hit had failed? 'Yes, but—'

'They are asking for interview access to you, and they requested that we withdraw our permit for him too, although that was before this arrest. He's wanted as a direct associate to James Hanslow, you know? They were seen together the week before the assassination.'

Lina leaned back. They were?

'At the moment, London seem only to view you both as associates, nothing ... more serious. But there has been the suggestion,' Isla hesitated and Lina's fingertips ached, 'that your father's situation is further endangering you. You are our priority, Lina. But don't panic. That isn't as bad as it sounds.'

And yet how could it be anything else? 'Isla—'

'There have been some attempts to hack into your ESF file. The security is solid, but I just thought you ought to know.'

'Xander,' Lina whispered. Isla tilted her head questioningly, but Lina said only, 'I'm safe here. And my dad is innocent. Please, will you ask if someone can talk to Slovak State? Please, Isla.'

She remembered whispering her mother's name in the dark, fingers on her lips to trace the shape of the word, make it physical.

Isla looked down at her desk again, lifted a slim sheaf of papers restlessly then let them drop. A gust of wind threw rain recklessly against the window behind her. 'I'll ask,' she said eventually. 'But this is attracting attention.'

Lina couldn't bear to ask, but she thought that Isla meant within ESF rather than outside it, and Thiago had told her what ESF would do if her family became a liability to her. 'Thank you,' she said. 'But he's—' Isla's image vanished, and instead of a blank screen, the thin faced man appeared as if he had been waiting.

'Dr Stephenson, a word, if you don't mind?' he said. When she stared at him without answering, he cleared his throat lightly. 'I assume Dr MacKenzie told you about the hack attempts?'

Lina nodded. In the corner of her eye a camera image held the slim silhouette of a wolf, the next image held two, one facing towards the camera with long light painting its coat the same colour as this man's eyes.

'Whoever they are, they are very good and rather determined.' He gave her a narrow indecipherable smile. 'I thought to check around the ... shadier parts of the web, and someone, I assume the same person, has been asking questions about you and your family.'

'Oh,' she said, almost numb.

'Dr MacKenzie has perhaps not followed through to the obvious conclusion,' the man said, not critically, 'but if this person were to unravel certain aspects of your past, and share them with London State...'

'Then,' she finished for him slowly, 'they would put a lot more pressure on ESF to hand me over. Enough perhaps for ESF to do so.'

The man, who had never given his name, made a small moue of distaste. 'Hardly,' he said. 'That is not what I meant.'

'Then what?' But she was piecing it together. She perhaps was safe, and Genni was now, as well. But her father was not. 'My dad,' she whispered.

The man nodded. 'Quite. With him as leverage they would effectively have you, I imagine.'

Because she would go to him. Exchange herself for him if that was what London asked. 'Oh god,' she said, holding still as if stillness would give fear no traction, nor heartbreak.

'Yes, well.' The man lifted a hand to touch the side of his glasses, gave her that small smile again and this time she saw something kinder in it. Beneath warning and perceptiveness, pity. 'You cannot do a great deal about your father's ... situation, so I'd advise addressing the potential leak. You have the means at your disposal, I believe. Good luck, Dr Stephenson.'

He knew it was Xander, she realised. Or suspected. *You have the means.* She was not naive, or stupid, so she knew what he was suggesting. But her mind skipped over it as if such a thought were a trap, which it was.

The camera images were slideshowing across her screen as they loaded. There was code running to filter them, so it ought to have been easy to find any people. But so far there was only two shepherds with their dogs and long-legged flock on a track between meadows. Lina's hands moved without her, widening the filter to catch any large mammal in case his pack was confusing the detection, which was more likely than that he had evaded all the cameras between his camp and here.

She watched the photos load and vanish, load and vanish, aware that she was cold despite the day's heat pressing through the open door like the edge of a wave, aware that there were a dozen things she ought to be thinking about but, for the moment, could not.

Xander, she thought. The tablet pulled up a photo of a bear, a large male, raised up on his hind legs to drag his massive claws down a tree, shedding bark like confetti. Another of him doing the same, then a third at the next camera, head low to some bushes. Sloes, Lina thought. Early, but perhaps the bear did not mind.

Xander turning over the earth of her secrets. Her father meeting James. ESF weighing the risk of him as political friction, as a hostage. London knowing they had both known James, but not knowing how deeply, not yet. And certainly not knowing what other secrets Lina and her father were hiding.

ESF had promised to protect her from her own past, but her mother's... Thiago had put it more bluntly than she would dare. *If a State were determined enough, there's always someone who'll take the job.* This place was safe as long as that oldest, deepest secret stayed hidden, the one James had not betrayed, although she would have forgiven him a thousand times over if he had. But he had not, and London did not know, and so there was hope.

Why had he been with her father though?

'Jeric... Genni,' she said, jerking into movement.

Genni was listening to music, head moving, and did not look up when Lina opened the door.

'You got a call through with Dad?'

Lina took a breath and came into the room, lowered herself to sitting on the floor by the bed. 'Not yet.' She would have to tell her at some point. But not yet. Genni narrowed her eyes and moved to turn her music up, but Lina touched her hand, stopping her. 'I need to ask you something.'

Genni pulled away, her dark eyes wary suddenly. Too quick, Lina thought. Still too quick to fear. And bloodstained messages left for her to find were not helping.

'Can you remember Dad meeting a man called James? He was...' she stopped, pressing a hand into her solar plexus. 'He was taller than Dad, black, a little darker than you. Shaved head, my age, he had...' The room fractured at the edges. 'He had a soft voice, a Bristol accent. He–' But she couldn't. His hand touching the nape of her neck, the way he would smile before opening his eyes in the morning. She couldn't. She lifted her chin and blinked desperately up at the wall above the window where ladybirds were gathered in a small, vermilion cluster.

'Yeah,' Genni said when Lina had almost forgotten what she had been asking. 'He came to the house one night. They talked. I didn't hear what about.'

Lina nodded, still avoiding Genni's eyes.

'Lina,' Genni did not sound angry anymore, more timorous, which was almost worse. 'Why? Does it matter? It was only that one time.'

She blinked and forced herself to look at her sister, who had come so far, and half of it alone. 'It's okay,' she said. 'It doesn't change anything, but you're sure you didn't hear anything they said?'

'Was he your friend? Is he the reason we–' Genni stopped, her small face showing that anger again, concern, anger.

No, Lina wanted to say. I am the reason. Whatever had taken James to her father's door, he would never have been there if he and Lina had not known one another, loved one another. 'Maybe,' she said weakly. 'I think it's why London was bothered about you guys getting away.'

'So it *was* about you.'

Genni's breath hitched and she began to bite her fingernails; there was blood in the corner of one as if she had bitten into the skin. Lina reached up and pulled her hand away.

'You'll hurt yourself,' she said quietly. 'No. He would never have gone to Dad unless it was important, and I ... I am not important anymore.' Her voice and the words were far more forlorn than she had intended.

'Bullshit,' Genni said, and Lina pulled away, shocked. 'You're all he ever talks about. Lina this and Lina that. So brave and clever and good.' She scooted back on the bed. 'But you ran away didn't you, so you're not *that* brave. And when you and ... *James* made trouble, you didn't come and get us, did you? You sat here and made us go through... There were *dogs*, and the boat was ... the waves, it was so dark, and then Dad, I saw the man knock into him and I didn't know, I thought he just stumbled but he *didn't*, and he didn't say *anything* till we were at the house then he *collapsed* and *there was blood all over him*, and *you weren't there cos you were hiding here*. So you *aren't* good or brave, are you? And it's your fault, Lina. It's yours.' She stopped, hauled in a breath that was as jagged as a wound and Lina fell into the silence with her whole heart.

'I know,' she said, her hands on the bed inches from Genni's drawn-up feet, Genni's breathing almost frantic. 'I know it's my fault, and you're right, I'm not brave, and I am hiding here, but I *can't* leave because that would just make everything worse.'

'How?'

Lina shook her head, tears finally escaping. 'I can't explain,' Genni reared back and Lina couldn't blame her. 'It's to keep you safe, Genni. I know you don't believe me, but everything I've done has been to try to keep you safe.'

'I don't believe you.' She was shutting down, the anger being pulled behind some terrible wall, and Lina had no idea how to stop it.

'I know,' she said. But if she told Genni who Xander and Silene were and how Xander was probing and probing, how their father was waiting in a Slovak jail to see which way the chips would fall, then would Genni be able to say nothing? Show nothing? Xander was both a hacker and State, and perhaps greatest of all he was a son in need of revenge. Silene was State, and ... more than a little odd, and Lina was frightened by her unpredictability, the harm an irrational act could inflict.

'When Dad is here, I'll be able to explain everything because we'll all be safe. But until then, you have to trust me.'

'Get out,' Genni spat the words, raising her voice raggedly. '*Get out!*'

Chapter Sixteen

Thiago got back before the software had finished filtering camera images. Lina only realised he was there when he laid a warm hand on her shoulder, and when she flinched he held himself still until she relaxed again. Just that warm touch and his unshakable presence. She wanted to lean into him but dared not.

'No luck?' he said, watching the images on one screen as she opened up a map window on another.

'Not yet,' she said. 'But look.'

She had taken the map layer of camera locations and run them by motion capture and by time. The time lapse played once, then again.

'The shadow.' Thiago removed his hand and Lina fought the urge to pull it back. He dragged up a stool next to hers and scrubbed a hand roughly over his face and scalp. 'Fuck.'

'I'm just checking the beginning and end of its track,' she said. It had not been present long, nor travelled far. She returned to a file window, searching for camera ID and timestamp.

'Lina,' Thiago said.

His voice had changed and she spoke to stop him speaking. 'I thought it had stopped, but now with this guy vanishing and the shadow ... what if it was him all along? Hiding? They said he was ex-military, and he's Drowned State – what if it's some tech? It could–'

'You've been crying.'

'–be electromagnetic. That would–'

'Lina.'

She stopped talking, stopped scrolling blindly through filenames.

'Lina,' he repeated very gently.

Staring at her screen because she couldn't look at him, she whispered, 'Slovak State have Dad. And James is dead.' And if Xander unearthed her secrets then her father was as good as dead and so was she. 'Genni blames me, and she's right.' She was not crying now, although it felt like she was. Thiago's gaze was on her as warm and steady as his hand had been.

'Slovak State aren't like London. He'll be okay,' he said finally.

It was what she had been telling herself, but only with Thiago saying so did she believe it. 'He's hurt,' she said.

'They'll take care of him,' he paused. 'I'm sorry about James.'

She turned to look at him finally and his eyes were softer than they'd ever been, reflecting heartbreak. 'I know,' she said. 'T, I can't–' Believe it, grieve him, forgive myself for leaving him...

'I know,' Thiago said. Then, 'Let me deal with this.' Thiago nodded his head at the tablets. 'You spend some time with Genni. She'll come around. She loves you.'

Lina shook her head. 'I'm not so sure.'

Pulling the screens towards himself, Thiago shot her a half-smile, leavened. 'I am.' Then he looked at the screens and paused, one hand raised.

Lina leaned forward slowly. 'What's that?' she said, but it was obvious. Even with branches swaying and the night-vision image turning everything greyscale, the shape on the ground at the edge of the picture was perfectly clear.

This was why neither the human filter nor the large mammal filter had picked him up.

Thiago swore a low stream of impenetrable Spanish and Lina could not stop looking at the figure in the image. His pack was still on his back so he had fallen awkwardly, his face half in moonlight a theatre mask of high cheekbones and black hair. There was no-one else in the image, and no-one in the image before. Then the shadow, and the camera had only triggered again two hours later when a fox crossed the corner of the screen, tail held high.

Thiago pushed to his feet, his blade scraping against the floor in protest. 'I'm going out. Don't tell the kid.'

'I'll come with you.' She was standing too, for the moment feeling nothing but a strange buzzing tension. 'I was going to go to Beli Iskar anyway, there was another–'

'No!' Thiago caught himself, consciously softened his voice. 'Stay, Lina. It'll be easier for me to do it alone.'

'T, don't be stupid.'

He grinned at her, but there was a darkness behind it. 'Stay with Genni. She needs you.'

Watching him swing into the truck again, she tried to fathom why he had said it would be easier. Was it that they would talk to him more freely without her, or that he meant to threaten them and did not want her to watch him do so. From the way he had moved, the tension, she guessed the latter and wished she could tell him that the parts of himself that were capable of violence did not disgust her, nor frighten her. It would have been hypocrisy in a way; they were both only products of a world made by evil men.

Xander pushed the door wide and came into the room breathing heavily. 'Where's he gone?'

Lina closed the image on the tablet. 'Gone to ask for help from the locals.' She looked up at him and realised the time. How was it still early? She felt husked and a little beyond herself, like she might not be able to stop herself from saying unspeakable things simply because there were so many of them overspilling her mind.

What are you looking for, she could say, *when you search the net for me? And what will you do with what you find?* Perhaps even, *What will it take to make you stop?*

'It's lunchtime,' she said instead. 'Shall we go up?' When he didn't move out of the doorway, she added, 'He won't be back for a while. You may as well eat.'

Her sister was curled on the bed, headphones on and her fingers moving across her screen. Fear grabbed at Lina's throat but she had to trust her, didn't she? 'Genni,' she said, 'coming for lunch?'

'No.'

Lina studied the floor at her feet, indecision and heartache vying for control. 'I'll bring some food back,' she said eventually.

'But you will come up for supper, okay?'

No answer. Still typing.

Better anger than mistakes, she thought, and straightened her shoulders. 'You are being careful, aren't you?'

'Of course I am. I'm not stupid.'

Lina left her there. It should not hurt really, being the target of a child's directionless anger, but it did.

Silene was in the main room, staring red-eyed at nothing Lina could see. Xander was already loading his plate from the food waiting out, and Kai was sitting on the balcony again. He had fitted his thin limbs through the railing and was humming softly. She could not see his face or hands from where she watched him, but she thought he was holding something, studying it as his feet swung over the empty air. The sun was on his bare arms but he was still so very pale. 'Be careful you don't burn, won't you?' she said, and he turned his face enough to cast a glance at her, then at Silene.

'Hello,' he said.

'Why don't you come in and eat.'

Silene was watching her, and her eyes were widening, a hand coming up to press over her mouth, painted nails digging into the cheek. 'Stop it,' she said, a whisper like a shout. 'Stop it.'

Lina looked at her; Kai and Xander both turning as well.

'You have to ignore them,' Silene said in that same brutal whisper and Lina could not help herself.

'He's a *child*, for Christ's sake. He's *your* child!'

Silene was shaking her head, her hand slipping from her face leaving red crescents in her cheek, touching her skirt pocket as if for reassurance and backing away. 'No,' she gasped. 'No, no, you don't understand. He's not–'

'Mum, what the fuck?' Xander cut her off and Lina wanted to kiss him for sparing Kai whatever their mother had been about to say. Wanted to weep, too, because this was not what mothers were meant to be, and was it not bitterly ironic that a mother who did not love her child got to live, yet a mother who did, died. Although...

No. Lina stopped herself. It was unfair and a betrayal, and she had done exactly the same, so how could she fail to understand, to forgive.

'Who *are* you?' Silene said suddenly, her eyes on Lina almost feverish. 'Who are you working for? Did they send you to watch me? Because I won't let you. I'll stop you; you know I will.'

'Silene,' Lina began.

Silene threw herself towards Xander. 'Darling, tell her it wasn't my fault.' Clutching at his arm. 'It was him, I always said, didn't I? I always said he would go too far one day but he didn't listen, darling. You know. Tell her.'

Who was she talking about? Lina thought. Kai had risen to his feet now, disentangled from the railings and distantly Lina realised what he was holding. A rib bone from something medium-sized. Badger, cat, fox. A boy clutching a bladed bone.

'What the fuck are you on about?' Xander said, pulling away with a jerk that made his mother stumble. 'Jesus,' he said. 'Just go and lie down or something, you're acting crazy.'

The word hung in the silence and Silene's face yellowed to parchment, old bones. She looked like she might faint, but instead breathed in sharply and somehow straightened. 'Alexander Wiley!' Xander folded his arms across his stomach but faced her without blinking. 'Everything I have done has been to protect you. Your father did not understand. He put his career first and didn't care if that put you at risk. He–'

'What? How did he put me at risk?'

'Oh darling.' her anger was gone as quickly as it had come, her hand coming up as if she might stroke Xander's face. 'The things you do online. They would arrest you if they knew. And Christof ... not everyone liked what he was doing, you know, with the camps.'

At the edge of Lina's vision, Kai seemed to flicker as if the sun and his own past were trying to erase him. Silene saw her looking and stepped in front of Xander. 'Leave us alone,' she hissed, her gaze flicking from Lina to the balcony and back, strangely unfocused, one hand slipping into the pocket of her skirt, clutching at something. Tablets, Lina thought. Tablets. 'Just leave us alone.

It wasn't us. It wasn't me.'

'Jesus, Mum!' Xander was the one grabbing at her now, pulling her towards the stairs and for a blind moment it looked like he might push her down them, but he went with her, half-dragging. 'Would you shut the fuck up?' he was saying. 'She knows it wasn't you, okay? She knows that.'

'Not her,' Silene said. They were on the second floor now, their voices slowly muffling. 'I didn't mean her.'

Xander replied, exasperation making his voice rise, but Lina didn't catch the words because Kai had moved out of the sunlight into shade, still oddly ephemeral, which was no surprise really. None at all. He here with his lovelessness and Genni across the courtyard with her anger; Lina could hate the world so vastly at moments like these that it felt impossible to be so full of rage and still breathe.

She set plates at the table for Kai and herself, unsure where Iva or Anais were but suspecting they were timing their work to avoid seeing anyone. Perhaps Lina could have done the same, but although at first she hadn't done so because she needed to look unremarkable, now, she realised, she was here because of this child. His thin fingers toying with the bread and refracted sunlight making his eyes gold.

'I don't think he'll find Dev,' Kai said eventually, jolting Lina out of tangling thoughts of abandoned children and her father, blood on concrete and James' face when they had said goodbye. Silene saying, *Who are you? I'll stop you.*

She looked at the child beside her and said carefully, 'Have you met Dev? Do you like him?'

Kai shrugged very slightly. 'He came when Christopher Wiley died. Then he left again.'

'What's he like?' she asked, tiptoeing around the minefield of this boy's life.

He shrugged again, scattered breadcrumbs over the table like seeds. 'He catches pirates.'

'Is that good?' Lina remembered Anais in the barn over lunch.

'It's better than burning slums.' Kai lifted his eyes to the landscape beyond the windows, dark forest climbing to grey rock to shreds of summer snow. Lina studied his half-averted face, trying to fathom being saved by the very man who had destroyed you.

'Yes, I suppose it is,' she said, and then added, 'I imagine that makes him good at chasing monsters away, too. Don't you think?'

Kai turned his head, his eyes like low fires. 'I think the monster has already caught him.'

Chapter Seventeen

Neither Silene nor Xander returned to the main room for lunch. Thiago would probably not be back for hours, and Lina wished she had gone with him, if only because then she might be too busy to think.

She would go to Beli Iskar with or without Thiago. Perhaps he was more suited to threatening, or bribing, but she was the one with a child to protect and they might bend to that more readily than anything else. And if she did that today then tomorrow, she thought like a promise, tomorrow she would go out early and do some work, and perhaps for a few hours pretend that her data and the morning were all there was. So Beli Iskar first, then she would deal with the warnings from both Isla and her unnamed assistant. The blood on the martenitsa was waiting down in the lab too, but it scarcely mattered. They knew who was leaving the dolls, and why. Lina said goodbye to Kai where he had returned to the balcony, turning the rib bone in his hand, running its narrow edge along his palm as if it were a knife and he was casting a spell.

On the second floor she heard voices, and if the thin-faced man had not said anything, she would have carried on without trying to listen. Or perhaps not, but he *had* spoken, and she did stop.

'You have to stop talking like that, Mum.'

Bedcovers rustling restlessly. 'But she knows, darling, I can tell. You have to stop her saying anything.'

'Knows *what*, for fuck's sake? It wasn't you, and what else can possibly bloody matter?'

'But darling ... you can't see it–'

'You fought, Mum. I know that. So fucking what?' Footfalls crossing the room, and Lina jerked away but then they retreated again. Xander pacing. 'Everyone has affairs, right? It's not like Dad didn't get around. Oh for fuck's sake don't bother, I'm not stupid.'

'How...'

'Because I looked.' The footsteps stopped at the far side of the room. Curtain rings clattered and something thudded softly against the glass. 'I'm a *hacker*, Mum, remember. That thing you said I'd get arrested for? It's not hard to find stuff if you want to.'

Lina closed her eyes and leaned her head against the wall.

'Oh Xander.' Silene sounded forlorn, more now than when talking about her husband's death. 'We never meant to hurt you.'

A croak of laughter. 'The only thing that hurt me was your taste in men, Mum. I mean *Paul Ellis*, for fuck's sake? But that's not...' Lina thought he might have sat down because his voice softened. 'That doesn't matter anymore. Mum. You need to stop talking shit. It makes you sound guilty. What ... what is it you've been taking?'

'Alexander!' But it was half-hearted. Almost ... drowsy, as if Xander's question had come too late. 'It helps me sleep, darling. I get these ... it's like I'm dreaming awake and I see... Darling, I'm just tired, that's all.'

'Maybe you're taking too much.' Xander's sigh was achingly sad and Lina feared him so much, but she bled for him too. 'They said they're rounding up the last few terrorists, that they'll get some confessions and then... Mum, are you listening? Just a few more days, right? Then we can go home again. But we're safe here till then, unless you make these people suspect you. ESF might kick us out, and we can't go home until they've got those confessions, can we?'

He had sounded so adult and soothing until those last two words, turning the whole thing into a fabrication for himself as much as her. *They'll get some confessions.* Lina held her breath, touched her fingertips to the cool plaster of the wall, feeling grit subtle beneath her skin.

'She's one of them,' Silene said, her voice lower, slower, slipping towards sleep. 'She sees it, darling. You've got to stop her.'

Silence, Lina's lungs aching.

'She's... Look, yeah, she's on some lists and shit but don't ... just, I'll find out what that's about. But she doesn't know anything, Mum, alright?'

'We have to keep each other safe, don't we, darling?' Even quieter.

Xander did not answer and Lina pushed herself away from the wall. What would he think if he opened the door and saw her there, listening? She stepped light as rain across the landing and down the stairs. The one second from the bottom creaked, so she skipped it and fled silently into the blaze of light, heat, the calls of willow tits like a low stuttering distress.

You have the means at your disposal, I believe. There were other options though, and she would find them.

She had not been down to Beli Iskar since that day retrieving the deer tag, before James' arrest had unfolded her world. It was the same old woman she saw first though, standing on a stool to tie vine stems up into the overhead frame. The river's voice was summer-hushed, and somewhere a radio played through an open window.

'Dobro den,' she said quietly, wanting to reach for the woman in case she fell. 'May I help?'

The woman looked at her with her arms still raised, lifted her gaze to study the empty road, then nodded slowly. 'Molya,' she murmured, taking Lina's proffered hand to step back down.

'I am Lina,' Lina said, taking hold of a long vine full of tensile strength, weaving it carefully through the older branches.

'I know this,' the woman said, 'and I am Baba Ruzha.' Grandmother Rose; Lina could not tell whether the informality was a kindness or simple habit. Baba Ruzha passed her a length of twine and Lina took it, holding the vine in place one handed.

'Baba Ruzha,' she said, her face turned up to the leaf-layered sky, 'I wonder if you could tell me who the woman was that I met when I was last here.' She reached for another vine. Chickens muttered argumentatively somewhere nearby and the old lady held up another bit of twine, waiting for Lina to take it before speaking.

'What is it you want with her?'

Lina had been right then, about who had been in charge, and

what of. 'I mean no harm,' she said, turning to look at Baba Ruzha. 'Or trouble.'

'No? And yet what else would bring you here?'

'My sister has come to live with me,' she said, shaking loosened vinebark from her face. 'She is nine, and adopted.'

Baba Ruzha nodded, folding her arms across the faded cotton of her dress. The chickens' argument rose to a peak then subsided.

'She has lived through ... a lot of danger to get here. Our father was wounded and she had to leave him behind. She is...' Lina sighed, dropped her arms and turned to look at the other woman. 'She is frightened, and I do not want her to be frightened anymore.'

Baba Ruzha did not pretend to misunderstand her. 'So,' she said, 'you do not perhaps agree with your friend in this thing.'

Had Thiago really been so explicitly permissive? 'Can I speak with her?' she said instead of answering.

Baba Ruzha studied the street again, looking both ancient and unshakeable. 'Her name is Ognyana,' she said eventually. 'House seventeen, if she is at home.'

'Thank you,' Lina said, but Baba Ruzha only waved Lina away. 'Thank you,' Lina repeated, turning away.

'You know about the old ways, yes?'

Lina looked back at the woman, the twisted trunks of vines rising behind her like an archway. 'Some,' she said, thinking of Iva's carvings above the doors, her bowl of milk in the hearth.

'Yes,' Baba Ruzha said. 'Then you will understand perhaps there can be a great anger in the forests, if they are threatened. Anger that is not about,' she turned a palm over in a slicing gesture, '*politics*, but is about belonging.'

Lina frowned. 'This is *people* choosing to act, not ... myths and monsters.'

'Monsters?' Baba Ruzha repeated, and Lina heard the word again in a very different voice. 'Not monsters, no, but our people belong to these *myths*, so it is not possible to have one without the other. You do not understand this, I think. Although the lost boy does.'

She could only mean Kai with his moonlit hair and translucent eyes, but how had she heard of him? 'You are saying that the martenitsas and the *blood*,' and the missing man, but Lina daren't mention him, 'are the work of an old god?'

Baba Ruzha made a sound that was part laugh and part pure derision. 'I am saying, Doctor, that the old gods are become angry, and my people are bound to those gods just as they are bound to this land.'

There was nothing in the woman's story beyond folklore and perhaps the need to feel protected by something more than ESF's impersonal possessiveness. But Lina laid her palm on the warm slabs of the wall. 'Why are they angry, your gods?'

Nodding as if Lina had finally said something worthy, Baba Ruzha said, 'Because you have brought monsters here, and if you do not banish them, then the forests will.'

Lina could think of no answer to that; after a long moment, Baba Ruzha nodded again and turned back to her vines. Further into the village a donkey brayed harshly and Lina shivered, turning towards the noise and trying to push the word *monster* from her mind.

She had gone back to the news sites last night, searching not for Christopher Wiley's murder, but for his work. She wanted to say to Baba Ruzha that the monster was already dead, and if he was here then it was only as a ghost, manifested from the grief of his wife and sons.

In the week before his death he had ordered and accompanied the State military to a south London slum and he had watched from an armoured car as armoured men went from door to door and speakers announced the clearance. They gave them half an hour to get out before the bulldozers came in, and what could not be flattened was instead set alight. It was not in itself unprecedented, or sensational, but the death toll made a brief flurry even in the State papers, someone somewhere seeking to benefit from Christopher Wiley giving the murder of children such visible ... patronage. It had been foolish of him to be there in person and Lina wondered whether Kai's adoption had happened just before or just after, cause or effect.

She had found no record of the adoption, but perhaps they had not bothered to formalise it, buying him instead like they might a new piece of art.

So why, if the monster was already dead, were both Kai and this old woman still seeing them? And yet why not? The thing with seeing a monster killed was that it proved they existed. Lina inhaled slowly, smelling ripening pears and the sun-warmed road, realising that she had not been looking for house numbers painted in amongst the notices of the dead.

Number seventeen was over the river and up a steep side path so that Lina could look down from here onto the ochre-red tiles of the houses below. She stood at the closed gate for a long moment before pushing it open, avoiding contact with those sheets of paper detailing the household's lost, their black and white images staring half-averted out at her as if in warning, or despair.

'Hello?' she called, and a dog answered, running from behind the house barking in a deep and warning frenzy, but Lina was used to bears and wolves, and did not move, holding the dog's gaze.

'*Teech!*' A man shouted, but the dog had already halted, his head up but teeth unbared. Kolev Asenov came out from a barn, a hammer in one hand, and stopped when he saw her. 'Here,' he said, and the dog came to him. Better trained than many, Lina thought, wondering what it had been trained for.

'Dobro den,' she repeated as he moved a few steps into the sunlight, the muscles of his forearms defined and brown. 'Baba Ruzha said that Ognyana lived here.'

His expression sharpened at the name. 'What do you want with her?'

'Is she here?'

'No.'

She believed him. 'Can you pass a message to her?'

He did not answer straight away, so she said what she had said to Baba Ruzha already, not moving from the gate even though the dog had retreated to sprawl against the barn wall. 'I wanted to say that it is not needed, the things that have been done. And only risks the villages, yourselves.' Arguments were gathering on his face so she carried on quickly. 'I am asking that...' she thought of Baba Ruzha's words, 'that my sister be allowed to feel safe here.'

'As we are allowed to feel safe here?' Kolev had not moved from the centre of his courtyard, but he, like Baba Ruzha had done, flicked his gaze past her to the street and then jerked his head for her to come in away from the gate. He sat in a sun-crackled plastic chair and she sat in another, mismatched. The hammer was still in his hands but he was turning it absently, as if forgotten. Lina had not forgotten though, the anger and the images of him carrying a bloody trophy through the forest to her door. She kept her feet balanced on the ground.

'Thiago, Mr Ferdinando, is working on getting the tag decision reviewed,' she said carefully. 'What you have done, it has worked. But any more might begin to do harm.' The hammer turned again, the head falling heavily earthward. 'I am asking you to stop. Please.'

'Please,' he repeated quietly. He had kept his gaze on her the whole time she had been talking, eyes the colour of peat and full of an anger that seemed as timeless as Baba Ruzha had said. 'And what about the rest? The others you have brought?'

Lina laughed, surprising them both. '*I* brought? God, I don't want them here.' She took a breath. 'We all want them gone, I think, yes?'

Kolev curled a lip and she remembered the missing man again. Devendra Kapoor.

'Unless we want ESF and London sending investigators in, or a taskforce, we need to let them leave quietly. Without trouble.' Not that ESF would let London in, she thought, but Kolev might not know that.

He leaned back with an outrush of breath, the sun catching a slim sheen of sweat along his hairline. 'You are protecting them. You feel sorry for them maybe.'

'No,' Lina said, two thirds of a lie. 'I don't ... I don't want them to start asking questions about you.' Another partial lie because his were not the secrets she most feared them unearthing. 'If you frighten them too much, or ... hurt one of them,' and if she had not been watching she might have missed the flicker in Kolev's eyes, 'then they will make sure you are hurt too.'

'And if we only want to show them that we will protect our own, what then? If we show them that we *can* hurt them, if we choose, but will let them go?'

Lina met his hard gaze for a long moment then shook her head and studied the hammer lying across his knees, his scarred fingers pale with wood dust. 'How would you do that, Kolev?' He moved slightly and she realised he had not expected her to know his name. 'Show off your strength without making it a threat?' She tried a smile and failed. 'If it was that easy, then perhaps we would have fewer wars.'

Kolev's knuckles rose where he held the hammer, his wrists flexing. 'I do not know,' he said finally, and pushed to his feet. 'I do not know, but we will not do nothing, Doctor. You want to take our privacy. You bring outsiders who *drowned our people*. If we do nothing then we are saying that yes, it is okay to do these things. Then next time you will take more, and more, and more until we have lost everything.'

Lina rose as well, took a step away because Kolev would not. Although fearlessness might work with a dog, or a wolf, it would only aggravate a young man fighting for his own hope. 'Kolev, please don't make this worse than it is.' But he would not hear her. She had thought when he had gestured her into the courtyard ... but no. 'Will you tell Ognyana what I have said?'

He looked at the hammer in his hand, his face averted.

'Please. Just tell her. Let her decide.' Because she is your boss, Lina thought at him, and must also be your family.

'Yes,' Kolev said eventually, angrily. 'Yes, I will. Now you should go.'

She did, and her hands only began to shake when she had left the last house behind her, her shadow and the bike's leading her home. Had it done any good at all, her coming down here? At least she had tried though, and made nothing worse. But she wished Kolev had not so frequently fused her and ESF into one enemy entity. He knew, or he should, that she did not agree with the tagging policy. Unless he simply did not care to make the distinction. It left her uneasy.

Chapter Eighteen

Thiago returned home in the early evening barely more than an hour after Lina. Glancing up, she thought she saw Kai jump down from the flatbed of the truck and vanish behind a stack of logs, but then Thiago walked past and the very calmness of his face made her forget Kai and forget the ESF access log for Xander's tablet.

'What is it?' she said before he was fully into the lab, his shadow behind him. She thought she saw Kai again, his pale head slipping into view and then away. 'T?' She got up to close the door and Thiago raised an eyebrow because they rarely did so except in winter. He sat at his desk and stretched his false leg out, rubbing at the points where electronics met flesh. Sometimes he did this because he had pushed himself hard and the leg was aching, but sometimes, like now, Lina thought it was a reflex born of remembered pain.

'Did you find anyone who knew anything? What did they say?' If she had it in her to feel intimidated by him, the look on his face might have silenced her.

'Yes,' he said eventually. 'They say the BB have him.'

The Balanitse za Budeshte, the rebels, resistance; terrorists, if you were State. 'He's alive?' She hadn't been sure.

Thiago gave an abbreviated upward nod.

'Who told you?'

Lifting one shoulder a fraction, Thiago said, 'Iva's mother at first, then a contact over in Panichishte.'

'Do you think they're telling the truth?' It would not be the first time people laid claim to an act they had not carried out.

'It's likely.'

'But he was, is–' Lina stopped.

'More than capable of fighting them off?' That fractional shrug again. 'On unfamiliar terrain though, against a group...'

Lina nodded; he would know better than her. 'Why would they want him then?' she said. 'Ransom?' There was another option but it was not one the BB had ever used as far as she was aware. Swords and vid files. Or guns, but they so often seemed to prefer swords. 'To French State or ... or Silene?'

Thiago stopped massaging his leg and shot her a look full of forewarning. 'Blackmail, of a sort.'

Lina breathed out. She had not thought of that. 'For the tags? But that will just bring ESF down on the villages. It will...' Decimate or destroy or exile them. Kai had said that the monster had caught Dev, but monsters were complex things, and were sometimes also heroes.

'Partly,' Thiago said. 'Yes, but they want ESF to kick the Wileys out too. The repatriations.'

'Yes, Iva said. That's an admission that the villages are connected to the BB though. Why would they do that?'

'Mmm.' Thiago rubbed the black stubble of his head and frowned at a map on the wall.

'T?'

She thought he was simply going to pretend he hadn't heard her, but then he rose and came to stand beside her, his gaze searching and oddly cautious. 'I don't know,' he said slowly. 'They'll see sense. Some people are going down to talk to them tonight.' Which meant they had taken the injured stranger down onto the plains out of reach of ESF's cameras. Easy enough to keep an immobilised man hidden in one of the multitude of villages made secretive and brutal by the cruelties of State and climate.

'We can send drones out to search for his tag,' she said, already calculating numbers, battery longevity, range.

'Wait till I've spoken to them again tomorrow,' Thiago said, and then, seeing her screen, added, 'What are you doing?'

Lina turned to look at the text file she had been slowly interpreting. 'Just checking–'

'Xander or Silene?' Thiago interrupted.

Lina touched the screen with one finger, the tablet ID a long number at the top of the window. 'Xander,' she said. She was about to tell Thiago about the conversation she had overheard, Xander's determination to hunt her, but when she looked up, his anger about Dev was still there, and she didn't speak. It perplexed her in a way, because she would have expected some anger, yes, but mostly frustration at the stupidity of others, even a little dry amusement. Not this.

But then it was wearing on him as well, the joint stresses of the Wileys and the ESF tagging programme. Where Lina was able to almost disregard the latter, he was not. She reached to touch his arm, his skin warm beneath hers. 'They'll let him go,' she said, not entirely believing it. 'They can't have thought it through, so we just need to make sure they can get out of it smoothly.' Not back them into a corner, definitely not tell the Wileys.

Thiago looked down at her hand and smiled slightly for the first time. 'I'll go get coffee,' he said. 'Looks like you might need it.'

Lina turned to her screen and Thiago went towards the door, the light in the room swelling and condensing as he opened it. She had not told him about going to Beli Iskar, she realised, but it felt unimportant now.

At supper time Genni came unresisting, eyeing the meadow and forests warily.

'Shall we go and watch the fox den tomorrow evening?' Lina said lightly, as if none of their previous conversations had happened. 'We'd leave about four to be there before they wake. It's about a mile away, so we can either cycle or walk?'

They had reached the new house door and Genni looked back out at the forest again. 'I dunno,' she said.

'It's safe,' Lina said, thinking of the missing man and the bloodstained doll. 'Much safer than any city.' Which was still true.

The door closed, leaving them with shadows and the faint smell of cooked tomatoes from upstairs. Lina could not see Genni's face in the half-light, but she thought she could interpret her sister's silence. The lure of foxes, the unknown of the forest, loneliness, boredom and an unyielding blame. She sighed, their footsteps on the wooden stairs a muffled syncopation and the voices from the top floor insistent.

Xander's headphones lay around his neck leaking flattened music and Genni drifted towards him, perched herself on the far end of the sofa, setting her tablet in the same way he had his. Lina was so busy watching this quiet mimicry she did not notice Xander's eyes on her.

She smiled quickly and looked away, moving into the kitchen where Thiago offered her a beer and she shook her head. She had managed to trawl through his internet history for only the last thirty-six hours and had no idea when the boy slept, because there were no breaks in activity. Automated bots, she guessed, hunting while he slept. She had realised though that she was not skilled enough to untangle his tracks, because in amongst the normal news sites and blog sites, even grey markets and pirate stations, there were long visits to sites that made no sense. A laundromat in drowned Manhattan, an Igbo evening class web page in Hokkaido, a couple of others less strange but still not sitting quite right. And those bot connections running and running and running.

She stood watching the kettle's first curls of steam, and when Xander shifted his weight on the sofa she felt it as clearly as if she had been beside him. If he was clever enough to access London State's arrest lists, he was undoubtedly clever enough to find out she had been checking. If he looked. Lina wrapped her cold hands around her empty mug.

'Who's that?' Genni said to Xander, gesturing at his headphones.

Xander gave a name that Lina did not catch. Genni shifted a little closer to him, and he looked up again at Lina. Thiago had told him that Dev must have moved downslope out of ESF range, had likely decided he would make quicker progress bypassing the steep slopes around Ibar. It was nonsense, logistically, but neither Xander nor his mother could know that. Perhaps the blank suspicion in his face was just doubt and nothing to do with Lina's searches, or with his mother's words earlier.

Two of the bots had been set running three hours ago.

'What blog is that?' Genni asked. Xander sighed audibly, looking away from Lina to his screen.

'An old one. It's been locked.'

'What does that mean?' Genni was typing and frowning when a blank error window opened on her screen. 'I can't get it to open.'

'The guy got arrested.'

Lina had just finished pouring water into her mug and for a moment she could not move. Surely not, she thought. Without turning her head, she saw Genni lean over to look at Xander's screen.

No, Lina thought. Please don't ask.

'Who is he? What's the blog about?'

'The Low Hand. Some "resister",' the quotes as clear as if he'd gestured. 'He might have killed my dad.'

No, Lina thought again. Thiago was standing beside her as though he had been there all along, his hand brushed hers where it held the edge of the worktop, and how did his smallest touch feel like such a bulwark.

'Xander, do you want to get your mother?' Thiago said, turning around but still close enough for Lina to lean into him, if she wanted to.

'That's...' Genni was looking at Lina, her eyes wide, the low sun turning them into black holes in a gold-dark face. 'Wow. That was *your dad*?'

Oh god, Lina thought. She should have told Genni. She should have risked it.

Xander did not answer, hunching his shoulders.

'OMG,' Genni said quietly.

'Whatever,' he said, standing suddenly. 'Gonna post about it? Look at who I met, son who found his dad's body. Cool. Gotta be worth a few likes, right?'

He reached the top of the stairs and directed all of that grief-stricken anger at Thiago. 'No, I'm fucking not going to get my mum. And I'm not gonna to sit here while you gawk at me. Not like you guys don't have secrets, huh? You turn me into clickbait and I'll destroy you, just watch me.' He vanished noisily from sight and Genni's vast eyes blinked.

'Why didn't you tell me?' she said slowly. 'This is that James, isn't it? He got arrested *for this!*' She pulled herself sharply upright. '*That's* why we had to leave. 'Cos you used to–'

Lina had thrown herself across the room, landed at her sister's feet looking up into her face and folding one small hand within both of hers. Thiago moved to stand at the top of the stairs, listening.

'Hush, sweetheart,' Lina whispered. 'Please hush.' The shock in Genni's face was morphing into something else, and Lina spoke in a rush. 'You're right. It was James who was arrested, and my, our, connection with him that meant you and Dad had to leave. And I should have warned you who these people were but Dad hadn't and I didn't want to frighten you.' Genni pulled her hand away. 'I didn't want you to have to worry about giving anything away, watching yourself all the time. Because, darling, we can't let them know anything, do you understand? They know you escaped London without permission, but that's it. That's all, and we need to keep it like that, do you see?'

She halted, almost breathless. Thiago shifted his weight to lean against the wall, his eyes on her even though he was still listening for movement downstairs. Genni looked at her tablet with the error message still showing. Even that hurt, Lina realised. James' blog page locked by the police like an excision of him from the world.

'He's dead,' she said so quietly that Genni leaned forward to hear. 'They killed James. We have to be so careful, Genni love. Can you be careful?'

Genni watched her for a long moment before saying slowly, 'So what do I say?'

Lina gave a small sobbing laugh. 'As little as possible about London or why you came here, and especially not about their father.' Thiago blinked, looked away. 'You don't have to lie, just be vague. They aren't much interested in us anyway, so we need to keep it that way.'

Genni did not need to lie, but Lina did. Mirrors and smoke and ashes. Her sister looked up to Thiago, who shook his head infinitesimally. 'Your sister's right,' he said. 'Avoid talking about the last couple of weeks, and you'll be fine.'

Lina watched her near-stranger sister with her new name and trembling hands. She wanted to tell her that she was safe, that this place was safe, that their dad was safe. She stayed silent.

'I want to talk to Dad,' Genni said. 'You promised I could.'

Below them, music burst against the floor like a tremor. Lina fought not to bury her head in her hands and weep. 'I'm trying,' she said helplessly.

'Come and eat,' Thiago said. 'Before it goes cold.'

Chapter Nineteen

Lina had never imagined that her alarm waking her at four in the morning could be a relief, but this morning it truly was because she was going out. She was going to, if only briefly, put altitude and the forest's own presence between her and this place.

Her mood faltered as she passed Genni's room and saw a thin line of light beneath the door. She had slept with the light on since she had arrived, and after pausing with her hand against the wood, Lina went silently on downstairs, pushed the door open onto a waning night full of the scent of crannies beneath stones, wet grass and amphibians.

Xander's skilled pursuit could wait, as could another call to Isla, and please let Genni sleep until she was back; let Kolev Asenov leave no more bloody proofs of defiance. But as Lina was packing the panniers on her bike, the main house door opened and she turned to see Silene leaning against the frame, shockingly wan in the low light, pained and drawn.

'Silene,' Lina said, 'What are you...' the other woman was wearing shorts but her feet were bare. 'You wanted to come out?'

'Thiago mentioned it, and I couldn't sleep, so when I heard you...' Silene held a hand against her face, her eyes drifting from Lina to the meadow and back again. 'I thought ... But I'm not ... it's very dark still, isn't it?' Her head dipped and rose again as if fighting sleep, but her eyes were still scanning the shadows.

'Are you okay?' Spoken reflexively, with so little interest in the answer.

Silene's fingers moved from her face to her throat. 'I thought I heard someone.'

'Just me.' Lina closed the panniers and straightened her bike.

'I thought it might be him, or maybe Dev.'

Lina studied the other woman's face, greyed by the fading night. There was none of yesterday's frenetic accusation there now, just a vague, weary anxiousness. 'I'm sure he'll be here soon. You should get some sleep. I can take you out another time.'

Silene nodded but did not move, her eyes on Lina, yet Lina's face must be mostly shadowed. She said dreamily, 'You don't want me to come anyway, do you? Lina Stephenson and her adopted sibling. My Xander says you have secrets. He says you are hiding things and I think he's right, because otherwise you wouldn't be able to see him.'

It was not fair, Lina thought angrily, that one half-insensate widow could hold this kind of power. It was not fair. But then, there were a lot of things that were not fair and self-pity had never saved anyone.

'I don't know what you're talking about,' she said, forcibly gentle. 'All I want is for you and your sons to be safe here and then go safely home.'

'See?' Silene said as if to someone else. 'They're working together so she'll say he wasn't there. But the *blood* ... I didn't ... We need to stop her, or she will put my boy in danger.'

Out in the whispering dark of the meadow something moved, and Lina knew without turning that it was Kai. Dear god, she thought, there was nothing good or right about any of this. 'I really must get on,' she said, pushing the bike forward and mounting it, brushing her hair back from her face.

Kai laughed in the darkness and Silene flinched. 'I won't let you,' she said, her gaze so drifting and unfocused she might have been speaking to her young son or Lina, or even herself. Lina pushed away and left the woman there against the door, her son's figure half-visible. Lina might have called to him, but he laughed again and ran towards the house. Lina heard the door slam behind her and did not look back. Just a few hours, she thought, away from this.

It was a monthly habitat survey that she was going to do; fixed quadrats for canopy cover, fruit loads, perennial species diversity. Perhaps not urgent, or even particularly important. But it was hers, and real, and right now felt like a gift.

With one horizon bleeding towards morning, lightning was painting the far north with fleeting silver images of black cloud and the unmistakable whisper of a wildfire. Iva's Svarog god, Lina thought, it was his season again. Then she was beneath trees and both the dawn and the distant weather were cut off, leaving her alone with the thin beam of her head-torch. An occasional late returning bat tipped its wings into her wavering light, and the forest whispered.

By the time she reached the start coordinates, bursting into an opening on a small, boulder-strewn rise, the sun was painting every shade of orange across the undersides of clouds and the air in the clearing scintillated like it was hung with crystals. She climbed one of the boulders to drink coffee and checked in.

- *T, doing veg transects W2-5. On site.*
- *OK. Check in 0900h.*
- *You going to the villages this am?*
A pause.
- *Yes. Talk when you're back.*
- *:-)*
- *Negative*

Lina laughed and a blackcap cut off mid-syllable, staring at her from the edge of a hawthorn. She smiled at him and spotted a martenitsa, another scarlet girl pirouetting slowly just beside him.

Her tablet sounded another alarm and *Oh thank god*, Lina thought; the blackcap began to sing.

- *Update on your father,* Isla typed. *He is still in Kosice but there's talk of moving him to Bratislava. He's been seen by a medic.*

What sort of medic? Lina thought. A good one or a bought one, and what did they say? – *Why the move?*

- *Not sure. They cite security and overcrowding in Kosice. He was able to write a short message to you. I'll attach it below but first, we're not going to interfere with the Slovak state case. We'll provide your father a lawyer who will keep you, and us, updated.*

The world spun on, not caring about blackcaps or dawn-lit clearings, or how desperately Lina had wanted a different reply.

- *How good is their security?*

Isla's reply was slow and Lina listened to the hundreds of miles between them, a clutch of nestlings begging in the brush behind her, the high calls of rodents in the grass. She wished she had found the courage to confess absolutely everything to Isla at the start. It might have made a difference now, but she had left it too late.

- *It's good. But there are complications with the murder investigation in London and I'm afraid there may be ramifications for you, although I'm not yet sure how.*

- *Complications?* Lina rested one palm against the rock, the chill damp of it reminiscent of caves.

- *Perhaps nothing. But our Investigators suspect that State are looking for someone internally as a co-conspirator. And they think it was a response to the latest slum clearances in South London. Your friend's last blog posts were about that, I believe, the child fatality figures.* A pause during which Lina lifted her hands to type but could think of nothing to say. Isla carried on, *If it was an inside job, that helps you.*

Unless they wanted to bury that fact. Unless Xander succeeded. If Xander knew about this then his fear for his mother would only increase. If Silene knew it might explain her ... paranoia. - *I'm in the field just now, but can you send through my dad's message? Can I reply?*

- *Only through the lawyer (and therefore us). I'll send you their contact. Here's the message. Speak soon.*

Isla's chat window closed and another opened, three short paragraphs in it. Too short, Lina thought.

Lina my love,

I am well and safe, so please don't worry. The Slovaks are being considerate and very humane compared to the alternative. I hear that Jericho is with you and, Lina, it makes me so happy to know that my two beautiful children are together and protected. I suspect that you have learned by now of another connection between myself and your friend and I don't know what I can say about that except that I am glad I saw him, and that he still loved you, Lina. Although that came as no surprise to me, of course. The women of our family are not easily forgotten.

He only wished to talk. and even with what has come after, I am glad that he came. I told you once that love was the only thing we had, but I have thought since that I was wrong, Lina love. It is the best thing, yes, but if anything is ever to change then we need our anger too. We need to forgive ourselves our anger.

I am out of time, it seems. Keep your brother safe, and yourself, and I do not regret anything that has brought me to this place. I am so very, very proud of you and will be with you soon.

All my love, your father.

He used her name so often, Lina knew, because he feared forgetting it. She sat there as the blackcap sang and the first hoverflies rose sleepily from the grass, and thought that if she moved, all the pieces of her heart might fall out between her ribs like moths. But she must move, and she must think, and if she was to face Genni then she needed to cocoon her pain. She climbed back down into shade and moved though dew-damp vegetation to the first white-painted quadrat stake and began working a routine too familiar to occupy her mind.

These were the things she could do nothing about, she thought: Her father's freedom, Genni's anger, Silene's paranoia, London's pursuit.

These were the things that, with luck or creativity, she *could* do something about: Xander's hunting for her secrets, Silene's drugs, the locals and Devendra Kapoor, and perhaps, perhaps, her father's safety.

So. There were four birch saplings in this plot, all less than three metres tall. Would Silene be more or less likely to lash out if her drugs were switched to something less mind-altering? Lina was not actually sure, nor was she sure whether taking her off them could be deadly. She paused with a hand on a lovely arching *Rosa gallica*, dense with late flowers and early hips. Perhaps not that then.

Xander. She saw no way in which she or Thiago could match his skill, so she had two options: find someone to erase her and Genni and their father's footprints before they led Xander anywhere, or persuade him that she was not his enemy. She thought of Genni angling her body towards him on the sofa and folded the long leaf of a rose between her fingers until it snapped.

Meadowsweet and foxglove, the old leaves of hellebores.

Devendra Kapoor. Did she even want him to be found and brought to the station? It would calm Xander and his mother, but would that only be replacing two smaller threats with one powerful one? She could not forget the raptorine angle of his face in the first images they had found. She would go with Thiago to Govedartsi, she thought, or back to Baba Ruzha. If she could learn more about Devendra Kapoor then she could calibrate his threat.

The next quadrat lay beneath trees, the understorey transitioning abruptly to pine needles, dwarf shrubs and resinous, confiding air.

Oh god, Genni, Lina thought, stilling in the act of entering a measurement, heartbreak threatening to subsume her all over again. *Keep your brother safe, and yourself and I do not regret anything that has brought me to this place.*

Her tablet rang a proximity notice, wild boar close by, so she spoke aloud. 'He will be fine. I'll speak to Vitaly, or someone, see if they can put someone to watch him.'

Lina ran the waxy leaf of an arum through her fingers, counted nine within the quadrat. Thiago might know someone if Vitaly did not. But could she involve Thiago in this? She thought of his strained face, the anger, and the fact that he, too, had come here to escape, and thought, *no*. Not yet. If London were watching, or the PeaceKeepers, then she daren't do anything that might make them take notice of Thiago too. 'No,' she said aloud.

I am so very, very proud of you, her father had written. Which was one forgiveness, she thought, and he had also said that you needed your anger, which was another, although this one not just for her. Lina pressed a hand against an ache in her sternum, because perhaps she had never managed that forgiveness. Her life had been one delineated by love and by anger, and by her mother's belief that the fight was worth abandoning her child.

No. Lina stood up, brushing from her knees wormcasts and lichen fragments like tiny swords.

No, she thought again, walking on to the next quadrat without really looking. Back into the burgeoning heat, cobwebs fluorescing and sun-hungry bees motile above the vegetation. She was not even sure what she was negating. The laying of blame on the wrong person, or the suggestion that she had not done the same.

Love for strength, she thought, and anger for change. It would be good to remember that.

The next quadrat stake was five metres away. Lina moved slowly, thorns snagging and a hoverfly making her flick her head instinctively.

Talk to Xander, hint concern at Silene's self-medication. Go to Govedartsi. Get Genni to write to their father. Contact Vitaly. Something had moved through here during the night, a badger perhaps, leaving a dewy trail in the vegetation. Four things to do; Lina almost smiled.

She stepped into the badger's trail. Into the bent-over grasses right next to the stake.

A quiet, vast *snick*.

Pain.

And pain.

Oh god, *agony*. Red and white and *pain*. Sweeping up from her ankle, and Lina was on the ground, rocks beneath her knee and *pain* and her hands cradling, scrabbling at ...

The shock like ice. For a second, or two. Long enough for her to think with perfect precision:

Leg-hold trap. And: Meant for me.

But not just that. The *pain*. Teeth. Metal teeth, pain and steel and fury.

Someone was whimpering great gasping sobs, half-blind, hands pulling at those teeth, but *No!* Retching, teetering on unconsciousness. Fingers quivering, cradling a ghastly, nightmare monstrous ankle. Think! But she couldn't. Roaring in her ears and a scream in her throat, her locked teeth, nothing in her head but *No*, and *Please*, and *Stop. Make it stop. Make it stop.*

And *pull*, and *don't move*, and *get it off get it OFF GET IT OFF.*

Then an image of a packet, a needle. *The pain.* Needle. Her bag.

Blackness dragging and everything shrunk down to teeth in her skin eating muscles chewing bones.

Needle. Her bag.

Morphine.

Fumbling the bag, every movement making her lungs spasm. Fingers searching, and not this, *ohgodplease* or this or … first aid kit. Morphine.

Pushing it through trousers into thigh and how could this tiny wound hurt, when *that*, when *that* was every neurone and neurotransmitter and breath and molecule of oxygen and there was nothing beyond *pain*. Black swimming shrieking fury, pain pain pain. Nothing but metal in flesh and terror and the world plunging and...

...and this breath...

...and *this* one.

And this one … was not a scream.

She bent her head forward onto her left knee, the safe one. Breathing. Just breathing with the ebb and rise of agony, closed eyes and pain condensing heartbeat by heartbeat ununiversal, not apocalyptic. Just terrible, and frightening, and she was very, very alone.

Chapter Twenty

Lina touched the wet earth with one fingertip, saw pain stain her skin the colour of poppies, pure as birdsong. It had never occurred to her before that pain had its own music, but of course it did. Everything held song, she thought, watching her hands cradling air; red metal and chords trailing downward like the wound was singing to the earth.

She moved, cried out, small and mewling underneath sonatas. Her water bottle rolled loose from her bag, hitting her tablet and she studied both, songless. Thirst, she thought. A monster in her throat, her lungs full of sand. How hadn't she noticed? But she didn't dare reach for it, watching blood blossom on the soil and the silent tablet. Please, she thought at it, not sure why, but desperately. Please.

The pain sang and the world tilted beneath her and if she were not anchored by teeth and blood and metal she might have fallen off, slipped away. Please, she thought. Endlessly. Without end, outwith endings.

Please. Red songs and blackness.

Please. And blackness, and pain choral on her skin, her bones never ending, never ending, never ending...

...

'Lina!'

The song paused, minor keys sibilant. The world drifted, burned, echoed.

'Lina.' A crashing and voices and Thiago was there. Thiago beside her, his hands over hers so that they formed concentric layers over the metal and blood. A planet, an atom. Thiago was here and Lina began to cry. Because it would be okay now. It would be okay.

He had one arm bracing her, speaking to her, his voice an anchor in the same way the pain was an anchor. She could hear her own breath and could not tell if she was still crying because Thiago was asking her questions and it was so hard to understand.

'How much morphine,' he said as if he'd said it already. 'I can see one vial. Is that all you took, Lina?'

Scrabbling in her bag, the needle, the short, separate pain like a piccolo in the dark. 'Yes,' she said. 'Yes, one.'

'Good,' he said. 'I'm giving you another, okay? And I'm going to lie you down here.' She didn't think she would be able to move, but his hands on her were so solid and gentle that she went where they led her and then the ground held her along the length of her spine and she was so tired that the sky and the broken canopy above her looked like dreams.

'Fuck, oh my god, fuck, she's ... oh my god. What do we–'

Xander? He was here? Lina closed her eyes and the voice cut off as if blindness was silence. The pain sang a constant contralto and someone touched her hair very gently.

'Lina,' Thiago said. The fingers on her hair lifted, then returned, stroking. 'Lina, we're going to get the trap off you. I need you to hold still. I've got you, but try to hold yourself still, okay?'

'T,' Lina whispered.

'Jesus fuck, I can't see. All the blood, I think I'm going to be–' cutting off again.

'The spring is broken,' Thiago said, and Lina thought he was talking to that other voice because he sounded so different. 'You will pull it apart by hand. I'll do everything else.' There was a strange, strangled noise, but it was moving away from her or perhaps she was moving away from it. The pain and her pulse in her ears were shaking her into pieces and she needed Thiago's voice but he was further away too. 'Save it, Xander. We don't have time. You'll do what I tell you. Now.'

Xander, Lina thought. He was ... there was danger. She began to open her eyes, although it seemed surprisingly difficult, and the fingers moved from her hair to her eyelids, cool on her skin until she gave up the effort. A voice next to her ear whispered, 'It's okay, Lina. We'll save you from the monster.'

The monster, Lina thought. The roaring and the pain. 'Kai?' she whispered.

'Hush,' he said, his fingers stroking her hair again. And then she could hear him singing. Her heart and the pain and his thin bird's voice, they were holding her like water, pulling her deeper and looser and far away she heard other voices, and the pain screamed and screamed again but the sea was carrying her away, a pale boy singing her under, and she sank.

She drowned. She hung drifting.

There were figures by her side sometimes, her half-surfacing, fog heavy between her and them like distance or the passage of time. She thought once they were a child, or two. They sang and she remembered her brother, but it wasn't him because ... no, she had a sister, but hadn't she lost them both? She remembered fearing that. She remembered powerlessness. And now it wasn't a child, although how could she know? The skin of her arms knew, the air. Unless they had been there, but weren't anymore, unless it was their ghost brushing her skin. Memories of love.

'James?' she whispered. Or thought she did. Everything was soughing like the sea after a storm, refracting sunlight and nausea with wrongness worming inward, a rank, dank fear that moved like fish in the shadows.

A touch on her arm, stroking. A child saying 'Lina,' and she wondered who they were calling, their voice so full of tears. 'Lina.' As if they were talking to her, but that was not her name. Wrongness and fear.

'James?' she whispered again. The word like an echo in her skull, slipping between hippocampus and prefrontal cortex, murmuring to her cerebellum.

A different voice answered. Male, calm. Safe.

No, she thought. 'James, be careful. Don't...' Don't what? She tried to move but her body drifted away from her, her arms

and her ribs distant archipelagos, the sea washing her further
away.

'Don't tell them,' she whispered. If she could tell him this maybe
that would make it better, maybe then they could both come back.
'My Mum, please don't tell them.'

Silence.

'What shouldn't I tell them?' James said.

Lina drifted anchorless. He must remember, she thought. He
had held her through the nightmares and he was not holding her
now, longing and the sea washed over her. Shadows.

'Dad?' She tried again. But Dad knew, and James knew and no-
one else could ever know because they had been calling her Lina,
which meant ... grief, but so familiar it was like coming home. She
had lost half of herself. Her voice crackled like an old radio, like
dead voices from dead times.

Silence. The tide rose, her lungs filling with dreams.

'Hush,' the man said. 'Hush, Lina. It will be okay.'

Another moment. Light beyond her eyelids, and voices, and
someone singing fingers on her closed eyes, company on the
sea.

'Why isn't she awake yet?' The song gone, tenderness filling
Lina like a tide. 'You said she'd wake up soon.'

'She lost a lot of blood, and I had to keep her sedated while
I removed a couple of bone fragments. She's not in any danger.'
There was a warm hand on her calf, its weight like a gift, and
she felt the tension of it as the man spoke. Thiago, she thought.
Thiago's here.

'What if she gets infected? What if it's drug resistant? She'll
die. I'm not stupid; everybody knows you die if it's drug
resistant.'

Lina wanted to reach for that voice, touch it, hold it. Felt words
rising in her lungs but they rose no further, dissolving like ink.

'The wounds are clean. And we have the best possible antibiotics.
She won't die.' The fingers on her calf tightening, relaxing.

There were memories of a nut-brown boy turning his body into
music, but that boy was a girl and no longer danced, and Lina

hung in water the colour of the underside of a wave with forgotten music rising and falling in time with her heart.

The room was dark when Lina woke, but this time, for the first time, she knew she was properly awake. Fully present at last. Even the parts that hurt were a comfort, because at least they were there; at least if they hurt, then she was there too.

She needed the toilet. A drink, a wash, crusted with pain and sleep and drugs like detritus on her skin. Lying still, she thought about these things, about how enormous it was to brace yourself against pain. Aware, distantly, that it was far easier to think about this hurt, this physical thing than about all the other things lingering blackly in the doorways of her mind.

Then she hauled herself upright. Air whining between her teeth, machinery sending out alerts, her ankle mercifully bound up so that she couldn't see what lay beneath. The alert sounded again. Remote medics asking how she was feeling, telling her she'd needed blood and sutures, that they'd removed minor bone fragments, that she had been asleep for two days. The screen was very bright in the unlit room, casting ugly, angular shadows.

Two days. The advantage, she realised, of remote medical care, was that as long as she remembered to remove her I.V. line first, when they told her to stay in bed they had no way of actually making her.

Thiago had left crutches against her bed, with a note saying, 'NOT downstairs.' She might have obeyed him. Dizziness, agony, a faint, lurching nausea, were nearly flooring her. But a heavy gibbous moon cast silvery light across the bathroom floor and an eagle owl was calling soft and sonorous, laden with shadows and starlight and the cool smell of pines at night. And she needed that.

There was also this: she needed to be able to run.

She could not entirely recall why, only that it might be terribly important. That if certain things happened then she would need to. ... her mind wavered, as if debating whether to let her remember. She would need to ... go to her father, to save him. The top of the staircase yawed black before her. She remembered. If there came a moment when she had to choose between her father's life and her own, then she would run to him the same way she had once run away.

More truths hung above her, but she ignored them because the stairs were wavering beneath her feet. She ought to go back to bed, painfully aware of the flimsy wall between her and where Thiago was sleeping and what he'd say if he woke. Hidden stitches were screaming, but she just wanted to stand in the darkness, her forest around her like a blanket. So she lurched vertiginous downstairs, doggedly on through the lab, and then out.

There were no lights in either of the houses, only one out of sight in the barn turning the courtyard into a soft-lit well, and the meadow beyond an etching that could have been of fog, or water, or nothing on earth. Lina filled her lungs with starlit air, her ankle wept and a swimming faintness clawed at her skull. If she wanted to stay out here, she realised, then she needed to sit. The tree stump only a short distance into the meadow seemed almost beyond reach and yet moving out from shadow into moonlight was like moving into a waterfall, becoming cleansed. Here was her forest. She took a long unsteady breath when she finally sat. The tideline of the trees, the voices of crickets like a second skin, the breath of the mountains against her cheek, something called distantly and Lina thought, *Tengmalm's owl*, almost smiling.

And then voices. Every muscle in Lina's body tensed, her ankle howled and her eyes strained wide against the pain and the dark. Because someone had set a trap in the grass where she would walk, and she had bled into the earth because someone had wanted her to bleed. And now someone had come to finish what the trap had begun.

...Her mind caught up. The voices were coming from the barn, where that lone, yellow light was shining, and she knew them both. She knew them. Although that did not make one of them any more innocent.

Xander was speaking with raw fury; perhaps he had been talking quietly before or perhaps he had slunk past with her still half-adrift on painkillers.

'It was those fucking locals, you know it was, and I want to know what you're gonna do about them?'

Thiago's voice was too level and quiet for her to hear. Lina wanted to go to him, stand within his line of sight so that she felt safe.

'It had to be them. Who the fuck else would it have been?'

Thiago said something very brief, and Xander's voice rose to a shout. '*Dev?*'

Lina watched that occluded light as if she would be able to see through it to Thiago, map out his thoughts from the infinitesimals of his face.

'Yeah well you're totally fucking wrong, cos they weren't even after your precious fucking Lina, were they? They were after my mum.'

'What?' Not louder so much as sharper.

'Yeah she said she was going to go with her that morning. So who heard her say that, then? That cook and her niece? You? Cos that seems a bit more fucking likely than someone suddenly taking against Lina when they've been threatening us since we got here. And a shitload more likely than Dev hiding out in the woods to attack you guys. I mean, why the fuck?'

Silence. Lina closed her eyes and the owl called again.

'I heard you talking to the cook, you know? Saying you were done with it, so I know you were totally in with it before. All those dolls and shit. Thought you could scare us away, right? Well, fuck, that kind of backfired didn't it?'

The sound of metal hitting metal, Thiago talking again even softer than before and Lina was not even a little surprised at Xander's changed tone.

'I just... I ... look, if they were after my mum then I have a right, yeah? To know what you're gonna do. That's all I meant, okay?' A pause. Lina held Xander's angry young face in her mind and felt all those suspended memories slipping back into place. 'She's ... she's not right. You can see that, right? She thinks... Doesn't matter, just, if she's not safe then you need to get us out of here. We can stay in Sofia or something.'

He sounded cowed and tired and a little bewildered and Lina thought, not for the first time, that Silene's drug-addled, wilful neglect was more deadly to her sons than their father's death had been. There were more words, but the heat had gone from Xander's, and the cold from Thiago's and this time Lina did see the teenager cross the courtyard, although he did not see her in her grey tunic against the silver sea of grass.

Rewoken worries wove drowsily through her mind and Lina spread her palms upturned to the moonlight as if she might gather it and then paint herself in it like armour. It did not surprise her that Thiago would cut himself off from the BB. But Xander knew he had supported them, and the mountain's slow breeze plucked shivers from her skin. Not Thiago, she thought; the idea of him vulnerable made her want to cry and she remembered crying against him with the trap in her flesh, then for the first time remembered Kai too, singing and stroking his thin fingers through her hair. Why had Thiago let him come and see her like that, and had Genni been waiting here with only Silene to stop her from being entirely alone?

Silene. Lina tipped her palms, half-expecting moonlight to run molten from them, then pressed her fingertips against her knees, wanting to move her leg against the pain but staying still. Xander had said the trap was meant for Silene, whereas Lina had assumed it had been meant for her.

But Silene had been waiting for her in the greyed shadows before dawn, with only drugs and the darkness stopping her coming. So who had known about that strange, restless whim? Lina herself. Anais. Thiago had told Silene that Lina was going out, but he would not have done so if he had known she might want to tag along. Anais would have told Iva, if the information had mattered. Which would mean it could have been for Silene ... and yet Lina struggled to believe it ... Kolev saying 'you' when he meant 'ESF'. Her saying to him, *'How would you do that, Kolev? Show off your strength without making it a threat?* Him replying furiously, *'I do not know, but we will not do nothing, Doctor.'* Wanting to scare off the Wileys and hating ESF, the hammer in his hands and the old woman talking of angry gods in the forest.

Lina pushed herself to standing with a hiss of pain, the skyline rippling like a blown sheet, then settling again. Perhaps he had thought that hurting her was the answer. Frighten the Wileys into leaving without angering them enough for London to demand retribution. Perhaps he had thought that it could be passed off to ESF as a poaching accident. Lina paused between one awkward step and the next, her wounded foot hanging, humming pain. Perhaps Kolev had thought *Thiago* would pass it off to ESF as a poaching accident. Perhaps he had thought that because Thiago had said so.

She only stopped again once she was at the door to the lab, turned towards the barn and the light that meant Thiago was still there although she could hear no sound at all. She took one slow breath and then another, the lure of bed and painkillers like a weight, Thiago's presence, Thiago's reassurance the counterweight. Tomorrow, she thought. If Thiago had agreed to the trap then it had been for Silene.

If they had thought Thiago sufficiently loyal to them though, that he'd forgive them either target, then she could not handle that pain right now. It shouldn't hurt because it could never be true; was ridiculous that it might feel even a little like betrayal. But it did, and she was dizzy and where the starlight had comforted her before, now the sleeping houses and that quiet light made her feel alone.

Tomorrow, she thought, and went quietly inside.

Chapter Twenty-One

'You disconnected the medic.'

Lina's dreams had been full of all the people she had lost and all the names, but now it was morning and Thiago was leaning against the doorframe, scowling at her with the dawn painting his black eyes fiery.

'They kept on wanting to talk to me.'

He huffed a laugh and came closer, peeling the blanket back from her ankle without ceremony and narrowing his eyes at the red-black Rorschach patterns on the dressings. 'Brace yourself.' He began to peel the wrappings off.

Lina tried not to yelp at the pain, tendons shifting over knuckles as her hands tightened on the blanket.

'Sorry,' he added, belatedly.

You could not do what Lina did and be squeamish. She was used to death, the intricate, intimate wonder that lay beneath fur and feathers and skin. But this was *her* skin, and *her* pain, and the vision overlaid on black-stitched bruises of metal teeth and ribbons of blood trailing down to the ground.

'Yuck,' she said very faintly and lay back childlike, holding her breath as he cleaned and re-covered each wound with his blunt fingers incredibly gentle. 'Where's Genni?'

'The new house. With Xander.'

So Lina would go to her there. Show herself whole.

'You'll live, I expect,' Thiago said once he'd finished, and Lina smiled at him with relief. He was quarter-turned away from her, tidying up, and his voice when he spoke again was very different.

'You frightened me, Lina.'

She had always liked the way he pronounced her name. He made the word more hers than her father had ever managed however often he said it. Pushing herself upright and lifting her legs carefully over the edge of the bed, sitting close to Thiago but not touching. He still didn't look up.

'Me too,' she said quietly. In the gilded light she could not fathom how someone else's assumptions could hurt her or ever diminish this. 'Thank you, T.' For coming to get her, for coming so fast, for caring enough to fear for her.

'Don't. It shouldn't have happened.'

She looked at him and her heart ached quietly. 'It's not your fault, T.'

He didn't answer, casting her a sideways look that she could not entirely read. 'You're meant to stay in bed,' he said. 'I'll bring you some food.' He did not move though, as if he knew there were questions she wanted to ask.

'T?' she said softly. His eyes held hers unblinking, so she took a breath and said, 'It was them, the locals, or the BB.'

Thiago tilted his head but then nodded slowly, not saying which. Perhaps it did not matter. He had accused Devendra Kapoor last night, to Xander, and Lina wanted to ask about that, but he did not know she had overheard, and she shied away from it.

'For me or Silene?' she asked instead.

He frowned directionlessly. 'I wish I knew. Lina–'

'T,' she cut him off. 'Did they think you'd cover it up for them?'

He stepped forward and sank into the chair, looking up at her with elbows on knees and his hands hanging loose. 'They ought to have known better. I would never–' he stopped, frowned, started again, 'They crossed a line, Lina. Iva is furious as well.'

Lina smiled, but he did not.

'I didn't know about Silene,' he added. 'Doesn't mean I'll let it go though. I wouldn't.'

'I know,' Lina said, her heart hurting all over again because she *did* know. 'Anything could have stepped on it,' she said, only now realising and the horror of it hitting her like ice. 'It's *breeding season*. They could have got *anything*, T.'

He was laughing, lifting a hand to rub over his face. 'Which would have been worse than this?' gesturing at her leg. 'Christ, Lina.'

She had to laugh too, although the movement made her ankle spark pain, because yes it might be a little ridiculous to think like that, but she couldn't help it. Thiago would probably have felt the same if it had been him, and he knew that.

She gathered the crutches and Thiago looked at her levelly. 'You are meant to stay in bed,' he repeated but made no other comment when she shooed him out of the room so that she could dress, nor as he went down the stairs beside her, not touching but ready to.

'Something happened last night,' Thiago said when she was two steps from the bottom, him below her looking up, his pupils contracting. Lina could see the strain of the last two days in his face, the way he was favouring his leg.

She stopped, foot suspended over the next drop. 'W-what?' she managed, thinking of the conversation overheard.

But it wasn't that, and the words were so nonsensical that it took her a moment to make sense of them. Maybe she was not entirely coherent yet.

'There was,' she repeated him, 'a dead fox nailed to the new house door.' Thiago nodded. 'And Genni found it this morning.'

They reached the lab. 'Wow,' she whispered. Then, more usefully. 'Tag?'

'No.' Not all foxes were. Enough only for population monitoring.

'How old?' She meant how long dead, but Thiago understood.

He shrugged. 'Soil type places it high up. I'd say three weeks, maybe four.'

This at least was familiar. She rested her crutches against the desk and reached for gloves. A soiled, crushed martenitsa lay within the fox's decayed jaws, and touching it, she raised an eyebrow at Thiago.

'Young male. No obvious cause,' he said. The calling card didn't really need discussing.

Lina nodded. Winters were hard on the juveniles, and spring

was harder still on the young males, who could not yet compete
with their elders. She ran her fingertip over the clean edges of his
teeth, the perfect knife-tip canines. With an untagged fox she'd
normally leave it at that. But – Lina half-turned to where Thiago
was waiting without impatience – this was different. She found
that she was stroking the pared skeleton of the fox's front paw,
soothing.

'He was nailed to...' trying to anchor this wrongness in amongst
all the others. 'Cameras?'

Thaigo gave a single upward nod. 'On it,' he said. There was a
blankness in his face that held rage and Lina thought that the trap
had flicked a switch in him which didn't bode well.

'Genetics,' she said calmly, 'and soil samples. I'll try to get a
location. We might get lucky.' She reached for her tablet and was
already setting up a new file when another thing occurred to her.
'The cameras at the trap, did they–'

Thiago almost imperceptibly flinched and she wanted to say
again, *It's not your fault*, but he spoke first.

'They were down.'

'Oh.' She ran a hand over the fox's fur. 'The shadow ... Then it
really was the BB,' meaning the trap, 'and they really do have EM
tech.'

Thiago touched the nail still in the fox's skull, said after a long
pause, 'So it would seem.'

Oh god, she thought, he's going to kill them all. She was about
to say, *How did they get something like that, and why would they go
this far? They would know where it would end, why risk it?* But he
spoke first.

'I've called a taskforce in.'

There it was.

'No! The villagers–' The expression on Thiago's face cut her off.

It wasn't for the martenitsas or the tag or even this macabre fox,
but for the trap. She couldn't hate the rebels for any of it though,
she realised. She honestly couldn't. 'Not for me,' she said softly.

'Why not?'

'Because I understand them,' she said. 'And I forgive them. And
there must be another way.'

'There isn't.'

There's compassion, she thought, and patience. But it wasn't just about her; Genni was here, and where might this end if they did nothing to stop it?

Thiago was searching her face and she couldn't answer. After a long moment, she saw him relax.

So the taskforce would come in then.

But what would that mean for Silene and Xander and Kai? Would they leave rather than see it, or would they not care, hardened to brutality the way Lina had so determinedly unhardened herself? They might see only retribution for an imagined sin. Her ankle pulsed when she moved, the stitches needle-points of fire. Not imagined then, but she remembered Kai whispering of monsters and the things she had read about Christopher Wiley, and would risk the trap again rather than see Iva's people pay for any of this.

Kolev had said, *If we do nothing then we are saying that yes, it is okay to do these things.* And Lina had always known this, her father had always known. So there must be a way, she thought, her fingers touching broken skin, bared bones. To not become a monster.

Thiago had asked Silene and Xander to come to the lounge and they came perhaps because they had the same dreadful sense of momentum that Lina had. Or they came hoping for deliverance.

Lina struggled up the stairs behind Thiago, irritably, determinedly mobile, not wanting anyone to see her any weaker than she already looked.

Iva and Anais were not there, and it looked like they might not have come in at all. Crumbs were scattered on the counter from yesterday's bread, and both Xander and Genni were at the table with plates of toast half-eaten in front of them. Xander had been saying something but stopped as Lina appeared, Genni leaning towards him, her eyes on both their tablets with a small frown of concentration on her face. Lina sat carefully opposite them both, the mountains secreted behind morning mist, the meadow slipping into view and away again like the station were floating. It would burn off soon and by late morning it would become hard to imagine this moment here, cool and grey and water-spangled.

Thiago caught one of Lina's crutches as it began to slide from the bench, touched her shoulder lightly and turned to the kitchen. Silene was curled into the corner of the sofa as if sleeping, and Lina caught Kai's slantwise gaze on the balcony and smiled at him.

Genni had not looked up at her yet, but Lina thought she remembered her sister's voice when she had been adrift. She reached across the scarred wood to touch her hand, her own gold-tanned skin and Genni's rich brown. 'Hey,' she said quietly, and Genni looked up. Her fingers beneath Lina's were fibrillating like a heart. 'You okay?'

Genni nodded mutely, her eyes scanning Lina as if looking for signs of breakage. She was breathing quick and shallow.

'You guys looked after me well, thank you.'

She nodded again. 'Who did it?' she said. Xander looked up from his tablet, slice of toast in one hand; Kai was floating silently towards them and Silene had opened her eyes.

'We'll get to that,' Thiago said before Lina could answer. 'Coffee first.' He set some in front of Lina, along with a plate of bread and honey, and she tilted her head back to smile at him. He did not smile back.

'Thiago said you found the fox, love,' Lina said to her sister, cradling the mug in both hands, gathering strength from the heat. 'I'm sorry you had to see that. It's a bit yucky, huh?'

Xander snorted and Kai reached Lina's side, lingering like a pale shadow, resting his fingertips on the table but not sitting.

'Yeah,' Genni said, edgy, holding herself tightly. 'Was that the same people?'

'It died in the forest,' Kai whispered and Lina glanced at him, wondering.

'It did,' she said to him, Genni's gaze flicked from Lina to Kai, frowning. Silene rose to her feet sharply. 'We'll find out who it was from all our cameras. It was a very silly thing for them to do.'

Xander snorted again and muttered something derisive under his breath. Another time, with another boy, Lina might have challenged that. Silene came to the table, giving Kai a wide berth before pulling a bottle from her pocket and shaking tablets into it.

Xander looked from the tablets to his mother's face, colour rising beneath his thin stubble.

'They were after me,' Silene whispered, dry swallowing the tablets. Lina winced and Thiago passed behind her so closely that Kai had to slip out of the way at the last minute. Lina frowned at Thiago as he leaned against a window, but his eyes were on Silene.

'The monster's coming,' Kai whispered. Silene flinched. 'He's hungry.'

'Why were they after you?' Genni asked Silene as if Kai had not spoken. Lina felt cold trace a pattern down her spine. Had Genni spoken to Kai at all? She could not remember.

'Why?' Silene said on a gasp. 'Because they hate me. They want to get rid of me. Someone always wants to get rid of you. And they want to punish me for—'

'Mum,' Xander cut her off, tension bulking his shoulders.

'But it's *true*, darling. I thought we could leave it behind, but it's *here too*. You don't see it, so you think if they arrest them all it will be over, but it won't and *she knows why*.' Pointing a ringed, unsteady finger at Lina, and Lina saw their eyes all turn to her, aware of the slow pulse of pain in her ankle, her woundedness.

'I think,' Thiago said, and the eyes all slid away. Lina took a breath, then another. 'I should update you on ESF's response to these events.'

Lina had reached decisions in the moments before the trap, and she needed to act on them now. Remember that the trap was not the end of anything. Xander was still trying to protect Silene from rumours of her guilt. Or from actual guilt; a fight gone wrong over infidelity or that last attack in South London where so many children had died. Thiago was telling them about the taskforce while Lina watched low gilded sunlight touch the upper edges of the mist. It was quiet outside, the meadow birds waiting for warmth as the swifts climbed above the mist to feed.

'So when will they come, this taskforce?' Xander said challengingly. Silene was resting her head on one hand, the other flexing on the table, almost vibrating.

'That depends on the weather.'

Xander was silent for a moment, thinking, and then looked

at his mum. She smiled, but her eyes were slipping in and out of focus, and Lina thought she might fall asleep right there.

'Then you need to get us out. We'll stay in Sofia.'

'What was that, darling?' Silene opened her eyes wide and straightened like a drunk might when accused of being drunk. 'But we can't leave. Not until someone confesses and they call it off, then maybe.' She shuddered, glanced at Kai and shuddered again. Lina touched the back of Kai's hand, Thiago and Silene watched her. 'They sent it here after me, look, and *she's* helping it. And...' Inhaling raggedly. 'They'd rather it was me, don't you see? Better a jealous wife than a security failure.' She laughed gaspingly, too high. 'So they won't give up until they can prove it or until they kill me. Look at her father. *He* knew it wasn't them and they *stabbed* him, darling! Just like ... just ... I never wanted the *blood*, darling. We can't leave. Not until Dev is here to protect us.'

Lina held herself still and met her sister's too-bright eyes steadily. *Yes*, she wanted to say. *He was stabbed, but he survived, just like we will survive.* And, *It's okay, it's okay, it's okay.*

'Fuck's sake,' Xander muttered, his hands fisted, 'So what then? We just hide in the house? Wait till they find the balls to come for us here?' Kai laughed sibilantly. 'And what *about* Dev anyway? What the fuck are you doing about him?'

'You could find him, couldn't you?' Genni said to Xander as if utterly sure of the answer. 'With his tag and all the cameras and things, you'd be able to find him easy.'

Xander shifted, ran his fingers over his tablet, opened his mouth and closed it again.

'I doubt it,' Thiago said. He knew something, Lina realised, or suspected it. Was the EM tech being used to hide Dev from both satellites and Lina's waiting drones?

'He's coming to protect us,' Silene said, beginning to sag again, focus drifting. A tracery of sunlight blossomed across the table. Lina reached both hands into it, and outside a swallow began to sing.

'When he's here, he'll stop it. He'll know how. And he'll know about you too,' looking at Lina again, through her. 'You're working with them, I know it. Xander said you ... darling? Was it so they leave her father alone? Or to keep that man alive? Dev will stop you though, stop you...' gesturing with one hand and Kai shifted. Stop her from talking to Kai, befriending Kai, stop her from hearing something that Kai knew?

'Stop her, will he?' Thiago said, and the sound of his voice made Lina almost rise from her seat to go to him. But Xander's head came up like a wounded beast.

'He won't need to. She won't tell anyone anything, because otherwise I'll tell everyone what I know.'

The sunlight strengthened and a green woodpecker laughed, the treeline visible through the mist now as a lacework of shadows. Oh Genni, Lina thought sadly, you did not deserve any of this.

'And what's that?' Thiago spoke very quietly, but Xander looked at Lina rather than meet his eyes.

'That she used to sleep with one of the guys who killed my dad.'

Genni's head was bent, as if frightened of what she might see, or say, and Kai drifted slowly around the table, his eyes moving between Xander and Genni thoughtfully.

'See?' Silene whispered. 'Darling, see? That's how she knows.'

Thiago laughed and Xander flinched. 'That's it? London already know that. So does ESF. It means nothing. And she's working with no-one. It was her caught in a trap two days ago, in case you'd forgotten.' He made a fractious, restless movement and Lina wanted to touch his wrist, to say, *I'm okay, T. We'll sort this. Don't worry*. Not so much because she believed it but because it was what he needed to hear.

Xander stared at Lina as if it had never occurred to him that ESF might know and still protect her. As if he had also forgotten about the trap and her blood. But then his face shifted, his heavy hands pulling his tablet against him like a shield. 'Yeah well, I'll bet there's more.'

'Why is it important?' Genni asked, and Xander froze in the act of pushing away from the table.

'Cos...' He looked at his mother, 'cos anyone who was behind my dad's murder deserves to die. That's why.'

Genni looked at Lina and for a moment, for a heartbeat, Lina saw agreement on her face. Not sympathy for the dead man but empathy for the son, and that same anger as before. Someone must be to blame for all this hurt, and perhaps it was Lina. Kai moved closer to Genni, watching her, his amber eyes narrowed catlike.

'No,' Lina said, not sure which child she was speaking to. 'No, don't–'

'Xander, darling,' Silene's voice was brittle as a husk and as she rose to her feet, she wavered. 'I cannot ... all the blood ... help me, darling.' Xander hesitated and Lina's ankle sang, but when she thought he might stay, hold onto his vengeance, his shoulders dropped and he grabbed at his mother's arm not gently but bearing her up. Silene looked at Thiago where he was leaning darkly against the window. There was blue in the sky now, Lina's leg was burning miniature suns.

'You have to stop them getting me. You and Dev. It wasn't my fault, I told him–' Xander pulled and she fell silent, her free hand cradling her cheek, fingernails making craters on her skin.

Chapter Twenty-Two

Lina sighed into the silence that followed, watching the shades of brown pulled from Genni's hair by the backlit sun. 'We need to sort your hair out, don't we?' she said. 'I've got some conditioner that should suit it, and some oils, I think.'

'Why's she think someone wants to kill her?'

Thiago was looking out to the leavening sky, his eyes black slashes. Kai sat beside Genni, mimicking the placement of her hands. She still did not look at him and that same icy spider trailed Lina's skin. Something was very wrong here, but she could not fathom what it was.

'I think,' she said slowly, 'she is frightened someone from London blames her for her husband's death, and will either arrest or ... send someone to kill her.'

Once upon a time a child might have questioned why the government might kill a murder suspect, but Genni did not even blink. 'The same people that tried to kill Dad. But if they think the resistance did it, then why would they be after her too?'

Lina tried to untangle Silene's incoherent words, cold in her stomach and a wooziness creeping up her limbs. 'I'm not sure she's thinking anything very clearly, to be honest. But she thinks Dad knows it *wasn't* the resistance. She said: *He knew it wasn't them, so they stabbed him.*'

Genni hands were running over her arms, plucking at the cloth. Lina forced herself to smile, to shrug off the unease and confusion. 'She's quite unwell, I think, love. Don't pay her any attention. Dad's okay and we're okay.'

Thiago pushed away from the window. 'I'm going to Panichishte.'

To see if his contact in the BB would tell him any more. 'Will you warn them,' she said, 'about the taskforce?'

'No.'

'T,' she said quietly.

'No.'

'We're warning Iva,' she said.

His anger faltered and he breathed out harshly. It was as much agreement as Lina would get, but it was enough, so she changed the subject. 'How are we going to get Devendra Kapoor back?' Genni tilted her head and Kai did the same. Dark and light, shadowy eyes and translucent, but in a multitude of ways exactly the same.

Thiago studied her face. 'That's what I want to find out.' Lina nodded. 'You should rest. Need a hand down the stairs?'

'No thanks.' Although she wasn't entirely sure about that. After another careful examination of her, he left.

Genni and Kai were both watching her expectantly, and it took Lina a moment to realise Genni had asked a question. 'Sorry, love?' she said.

'Who is it after Silene and *are* you part of it? *Is* it the resistance? But why did you–' cutting herself off, fingers digging into flesh. Kai tilted his head and hummed a quiet descending chord. Lina closed her eyes. She had earned that suspicion perhaps, but dear god it still hurt.

'She thinks it's the State,' she said. 'No, I'm not part of anything and god knows why she thinks I'd be helping them. I guess no-one has confessed,' however meaningless such a confession would be, 'and she said State won't want to admit that terrorists could kill someone so important without inside help. She's a political reporter, so she'll have enemies who might want to see her … removed.' She looked at Kai, wrestling sorrow and ghosts. 'Xander is trying to protect her from all of that, I think.'

'He's a *hacker*.' Genni said it with wonder, releasing her hold on her arms. 'He's teaching me.'

Kai had something in his hands, although Lina had not seen where it came from. The rib bone, she realised, and remembered the fox waiting for her down in the lab.

'She doesn't see what he is,' he said. 'And she wouldn't protect you if the monsters came, would she?' He turned the rib bone and pressed the tip into the table as if it were a blade. Genni shifted but did not speak, and Lina chose to address the easier statement.

'You will be careful, won't you?' Genni looked up, that ready anger rising like a fire. 'Not just about what you say to him, but ... it's very, very illegal,' she said. 'The things he does. And you don't have State status to protect you.'

'I thought you said I was safe here.'

'Yes,' Lina wanted to sigh. Her leg was agony and she was so tired. She held herself still and spoke quietly, remembering Thiago saying that enough money would buy someone willing to risk coming even here. 'But it's not worth the risk, Genni love. It really isn't. Dad would say the same; you know he would.'

Genni did know, that much was obvious, but she wasn't about to admit to it. Instead she rose and moved towards the sofas. 'Yeah well he's not here, is he? And whose fault's that?'

Lina closed her eyes.

'She blames you for the monsters,' Kai whispered, the bone held out before him. 'I don't.'

'I know,' Lina said, wondering if her mother were here, would Lina blame her. Would she have done when she was a child? 'I'm going to go do something with that fox,' she said, but neither child answered her. Genni bent over her tablet with headphones over her ears, Kai watching her with his shining eyes unfathomable. She paused. 'I didn't say thank you for helping me when I was in the trap. Singing to me.'

Kai turned so that the sunlight fell slantwise across his face, the bones too clear. 'I won't let the monster hurt you again,' he said.

'Why did you come with Thiago and Xander?' she said. 'You should have stayed here with your mum and Genni.'

He blinked slowly. 'I didn't know who the monster was hunting.'

'I don't think it meant to hurt me,' she said, although it was a partial lie and Kai probably knew that. 'But thank you for looking after me. It was very brave and kind of you.'

'You have to be brave,' Kai said, turning those wild eyes on her. 'To defeat the monsters.'

'Yes, I suppose you do.' She thought of him in the meadow in the dark, laying out iron nails in the barn. 'But sometimes you have to let other people fight the monsters for you.'

Kai only smiled. The bone held like a knife was almost glowing. 'I fought one monster already,' he said. 'And I thought if I fought the others too then she'd keep me. But I don't want that anymore. If I stop the monster from hurting you then I can stay here, can't I?'

'Oh, Kai.' Lina faltered, sunlight coruscating at the edges of her vision. She had found no record of his adoption. 'I'd love that,' she said, and realised she meant it. This strange, wild, lost boy. Where better for him to live than here in the wilderness? She thought her father would love him.

Kai blinked catlike. 'I don't mind if the monsters get them anymore. But I won't let them hurt you.'

Lina reached out to touch his cheek, his skin beneath her fingers cool as the surface of still water. 'You don't have to fight monsters for me, sweetie. You never have to fight monsters for me.'

He leaned into her touch then pulled away, casting a look at Genni's averted back. 'I'm going to keep watch,' he said and moved to the balcony as if his feet were not quite touching the ground.

'Genni,' Lina called, and when her sister's head half-turned, said, 'want to come down and do your hair?'

'No.'

She did not look at Lina. There were so many things Lina wanted to say, but no words with which to say them, so she gathered herself onto her crutches and turned quietly towards the stairs.

An hour or so later Silene appeared in the doorway to the lab. Lina carefully laid down the saw she had been using to section the fox's femur as Kai slipped through the door in his mother's wake. Lina realised, thinking that, how little she still believed in that relationship. Silene was no more this child's mother than she was Genni's, and if there was a way for both of them to stay then Lina wanted to find it. Silene ignored both Kai and the fox which was, even with the door wide, filling the air with old death.

Lina's fingers tensed and relaxed, then she smiled. 'Can I help you?'

'You see,' Silene said, as if carrying on a conversation already begun. 'You see, Dr Stephenson,' flattening her hands against her stomach and then sitting very precisely, 'It could hurt Xander.'

The fox and the widow watched Lina, and neither made sense. Because it didn't matter if she pinpointed his death, where had the locals obtained tech that would take out the cameras? Surely *that* mattered more than who had actually set the trap, or swung the hammer?

Only, all she wanted was for this woman and her angry son to leave, which they would only do once Devendra Kapoor was here; and she really, really did not want the taskforce to come. Even though it had to happen, and she ought not care about relative guilt when what they'd done was bad enough. But if Iva, forewarned by Lina, *did* warn the nationalists, then perhaps that would be enough. Xander and Silene would feel defended, Kai perhaps would cease to watch for monsters, and the only-partially-guilty would not pay too heavy a price.

'It could hurt Xander,' Silene said again.

Lina forced concerned puzzlement onto her face.

'Yes,' Silene said, taking Lina's silence, her expression, for agreement. 'You can see it too,' her eyes sliding sideways to Kai, sliding back again. 'So I knew you understood. Someone has to be guilty and then Xander and I will be safe. You understand?'

Lina did not move or speak.

'My boy is very clever, you know?' She could have been at a dinner party. 'Of course you do. If he weren't so very talented, it wouldn't ... he said to me...' She leaned forward and smiled in a way that made Lina want to scratch her eyes out. 'He said Dr Stephenson has secrets. Yes, he did. So you can't hurt me, otherwise he'll tell.'

'I'm sorry,' Lina said meticulously. 'I have no idea what you mean, and I am very busy–'

'You see you cannot keep secrets from my boy, and *it has to be someone else*. Doesn't it? Otherwise how will I protect my son?'

There were tears in Silene Wiley's eyes, and they were genuine. It made it harder to distinguish drugs and grief and guilt when this love for her son was real. It didn't change how much Lina could hate her.

'Mrs Wiley,' she said slowly, 'no-one here is connected to London and the threat from the locals is over now. ESF will capture them. I don't understand what you want.'

Silene laughed then slapped a hand over her mouth as if startled. 'What I want?' she hissed. 'I want Christof never to have *watched* that day and never to have brought back that, that *thing*. I want it *gone* before it tells you. I want them all to hang, because they're all guilty of *something* so it hardly matters. I want my boy safe. I want him safe. I want him safe.' Sobbing through her fingers, nails digging viciously into her cheek. Then she dropped her hand. 'And if *you* have to hang so that he is safe, then Dr Stephenson, I want that too.'

Lina did not move, listening to her own quiet breathing, wishing her flesh, her bones subsumed into the rocks and trees.

'Oh yes,' Silene murmured as if Lina had spoken. 'If you tell London, then no,' drawing the word out. 'They would rather it was me, do you see? Makes them look less weak. And I can't risk it. No, I can't.'

The sun canted gently through the window, and it seemed impossible that it was not night-time, that this was not all happening in the darkness.

'I think,' Silene said, her voice coming at Lina through miles of space. 'Yes, you understand don't you? I'm very sorry for all this. It's all rather ghastly, really. Exhausting.' Pale hand fluttering around a pale face and Silene rose. The light from the doorway darkening then brightening again, and Lina could not move, retreated so far inside herself that she barely remembered how.

It didn't matter, Lina realised. It didn't matter who was guilty of Christopher Wiley's death or even the trap in the grass. Because in Silene Wiley's shattered mind there was only her own fear or guilt, and her love for her son, and Lina had no defences against her because Lina was guilty of things that would see her hang. No, not hang. Blood on stained concrete, fractured doorways. Her breath catching and stopping, catching, stopping.

For a long time Lina had not known what had taken her mother away, had not understood how a mother could end up there. And that child had become someone who *needed* to know. Knowledge kept you safe. Hiding your fear kept you alive, but knowledge kept you ahead. And then she'd come here, where knowledge was not about fear at all but about joy and Thiago and peace.

Until now, when a broken, corrupted, frightened woman had set her son to find Lina's last secret, to turn Lina into the card that would win Silene the game. And Lina would go willingly, because Genni needed their father more than Lina needed anything at all.

Unless...

The swifts screamed but Lina did not move.

Unless...

Silene thought Kai knew something. Xander doubted his mother's sanity and Devendra Kapoor might, *might*, be able to calm her, would surely want to. He might actually be able to save them all.

Vitaly and Kolya might be able to protect her dad. Thiago would get Devendra released, and Lina could talk to two wounded boys, and if she was pressing at their wounds then she must simply fight that guilt down.

Chapter Twenty-Three

- T. Where are you?

It took a couple of minutes for him to respond, and Lina opened another window, sending messages to both Vitaly and Kolya. She could not know if they could get anyone inside the prison holding her dad, but they were her best chance. Although ... PeaceKeepers could get in, and even if Thiago never talked about it he must still know people...

- T?

- You ok?

She took a breath. *— Would ESF call off the taskforce for DK's release?*

- ?

- It would be worth it.

Nothing. If he was not alone his face would be giving nothing away at all, but if he was alone, he would be scowling ferociously and cursing in Spanish.

- This isn't about me, she typed. Or at least was not about the trap, the blood beating at the stitches in her skin. *— They'll leave if he's released, and then the BB will stop anyway. Please, T.*

Still nothing. If he did this then the locals would know about the taskforce only once the threat was gone. If he did not, she would have to get to Govedartsi to tell Iva. Aware of her own brokenness all over again.

- Lina, I can't let this go.

She sighed. *- I know. But please, T.*

- I'll see.

If he negotiated Devendra for the taskforce then there would be no outlet for either his anger or his unwarranted guilt. But he could live with that, she thought, if she could. And she needed Devendra here more than she needed the mixed comfort of Thiago's retribution.

She went in search of Genni next, and found her where she had expected, perhaps dreaded. On one of the sofas facing Xander, their tablets resting on their identically raised knees. Various chat and code windows were open on Genni's screen, and Lina guessed one of those chat windows would match another on Xander's. She thought of the programmes he still had running like hounds quartering and wished she could predict what Genni's reaction would be if she knew about them.

'Hey,' she said quietly.

Genni looked up then away again. The skin of her hands was dry and Lina wanted to take her out of here into the sun and the kind air of the forests. Wanted her to love this place. Lina lowered herself beside Genni, positioning her bandaged foot gingerly on the floor, setting hair moisturiser on the table and mustering words that could be said in front of her enemy's child.

'I wondered if you could write a message for Dad.'

Genni did look up now, her hands falling away from the tablet. The brown of her eyes as dense and rich as treacle.

'He'd love to hear from you.'

'Where is he? Is he still in—' Genni stopped and Lina breathed out.

'Yes,' she said. She did not know if Xander knew about her father's arrest. 'He's being seen by a doctor now, and he's okay. We can't call him yet, but we can send messages.'

Genni stared at her, shadows beneath her eyes, worrying at the inside of her cheek.

'Send anything you write to me and I'll send it on.'

'What? Why can't I send it straight to him?'

Lina turned the pot of moisturiser in her hand. 'Because ESF needs to check that everything we say is … safe.'

'So I can send it straight to them then.'

'I won't read it,' Lina said. She remembered Kai saying, *She wouldn't protect you if the monsters came.* And it was foolish to expect a child who barely knew her to forgive Lina for bringing the monsters to her door, but perhaps Lina was a fool. 'I won't, Genni. I promise. Just someone at ESF and then Dad.'

Genni turned back to the screen that she had angled away from Lina. She read something there, shot a strange, quick glance across the room to Xander and said, 'Okay. You better not.'

Xander was ignoring both of them.

'I won't,' Lina said. She waited to see if Genni might argue further but then said cautiously, 'Do you want me to use Genni or Jericho in my message?'

Genni stared at her, colour rising in her face, turning the brown darker. 'Why are you writing about me?'

'I can hardly not, sweetie.'

Perhaps she realised that, because after another long minute she looked away and spoke more to her screen than Lina. 'Whatever, Genni then.'

'Okay,' Lina said, then because she had no idea what else to say, she turned away and said, 'Could I have a word, Xander? Outside perhaps?'

He stared at her, first bemused and then suspicious, but when she tilted her head and moved to the stairs he rose, still holding his tablet, and followed her. Once they were out in the meadow where no-one would overhear, she turned to face him, the sun on her shoulders a reassurance and a short-toed lark singing above.

'Thank you,' she said. He sat down on his mother's deckchair and scowled up at her. She thought how very unguarded that expression was compared to his face when he was with his mother, and hoped.

'I wanted to ask you about your mother.' She had thought carefully about what to say and spoke gently, using her crutches to sink down into the vetches and grass, lower than him. 'Whether there's anything I can do to help.'

'What?' His eyes shifted away from hers.

Carefully, she thought. 'I've noticed that she's on a lot of medication and I wondered if ... perhaps there is something less powerful that would be better for her. We have a lot of meds here, and the ESF medical support is really very good.'

Xander looked at her. He had short, dense eyelashes the colour of rust and there was red around his eyes as if he had not been sleeping, or had been weeping.

'Why do you care?'

Carefully, resting a hand over her bandages, 'The situation here is frightening her, isn't it? And I think the stuff she is taking might be exacerbating that, making her prone to ... irrationality maybe. I thought it might be easier for you both if she was ... more settled.'

Behind Xander, Kai was drifting slantwise through the meadow towards them, but Lina had reached the point now where Kai was so separate in her mind from either Xander or Silene that she didn't care if he overheard.

'So it's nothing to do with you being guilty of anything,' Xander said, his arms folding over his chest, his shoulders rising. 'How do I know what you'd try to give her? She reckons you want to kill her. D'you think I'm stupid?'

'No,' she said. 'I really don't, actually. I think you are trying very hard to protect your mum, which must be exhausting.' It startled him, her saying that, and she wondered how many people had seen anything other than his size or his surliness. 'I'm not a medical doctor,' she added, 'but I am a biologist, and I know what too many of the wrong drugs can do to someone.' She lifted her hands, palms up, watching him watch her. 'I'm just saying that they might be affecting her more and more, and that I'm here to help, if you like.'

She had always been good at hiding secrets, because she had to be, but she had not known she had it in her to lie so selfishly and baldly to someone who was still mostly a child. Kai was within earshot now, watching something in the grass, his pale form heartbreakingly adrift. She wished Thiago were back already. Using her hands to push upright, she bent to gather her crutches, the change in position sending blood and agony into her ankle strong enough to make her hiss.

'Lina,' Kai sang, and Lina took a swinging step towards him when Xander spoke again, not looking up at her.

'I don't trust you. You're one of *them*. Or you were once.'

Lina looked down at his averted face and knew she had won the tiny victory she had hoped for. He didn't trust her, but she had seeded more doubt about his mother's lucidity, which might be all she could hope for. She said slowly, 'You want to leave, don't you? Once Devendra Kapoor is here?' He lifted his gaze to hers, pupils contracting. 'What will they think of her if she's like this at home?'

He drew back sharply, lips pulling into a snarl, or a flinch. She turned away before he could recover, moving painfully through the flowers towards Xander's pariah brother, fritillaries rising from her path.

'Will they lock her up?' Kai said. He was pulling apart early thistle seedheads, scattering down around his feet. Lina leaned carefully against the trunk of the lone pine, weariness and pain occluding her.

'Pardon?' she said.

Kai glanced up at her, thistledown falling from his fingers turned phosphorescent by the sunlight. 'Will they lock her up if they think she's mad?'

She would have tried to reassure him not long ago. Instead she was honest. 'I doubt it. She's too important. Unless they do pin the murder on her.'

'Christopher Wiley,' Kai said, smiling. He had never called either of them 'Mum' or 'Dad', she realised. Perhaps there had not been time, or invitation. Had he even spoken directly to Silene, or Xander? Or anyone other than her? Lina tried to think, but the sun was painting the flowers into kaleidoscopic fires and there was something more important she needed to ask.

'Kai, sweetie,' she said slowly. 'Do you know what happened when Christopher Wiley died?'

Kai did not answer, gathering white billowing seeds into his palms. Then he turned to face her and tossed both hands skyward, thistledown falling around him like snow or wonder and he laughed at the sun. 'Yes,' he said.

Across the meadow, Xander rose from the chair so rapidly that Lina thought he might have heard, but he was not looking at them. He strode away beyond the house, plunging into the scattered treeline there without pausing, lifting his hands to cup the back of his skull.

Lina looked back at Kai and said slowly, 'Were you there?'

He made an odd little gesture, shaking one fist over an upturned palm. 'She was,' he said. 'She was there.'

One of her crutches fell to the floor as Lina's hand scrabbled for support against the tree. Her legs wavered and she thought she might follow her crutch downward, but she didn't. That was it then. Was Silene guilty of murdering her husband after all? It would make all her paranoias less paranoid.

'And then I was there.' He was studying his hands as if they were wondrous.

'Christ, Kai,' she whispered, but he did not look even mildly distressed. He never really did, she realised, and perhaps that meant nothing in a child raised on trauma so she should be being more gentle, less selfish. 'That must have been ... scary to see, sweetie.'

He glanced up at her curiously, repeated the adjective silently to himself, his hands reaching for more thistleheads. 'Not really,' he said. 'Anyway, *I* fought the monster.'

He had said it before. What was the monster in Kai's mind? Or who? Something terrible enough that it could put witnessing a man's death into insignificance.

'Why did–' she stopped herself. Why did he want to stay with Silene after that? What else would he choose? To return to the slums alone? She shook her head and the treeline spun, tipped; breathing deeply until pine resin and hot grasses settled her. 'Thank you for telling me, sweetie. Are you okay here? I need to get a drink of water – will you come in?'

He lifted her hand in both of his, studying scratches she had not noticed, his fingers cool. Then he let her go and smiled his slight, orange-eyed smile. 'I'm okay,' he said. 'I'm keeping watch.'

She ought to have gathered him inside with her, not because he should not be alone but because he should not think he needed to be. But if she waited any longer she might not make it back to the lab, so she left. Hating her weakness and reeling from pain and revelation.

Chapter Twenty-Four

Thiago did not get back until mid-afternoon, by which time Lina was fractious with impatience and her refusal to dull herself with painkillers. Neither Vitaly nor Kolya had responded to her messages, which was not unexpected so quickly, but she kept checking anyway. Genni had not sent anything through yet, and Lina needed to write something herself but had no idea what to say and what to hide.

'T,' she said as soon as he appeared in the lab doorway. 'How did it—'

'Jesus, Lina.'

She fell silent, staring at him. And then smiled. If he had failed, or decided against, then he would not be so angry. 'They agreed,' she said, still smiling.

He muttered something rude and came towards her, one broad hand touching her cheek then cupping her shoulder. 'You look like shit. What the fuck have you been doing?'

'When do they hand him over? Did you see him?'

'You're supposed to be resting. Have you even taken your meds?' His hand shook her, his strength and frustration held tautly back.

She lifted her own hand to cover his and tilted her head. She had sat alone here, repeating every one of the morning's conversations endlessly in her head until she felt sick, but now Thiago was here and so cross with her that the world felt just a little more solid. 'When, T?'

He growled faintly and released her, turning around to reach for the medicines waiting on her desk. 'I'll tell you once you've taken these,' he said, holding them out then sitting on the stool beside hers, studying his hands intently. 'Yes, they agreed.'

Lina swallowed the concoction of painkillers, antibiotics and anti-inflammatories obediently and waited for him to continue.

'Handover in Govedartsi ten am tomorrow. I saw some video. He's fine.'

'In return for calling off the taskforce?'

Thiago scrubbed a hand over his face and scalp then dropped it again with a harsh sigh. 'Yes.'

Across the courtyard, Xander must have opened a window because the thump of music abruptly drowned the birdsong. On top of everything else, Lina thought, she resented this too. She watched Thiago's face though, and took a guess. 'How did they react about the taskforce? Was it bad?' She did not know if he had gone armed, but ought to have insisted on him carrying a jacket cam.

He lifted one shoulder and smiled faintly. 'They weren't happy. It was fine.'

Of course it was. She smiled, found her gaze drifting back to her tablet again and, as if reading her mind, he said quietly, 'Any news?'

She shook her head. 'I want to see if anyone can keep an eye on him. You know? Make sure no-one gets to him.' She woke her tablet screen and frowned at it abstractedly, her mind hundreds of miles away.

Thiago shifted on his stool and she realised that he had thought of offering too, but that it was not a simple thing to do. For him to do. She wondered again what it was he had run from.

'I know someone,' he said, but she cut him off.

'It's okay,' her heart falling just a little. 'I've asked the people who got Genni here.'

He narrowed his eyes at her and at least he had forgotten his anger, if only briefly. 'I'll ask too. Likely my ... friend is better positioned.'

'They're PK?' she said and at his curtailed nod, added quickly, 'There's no need, I–'

'Lina.' It was back. The anger that was only as sharp as it was because he felt guilty.

She held his gaze doubtfully, aware that her spine was already loosening with relief. 'Thanks,' she said eventually, and reached to touch his knee where the uneven topography of muscle and scars met robotics. He didn't smile, but the guilt banked down just a little and she wondered if they would ever tell each other everything about their pasts. Whether all of this would bring it out and whether that would change anything between them. She did not know if anything *could* change this, and she did not know what she would do if anything damaged it.

A message finally arrived from Genni and Lina made herself write to their father. Teasing out comfort, reassurance and love from the truth that she and Genni were not as safe here as he believed. The urge to read Genni's message was terrible, because she wanted, needed, to know whether Genni had repeated her accusations to their father. But Lina resisted and wrote with Isla's assistant's clever eyes in her mind. She sent both messages just as the sun was painting the sky copper and violet, then she searched again for news from London, dug further back from the murder to Christopher Wiley's career and Silene's as well.

Silene had said to Lina that she wished her husband had never watched something, assuredly referring to the slum clearance in South London days before his death. And it was this that Lina kept circling back to. The State media played up words like 'revitalising', 'reclaiming' and 'modernising' with images alongside of the rubble and the aftermath. Silene might have written one of those articles.

Xander, she thought. He had accessed James' blog, and someone, she could not remember who, said James had posted about the clearances, so had Xander read that very different version, and if so what had he felt? He was clever and angry and both of those things meant he might see one thing, but he was also comfortable and unimaginably cocooned, which meant he might see nothing at all.

She found a newer article citing a police source that the post-mortem had shown irregularities, that the stab wounds may not have been the primary cause of death. The article hinted at family secrets and alluded to the long lists of arrested resistance.

Suggestions and rumours only, but was this Silene's fear becoming reality? Lina clicked away, frowning.

She found the unofficial photos. People, children running, State police and military, masonry falling. In one, bodies.

Simply surviving this meant that Kai had defeated a monster, she thought. Remaining standing at the end of each day meant that he was strong. Perhaps it was no wonder he loved the meadow so much, its stillness, its gentleness.

If she suggested he stay, she could not imagine that Silene would argue. It was only her ego and ... hostility, hatred, paranoia that might stop her letting him go. Lina had no idea how to have that conversation though, after their last one. How to have any conversation with her now.

I will see you hang.

But she would not hang. She would be shot.

Or she would do what Autumn had done, take the option waiting in her father's silver blue tin. Whisper her mother's name when all else was gone.

'Dinner,' Thiago said from the doorway, the light painting his skin ochre and the courtyard behind him darker.

Lina reached for her crutches and when they were climbing the stairs, he stayed just behind her in case she fell.

Genni and Kai were both on the balcony, Kai's legs dangling through the bars, her arms resting on the railing. Oh, Lina thought, there they were, and from where she stood it seemed like closeness, but then Genni heard Thiago and turned to come in, brushing past Kai without caring that he had to lean aside. Without even glancing down. Oh, Lina thought again. Stars were wakening in the wide sky and the air slipping into the room tasted of rocks and high places even though it was still warm.

'You sent it,' Genni said.

'I did.'

'And didn't read it.'

That bitter little pain again. Thiago glanced across from where he stood at the kitchen counter. Lina set her crutches aside, lowering herself to sitting on the sofa facing Genni. 'No,' she said. 'I promise.'

Tilting her head, Genni almost smiled. 'I know,' she said. 'Xander told me.'

Lina stared.

Genni blinked and looked away. 'What?' she muttered.

Xander wasn't here, Lina realised belatedly. Thiago was pouring wine and Iva must have come in at some point, either that or Thiago had prepared food earlier, and Xander must be down in his room but doing what, now that she was up here and he could not track her keystrokes from across the courtyard.

Dear god, had he been tracking her keystrokes?

'What?' Genni said again, not quite meeting Lina's gaze, but the whites of her eyes reflected the light like a deer.

Lina shifted, hissing at the pain, and tried to remember everything she had done on her tablet since ... since when? How long had he been tracking her so closely, because she had absolutely no doubt he could have evaded her notice and surely she had done something to condemn herself.

Thiago held a glass of wine in front of her and she took it, sipped it automatically, grounded by the act and the taste. Repositioning her foot gingerly, she smiled at Genni a little unsteadily.

'Did he show you how he knew?' she said carefully.

'No.'

Kai lifted his head as if he had heard something out in the forest, his hands coming up to weave shapes out of the evening air.

'But you believed him?' Lina did not wait for an answer because she could see Genni bridling a little at the question and felt the quiet hurt turn for the first time into anger. 'Did he say whether *he* read it?'

Genni's mouth opened and Lina kept her face calm as she took another sip of wine.

'No!' Genni said. 'Why would he?'

'Why would he read it?' It was a struggle, holding onto that calm. 'Why wouldn't he? Genni love, he wants to find his dad's killers, and he is trying to link me, us, to them. If I were him, I'd read your emails. And mine.' Oh god, she thought again. Dear god, what had she given away?

There had been nothing in her own message to their father, and her reading up on his father might only be curiosity or spite; he could hardly pin culpability on that. But she had sent messages to Vitaly and Kolya. Meaningless on their own, and encrypted besides. But to a suspicious boy...

'He's not out to get me. It's only you who did anything, and that's not my fault.' But Genni's breathing was audible over the crickets and Kai's near-silent humming. She was hunched forward, glaring at Lina. 'It's not my fault,' she repeated.

Lina reached to take Genni's hand, not letting her pull away. 'No,' she said. 'None of this is your fault. But you are still involved, love.' Squeezing the rigid brown fingers within hers as Genni's breathing worsened. 'We talked about this, about being careful. I know you like Xander, but...' it was a cruel card to play and Lina winced. 'But if you want Dad to be safe, then you need to not trust him.'

Genni's chest shuddered and Kai turned from the view of the night to stare at her. 'Hush, love,' she whispered, but Genni was breathing rapid and thin. 'Hush, love. It's okay. It's okay. It's okay.' She touched Genni's back, hating herself, wanting to wrap her arms around Genni's hunched frame but just stroking instead, murmuring.

'Xander is telling her things,' Kai whispered. He was holding a hand over Genni's hair, so close that Lina could not tell if he was touching Genni or simply cradling the air. She remembered his fingers holding her eyes closed as he sang to her when she had been drowning.

'Hush,' she whispered, to both children.

'He's a monster too,' Kai whispered quieter still. 'Maybe he wasn't, but he is now.'

He moved his hand and Genni shivered. 'He's not bad,' Lina said. 'He's just very angry and very sad, and this is his way of dealing with that.' Kai opened his mouth but Lina added, 'Which makes him dangerous, sweetie, but not a monster.'

She believed it. Which seemed flawed, given what she had just discovered, but she still believed it and it would have been easier if she had not. If, like in his mother, she could see only maliciousness and corrupted power, then she could have hated him. It was so much easier to hate your enemy than to pity them.

'Lina,' Thiago murmured, making her realise there were footsteps on the stairs. Genni must have heard them too, because she jerked straighter, Lina's hand falling away, and with a great, painful swallow, she seemed to return to herself, stiffening as if those long minutes of panic and Lina's touch were something to be ashamed of.

Silene did not come up for dinner but Thiago told Xander a pared-down version of Devendra Kapoor's captivity; simply that locals had found him, held him, and would hand him over in the morning. If Xander noticed the glaring gaps in the story, he seemed too relieved to care. He helped himself to the wine and loosened to the point where he laughed at something Thiago said. A laugh that was pure amusement untouched by bitterness, and Lina thought the sound of it startled him as much as it did her. She did not hate him; she understood him, and pitied him. And he could kill her father, kill Genni, kill her.

He drank more wine and Thiago tipped back in his chair, watching him thoughtfully as Lina watched their reflections in the wide windows, wondering if her father had got their messages yet and what he would do if he was here now. She thought that he would not know, that the choices he had made would not have prepared him for the choices Lina now faced.

'So what'll Dev do when he gets here?' Thiago asked Xander. Kai turned from where he stood at the window, tilting his head.

Xander smiled and, like the laugh, it was lovely. 'I don't know,' he said, but then his face shifted, his eyes slipped to Lina. 'He'll sort everything out. He's good at that.'

Thiago tipped his head as if in agreement and Lina wondered what he was doing. 'He's had a tough time. Might want to get home straight away.'

Xander looked at his wine, his mouth twisting as if he had been hit by nausea. He had not contemplated a Dev less than perfectly capable of rescuing them, Lina thought. Thiago raised his own glass and glanced at Lina over the rim.

'He owes ESF his freedom,' he said quietly, as if thinking aloud. 'Probably his life.'

Lina looked at Genni so that she did not look at Xander, because doing so might remind him of his anger, and Thiago wanted him to doubt, instead.

Chapter Twenty-Five

Lina insisted Thiago take her with him to Govedartsi. 'You can't talk, and watch Devendra, and watch everyone else at the same time,' she said and waited as he failed to find any answer other than blind insistence. 'You watch people and look scary,' she said and smiled. 'I'll do the rest.'

She did not want to go at all. Face the people who had set a trap and brought her so much pain? The idea made her a little sick, but Thiago should not do it alone, and he was riding his anger on such a tight rein that she daren't let him try.

Xander came outside as they were getting into the truck and Lina spoke before he could ask. 'Wait here. We won't be long.'

'I want–'

'I know,' she said gently, thinking that he was more frightening to her than another trap, than blood and pain. 'But it's a delicate thing and they won't like you being there. It might tip things out of balance.'

'But–'

His mother's voice from inside the house cut him off, clear through the closed windows.

'Get out! Get *out! Get out!*'

Xander flinched but did not look around.

'Why can't you leave me alone? It wasn't my fault! It wasn't me!'

Kai, Lina realised belatedly. She was shouting at Kai and Lina moved towards the door. Xander grabbed her, shoving himself in the way, twisting her ankle so that she yelped, Thiago at her side already and Silene's voice still rising.

'I didn't know about the children!'

'Leave her the fuck alone,' Xander snarled, turning and barrelling into the house, the door swinging resoundingly shut.

Thiago had a hand under Lina's elbow, steadying her. Silene fell silent then spoke pleadingly.

'You have to make it leave us alone, darling. It likes her; it'll leave us alone if she tells it.'

Thiago switched from studying the empty doorway to frowning at Lina. She moved, resettling her crutch, turning to the truck, avoiding Thiago's eyes because there were things that weren't making sense and if he spoke some vital logic might crumble. And she needed logic, all her careful, clever thought, to give her any sense at all of control.

Thiago did not speak until the truck had fallen from meadow into forest, the canopy closing overhead like the ocean.

'Who was she talking to?' he said, watching the shadowy track. It was not far to the village. Iva walked it every day and normally they would never have driven such a wasteful distance. But today it was necessary.

Kai, she wanted to say. Of course Kai. But she watched the gradations of sleepy green outside the window and realised she did not dare, and did not entirely know why.

'She wasn't on a call.'

'She might have been,' Lina said.

The track turned downhill then swung up again sharply. Two squirrels fled from the road, black tails flicking, Thiago glanced at her, but they were nearly at the village so he changed the subject. 'It should be Ognyana Asenov and a couple of her men. It's in the middle of the village so–' he shrugged and Lina nodded without speaking. So they too would want nothing to go wrong. 'You deal with her. Don't worry about Kapoor, I'll get him out of the way.'

'Okay.'

'Lina.'

She looked at him. The forest broke apart and they were coming into the village with no transition at all.

'Stay close to the truck.'

Because she could hardly move above a child's pace. Lina grimaced and glared at her ankle. It occurred to her that this too was why Thiago had agreed to her coming. That her woundedness would remind them of the thinness of the ice they were skating.

There were villagers leaning on the wide slabs topping their garden walls, standing in the street beneath walnut trees just beginning to shed underripe nuts. This was good, Lina thought. If they had truly feared, there would have been only the empty road. Ognyana Asenov stood beneath a vast, ancient walnut tree in the middle of a stretch of bare earth that might pass as a village square. She appeared to be alone, but as the truck came to a halt, a man stepped away from where he had been talking to an elderly man. Father or grandfather perhaps, although if so then it had been foolish to reveal the link.

'Dr Stephenson,' Ognyana said once Lina stood in front of the truck. 'I am sorry you are hurt.' She made a small gesture towards Lina's ankle, her face revealing nothing but her gaze determinedly on Lina, not Thiago.

'Thank you,' Lina said. 'You are still happy to proceed, I hope?'

Ognyana turned her head a fraction and two men came out from a narrow lane between two houses that Lina had not noticed, although Thiago would have. One of the men looked familiar but her attention was on the other man. Silene's saviour, Xander's hero, bruised and a little ragged, held firmly by his bound hands. Damaged and defeated and yet the angle of his head, the way he scanned the entire area and settled his gaze on where Thiago was standing, was somehow still imperious. And dangerous, she thought.

He would take them away, she reminded herself fervently. It did not matter if he was dangerous, he owed Thiago and he owed ESF, and he would take the Wileys away.

'Mr Kapoor,' she said to him.

His eyes shifted from Thiago to her, to her bound ankle and crutches, curiosity flickering. 'Pleasure to meet you,' he said, incongruously charming.

'Ms Asenov,' Lina said. 'ESF will take no further action. They are content to let this be an end to it.'

'How do we know this is true?' she said. Not quite a challenge but treading the line. Lina heard Thiago's feet shift in the dust and opened the palm of a hand, knowing he would see the small movement. He stilled.

'I cannot prove anything,' she said. 'I could show you the transcripts of the discussion, but they would still prove nothing. You have my word. And Mr Ferdinando's. That is all I can offer.'

'And if ESF change their minds once Mr Kapoor here is safely away?'

Brief murmurs from the watching figures. The man beside Ognyana shifted, muttered something to her.

Lina mapped the tension in Ognyana's shoulders, the way her legs were not entirely straight. Poised to fight, or flee. How much courage she had, to face down people backed by an entire military force and not waver. To keep fighting, to keep believing that there were better ways, better worlds. The stitches in Lina's ankle throbbed insistently, but even with that, with the bruises black on Devendra Kapoor's brown skin, she felt only a faint, awe-filled sadness.

'Then I will warn you,' she said eventually.

Ognyana watched her for a long minute. Somewhere a dog barked once, the man holding Devendra shifted his weight, watching his boss rather than Thiago. The world held still while Ognyana read Lina's face, weighed her promise and eventually smiled.

'What?' the man beside her said. 'You can't believe that.'

'So,' Ognyana said, ignoring him, turning, 'Mr Kapoor, it was a pleasure.' The man released him. 'And I hope you keep your promises, Dr Stephenson.'

'Wait,' the man beside Ognyana said. 'Ognyana!'

From the corner of her eye, Lina saw Devendra hesitate, then begin walking.

'Wait.' Grabbing Ognyana's arm one-handed, the other reaching behind his back, his eyes on Thiago. 'We can't trust them, look at him, we can't–'

Ogynana turning, mouth opening, the man's hidden hand coming up, movement behind Lina and Devendra falling, rolling, the man staggering back; the sound of the gunshot suffocating everything. Thiago occluding Lina but she saw Ognyana, gun raised, Devendra near the truck somehow coming up into a crouch, Thiago's broad shoulders and the man on his knees, blood spilling over his hands.

'That was stupid,' Thiago said. Devendra did not move and Ognyana ignored the man bleeding at her feet, watching Thiago unblinking.

'Are you going to make it worse?' Thiago's voice was calm, almost cheerful. Lina's pulse reverberated in her ears like an echo of the shot. The man moaned and swore, his gun fallen mercifully out of reach.

The dog barked again and Lina whispered, 'The villagers.' Saw Ognyana hear her and waver.

Thiago sighed. 'Get that idiot and go,' he said. 'If he lives, I'd recommend shooting him again. Kapoor, Lina, get in the truck, would you?'

Lina did, her hands barely obeying, beginning to shake, then Thiago was beside her and Ognyana raised her voice over the engine.

'The taskforce?'

Thiago laughed, but Lina saw a brave woman kneeling in the dust beside her friend and shouted, 'They won't come. They won't come.'

Ognyana bent her head and Thiago pulled the truck away, raising dust over the bleeding man.

As they came into the meadow, Lina found that she could speak. 'Are you hurt?' she said to the man in the back seat, turning to study the bruises on his face, the sharp lines of the smile he gave her.

'No,' he said. But his smile faded quickly, his head tipped back to rest against the chair, and she wondered how much he was lying.

Xander was waiting outside as they pulled into the courtyard and Lina heard Devendra take a long breath out, then in again, before he opened his door.

'Dev!' Xander said, coming forward then halting so quickly he nearly overbalanced. 'What–'

'Just a few bruises,' Devendra's voice was light. 'Good to see you. Sorry for the delay.'

Xander laughed, Thiago opened Lina's door as she finally pulled a crutch free. When she had got to her feet and Thiago was pulling the truck forward into the barn, she watched Devendra and Xander and thought that, despite the colour of the man's skin, they were the same. Rich and privileged; complicit.

'Where's your mother?' Devendra was saying, laying a hand on Xander's shoulder.

Xander shrugged. 'Sleeping, I guess. Dev, she's...' he trailed off. 'She's not...'

'Okay,' Dev said. 'It's okay. We'll sort this out. Hey, Xander,' Xander lifted his head. 'I'll sort it.'

Xander nodded, then noticed Lina and the frown returned. Devendra looked around and released Xander's shoulder.

'Ah,' he said softly. 'I didn't say thank you. Rather paltry, I know.' He smiled disarmingly, marred only a little by the swelling around one eye. 'Devendra Kapoor. Call me Dev.'

'Lina Stephenson,' Lina said, shaking the proffered hand. It felt strange to do this when they had just rescued him from kidnappers. More strange that they had not yet met when his absence had been so profound a presence. 'And this is Thiago Ferdinando,' she said.

With his attention off her, she realised how Devendra's irises were blown, his gaze slipping fractionally in and out of focus. She remembered him splayed on the greyscale forest floor.

'You're concussed,' she said, seeing it now. The way he turned his head with a deliberation that spoke of someone in pain and determined to hide it.

'I'm not,' he said. 'Just tired. I assure you. I'd kill for a shower though. Xander, mind if I beg some supplies off you? Seem to have mislaid mine.'

Thiago was scrutinising him now too, but as the other two turned away, he simply raised an eyebrow at Lina and crossed the courtyard to the old house.

'Dev,' Lina said. He hesitated, face half-averted. It did not matter to her if he was battling concussion, she thought, so long as he controlled Silene and took Xander away. She certainly did not care that the BB might have wounded one of the people she had fought against for so long.

'Will you let me check your injuries, after you are showered?'

He met her eyes, and even dazed as they were, tired and bruised, she saw the flicker of surprised interest and cursed herself. 'Thank you, but there's no need,' he said. 'If you have some painkillers, I'd be grateful though.'

'Sure,' she said. 'I'll bring some over.'

'Come on,' Xander said from the doorway, and Lina turned to follow Thiago.

'You okay?' Thiago said to her as soon as she was seated at her desk.

Lina nodded. 'You?'

Thiago laid his handgun on his desk, began to unload it without looking. 'Yes. He'll live if they're quick, sadly.'

She hadn't been sure. 'And the deal is still on. Ognyana didn't know he was going to do that.' It had been Thiago's unhidden anger, she thought, which had triggered it. So unlike him not to be able to mask himself.

Thiago shrugged. 'Maybe,' raising a hand to waylay her. 'Later, Lina.' Wearily, rattling bullets in his palm.

Lina closed her eyes, because she could not erase the man on his knees from her mind. The gunshot, the fact that she did not know who he would have shot if Thiago had not been faster, the fact that it might have been Thiago.

'What do you make of Kapoor?' he said eventually.

Lina opened her eyes, tried to collate her thoughts. 'He is concussed,' she said and Thiago laughed. 'I don't think he'll want to stay,' she added.

'No.'

'Have they arranged anything about leaving?'

Thiago lifted a shoulder fractionally. 'No. I'll talk to him later and do it myself if necessary.'

But would Silene go? Lina had no idea. And would he force

her? She had no idea about that either.

'I'll hear about your dad tonight,' Thiago said, and Devendra Kapoor was forgotten. 'She's got access. It's not a hundred percent, but–'

'Oh god.' Lina covered her face with her hands, not sure if the thing she was holding back was joy or tears. She had not realised how frightened she was for him until now, knowing someone would be keeping him safe. 'T,' she said, dropping her hands. 'Thank you. Tell her thank you.'

He did not smile, but there was such gentleness in his eyes. 'It's nothing.'

It was not nothing. To her or for him. He was risking something in doing this, and if that was not physical safety then it was psychological safety, but he'd done it anyway and Lina wanted to cross the distance between them and put her arms around him but daren't move because she *would* cry then and she needed to remember that even if her father was safer now, that did not stop him being made leverage and lure.

'What is it?' Genni stood at the base of the stairs, hands at her waist, her fingers flexing as if clutching at the air.

Lina turned her smile on her sister. 'Nothing, love. Are you okay?'

Genni stared at her and Lina could almost feel the hostility rising between them, all her joy and relief falling away. 'Have you heard from Dad yet? Why isn't he well enough to travel yet? He said it wouldn't take this long.'

Thiago rose and moved past Genni to his office. Lina knew he would still be able to hear and that he had only gone to make Genni feel less outnumbered, but still wished he'd stayed.

'He's much better, you're right.' Lina patted the stool beside her but Genni did not move, her fingers gripping her upper arm now, the skin indenting. Lina sighed. 'But isn't allowed to travel just yet.' She had never minded the lies before, but did now. Lying to this child.

'I'm working on it, Genni,' she said. 'He's safe, and being looked after, and hopefully soon he will be allowed to finish the journey.'

The light was bringing out the gold tones in Genni's dark skin, like she was lit from within. 'Was that that man back?' she said finally.

'Dev,' Lina said. 'Yes.'

'So the people who put the trap out are going to get away with it.'

Was this the love Thiago was so determined to see? Or was it simply overspilling anger at all the injustices and cruelties and powerlessness in her short, difficult life?

'Yes,' Lina said. 'They messed up. They won't do it again.' She tried a smile. 'Hey, fancy going to find those foxes tomorrow?' Wanting Genni to see the forest as safe, as more than shadowy dangers and blood.

Genni shrugged, but her clenching hand fell still and Lina's heart felt almost weightless. 'Dunno. Maybe, I guess,' her sister said, and for the first time Lina thought that perhaps it would be okay. Perhaps she could save all of them, and their secrets, and herself.

Chapter Twenty-Six

Lina went out the next morning. Not far, but taking the truck up past an abandoned village to the point where the forest became solely pine. Driving hurt but she swung on her crutches almost fluidly along a track of needles and black earth, buoyed by birdsong and the scent of old resin, a hint of musk. There was no real reason to be here, and Thiago would scowl at her for coming out at all, but she had put dormouse nestboxes along this track and wanted to check them for occupancy. She needed to be away, if only for an hour or two.

In the first box the bedding she had provided was hollowed to the shape of a sleeping body, but no nest, no young. She moved on. There was mist lower down but here the pine trees were dusky amber and tawny in the rising sun, the exact colour of Dev's skin where it was not bruised. Off to the right a black woodpecker drummed sonorously, unanswered, and the next box held great tit chicks, their yellow gapes opening for her blindly. The next box, and the next, held dormice and their young. Lina closed those lids immediately, smiling. Then the track ahead became wetter and she studied the mud and the already filthy ends of her crutches forlornly. She had not truly valued this, she thought. Not just the refuge but its effortless, untainted joy. She stood there for a long time before turning around. Genni would wake soon, and it was stupid to risk dirtying her healing wounds for the sake of a little more resinous peace.

Back at the station, she changed her dressing. Soon, she would go without them, she thought, begin walking unaided, and then if she needed to leave she would be able to.

'Breakfast?' she said to Genni when her sister appeared in her bedroom doorway. She set the medical supplies to one side and lowered her foot testingly.

Genni nodded, not waiting for Lina but also not moving away faster than Lina could manage.

'You did your hair,' she said. Genni touched it gingerly.

'Not very well.'

'Shall I give it a go after breakfast? I'm sure we can figure it out together.' They crossed the courtyard, Lina's grip on her crutches tight as a fist.

Genni lifted her narrow shoulders.

'I'd like to learn,' Lina said.

She thought Genni would not answer and that she had asked too soon. But her injury had frightened her sister, she was sure of it. Her warning about Xander too, perhaps. She waited.

They reached the new house door and Genni pushed it open, then said with another shrug, 'Okay.'

Lina's fingers relaxed.

Iva was in the kitchen, although Anais was not, and Lina touched a hand to the older woman's briefly. 'It's good to see you,' she said.

Looking at the crutches, Iva said, 'It was a bad thing, yes? I told them this...' she paused, the lines around her mouth deepening. 'I am sorry for it.'

Lina had never once thought Iva was involved. 'You don't need to be sorry,' she said, and remembered telling Kai that he did not need to fight monsters for her. 'I'm fine.'

Raising her eyebrows, Iva turned back to the counter with an expressive huff. 'You sit,' she said, picking up a knife. But as Lina turned, Xander was coming up the stairs two at a time and looked so unfamiliarly relieved to see Lina that she froze.

'It's Dev,' he said. 'He's sick.'

More aware than ever of how slow she still was, Lina followed him back down the stairs, but just one flight down she saw Dev coming from his room. He looked up at her frowning.

'I'm perfectly fine,' he said to her rather than Xander.

It was hard to tell in the low light of the landing, but he did not look perfectly fine. The bruising around his eye was morphing to a low burgundy but his skin held a yellowish cast and his grip on the doorframe was fierce.

'You were being sick,' Xander said. He was standing at Dev's side, pallid in the clear light. Poor boy, Lina thought. He had invested so much faith in Dev and his saviour had proven fallible.

'I was—' Dev ran a hand over his face, wincing. Still directing his words up to Lina. 'I've got a killer headache, that's all it is. I'm capable of self-assessment.'

'Okay,' Lina said, shrugging lightly. She knew enough about stubbornness to recognise a refusal to admit to weakness, but wasn't sure of his reasons. Was it simple machismo reflex, or was it hostility? And if hostility, was that borne of captivity and associative blame, or was it something else?

Dev was watching her watching him, so Lina turned away, climbing slowly back up the stairs trying, like him, to look stronger than she was.

As Lina and Genni were tidying their plates away, Silene appeared, making Lina realise she had not seen Kai since that ghastly overheard conversation yesterday morning. She would find him though. Once she had checked for news of her father, and Genni was busy with something, she would search the meadow for Kai and try to talk to him about drugs and psychosis and thoughtless cruelty.

Silene sat meekly beside Dev at the table but instead of eating, kept lifting and setting down her mug of tea, one hand fidgeting with something in her lap until Dev set his hand over the top of hers and murmured something that Lina did not catch.

'Xander will tell you, won't you darling?' Silene said, turning her head but not focussing on anyone. 'He has been very good looking after me, you know? I just, Dev darling, I just want it to be over, and them to leave me alone. You understand?'

'Yes,' Dev said, his gaze flicking from Silene to Lina as Lina ushered Genni towards the stairs. It might have been good to hear this conversation but Lina doubted Dev would say anything as careless as Silene would, and Genni did not need to hear any of it at all.

She had recognised, belatedly, the gesture Kai had made as he told her that Silene had been there when her husband died. It had been the shaking out of tablets into a palm.

Dev came to find her, later. She had spent an hour sitting in the meadow with Genni, following an instruction video as she learned to treat and tame Genni's untamed hair, Genni listening to music and not speaking, but that was okay. It was okay. Then, Genni gone, Lina had lingered searching for a pale-haired child before seeing Dev in the courtyard waiting for her. The sun lay upon the meadow as dense as honey and although she would happily have stayed out here floating in heat, Dev nodded towards the old house and said, 'That's your office, Xander said. Can we talk?'

She made sure she smiled, and made sure to leave the door wide. A blue butterfly danced electric in the doorway then away and Lina pushed a stool towards Dev before sitting herself. She realised she did not know where Thiago was.

'How are you?' she said pointlessly, filling the silence as he studied her face the way she had done his in the stairwell earlier. Mapping weaknesses, she thought, and stilled her hands against her thighs, felt her breathing slow.

'I'm fine,' he said.

'I don't mean your head. I mean...' she searched for words that would not offend. 'It cannot have been very pleasant, the last few days.'

He smiled and again she was startled by how beautiful that smile was against his dark bones. 'They weren't that bad, actually.' Seeing Lina's gaze travel over his bruised face, he added. 'That was the initial scuffle. After that, they were perfectly civilised.'

Which was possibly a commentary on how he expected resistance fighters to behave, and a reminder of which side he was on.

'Would you like ESF to arrange travel home for you all?'

Another smile, this one a little edged. 'Ah, well. I'm not sure we will be leaving right away, if that's alright with you.' Not asking.

'Oh?' Lina said, aware of her pulse and the rising tide of sunlight across her desk. 'Is everything alright?' He tilted his head and she realised she was being improbably naive. She wished she knew what Silene and Xander had told him. 'Is it Silene's ... health?'

He leaned forward to rest elbows on knees, sunlight reflected in his eyes. She was backlit, she thought. It gave her a sense of protection.

'I wonder if you could tell me some things about my recent friends,' he said, without answering. 'You are familiar with them, I believe. Although perhaps not as much as your ... colleague.'

Also a question, which Lina likewise ignored. 'Everyone in the Balkan States is familiar with the BB,' she said. 'And a considerable number are sympathetic to their motives.'

'Your cook, is she sympathetic, Dr Stephenson? Are you?'

She wondered what he would do if she said yes. 'They caught my leg in a trap a few days ago.'

'Ah, yes. I heard. Ghastly.' Dev did not look at her ankle though, and there was only curiosity on his face, not sympathy. 'But you understand my position perhaps. That my captors spoke about certain links to this place, and I am not the sort of person who likes to leave puzzles unsolved.'

Lina's spine ached quietly with the effort of holding so straight. 'Mr Kapoor, Dev, while some of us may empathise with the BB's situation, I assure you no-one attached to this station had any involvement with, or condoned, the attack on you. If you got that impression from the people holding you, then you are mistaken.'

'Am I?' Dev said softly, and Lina ought not give way to the bitterness rising in her throat. but of all the things to be accused of, this was the only one she was fully innocent of. If it had not infuriated her, she might have laughed.

'Are you fluent in Bulgarian, Dev?' she said in Bulgarian. 'To be so sure of what they said?'

Dev started laughing, leaning back on the stool and appraising her anew. 'They spoke a little German, two of them,' he said eventually. 'And I speak a little Russian. Some of the words are similar.'

Lina said nothing. The sunlight reached the edge of her desk, poised to spill into her lap. She turned her palms up, waiting.

'Anyway,' Dev said, scanning the equipment lining the walls, 'I'd like to speak to Thiago, if he's around?'

Reaching into the light to check her tablet, she said. 'He's due back for lunch.' It was not like him to stick to such short trips, and he was only doing it for her. She touched her screen again, resisting the urge to check her emails.

'Xander tells me your father has shared my recent fate.'

It took a few seconds for Lina to turn her head and meet Dev's waiting gaze. 'Yes,' she said.

Dev nodded. 'Shame. ESF can't get him out?'

Like they had for him? No, Lina thought, they could but they wouldn't because the incentive was not there. 'We are trying,' she said.

'Hmm. It's a difficult journey from London. A lot to go wrong.'

Dear god, Lina thought. 'Yes.' Then to pre-empt him, 'I'm sure Xander has told you why my father and sister left London.'

A nuthatch landed on the window frame, hopped upwards, thrusting its slaty beak into crevices hunting spiders or long-ago stored seeds. Dev watched her. 'He did indeed. Funny coincidence, isn't it?'

She meted out a smile. 'Funny is not the term I would use, no.'

'It does cast a certain light over events, of course. You do see that, don't you?'

It was worse than Silene's accusations, Lina thought. Wild irrationality carried at least the possibility of being disbelieved. But this man. This man would be believed.

'I don't really,' she said, pressing her fingertips into the sunshine, the heat burning against the ice in her blood. 'My connection to … one of the people arrested was a long time ago, and purely romantic. There is nothing linking me or my family to any recent events in London.' It felt like she was betraying James, like he deserved her declaration of everything they had been to one another, deserved to hear her grief spoken aloud.

'Of course,' Dev said, smiling easily. 'Of course.' He looked around and said, 'Do you have a cat?'

Lina could not fathom him at all.

'The milk,' he said, pointing at Iva's bowl in the hearth, freshly filled this morning.

'Oh. No. It's a folk tradition, feeding the domovek who protects the house.' Although what could a domovek do against the evils within the walls, she thought. She remembered Baba Ruzha talking of monsters, and Kai, and counted her breaths, willing Dev away.

'Ah, I see. How fascinating. I'll have to ask your cook. Iva, wasn't it?' He rose and turned away. 'See you at lunch, I imagine. Hopefully Thiago will be back then.'

She saw him waver as he stepped into the sunlight, imagined the heat pressing against his bruised skull and felt a cruel pleasure at the thought of his pain. Then he was gone and her fingers curled in upon themselves, cold and shaking.

Thiago was not back in time for lunch and Lina took hers and Genni's out into the shade of the barn. They sat there in near silence, the fledging swallow brood overspilling their nest to perch tattily on the high beams. She had still not been able to find Kai, although she thought she had heard his laughter.

'Foxes later?' she said to Genni.

Genni had piled more bread than she could possibly eat onto her plate, and was now rearranging it carefully. 'How far away is it?' Her dark eyes full of shadows and sunlight. 'I don't want ... I don't want to go too far.'

'Why is that, sweetie?' Lina placed one of her tomatoes on Genni's plate. 'Is it because the forest seems scary or something else? I will be able to get messages while we're out. Emails and things.'

Lifting the tomato, weighing it in her palm before laying it back down and reaching for the knife. 'Are you worried about Dad? 'Cos you don't seem it.'

Lina laid her hands palms down on the table. How was she meant to answer this? Their father would have known. 'I am,' she said slowly. Genni's pupils contracted. 'How could I not worry? Just the way I worried for you until you got here. The way I still worry for you now.' She reached over to hook a finger around one of Genni's, braced for rejection. 'But I also believe he will be okay.

I do believe that, love.'

'But you said Xander might get people to hurt him.'

Had she said that? She did not think so, which meant Genni was assembling truths from half-truths. 'I think Xander and his mum, and now Dev, have a great deal of power with London State. And if we give them reason to ... to hate us, I guess, then they could use that power to hurt us.'

'Hurt Dad.' She had not pulled her hand away, but her fingers were hot and stiff.

'It's a possibility, yes. But sweetie, I have friends protecting him, and ESF protecting him, and these people will leave soon. This will pass and we can start again, the three of us here, together.'

And Kai, she thought. Maybe Kai too.

'You really believe that?'

'Yes,' Lina said, blinking away a rush of tears before they could show. What was belief anyway, she thought, other than hope so profound it could hold you up. What was a lie if it gave someone hope?

'I don't,' Genni said, and now she did pull her hand away, wrapping her arms around herself, fingers gripping her upper arms. 'I think Silene is mad and she'll make Xander do something. And I think if they hurt Dad it will be because of things you did.'

Chapter Twenty-Seven

'They are talking about you.'

Lina hadn't been back at her desk long. Genni had gone up to her room, leaving Lina to fool herself she was working by staring blindly at data that had never seemed irrelevant until now. She had not heard Kai coming into the lab, and yet here he was beside her, his head canted fiercely.

'Pardon?' she said.

'Xander and Dev. They're talking about you.'

'Oh,' she said softly. 'I see.'

'Do you want to know what they're saying?'

God no. Yes. No. 'Do *you* know?'

'Yes.'

Lina had not noticed the skull in his hands until he lifted it up. His index finger was stroking a slim canine and Lina studied it, disturbed. Then she checked the windowsill on the opposite side of the lab where an odd assortment of skulls and bones and feathers lay gathering dust and the corpses of flies. The fox skull there was not missing, so Lina looked back at Kai. 'Where did you find that?'

'I want to be a fox,' he said. 'Fierce and wild.'

Another camp child seeing something of the fox within themselves, she thought. How strange these tiny universals were. 'I think you already are like a fox,' and instead of asking again where he had found the skull, she said gently, 'Is that how you heard them talking, by being like a fox?'

Kai smiled and the skull smiled, and with his pale bones and gold eyes, for a moment he really was something other than human. As if the tawny, bright spirit of the dead fox has passed somehow into this lost child and was looking out through his eyes. Lina reached out to touch the faint ridge along the fox's cranium. Sagittal crest, she thought distantly.

'Xander told Dev that you aren't really Lina Stephenson.' Kai held the skull up to look slantwise through the eye socket. 'Is that true?'

Lina sat very still, her eyes on the skull's sharp teeth, aware of the wagtail alarm calling just beyond the house, aware of the weight her own lungs held within her. 'Who did he say I was then?' she said eventually.

'He said he'd find out.'

Sensation slipping back into her face, her fingers. It was not all lost then, not quite. But assuredly soon.

'Are you real, Lina?' Kai lifted the skull away from his face then returned it as if the fox's eyes would see her lies and her truths more easily than his own.

'I am real, sweetie,' she said. 'And I am really Lina Stephenson.'

'But you weren't before.'

'What did Dev say?' Thinking please don't ask again. Please don't ask, because this boy was perhaps even more fragile than Genni and she did not know what it might take to break him.

Kai studied her through the bones then lowered the skull. 'He said that he suspected Thiago more than you and he wanted to know what else he had planned, and who was paying him.' He frowned. 'He said if London really wanted Silene harmed, they'd hire the ex-PK. But they didn't know if London did want that.'

'Okay,' Lina said.

'But Xander said if London wanted his mum killed secretly, they'd blackmail the ex-terrorist with a dad in prison for like, leverage or whatever. And anyway you two were probably fucking so it didn't matter which way, did it?' Mimicking Xander almost perfectly.

Lina nodded slowly. So then, she thought. So then. She had told Genni that she believed, and told herself that her hope was unassailable. But if either had been true two hours ago, they were not now. So easily undone. 'Anything else?' she said. 'Did they say anything else?'

Kai opened the fox's jaws wide, closed them again with a snap. 'I don't know,' he said. 'That's when I came to tell you. Do you want me to go and listen again? They didn't know I was there.'

'I'll go,' she said. 'Where were you listening from?' Because they might be deciding what to do about the ex-PK and the ex-terrorist whose father was become the pawn in a game of threat and revenge and injustice.

Kai laughed and patted her arm as if she were the child, his touch cool as the morning in the heavy afternoon heat. 'They'd see you,' he said, spinning away from her as lightly as a turning leaf then pausing half in sunlight, luminescent. 'I won't save your sister from the monster, Lina. She said she'd help him.'

Lina recoiled. 'What with?' she said faintly, but the doorway held only excised light. Was this the choice Genni had reached from her reconstructed truths? That if she helped Xander pin blame, then he would keep their father safe? And if it was Lina pinned then that was only justice for all of Lina's own betrayals. It made a terrible kind of sense, bartering known brutalities, but for a long time Lina sat pressing her hands so hard against the desk that her wrists began to ache, holding herself still so that she did not go upstairs to her sister and shout, and plead, and rage.

When Thiago returned, he stood in the doorway watching her as she remembered to move, remembered that she was down here and reeling, not up there, letting all her pent-up anger fall on the wrong person.

'Okay?' he said quietly.

Lina took a breath, said, 'Dev wanted to talk to you. He knows you were working with the BB, before.'

'Not working with,' Thiago said a shade too quickly. Lina turned slowly to meet his eyes. 'Fuck,' he added.

'He's...' Lina paused, struggling to articulate how he had unnerved her. 'Slippery. And he's been talking to Xander.'

Should she tell Thiago about her mother? Before Xander found out and told? She had never had to put that story into words before though; never had to hear herself recount her mother's death, and she did not want to do so now. When she was a child she believed that the last thing she heard her mother say had been her name. Now, understanding terror a little more, she doubted it. But even fabricated memories were a way to remember being loved.

Thiago cast a quick glance out into the courtyard then closed the door. 'Tell me.'

She told him about London perhaps wanting Silene quietly killed, about Dev and Xander not knowing which of the two of them might be being paid to do so. She did not mention her old self.

'Leverage,' Thiago repeated. The one most terrifying word out of all of them, and Thiago understood. Lina pressed a hand over her heart.

'They know you overheard?'

Lina shook her head. 'Kai told me.'

Thiago frowned at her. 'Kai?'

'Yes,' Lina scanned his face for answers. 'What do we do, T?'

He carried on frowning but after a while laughed and scrubbed a hand roughly over his face. 'Give him back to the BB? Throw her in for free?'

Lina laughed. 'And Xander?'

'He's not a problem,' Thiago said, so quickly that Lina realised he had spent time on this too.

'Yes, he—'

'How did he find out all this stuff, Lina? To get anyone to listen to a kid, he'd have to show them how he found out. Not a chance.'

That had not occurred to her. Perhaps because she had never considered him as an entity separate from his mother's influence, and now Devendra Kapoor's as well. But Thiago was right. It would be a prison sentence. Hadn't that been one of Silene's many half-mad statements? That she must protect him from that risk, and his father had endangered him by ... by doing something as controversial and visible as the clearance, by attracting enemies.

'But they'd listen to Dev.'

Thiago did not answer; there was no need.

'They won't be able to link you to anything though,' she said.

All he had done was provide tacit consent for a few martenitsas hung on doorways and engineer Dev's release. But he hesitated, glanced at her and then away, and something that should have been obvious for a long time became clear. 'The EM tech,' she said. 'You gave it to them.'

He grimaced, rubbed at the conjoining of muscle and robotics.

Lina breathed in sharply. 'Because of the tagging programme. To help them hide. Oh, T.' Something sad and proud pooling beneath her ribs. 'Oh, T, why didn't you say?'

'Because,' he said tiredly.

'Because it's illegal and you didn't want me implicated. Because we're both too used to keeping secrets.' He looked up sharply at that, his fingers stilling on his leg, but did not speak so she added, 'So if Dev or Xander discover that, they might see it as proof of sufficient guilt.'

'It's not as clean as blackmail, but it would still work.' Meaning Lina would still be the most obvious even without her mother's crimes coming to light. 'And sounds like Kapoor won't leave till he has one of us, or both.'

Why not, Lina nearly asked. Why not just leave if he really thought they were planning Silene's murder? But she studied her reflection in her tablet screen, darkened and featureless, and knew the answer. Because if he could uncover a link, then he could trace it back to London, to whoever in State was trying to remove Silene, and by default Xander. If he left without knowing, then the danger in London would still be there waiting.

'But we're *not*!' she said, curling her hands into fists then forcing them loose again. 'Neither of us *wants* to kill her.'

Thiago smiled fleetingly. 'I wouldn't go that far.'

It hurt to laugh. 'Fair point,' she said. But then remembered Isla's assistant's advice and the room felt a little more full of shadows despite the angling sunlight. 'I meant there probably isn't any conspiracy in London at all. It's just her fabricating it.'

'Yeah. Why is that?'

Ignoring Kai, fearing for Xander, the affairs, opposing the slum clearance not for morals but for the attention it brought them. Children both living and dead. 'Guilt?' she said slowly. 'Either she did actually kill her husband or ... paranoia?' That the link between the clearance and his death *had* opened the door to rivalries and an opportunistic purge. Lina saw again the photos of the clearance, the bodies. Something tugged at her, something...

'Lina.' The thought vanished, Lina looked up. 'You can't go to your father. If they threaten him. You have to trust his protection.'

'T,' she said.

'Promise me. It would be suicide.'

She sighed. 'I can't promise that, T. You know I can't.'

He held her eyes for a long moment, then nodded shortly. 'So,' he said. 'Options.' And she softened with relief because he wasn't going to push, and she didn't have to refuse him again, and he was going to be cool and logical and steady about the wreck of their situation.

'We've got three that I can think of.' He ticked them off on his fingers. 'One: Do nothing, wait for them to give up, trusting our tracks are covered and your dad's safe.' Lina winced. 'Two: Push Silene. She's the weak link, she might reveal something incriminating enough to take the heat off us.'

'Which is what Xander is scared of, and why he's looking into me.' Lina shook her head. 'And he's bloody good, T.'

Thiago only nodded, touched his third finger. 'Three: Remove the threat.'

'You can't be serious.' She stared at him, but his smile was full of knives and she remembered the man bleeding in the dust.

'It would keep you safe.'

'No, it wouldn't. Don't you think London would check it out ... if it wasn't them? Or the Drowned State. Dev works for them, doesn't he? And what about Xander, you can't possibly–'

'I said Xander won't talk. And Dev's independent.' But Thiago curled his hand into a fist, knowing that he was still important enough to attract attention that they, and ESF of course, did not want. 'We could make it look an accident, or blame the BB.' A pause. 'They deserve it.'

'Jesus, Thiago.' Besides, she had not said Xander's name because he might talk, she had said it because Thiago was talking about making him an orphan. Make him one so that she could not be threatened with the same. Blood and empty doorways. 'No,' she said, bending forward abruptly and covering her face with her hands. 'No. Never.' She wouldn't mourn Silene, nor even Dev. But leave a boy motherless? Do to him what was done to her?

'I'd do it,' Thiago said, utterly calm. Lina remembered Genni was upstairs and sat up so fast her vision blurred, looking at the empty stairwell.

'I'd do it,' Thiago repeated. 'But it's your call. You've more at risk.'

Oh god, if only he wasn't right. If only ESF's mouthpiece had not already suggested the same. Oh god, she thought blankly, oh dear god.

'What do you think would happen to Genni if you went to your dad?'

The world slowed, the air in her lungs abruptly too heavy to breathe. She had not thought of that. Why had she never once thought of that? She stared at Thiago and saw him hurting because he had hurt her, but all she could think was that it was not a choice between her and her dad after all. It had never been as simple as that.

Even if she threw herself into the fire to save her father, he and Genni would not be saved.

She realised now how much she had been depending on having that last, terrible option.

'I'm sorry, Lina.'

'I know,' she said, her voice foreign, the sound in the room muted by the closed door. Birdsong and grasshoppers and the distant murmuring trees all absent and the air somehow heavier for the lack. 'But still, no,' she said slowly. Not sure it was still true but having to believe.

Chapter Twenty-Eight

She packed sandwiches and hot chocolate for her and Genni, then drove down into the forest below the station. Xander had been alone in the lounge when Lina went up there, and when she asked, listening to her own level voice with surprise, he told her Dev had taken Silene out for a walk. Brave of him, she thought, to go back into the forest he had just been rescued from. Let it swallow them up though. Let it reveal its teeth and consume them. She remembered Kai opening the fox's bone jaws and felt a flutter of guilt for not bringing him along this evening. But he had not been visible, and anyway she needed this time with her sister. Genni needed it too, she thought, she hoped. Besides, there was something about Kai that was scratching at her mind like claws and she wanted to escape that too.

Here, stepping out of the truck into the contented heat of the afternoon, she could pretend too that the things Thiago had said were not real. They didn't feel real here, a wood warbler singing above her and Genni watching Queen of Spain fritillaries fan their exquisite wings on the teasels.

'Come on then, love,' she said quietly. Genni looked at the sunlit flowers edging the forest ride, the dusty mass of the truck, then along the deertrack that Lina was standing on.

'In there?' she said, her eyes reflecting the shadows beneath the trees.

Lina tried to picture how this place looked to Genni, who had perhaps never been in woodland before coming here. But her imagination faltered – how could birdsong and this green dappled cathedral be anything other than wondrous after the camps, the city, the State? 'It's not far,' she said. 'And very safe.'

Genni came forward slowly, not looking back, her hands clenching and unclenching at her sides. And it wasn't far, just a few minutes through hornbeam and oak, a scramble up a bank and there was the den. Mounded earth smoothed by multitudinous paws. Lina took Genni's hand and led her past it to a spot where they could settle themselves against the bole of an oak. 'There, look,' she said, point to a tree directly ahead of them. 'See the camera? That's what the videos I sent you are from.'

Genni looked, but her gaze was skipping around and her hand had stayed miraculously in Lina's, faintly trembling. Without letting go of her, Lina pulled sandwiches out and handed one over. 'Eat,' she said. Food was such a weighted thing to a child who had gone without. Lina would never fully understand that, because her father had protected her so well, but she relaxed a little when Genni pulled her hand free of Lina to hold the sandwich.

They ate and did not talk much, although Lina pulled out her tablet to check her messages and showed Genni the screen so that she knew there was nothing from their father. Perhaps she should not have checked at all, or at least not waited until the sun was beginning to fall towards the hidden skyline, because Genni's small frame tensed against her own.

'It's getting dark,' Genni whispered, a long beam of sunlight turning scarlet against last year's fallen leaves. 'We should go. They aren't coming out.'

'They will,' Lina whispered. 'They'll be awake already. It won't be dark for a while yet.'

'We won't be able to see.' Genni was still whispering but breathlessly. 'No-one's coming.'

'They will,' Lina repeated, taking Genni's hand in hers again, stroking the brown fingers. 'They will come, love. We're safe, remember.'

'But what if...' Genni was looking at Lina's stretched out leg, her wounded ankle. 'What if we're not safe. What if–'

'Look,' Lina whispered. 'Look, here they are.'

And there they were. The mother fox standing in the entrance to her den, black nose tipped up as she scented the air. Lina had ensured they sat upwind of the den, so after a moment the vixen turned her head and, as if waiting for that signal, two small forms appeared, weaving between her legs investigating old bones and acorns.

'Oh,' Genni whispered and her breathing had calmed, her eyes wide enough to become white-haloed in the falling light.

Another cub emerged, and then a fourth, and as the mother sat patiently, they did what fox cubs did best, what Lina had most wanted Genni to see. They played and pounced and chased and growled, one coming within touching distance of where they sat silently, far too consumed by the game and the need to assault its siblings to notice them. Then the sun threw a last flare of bloody light across the forest and the night reared up from the shadows where it had been waiting. Genni flinched back and gave a high whimper, brief and faint but enough for the vixen to turn her gold eyes on them and with a low bark send her cubs scurrying for their den.

'Genni,' Lina whispered. The mother fox stared at them, black tail moving slowly, then she turned and disappeared lithely into the trees. 'Genni.'

But Genni did not seem to hear or notice that the foxes had gone. Her eyes were fixed on the slivers of pearly sunset between the branches and all of her muscles were tense. 'It's too dark,' she said. 'We have to–' scrambling to a crouch. 'We need to–'

'Genni, love,' Lina whispered, not moving because she thought if she did, Genni might startle away. 'We're safe, remember. We're safe, and it's still light. See? You can see me, can't you? Here,' she said, reaching into her bag. 'Here's a torch, would you like it?'

Genni grasped it but her eyes seemed blind. 'What if we're not safe,' she said. 'What if we're not...' Lina smoothed the hair from Genni's face and Genni turned to stare at her. 'Can you stop them? Can you stop them getting Dad and coming here. You have to stop them.'

'Yes,' Lina said without thinking. Remembering too late the choices Thiago had laid out so brutally, wanting to put her hands childishly over her ears and curl up here alone. But Genni was breathing fast again, her eyes focused on Lina's but unseeing, turned nightmarishly inward. Lina did not need to guess what that nightmare might be, too many miles crossed and hunted. 'Genni, you *are* safe here. You are.'

'What about...' a rasping breath, her eyes flickering shut but when Lina touched her she flinched. 'What about Dad? What if they get him?' another breath loud in the stirring forest, her voice rising. '*What if they get him?*'

'They won't–'

'You don't know,' Genni gasped. '*You don't know!*' Her head shaking too frantically and Lina so wanted to fold her into her arms, but held still. 'You have to save him, you have to save him, you have to–' her fingers clawing at her arms, she choked on her own words, and this time Lina spoke louder.

'Genni,' she moved so they were facing, her ankle flaring heat and pain. 'Genni, listen to me. It's alright. It's alright.' But it was not alright, and anger rose up in Lina like a stranger because she had been spending so much time worrying and fearing that she had forgotten to rage. 'Genni,' speaking a slow cadence, 'It will be alright. It will be alright. It will be alright. Breathe with me, love. Breathe with me. It will be alright.'

Darkness grew, the sky between leaves deepening to damson then an oceanic blue, the moon a narrow smile high above. Lina whispered, and Genni whimpered and breathed and whimpered, and slowly calmed. A roosting thrush called a last alarm and, almost too far away to hear, a nightingale's song rose up the slope. 'I can't see,' Genni whispered, more exhausted now than anything. Lina turned the torch on and as she had known it would, it made the night deeper around them, but that was not the point. It had never been about the darkness itself. Lina felt that anger again and realised that a small and brutally selfish part of it was at Genni. Or rather because Lina had to remain calm when she did not feel it, because she had two lives to protect instead of just one, and Thiago's voice kept murmuring the answer to a riddle she wished undone.

She closed her eyes, listening to the nightingale and realising she could smell wildfires from the plains, bitter on the evening air.

'Come on then,' she said eventually, rising awkwardly to her feet, wounds pulling. Only when they were in the truck, the cab light a cocoon, did she realised Genni was crying. Silent and furious, hunched over herself, and Lina's throat closed, but tears were better, she thought. Tears were healthier than gasping for breath on her knees. 'Oh, love,' she said softly, but Genni swiped at her face angrily and stared ahead. The light went out.

'I want to go home.'

Lina did not dare ask whether Genni meant London or the station because she thought she knew the answer.

'I want to go home.'

Lina started the engine and turned the truck, avoiding the tall teasels and hidden rocks more from memory than from the truck's muddied lights. 'I know, love,' she said.

'You don't,' Genni's voice sounded distant and calm, which was worse somehow than when she was shouting. 'You don't know because you left. You ran away. That's what you do. You leave people. You'll leave Dad there.'

'Jesus, Genni,' Lina said, startling herself. She stopped the truck, her hands on the wheel. 'I'm sorry, love, but you have no idea why I left, so you can't possibly understand.'

Genni made a harsh sound of disbelief.

'Genni. For god's sake, I left to save Dad. I left so that he and you got to hold on to that home you want to go back to. That life.' She stopped, dropped her hands into her lap where they curled in upon themselves. 'I gave up my life to keep you safe before,' she said. 'I'll do it again if I have to.'

She would. But it would still not be enough.

Genni's head turned, her eyes a low gleam in the dark. Lina had no idea what more to say, anger and sorrow spiralling slowly within her.

'Will you? How?'

Lina's hands moved to flatten themselves on her stomach, still the ache and the roil. 'However I need to,' she said.

'Xander said your friend killed his dad. Is that what you'll do? Kill people?'

Oh god, Lina thought, just as she had done earlier, sitting in the lab faced with Thiago's unassailable logic. 'James didn't kill him,' she said, remembering Kai sly gesture, the post-mortem results. 'State just want people to think so. Xander wants to think so.'

'I thought you said State wanted to blame Silene.'

'*Silene* thinks that. She thinks someone wants to pin this on her. Genni, I've no idea if that's true.'

Genni was silent for a minute. 'But it doesn't matter, does it? It's still because of you and James that we're not safe.'

She was right. And wrong. Their father had never told Genni about Lina's mother, against the unconscious indiscretion of a child, but also to spare Genni his own mourning. Lina could tell her now; it might excise her from guilt, her and James and all the things they had done. She turned the headlights onto full beam and drove the truck up the rough track that jostled them loosely, filling the silence with engine and rocks and gears.

When they pulled into the barn, Lina turned the headlights off, leaving only the light Thiago had kept on awaiting their return. Before Genni could move, she said levelly, 'I can't change the past, Genni. I can only fight *this* fight, here and now. So you can either carry on being angry with me for things I can't change, or you can accept that I am doing everything I can to keep you safe now and not make that even harder for me.'

'I'm not–'

'You are, actually,' Lina said. 'By blaming me, by fighting me, by not trusting me. They make it...' she cut off, her eyes becoming awash without warning. 'Just be careful with Xander and *trust me*, Genni. Please. Hang out with Kai, he'd like that.' She put her hand on the door. 'Can you do that for me?'

Genni did not answer.

'Genni?'

Genni sighed, shifted her weight. 'Okay. Okay.' Then swung herself out of the truck, Lina only catching up with her at the old house door. She pushed it open and Genni moved into the honeyed light as if reaching dry land. Lina began unloading her bag so she had her back turned when Genni spoke again.

'Who's Kai, anyway?'

Lina's hands stilled, and she stared at the mud beneath her

fingernails. She wondered where he was now, out in the meadow in the dark or hanging loosely over a balcony edge, fox skull in his pale hands. Oh Kai, she thought, and for a moment was too frightened to turn around and face Genni's question.

'The boy,' she said finally. Genni was standing at the foot of the stairs, weight canted and a frown between her brows. 'The boy who's with ... who lives here. Blond hair, your age...' she fell silent. No, she thought. No.

'What?' Genni's frown deepened.

No, Lina thought again, desperately. It was impossible. He was real, and she was not losing her mind, and all the tiny oddities that had been building to an answer were wrong, wrong, wrong.

'Perhaps you've missed him.' But he had held his hand over her bowed head, he had sat beside her mimicking her movements, he had sung to Lina while she was drowning. Genni studied her face and Lina had no idea what she might be reading there, but eventually she simply shrugged and muttered, 'Yeah maybe. Whatever,' and turned towards the stairs, her footfalls quick and light.

A moth had followed them in out of the dark and was flying bewildered orbits around the light. Lina watched it with her pulse a slow murmur in her ears.

'Kai,' Lina whispered into the empty lab. And then, 'Silene.' Silene talked to him, saw him, hated and feared him, and Lina's first surge of relief at the thought turned to ice when she realised what that meant. That the only other person who had ever noticed Kai was the delusional woman who had quite possibly murdered her husband.

Connections and stray words and the circling threat to her own friable sanity ravelled themselves in Lina's mind as the moth fell and rose, fell and rose. Then she moved, turned to her tablet, sat as if she might shatter and pulled up the news articles she had already read a dozen times. Pulled up the photos.

Chapter Twenty-Nine

Thiago found Lina just as the eastern horizon began to bleed from deep blue to cerulean. She was sitting on the tree stump in the meadow, both it and her chilled and dew-speckled, and she only moved when Thiago crouched at her side, touched the back of her hand.

'What is it?' he said quietly.

She looked at his familiar face and did not know what to say. That she could not forget his words yesterday, that she had come to care for a boy no-one else could see, that if she only had a finite number of days left then she wished she could have spent them here, alone, with him.

'He's doing well,' Thiago said when she did not answer. 'I got an update last night.'

She moved her head very slightly.

'I spoke to Kapoor,' Thiago continued, as if knowing that his voice might be what she needed to bring her back. The edge of the world became a line of fire, the vast arc of sky above them still alive with stars. 'He's ... interesting. I think he's conflicted. He knows he owes us his freedom, but he's suspicious. He isn't the type to act until he's certain though.'

'So...' It took an effort to speak; she had not slept and was far colder than she'd realised. 'So what will he do?' To become certain.

Thiago shook his head slowly, the bloody rising dawn painting his face, casting his eyes in shadow. 'I did mention Xander's hacking ESF. And I had another look at the reports around Wiley's death. He was dying before he was stabbed. Drugs.' He lifted a shoulder.

'If we push her, she might do our work for us.'

Drugs and knives, threat and counterthreat. And anything Lina and Thiago did would hurt Xander, who was grieving one parent and carrying the other. She lifted her eyes from Thiago to scan the indigo meadow, but there was no-one there. She wanted to talk to him but also dreaded doing so more than she could say.

'Yes,' she said. 'She's worsening, so...' So it would likely not be hard. 'Not in front of Xander though.'

'If possible.'

Lina shifted, her clothes moving damply against her skin. The air was incredibly still, mist laced against the trees like frost, the smell of water and the dying night. 'T,' she said, but then, faintly, the sound of alerts reached them through the open lab door, and they both turned.

'I'll go see,' Thiago said, rising, then reached down to her. 'Come in. You're freezing.' She put her hand in his, and knew he was right mostly because his skin was furnace hot against her own.

The alerts were for a super-storm. Not a storm, but a super-storm. She had not checked the weather for days, so had not seen this coming and it was rare for one to persist inland from the Atlantic coast. Lina read the words again and wanted to laugh. How utterly apt, she thought. But the humour faded almost before it formed. Perhaps the mountains would turn it aside, perhaps it would lose its fury as it barrelled across the continent.

'Forty-eight hours,' Thiago said. 'We should start prep now.'

'They might want to leave.' She looked up from her tablet to Thiago, who was scowling at the windows as if calculating their strength. 'They'd be safer in Sofia. Even Plovdiv.'

Thiago gave an abbreviated nod, still scanning the room. 'Ask them?'

'Gladly.' She did not look at her tablet again. Minimised in the corner was a photograph she had enhanced last night then stared at for a very long time wishing it unseen but unable to look away. The sky was a thinning blue now, cloudless and foretelling heat. Neither of the Wileys would be up yet. Devendra might be, but Lina went to shower and check on her sleeping sister without rushing.

He was there, a pot of coffee steaming beside him on the dining table, tablet propped up and his bruises fading fast now, yellow and mauve. Silene was curled on the sofa with her own tablet, and there was no sign of Xander. Lina had not checked his web activity again, but she pictured him sleeping sprawled between gear and cables, his hunting bots tireless.

Dev looked up and smiled infuriatingly pleasantly. 'Coffee?' Gesturing at the pot. 'It's fresh. I hope you like it strong.'

This was surreal, she thought, fetching a mug and letting him fill it, the blue sky and the storm raging towards them beyond the horizon. She set her tablet on a coffee table and went to open the patio doors, half expecting, dreading, Kai there but the balcony was empty, swift fledglings murmuring restlessly in the eaves above her. A flicker of white movement caught her eye within the barn and, with a shiver, she turned back inside.

'I'm not sure if you've checked the weather,' she said to them both. 'But there's a super-storm coming. It'll be here by the end of tomorrow probably.'

Silene looked up at her, frowning with the effort to understand. Dev canted his head expectantly and Lina said steadily. 'It will be dangerous here, so HQ have asked that we evacuate you to Plovdiv. We can arrange travel to Sofia if you'd rather. You'll need to leave this morning, I'm afraid.'

'What...' Silene looked to Dev, then back to Lina. 'A *super*-storm? But ... no, that cannot be right. Dev...'

He had turned back to his tablet, likely confirming Lina's news. Lina came to sit on the end of the sofa near Silene. 'A full super-storm cell, yes. They are extremely rare here, but...' she shrugged. 'The station isn't designed to withstand them, and the forest will be deadly. It really is vital you get to somewhere safer.'

'And you?' Devendra said softly. 'I assume that means you will be leaving too?'

Lina met his gaze. 'That depends. We have a lot of work to do preparing the station as much as possible. And it would be better if we were here to act if needed. We'll be watching the forecast.'

'You aren't leaving?' Silene said.

Lina looked at her dormant tablet, waiting in front of her and Silene. 'We have a duty to this place.'

'That's a hell of a strong sense of loyalty,' Dev said, smiling his sharp, devastating smile.

Trying to batten down a flare of anger, Lina said, 'It's our home, so yes, we will risk ourselves for it.' She took a breath. 'But we can't let you do so. Thiago is arranging transport at the moment. We might be able to get you an airlift if the winds on the plain stabilise. If they can't get clearance, we'll truck you out to the ESF border where a security team will meet you and take you the rest of the way.'

'We can't go,' Silene whispered. Her fingers were wrapped around her throat, their nails ragged, the polish chipped away. 'Dev, tell her. We can't go back.'

Lina glanced at Dev and then back to Silene. 'You'll be safe in Sofia,' she said. 'Won't you? You could stay there afterwards if you don't want to go home. Xander would prefer Sofia to here, I imagine.'

Silene shuddered and Dev leaned one elbow on the dining table, watching.

'I can't go back,' Silene whispered, staring at nothing. No, not at nothing, Lina realised. At the meadow still hung halfway between shadow and sun. 'You said they couldn't make me go back. So they can't, can they, even if they know? But the blood wasn't–' a tiny gasp that reminded Lina of Genni in the forest yesterday, fighting for breath. '*He was there, Dev!* It was *him*–'

'Silene,' Dev said impatiently. 'No-one knows anything, more's the pity. They only want to talk to you, and you aren't going to talk to them. But perhaps we ought to listen to Lina and get out of here.'

'No. You cannot make me, Dev darling. You simply cannot. I am staying here until it's safe.'

'It's not safe here,' Lina said.

More unnerving than the clutching hands and the glazed eyes, Silene laughed. 'Not safe? Oh, I know that. With that *thing* here, and *you*, how could I be safe here? But...' she turned jerkily to fix her gaze on Dev. He frowned at her. 'But I don't care about *my* safety, don't you see? They can kill *me*.' She laughed again. 'Yes, they can. But I won't let them get Xander. And if we leave here, they will take him away. You know they will.'

Dev looked at Lina and said musingly, 'Do I? Perhaps I do.' He scanned the room with the same analytical assessment as Thiago. 'This place looks quite sturdy. And the forecast suggests the storm eye will track north of us.' He gave Lina a wide, generous smile and she felt a weight press down on her lungs. 'If we stay we could help Thiago with the prep as you are ... not fighting fit.'

Lina had abandoned her crutches and the pain had become such a background presence that she forgot he might still see her as broken. Unless it was more warning than taunt. She opened her mouth to argue with him, but then a high trill of laughter rose in amongst the song of a blackcap, and she came to a decision. Leaning forward, she shifted her tablet to sit square to both her and Silene, and woke the screen. Looking at that, she said, 'The error margins are pretty wide at the moment, and even if it just brushes us here, we'd expect structural damage. ESF is not happy having guests here.' She did not mention Genni. Silene had gone deathly still beside her, but Lina did not look. 'They aren't willing to risk one of you becoming injured, especially in light of recent events.'

Silene began to make a high, high keening sound, and even though Lina had chosen to do this, she did not want to turn. Because seeing the truth on Silene's face might make it real, and the thing Lina had discovered in the night was something she desperately wanted to remain unreal.

'Silene,' Dev had risen to his feet, and Lina did look at the other woman's face then. Told herself to show neither cold horror nor cruelty; anger and heartache looming.

'Silene,' Dev repeated, sitting on the table in front of her. 'What is it? What's...' he followed her wide eyed gaze to the screen of Lina's tablet and picked it up. 'What's this?'

Although Lina was unsure who he was addressing, she answered as steadily as possible. 'It's a news photograph. Do you recognise it?'

Seeing Silene flinch back, her face so colourless she looked deathly. *Good,* Lina thought savagely. *This is exactly how you deserve to feel.* And for the first time, found something in this new impossible knowledge that seemed just, and right.

'From what?' Dev said. His voice held danger now, which was what Lina had told herself to expect, but it was still chilling.

'It wasn't me, Dev,' Silene whispered. 'You have to understand it wasn't me. I told him not to go. I said it would draw attention, but he wouldn't listen. He never listened, Dev, you know that. And if he hadn't gone then...' she shuddered so violently that the sofa vibrated, her eyes finding the photograph on the screen, shying away, raised a shaking finger to point. '*It followed me.*'

Dev looked at the screen and Lina found that she could not breathe, the air around her thinned to the point of vacuum.

'It was there too, Dev.' Silene's voice was dry and shriven. 'No-one sees it, but it followed him home and then ... and then...' She began to sob brokenly, her face haggard and twisted. She had been so poised and preened when she came, Lina thought numbly. Would anyone have guessed she would break so easily? Yes, perhaps.

Dev had not raised his head, still studying Lina's tablet, and she did not want to look at the photograph, but had memorised every pixel anyway. Of the small body lying on the ground, its pale face twisted towards the camera, blood outlining his torso.

So much blood, she thought just as she had done last night. So much blood from such a small body. He must have been so cold at the end. He still was.

'His name was Kai,' she whispered, her throat full of tears and blind disbelief. 'He was eight. He was murdered on Christopher Wiley's orders. As he watched.'

Chapter Thirty

'Silene thinks she can see him,' Lina said. Silene shrank back into the sofa, clawing at her face as if to obliviate herself. Lina spoke without looking at Dev, but he was listening so intently she could feel the weight of it. 'She says this boy, Kai, saw her with her husband just before he died.'

'She's told you this?' Dev said.

This was what she had wanted. Silene's innocence cast into doubt alongside her sanity so that Dev would have more reasons to take her quietly away than he had to hunt conspiracies. So why did it feel like it was her being unravelled, and her who was betraying that unutterably betrayed boy in the photograph.

'Yes,' she said very quietly, turning her face towards the balcony again, relieved to see that it was still empty. She could not have borne it if he had heard her claim not to see him.

'Silene,' Dev said, setting Lina's tablet down and leaning forward to pull Silene's hands away from her face. She yelped and resisted, but then surrendered and looked at him like a child expecting redemption. 'Silene, you aren't seeing any ... ghosts. They aren't real.' She was shaking her head mutely and he tightened his hold on her. 'Ghosts aren't real, Silene. This is just your grief. That's all. We'll get you to a doctor and all of this will get better.' He looked at Lina, catching her by surprise. 'What has she been taking? Have you supplied any of it?'

'What?' Lina frowned, her mind still full of his certain, soothing voice saying, *Ghosts aren't real*. Hysteria welled within her. 'We've given her nothing. I don't know what she's taking, but I...' treading such a fine line. 'I did mention my concerns that she has been overmedicating to Xander.'

'Overmedicating,' Dev repeated and Lina thought that he too had read the latest reports and was thinking of the unnamed sedatives in Christopher Wiley's blood.

'Hmm.' He brushed Silene's hair back from her face with a tenderness that Lina had not expected him to be capable of. He was too full of trickery and edges to be so gentle, or perhaps it was that he was so full of trickery that she did not *want* to think him also capable of gentleness. Monsters were easier to hate if they were only ever monsters. Her heart lurched a little at the word, and she thought that even if the impossible were true, even if she too was seeing a boy who had died hundreds of miles away, then that did not stop her wanting to protect him from harm now, here. She thought of James, and the fact that she could not bear him being accused of murder even though he too was beyond caring now, beyond being hurt.

Maybe that was why she was seeing Kai, she thought, her heart faltering, sharp and lonely. Maybe she was seeing an abandoned, innocent child and wanting to save him because she had abandoned James, and he was innocent, and no-one had saved him. Because she wished so much that she could have told him he was loved even after all this time, even though it had not been enough.

Maybe it takes a broken heart to see other broken things, she thought. In which case how could she wish to make herself blind?

'I must go,' she said abruptly, coming to her feet, cradling her tablet against her. Dev did not look up, murmuring to Silene just the way Lina had spoken Genni back from the darkness. At the top of the stairs, Lina remembered herself. 'Thiago will tell you the evacuation plans. You should pack.'

Dev did lift his head now, his eyes on her dark as coffee and deceptive, but she left before he could either answer or read the agony on her face.

'Kai,' she whispered coming out into the meadow, raising butterflies and silencing grasshoppers as she passed. 'Kai,' she said. 'Kai.'

But he did not come. Perhaps he couldn't, now that she knew.

Perhaps she had only ever dreamed him out of grief and fear and rage. She sat in the meadow, watching the mountains shimmer beneath the sun, waiting for the memory of a child, summoning the will to face a storm.

A swallowtail glided golden past her to dip and rise over the orlaya and Lina saw Thiago looking for her, so she rose. It hurt to walk without crutches, but the pain was a promise of healing. When she reached him, Thiago said:

'Airlift at thirteen hundred. How's the ankle?'

Lina smiled at him. 'It's fine. Is Genni up?'

Thiago lifted a shoulder. 'Listening to music.'

They needed to talk again, her and Genni, move them both forward from last night.

'She's staying here?'

Thiago was leaning against the doorframe and Lina sat on the bench against the wall. She looked up at the high blue sky framed by roofs, then at the light lying over the meadow, wavering above the forest and the slopes, smelling that taint of smoke again from the plains. Two years ago a tornado had seeded fire through a small village and she had gone down to help. A handful of people survived, far more died, ash and burnt flesh in her lungs and the vultures overhead, corvids on the stumps of walls.

They were so easily forgotten, the dead, and it shouldn't be that way. She thought of James again and gingerly, still resisting, of Kai.

'I can't send her away,' Lina said eventually. 'She's got to be safer here. Anyway, she'd be alone again, and I can't do that.'

Thiago's jaw tightened but he nodded. 'Then we'll keep her safe,' he said.

Lina tipped her head back against the warm bricks. 'One o'clock.' Less than four hours and then perhaps it would be over, if what she had just shown Dev was enough. 'What's the weather like?' Meaning on the firestrewn plains between here and Plovdiv, where small and deadly tornadoes could fill the air with smoke and collapsing wind patterns that no-one could predict, or fly in.

'Borderline.' Lina looked at him, but Thiago said nothing else and she had not really expected him to. Neither false reassurance nor unneeded explanations. 'I'm starting with the barn. You do the shutters?'

Lina nodded. There was so much work to do before tomorrow evening, and her injury would slow them. 'I'll check on Genni first,' she said, and Thiago pushed off from the doorframe, leaving her to drag herself out of the sun.

Far more readily than Lina had expected, Genni agreed to help unpack and check the storm shutters that would fit over the old house windows. Watching her intent face, Lina realised that Genni had gained a little weight since coming here and her lovely dark skin was two shades darker than it had been. Despite the anger, the hours hunched over her tablet, the lurking panic, she looked healthier now than she ever had before. Lina took a slow breath, brushed cobwebs from a shutter scattering spiders, and said, 'You know the others are leaving later?'

Genni nodded, eyeing the spiders dubiously.

'The storm might get…' Lina searched for a balance between truth and kindness. Thiago would not have bothered, and perhaps he was right, but she couldn't help herself. 'Pretty rough,' she said eventually. 'But we'll get through it, okay?'

Genni nodded again, but she threw a quick, dark glance out towards the forest. Lina touched her shoulder briefly, then scooped up one of the spiders and let it run across her palms. 'She's carrying her egg sac, look. Protecting it. She'll tuck herself into a hole during the storm and be perfectly safe.' Genni kept her gaze half-averted, so Lina set the spider down out of the way, wondering what she had been trying to achieve. 'We should write Dad another message today,' she said, and Genni's eyes became immediately wide and strained. 'We'll turn off the electricity before the storm arrives, and will probably lose the net as well.'

'He didn't write back.'

'No,' Lina said. It worried her, that. The ESF lawyer had replied, confirming he'd passed the messages on, but had advised they give it time. *The Slovaks will lose interest soon and let him go*, he'd written. *He's being treated well. Don't push. I'll check in weekly.*

'But they don't…' Lina cut off. Genni still believed him to be simply resting in a safe house, recovering more slowly than he had hoped. 'I think he's struggling to get safe access to the net. But we know he got our messages.'

'What will you say to him? About Xander?'

Lina shrugged, smiled. 'I'll tell him they are leaving. That's the important thing.'

'And I'm staying with you?' Genni was rubbing her dusty palms together, gathering spidersilk between her fingertips.

'Yes,' Lina said. But she could not tell from Genni's face whether that was the answer she had sought, or simply a reminder of their father's absence.

Neither Xander nor Kai had shown themselves yet, and both absences worried at Lina's mind as she stacked the shutters ready in the lab, as she got Genni to help her carry the sun lounger into the barn. But when Genni went inside in search of food, Lina turned from the barn to see Kai standing in the sunlight at the very edge of the courtyard. She studied him, her pulse pressing against her wrists and a voice in her head whispering, *this is madness. It cannot be true, this is madness.* His shadow lay at his feet and he watched her without blinking, eyes bleached almost yellow by the light and wariness.

'Hello, Kai,' she said, very aware of all the open windows around them, of the fact that she did not know quite where Thiago was. 'How are you?'

He did not move so she went to him, resting a hand against the old house as if that might lend her solidity. 'Kai,' she said again.

'Lina,' he replied. 'Xander has found something out.'

She stopped trying to measure the way the light hit his face, his mass compared to the air around him. 'Pardon?'

He moved his hands and their emptiness was a relief, ridiculously. 'I don't know what, but something.'

'Is it…' she glanced over her shoulder at the empty courtyard, the windows that reflected the sky blindly. 'Sweetie, is it about you?'

As he tilted his head the sun caught his eyes and some twist of gilding and shadow was exactly like the fox in yesterday's dusk.

Wariness and intensity and wildness. 'Me?'

Oh god, she thought. He looked like he might flee, vanishing foxlike too, only into light rather than darkness. Did he know? Did he even know? 'Nothing,' she said faintly. 'What's he doing?'

'He's on the net, reading things.'

'Lina?' It was Genni, calling down from the upstairs window. 'Can you come up? Are you on a call?'

Xander had asked her the same question, Lina remembered. She had been talking to Kai on the balcony and Xander had asked that question, and she had somehow failed to comprehend the myriad hints and oddities until she zoomed in on a photograph and ceased to understand anything about the world.

'What's up?' she said, seeing Kai take a step back from the wall to look upwards as well.

'Can you come up?' Genni repeated.

'Yes,' Lina said, turning back to Kai and abruptly unable to speak, Genni above looking down. Kai was watching Genni with a strange, twisted expression, and Lina remembered him running his fingers over the fox's sharp teeth and shivered. She knew nothing about any of this, she thought desperately. About him or what he wanted or even what he was thinking, not really. If he *could* think. If he was not simply a ... a gathering of memory and anger and grief given weight.

Realising she was watching him, he dropped his gaze to hers and said, 'You should send her away before the monster comes. She still wouldn't fight for you, you know?' Then he slipped around the corner of the house, and Lina realised that nothing on earth could have made her step forward to see if he was still visible.

'Chopper's five minutes out. I'll go round them up,' Thiago said as she stepped into the blinding shade of the lab. 'Looks messy though.'

Lina would have happily absented herself from their leaving, but Genni had overheard and whatever she had called Lina for was forgotten beneath the need to watch the helicopter collect these people in a blaze of wealth and privilege that she had never seen before, not like this.

They gathered outside, Silene slumped on a bench in a catatonia that perhaps she had been in ever since seeing Kai's photograph. Xander was plugged in to his tablet but he was watching Lina, pale-faced but strung with something that might have been victory. Fear tainted her throat with acid as she kept her gaze on the foothills where clouds had gathered in a sullen, straggled line.

'Fire twisters,' Thiago muttered beside her and another fear stirred, a different, impersonal one.

'It's here,' Lina said. A black shape lifting into sight in the east, skimming a line between the ravaged plain and the mountains, distorted by heat and the dirty air rising from the flatlands. Three kilometres away perhaps, then two and a half kilometres, the engine a low *whump whump* at the base of her spine, Genni's hand creeping into hers and Lina gripping it in return, watching the slow swirl of the rising air, the dense distorted horizon. Another few seconds, then Xander noticed the helicopter and moved towards his mother. Dev had been watching it already, perhaps had seen it even before her. The air behind the helicopter shifted colour from a tarnished blue to something leaden and Thiago swore.

A dust tornado rose behind them, but they looked clear.

Dev straightened and resettled his feet, and beside her Thiago did the same. Faster, Lina thought. The twister veered into the helicopter's wake, the sky above turned liquescent and then a thin tornado was leaping downward. Parallel to the machine, swinging precipitously, the helicopter's black mass there and gone in a cloud of rock dust. Lina closing her eyes reflexively, too late. The helicopter bucking on the tornado's cusp, rearing upwards then catching the edge of the fire twister, thrown sideways and downward and down. A fountain of rock and rotorblade and carapace fragments. Then black and oily smoke, half-concealed flames.

Thiago swore again. Dev and Xander speaking and Genni gasping a shrill note beside her, and Lina could think only, A crew of two. Smoke and ashes, she thought. Two people and she did not know their names.

Chapter Thirty-One

'Did you know that would happen?' Xander said, spinning on Thiago. 'Did you know they'd crash?'

'Xander,' Dev said quietly, but Xander's hands were balled at his sides and a crimson wave was climbing his cheeks. He took three steps towards them, his mum twitching as he passed.

'I fucking *knew* it,' he said. 'I *knew* you wouldn't let us leave. So this was just like a *stunt* or whatever. That's sick. It's fucking *sick*. There were *people* on that thing,' waving an arm towards the slow rising smoke.

Lina wrapped her other arm around Genni and bent to whisper that she should go inside, but Genni did not move. Thiago had not moved either. Dev went to stand beside Silene, his hand on her shoulder as if comforting her, although she seemed too far gone to need it.

'Two people,' Thiago said levelly. 'Andrei Mikailovsky and Denise Larsden. They both have young children.'

Genni flinched, Lina's own fingers tightening, and although Thiago's words made Xander shudder as well, they weren't enough to stop him.

'You couldn't just tell us we're prisoners here? Like, would it kill you?' He spread his arms wide like a bear rearing. 'Well, here we fucking are. Do your fucking worst, I dare you.'

Thiago crossed his arms, lifted one eyebrow almost infinitesimally, and it was Dev who spoke from behind Xander. 'Why on earth would they want us to stay so badly, Xander?'

This was what Kai had warned her of, Lina realised. The blood in her veins slowed, the world slowed. She could not look away from Xander's reddened, furious face.

'Because she's guilty as fucking sin. She wants to kill us like her fucking *boyfriend* killed Dad. Like her *mother*–' He took another two steps forward and Thiago shifted his weight but all Xander did was lift a hand to point at Lina, his whole body shaking. '*I know who you are* and I'm going to tell the *whole fucking world.*'

Spinning on his heel to leave, stumbling as Thiago caught his arm and yanked him back around and Dev had moved forward although Lina did not know which one he wanted to stop, and all she could think was, *No. No, no, no.* Everything asunder, terror and grief and horror and fury all unravelling. *No, no, no.* Too trapped within her own mind to hear anything other than the level, cold blankness of Thiago's voice, feeling his fury only undo her more.

'You are wrong,' he said. 'Whatever you think you know, you are wrong about the airlift and wrong about Lina. But you are right about this. If you endanger her, you will not leave this station.' He released Xander's arm dismissively and said to Dev, 'Get him under control or I will.'

No, Lina thought again, but at Thiago now as well as everything else. Genni moved against her and Lina's body was suddenly her own again. 'Come away,' she whispered painfully. Thiago began to turn towards her, Xander fled past Dev, Dev pivoting slowly in his wake, and Lina pulled Genni with her. 'Come away,' she said. Thiago back at her side again as if he had never left, reaching to touch her.

'Lina,' he said. 'Don't–'

But she did not slow because if she did she thought she might scream and once begun, never stop.

'You have to–' he tried again.

'Not now,' she said, and he stopped, letting her leave him behind as she took herself and Genni away, not into the lab because she thought walls might crush her now, and it was Thiago's space as well as hers, and his rage might crush her too. So instead away around the back of the old house to drop into a crouch against the wall amidst old peony leaves and fallen cherries. Genni sat beside her and for a long time neither of them said anything. She needed to speak, Lina knew, but she could only sit there with her heart pressing against her ribs, seeing the helicopter flip sideways over and over and over. Seeing Xander's pointed finger shaking.

The truck pulling away fast made both of them look up. It would be Thiago going to check on the helicopter, Lina thought, and she should have gone with him but did not move.

'What did he mean?'

Lina turned her head to look at Genni. 'He was just angry,' but prevaricating was beyond her. 'I'm going to have to go and get Dad.' Putting into words what Thiago had known she was thinking. They knew each other far too well, she thought, still shaking. 'Will you be okay staying with Thiago while I do that?'

Genni's arms were wrapped around her drawn-up knees and Lina watched her breathing, waiting for it to change.

'I want to come.'

'I know, but you're safer here,' adding quickly before Genni could protest, 'And I'll be faster and safer on my own.' And if it came to it, she did not want Genni to know what she was doing until it was done. 'And as long as you're here, ESF will make sure Dad gets here too.'

Genni thought about this, closing her eyes and resting her cheek against one knee. Lina expected more objections, so when Genni spoke it startled her. 'Who's Kai?'

Not this too, she thought, exhausted almost to the point of hysteria. She watched the forest now, the multitudinous greens, the silver scattered lindens. 'He's a boy I see here sometimes,' she said eventually.

'Was that who you were talking to earlier? I thought I saw...'

'What?'

'Nothing,' Genni lifted both shoulders enormously. 'Sometimes I think this place doesn't like me.'

'No!' Lina reached to touch her cheek with the backs of her fingers. 'That's not true at all.' But Kai's face as he had looked up at Genni, and his words, had held animosity. She tried to find something rational to say, something that did not include ghost children full of hurt and trauma. 'It must all feel very strange to you here,' she said slowly, 'but the wonderful thing about this place is that the mountains and the forest, and even the animals, they don't care about us at all. We just have to live respectfully and they carry on the way they've carried on for thousands of years. I've always liked that ... invisibility. It's peaceful.'

'Are you scared?'

Her fingers were tense, but she was still breathing calmly so Lina looked back to the forest and sighed. 'Yes,' she said. Yes and yes and yes. 'But never of the forest.'

'Of going to get Dad.'

'Yes,' she said again. Not of the journey, but of what she might give up to save him, and what might still happen to them regardless. Thiago would look after them, she told herself. But ESF likely would not, so how much could he realistically do?

'When will you go?'

It must be about half past one now, she thought. How much the world had shifted in those thirty minutes. 'Tonight,' she said. ESF would be slower to notice her departure at night. And once she was clear, she thought they would rather speed her trip than force her back. She hoped.

A low murmuring thunder rolled along the mountainsides although there were no storm clouds within view. She wished she knew what Dev was saying to Xander, and what Xander was saying to him. Although actually she did not want to know the latter, know how he would choose to tell the story.

Slowly, painfully, she pushed to her feet. 'I'd better speak to HQ. And check the weather.' Twenty-four hours until the superstorm hit. She had almost forgotten, and ought to leave sooner. Perhaps ESF would not even realise she had left until the storm had passed. Genni rose beside her and when Lina reached out a hand, she only hesitated briefly before taking it. There was no way to know whether this new détente was because of the panic and the fight, or the knowledge that she was leaving, but Lina held onto the slim comfort of it as if it were the only spar remaining.

Another message to Kolya first, and to Vitaly. Full of foreboding that neither had replied and wishing she had tried again sooner, set up a contingency plan sooner. Then to the lawyer asking again for news, telling him that they would soon be cut off. Then placing a call, and when Isla's assistant picked up she said quickly. 'Please don't put me through. I wanted to speak to you.'

He raised his eyebrows but said nothing.

'You've heard about the helicopter?'

'Of course. Mr Ferdinando called it in.' Although he would not have contacted Lina's department, which confirmed her suspicions. 'I believe trucks are being arranged as we speak.'

Good, Lina thought. That was good. 'Can I ask you something else? It's about net activity, search histories, that sort of thing.'

He glanced at another part of the screen then back to her. 'This is about Alexander Wiley, I imagine.'

Lina's fingertips pressed against the edge of the desk. Genni had gone upstairs, so Lina wanted this done before she returned. 'Yes,' she said. 'Is there a way to … wipe his downloads, anything he might have accessed recently? He's been using search bots I think. Can we destroy them?'

The still-unnamed man tilted his head, studying her. 'It is possible,' he said slowly. 'Why now? Any particular reason, beyond the obvious?'

An alert popped up in the corner of Lina's screen updating the storm warning, shifting it closer to the station. Her pulse sped up, she breathed out slowly. 'He's been hacking through ESF systems,' she said. 'If he starts making claims in public, it will lead back to our security.'

The man laughed, light from an unseen window turning his eyes metallic. He had positioned his desk so that he faced both window and door, Lina realised, whereas Isla set the window behind her as backdrop. 'Very good,' the man said. 'And yet I doubt that would hold up. If it were particularly important, however, the right person might be able to help.'

Music fibrillating across the courtyard and into the lab. 'I think I'm speaking to the right person now,' Lina said steadily.

'I assume we are disregarding the obvious solution to the issue?'

He had suggested it before. As had Thiago, differently, and it still made nausea rise in Lina's stomach. She could not answer but he must have read her face. 'Well, you've run out of time on that anyway, I imagine. How about a transcript of his code. I'm sure I can pull enough together for some mutually assured destruction.'

Which was what Thiago had reasoned as well, the two men suspiciously alike even if one was more subtle about it than the other. And yet Lina was not sure that Xander was thinking clearly enough to protect himself. Grief and the terrible pressure of caring for his mother had turned him inside out, she thought, so that he might be happy to immolate himself if it meant everyone else would burn.

'I can send you a programme that would wipe everything,' the man said. 'But it would have to be uploaded directly. I imagine his firewalls are insurmountable at short notice.'

Genni, Lina thought, appalled at the thought even as it formed. 'Yes,' she said anyway, 'Please–'

'It's only a short-term solution of course. A delay.'

'Yes, I–'

'And they will be leaving this evening I imagine.'

Dear god, she thought. How did you become someone for whom death was such an unremarkable option? But she knew how, and while she understood and forgave it in Thiago, that same reduction of life to weights on a scale was everything she hated about the States and Christopher Wiley and Silene. She would not let herself become them.

'Can you send me the programme?' she said. The bathroom door upstairs opened and closed.

'Of course,' the man said, smiling, knowing what she was thinking. Where Thiago would not have judged her, she thought this man saw weakness. 'Ah,' he added, 'The trucks are due ten pm your time. Which gives you eight hours, I believe.'

'Okay,' Lina said. Footsteps on the stairs and Genni coming into the room. 'Thank you.'

'Good luck, Dr Stephenson.' He cut the connection before she could and, although she had not seen him typing, an email from an unlabelled internal address arrived almost immediately, an .exe file attached.

Chapter Thirty-Two

Lina and Genni went up to the lounge, Lina needing coffee and with the programme saved onto a mini USB drive lying in her pocket like a prayer. They were all up, even Silene, her eyes flitting from Dev to Xander to the balcony and her whole body poised for flight. So whatever she had been given to get her on the helicopter had worn off then, Lina thought, and met Dev's gaze with that in the forefront of her mind like a shield.

'You've heard about the trucks,' she said to him. Xander was sitting at the table with Dev but after one quick glance at her had tucked his head down and lifted headphones over his ears. No more accusations then, not that they needed repeating. Genni went out onto the balcony, leaning out to search worriedly for tornadoes. Lina felt sick.

'In the dark,' Silene said. 'We can't leave in the dark.'

Lina turned away from all of them to put the kettle on, making work of setting things out so she did not have to answer. Eight hours and then they would be beyond her reach. Which she had wished for this morning, before Xander had revealed how much he knew.

'If Lina says it is safe, then I'm sure that's true,' Dev said, sounding, unbelievably, *amused*.

'I do,' she said, far more sharply than was wise. 'And it is.'

'There we are then,' he said, turning his hands up on the table, palms flashing pale. 'But what should we call you, instead of Lina? Xander hasn't said.'

The kettle reached boiling point beside her, steam occluding her view of Silene. She had not really expected them to say nothing, but his words still hit her like a fist, her breath becoming drowning. And yet, she realised, unless this was a feint, he did not know her old name, and so ... and so Xander had not told him everything. Why? Why not?

She did not answer, only held his gaze and waited, carbon dioxide burning her lungs. He tipped his head and gave her a feline smile but there was a softness to it that she had not seen before, or not aimed at her.

'Very few people have his skill, or his determination,' he said eventually, nodding at Xander's studiously unresponsive form.

What was she meant to take from that? Comfort, that no-one else might uncover her secret? She still could not speak, thinking of her unanswered messages to Kolya, hearing Genni say something about the smoke. Silene rose jerkily to her feet and came to Dev, laying an unsteady hand on his shoulder, and Lina saw his muscles twitch at her touch, as if he had begun to shrug her off but stopped himself.

'What is it, Dev darling?' Silene said. 'What has she done?'

'It is more what she hasn't,' he said slowly, his eyes not leaving Lina's face. 'Or what she wouldn't, perhaps.'

'Wouldn't? What ... what is she going to ... I don't understand.' Silene was looking fixedly at Dev, ignoring Lina as completely as her son was. Lina found her voice.

'There are many things I would not do,' she said more certainly than she felt. 'And many things I have never done. Which is more than can be said for State, or for you, I imagine.'

'Ah, but I am not State,' Dev said with the gentleness that was likely meant to unbalance her, and was working. Again she did not answer, but this time because the fallacy did not warrant one given the woman clutching his shoulder with cracked, bitten fingers.

'She's State,' Silene whispered. 'They've got her father, so she'll do anything they say, Dev. You have to stop her. You have to stop her before we leave.'

'Mum,' Xander said without warning. Lina had assumed his music was loud enough to deafen him. 'It's over, alright? Just shut up. That's all you have to do now.'

He thought he had won, Lina thought.

He knew she could say nothing without condemning her father and herself and Genni to death and if not now, for her and Genni, then inevitably, eventually. And yet why then the hunched shoulders, the fixed set of his averted face? As if aware of her gaze, his own shifted to Dev then away, and was that it, she thought, doubting. Had Dev not *wanted* to know Lina's secret, and was he holding Xander silent?

'Mutually assured destruction,' she said quietly, repeating Isla's unshakable assistant, wondering if it was possible that Isla's assistant could still be wrong and Thiago could be wrong and perhaps it would all simply end here with a teenager's dampened anger and the unreadable gaze of a deceptive man.

'Hmm,' Dev said.

'Dev?' Silene said, her hand crawling from his shoulder to her neck, her cheek. 'Dev?'

'Go and have a lie down, Silene,' he said, twisting to look at her for the first time. 'Xander, can you take your mum to her room, make sure she's comfortable?'

They both obeyed him without hesitation. What had he been in their lives before Christopher Wiley died? And what was he thinking? Dear god, what was he thinking?

She checked on Genni, sitting on the balcony now, tablet and headphones in place, her feet raised against the railing. Kai was outside, Lina realised. On the track leading away into the forest, his hair spindrift in the wind and something hanging from a raised hand, dancing. Something small and red as blood. Lina took two steps forward to be sure, aware of her ankle abruptly. Dev's voice was soft behind her, but relentless.

'Would you sit, Lina?'

But then the truck threw itself out from beneath the trees into the sun, Kai slipping into the grass as it passed, and Lina wondered whether he needed to. What would have happened if he had not moved? He watched the truck pull to a stop in the courtyard, closing his still-raised fist around the doll.

'I need to speak to Thiago,' Lina said, turning to Dev and hesitating. Wanting to ask but full of dread.

'Of course,' Dev nodded. 'Does he know your name? I'm sure you told ESF when you joined them, but does he know?'

It was too late for regrets, but god, if only she *had* told Thiago. 'I imagine that is irrelevant to you,' she said. 'Do *you* know it?'

He smiled less gently. 'I doubt anything concerning Thiago is irrelevant to you, however.' Leaning back, lifting a mug. 'I wish you no harm.'

She laughed. Three swifts screamed, knifing past the balcony. Genni flinched but Dev did not. He had not answered. 'And yet,' Lina said, 'you threaten it.'

'No,' he said, as if he believed it, as if it mattered to him that she did too. 'No, I am trying to understand you.'

The front door opened below them. Lina's heart rose and fell within her. 'Whatever for? When you have what you need?'

'I don't know,' he said, and laughed. 'Did you love him? James Hanslow.'

Thiago's two-tone footsteps were on the stairs, blade and boot, blade and boot. How could she want him here and yet be wishing him slower? It made no sense. This man made no sense. 'Yes,' she said helplessly. 'I did. Do you have children, Dev?' Perhaps hoping to unbalance him in turn but failing.

Thiago reached the last flight of stairs and paused momentarily when he saw her, but then came on up faster.

'I don't,' Dev said, and Thiago faltered again, minutely. 'Because I will not bring children into this world.' He glanced at Genni out on the balcony and Lina hated him then, for being able to read her, for being friends with the very man whose acts he now judged wrong.

'Lina,' Thiago said, reaching her side. 'Kapoor. Lina, alright?'

Lina nodded, but her thoughts were still full of Dev. 'So why then?' she said. Meaning why help the Wileys, why threaten her even if that was not what he was calling it?

For the first time, Dev's face showed something other than amusement and acuity. 'Old loyalties,' he said, looking away from her to study his hands, the heavy gold band on the wrong finger. 'Curious how they tie us in knots, isn't it?'

Thiago shifted and Lina felt the pull of his tension win out.

'What is it?' she said quietly.

'This is for you too, Kapoor,' Thiago said and Dev's face smoothed. 'No trucks. There's been a rockfall on the lower road. I can clear it but not till after the storm.'

'What? Where? How did–' Lina stopped. 'The wreck?'

Thiago's blade was shifting against the floor in a small repetitive movement, only noticeable because she knew to look for it when he would not meet her eyes. 'No, further down. The tornadoes, I think.'

'So we're staying after all.'

Lina and Thiago both looked at Dev but this time Lina's mind was still on the man beside her, the one she knew better perhaps than she knew herself.

'Yes. Sorry.' Thiago did not sound particularly sorry and Dev clearly noticed, raising his eyebrows slowly.

'We can't hike down past it?'

'T,' Lina said, but Thiago ignored her.

'You could. But the others?'

Dev grimaced faintly and did not bother to answer, instead he pulled his tablet towards him as if to check the weather forecast again, or to let Xander know. 'It seems everything must wait till after the storm,' he said softly, not looking up.

Lina stared at him but he only smiled faintly to himself and she turned away too fast. 'T,' she repeated. 'Can we talk?'

His foot moved again and he lifted a hand halfway to his face before dropping it. 'Right,' he said, and turned back to the stairs, watching her progress, more aware now of her injuries than she was.

They stood in the lab facing one another, him leaning a hip against the workbench, her crossing her arms around herself. 'What have you done?' she said finally, more disbelieving than anything.

He met her gaze, the lowering sun painting flames into his black eyes. 'Lina,' he said, but she did not let him finish. He was the only one who made her feel real, she thought. The person who was Lina and no-one else had only every really been present and whole here, with him.

'You knew I would go.'

He did not speak this time, but his shoulders shifted as if bracing.

'You knew I would go to Dad, so you blocked the road.'

'No.'

'Yes, T. Don't lie to me. Just ... don't.' She dropped her gaze, caught halfway between fury and tears.

'Lina,' moving quietly. 'It was to stop them leaving.'

She looked up. Because of Xander's threat. He had thought that trapping him here in a storm that would cut them off was keeping her safer than letting Xander loose into the world. And he might be right, Dev had just now proffered an oblique postponement. Thiago's eyes were bottomless and strained.

'Not just that though,' she said.

He ran a hand over his face, his fingers muddy along the knuckles and under the nails. 'It was suicide,' He saw her stiffen and raised a hand. 'It was *pointless* suicide, Lina. It would have saved no-one. You know that.'

'I can't just *sit* here,' fighting back a scream. 'I have to at least *try*. Jesus, Thiago. He's my dad, and he saved me so many times.'

Thiago's voice was soft and certain. 'And you saved me. So I get to fight for you, too.'

'Don't–' she turned away, setting her palms on the desk, staring at them as the room spun and plummeted beneath her. 'It's not fighting for me, T. It's taking away my choices.'

'I won't let you kill yourself.'

She couldn't look at him, because she had never once hated him, but she did now. A little, a lot. 'I won't let my dad die in my place.' He did not speak, but nor did he move away, and she hissed out a breath and turned around. 'Besides, aren't you curious about who I really am? How do you know I'm worth saving, T? What if I'm as bad as them?' Throwing a hand out towards the window, the courtyard beyond. 'What if this *makes* me as bad as them? I won't be worth saving then, will I?'

'Yes.'

'Jesus, Thiago.' She moved, needing the wild air and to be away from him and his terrible loyalty. If any of this led to Xander's

death, or even his becoming an orphan, then she would not want
to be saved

'Hello, Lina,' Kai said from the doorway. She was sure she had
closed the door but now it stood ajar and Kai was there shadowed
by the sun's westering light. She went to push the door wide, wind
skittering in around her feet.

'Let me carry it,' Thiago said to her back. 'I've done worse.'

She halted, a hand on the doorframe and the other reaching
blindly to touch Kai's cool, satiny hair. He was holding the
martenitsa, she realised, and Thiago had said that she had saved
him.

'Stop it, Thiago,' she said without turning. 'Christ, just stop it.
I won't let you.'

She threw herself out into the restless, hot wind, letting Kai
lead her beyond the shadow of the buildings and into the meadow.
He took her across to the treeline, where the lowering sunlight fell
into the forest beneath the trees, then turned and carefully hung
the martenitsa on a low branch.

'The monster is coming,' he said. 'You need to not let it get
you.'

'The monster?' she said, fighting herself calm.

'I don't think it wants you, but you need to hide when it comes.'

'You mean the storm? I will hide, I promise.' She studied him,
his skin too pale in the sun. 'Will you hide too?'

He smiled and bent, lifting the fox skull from the grass. 'I'm
going to watch it,' he said, holding the skull against his face and
talking through its bladed jaws like he had done before. 'I want to
know who it wants.'

What would being out in the storm do to a child who did not
exist? she wondered. Grief and fury were not so easily destructible,
and yet she still said, 'You must stay inside with us, sweetie. It's
going to be dangerous outside.'

He smiled, the fox's jaw opened, sharp-toothed. 'I'm going to
be dangerous.' And then, slyly, 'Silene is going to hurt you, so I'll
stop her.'

'What? Kai, no, don't–' don't what? And why should she stop
him? If his presence drove Silene deeper into an irrationality that

would undo anything she might say, then why on earth should Lina stop him? It would not leave Xander orphaned, and it would not be murder. She met Kai's gilded eye through its bone socket and sighed. 'You will be careful, won't you?' It was ridiculous, but she saw his fallen form made pixels every time she looked at him, and if protecting him now meant anything at all to the child he had been, then how could she not?

'I'm fierce,' he said. 'And then when the monsters are all gone, I can stay, can't I? Even though you've got Genni?'

'Yes, sweetie,' she said, swimming through bewilderment and weariness and infinite tangled sorrows. 'Of course you can.'

'Good,' he said, closing the fox's jaws and patting her hand with his cool fingers. 'Because she won't fight the monsters, but I will. You'd better get ready. The monster's coming.'

Chapter Thirty-Three

When Lina reached the track, Iva was walking up through the trees into the sun. She was carrying a bag of food and gave a short nod to Lina as they met, but did not slow.

'I've not seen you,' Lina said, feeling the pace pull at her ankle. 'Are you okay? Are you ready for the storm? You can stay with us, if you need to.' Although the station may not be any safer really, exposed as it was.

Iva threw her a sideways, shuttered look and said only, 'I will stay with my family.'

Lina had meant her family too, but she suspected Iva knew that. 'If you don't want to be here,' she said slowly, 'I can take that for you.' Gesturing at the bag, but Iva only shook her head.

'I have to talk to Mr Ferdinando.'

So stubbornly formal, Lina thought, even now. 'About the storm?'

Iva's stride faltered for the first time, but then sped up again. 'No.' She looked down and her face tensed, smoothed out again.

Her ankle, Lina thought, she had been looking at the place where her skin was building scars that would never fade. She stopped, forcing Iva to stop as well. 'It's not about the BB? Iva? I thought that was all over.' But she had just watched Kai hang a martenitsa into a fir tree and it had been fresh and soft and unstained.

Iva stared at her unblinking, but then huffed out a breath and set her hands on her hips. 'You ask Mr Ferdinando, yes? I think it is not at all over.'

'But–' But Thiago had shot someone and none of the BB's reasons for anger had gone away. Even without the taskforce, the Wileys were still here and a travesty, the tagging programme only delayed.

'The storm it is coming quicker, you know?' Iva said. 'Tomorrow morning. You...' she looked at the station then frowned at Lina, the lines around her eyes labyrinthine. 'You stay in the old house, yes? The domovek can protect you. The forest is ... there will be bad things in the storm, I think. You stay in the old house, Lina. You will be safe there.'

Lina looked at the station too, the new house with its smooth walls and wide windows, the old with bricks of straw and mud, built and repaired and mutated over hundreds of years. 'Yes,' she said, although they wouldn't. It was ESF protocol. 'We will.'

'So,' Iva said, nodding and turning away. 'Now, I will speak to Mr Ferdinando.'

Lina did not attempt to keep up this time, standing in the golding sunlight, worrying at the link Iva had drawn between the BB and the storm, the link Kai drew between the storm and his monsters.

'Genni?' The curled brown form on the top balcony did not move, headphones deafening her, and as Lina approached, she caught the smell of fires from the plains again. The rains would stop them, she thought, but that was no solace at all.

With Thiago and Iva in the lab, she borrowed Genni's tablet to check the weather. Iva had been right. The storm forecast had updated to an eighteen hour warning for first contact, twenty-four till peak winds.

'Damn,' she murmured, Genni watching her, hands flexing on the chair's armrests. Lina grimaced and then screwed up her nose, Genni's fingers stilled. 'I guess we better get our arses in gear,' she said. 'The storm is trying to race us.'

'Okay,' Genni said, leaning forward, eyes eclipsed moons in her tense face. She took two uneven breaths. 'Okay, we have to hurry, right? Do we have time? We have time though, right?'

'Yes,' Lina said, reaching for her hand. 'Come on then, let's chase up some help.'

And yet she lacked the will to knock on either Silene or Xander's bedroom doors. She remembered the memory stick lying in her pocket and wondered how the rockfall changed that, other than giving her more time. Genni looked at her and then away, then knocked on his door.

'Xander,' she shouted, then opened the door and Lina heard the rustle of bedcovers, a muttered curse. 'You have to come help prepare for the storm.'

'Like fuck,' he said, a little loudly, speaking over hidden music.

'Yeah. The storm is gonna be here in the morning, so everyone needs to help.' Genni moved into the room and Lina belatedly realised something. Genni was capable of acting with Xander, and acting with Thiago; but she had never acted with Lina. Lina leaned against the corridor wall and closed her eyes, missing her father viciously, missing her mother more. Or missing the knowledge of a motherhood that did not end.

'Not my job,' Xander said. 'Leave that to the traitors; it's their job.'

'Chicken,' Genni said, and Lina opened her eyes.

'What?'

'You're scared of the storm. And you're scared of my sister.'

'Like fuck,' he repeated, but he was moving. Lina stepped into view and he faltered, looming.

'We'll be in the courtyard,' she said unsmiling. 'Come out as soon as you're ready. Do you know where Dev is? His door's open.'

He glowered at a point just beyond her shoulder and shrugged. 'Why would I know?'

'Okay,' Lina said, and she and Genni went out into the sun. Iva was halfway down the track already, almost running, and Thiago was hitting something in the barn. Lina did not want to face him; they had never had to learn how to treat one another when they were fighting.

She checked her tablet, found, finally, a message from Vitaly, but not the one she had wanted. He was too far away, he had no connections beyond the one she already knew. He could ask, he said, but he doubted he could help.

The logical part of her had known this would be the case, but the hopeful part had not. And hope not strong enough for belief still hurt to lose.

So she must wait for Kolya then. And the lawyer.

Xander knew. The fact kept hitting her like a long fall ending. All the years of silence and lies and fragile safety ending. He knew, he knew, he knew.

They did the shutters first, then filled great bottles with water. Lina sent Xander to carry sacks of potatoes and rice up to the kitchen, seeing in his sweat and cursing a kind of vengeance. But also quixotically, unfathomably, still hoping that it was granting him at least a little peace. Thiago drained the truck's tank and locked the fuel away, then he scowled up at the solar panels on the roof and Lina came silently to stand beside him.

'You can't do it,' he said without turning. 'Your ankle's not up to it. I'll ask Kapoor. Where is he anyway?'

And there he was, coming around the house carrying two of the car batteries that Lina had queued up for Xander. He looked from them to the roof and smiled. The bruises were gone, Lina thought, or at least so faded that his colour hid them. You would never know watching him now, how he had looked walking away from his captors. 'Going up, are we?' he said. 'Not planning to throw me off, I trust?'

Lina left them there and took Genni around the lab storing equipment away, raising everything up off the ground. The milk in Iva's bowl on the hearth was fresh, and for a second she had to hold still, softened by kindness.

'Are you still leaving?' Genni said when they were in the back office, Thiago's office.

Lina set an invertebrate sampling net back down on the floor and looked across the room. 'There isn't time,' she said. 'It's a long hike out. I wouldn't make it.' Not half-healed, although she might have done before, and not with the rockfall where the climb around it would be its most precipitous. Thiago had planned it too well.

Genni studied her shoes, scuffing one against the other, vainly trying to dislodge cobwebs and dirt. 'So what about Dad? What if—'

Lowering herself gently into a chair, she tried to ease her ankle's rising pain. 'Nothing is going to happen until after the storm, either with Dad or here.' Although between Iva and Kai and her own frustration, she was not so sure. The monster was coming, something building, everyone here teetering on the edge of some darkness and Lina could tell herself it was simply dread of the storm and the normalisation of her fear, but she was not sure. She was not sure.

'What is it Xander knows?'

She had been expecting this question, was surprised Genni had not asked it earlier, but looking at her face now she realised how much courage it had taken to speak. Genni had already had one life stolen by the State, and then been forced to flee her second one. How much bravery it took to meet Lina's eyes and ask if she would lose another. 'Genni,' Lina said and reached her arms out, wanting to weep when Genni moved hesitantly into her embrace. 'Oh, love. I don't know what to tell you.' She brushed her fingers over her sister's cheek, up over her hair. 'It's about my mum. She'd have been your mum too, only she died.' Genni moved, but Lina placed a kiss on her temple. 'She'd have loved you so much,' she said.

'So what happened?' Genni whispered.

The door to the lab opened and closed, followed only by silence, so Lina spoke as steadily as she was able. 'She died. She ... did something and State took her away and she died.' *I can't*, she thought desperately. Couldn't say the words with her mind full of broken doorways and the television image of a concrete yard, the sound of her mother's laughter, a palm against her cheek in the night. *Please*, she thought, *I can't*. But Genni waited, and she spoke.

'The State wanted us too, because of what she did. They would have taken us too, so we changed our names.'

'They would have killed you because of what your mum did.'

Movement made Lina turn her head against Genni's hair. Thiago was standing in the office doorway. She had forgotten how silently he could move.

'Yes,' she said, to him and to her sister, stroking her sister's back. 'If they knew our old names, State would kill us.'

'Even though it was years ago.' Genni lifted her head, and Lina shifted her gaze from Thiago to her. She laid her palm on Genni's cheek just the way she remembered her mother doing to her, a breath away from weeping. She wondered if her mother had wept the night she had left her child sleeping and gone out to try to change the world.

'Yes, love,' she said. 'Even now.'

She could almost feel Thiago thinking, adding timelines to news events to Lina's silences, but she smiled at Genni and added, 'Our dad saved me. Just like he saved you. So we'll save him, okay? We'll keep this secret and bring him here, and we'll be safe.'

Genni looked at her for a long time without speaking, her head resting very lightly against Lina's palm. Then she straightened and wrapped her arms around herself and although her eyes were dry and steady, it had not been enough, Lina thought. She ought to have made up some safer lie, or turned the truth into sometime more certain.

'We'll never be safe. Not really. Not now Xander knows.'

'He can't prove it, not without admitting to hacking,' Lina said, but surely that would not stop him. If she did not stop him. She felt, rather than saw, Thiago move away. Genni nodded, but again, it was not enough.

'What did Iva say?' Lina said to Thiago in a moment alone in the barn, cinching straps tight around the truck's cab. She did not want to know what he had managed to calculate of her past, so she would instead insist on knowing this.

'Nothing important.'

'So not about the BB then?'

He looked up at her sharply and winced. 'She said.'

'Not much. Only that they aren't finished with us ... this.' She nodded her head at the new house.

Thiago narrowed his eyes. Beyond the courtyard the meadow was a field of gold, umbellifers turned incandescent and butterflies falling to earth like jewelled snow. It would be dark soon, and then the waiting night, and then the storm.

'Do they still have the tech?' she said, only now remembering it.

Thiago did not move, even when Lina took up the next strap. 'Yes,' he said eventually. 'They'll give it back.'

Smoothing the tarp beneath her hands, Lina watched him. 'In exchange for what?'

'Nothing.'

'T.'

'It doesn't matter. I'm not going to be blackmailed.'

'What are they–' Lina stopped, looking from his stubborn face to the new house. 'Them. They want ... Dev back? No,' Thiago met her gaze, frowning. 'Xander or Silene. Because of Christopher Wiley. But what good... Oh god.'

'A video. They could post it online. They've decided it's payback for the deportations.'

'Kill them.' She pressed her hands down until the metal of the truck hurt her palms. 'Why in god's name are you all so obsessed with killing things?'

Thiago flinched and guilt swept over Lina. 'Oh, T. I didn't mean...' he looked at her and she fell silent. She *had* meant him, even if she forgave him what she could not forgive in others. Which made so little sense that she could not begin to explain. 'But you won't,' she said instead. Not asking, giving him at least that much.

'Not out of fondness,' he said. 'I said I'd give them nothing. I meant it.'

Because of her then. And yet it felt so distant now, the pain, the trap, his guilt. So long ago and irrelevant. 'Well,' she said fiercely, 'we aren't leaving Xander an orphan, and we aren't letting a child die. So we'll get your tech back another way. After the storm.'

Thiago's eyes blinkered, he moved to the next strap, pulling on it violently. 'Yes,' he said, then muttered something else in Spanish. There was a secret in his averted face, but she was too full of her own lies to fathom it. Too full of the coming storm and her father's last words; a USB stick and futility. And then someone calling her name from the balcony of the new house, above and out of view.

She came to the barn entrance and looked up into Dev's face, the last of the sun turning his lines and bones and darkness into a moment of Mughal art.

'It's Genni,' he said, and she was running before he had finished.

Chapter Thirty-Four

Genni was crouched beside the sofa, her palms pressed against the floor and her head bent, keening a high, breathless note. Lina fell beside her, whispering her name, running a palm feather-light down the curve of her spine.

'What did you say?' she said, looking up. Stroking, stroking. Genni's eyes were wide and blank. 'What the fuck did you say to her?'

Xander stood three paces away, shoulders forward and chin up, 'Nothing! She's crazy!'

Lina glared, Genni's ribs rose and fell beneath Lina's hand. 'What did you say?'

'Oh my god, nothing!'

Dev turned to Xander and folded his arms silently.

'It was just about camp kids. It was nothing. It's not like she is one anymore.'

Disgust made Lina speechless. She lowered her head to Genni, whispering. 'You're safe, love. Gently now. You're safe. You're safe.' Distantly aware of Dev speaking to Xander, Xander's protest cut short and then his retreat; Dev sitting on the sofa, leaning back and staring up at the ceiling as Genni breathed and breathed and breathed. 'You're safe, love. I'm here. You're safe.'

She took Genni up to bed when she was calmer, sitting with her in the shadows without speaking. And once she was asleep, dark against the pale sheets and the moonlight, Lina went outside into the meadow where mist was beginning to rise from the trees. There was still work to do. Thiago was somewhere, perhaps taking down the antennae from the back of the barn, but the sky above had cleared and she tipped her face up to the filigree stars, still hearing Genni's birdlike breaths.

'I'm sorry.'

She did not turn or move. Startled and yet unafraid. 'What for?'

Dev came to stand beside her, the grasses whispering. 'For Xander. He's a good kid, he's just—'

'Grieving, yes, I know.' Too tersely to be empathy. She felt Dev's attention on her. 'And also spoiled, blinkered and wilfully cruel.'

'Not wilfully,' Dev said, and she turned to him, his face a map of indigo shadows and the whites of his eyes. Starlight reflected.

'No?' she said softly. 'And yet he knows his father killed those children. And yet he will destroy me and Genni and my father. Perhaps he is a 'good kid', Dev, but only in your world. Only by your reckoning.' She meant it, and also did not mean it, because she could not believe any child culpable for the bigotry their parents trained them in. There was a point, she thought, where the child became responsible for their own blindness, and choices, but she had no idea where in Xander's life that point lay. Whether he was beyond it or not.

'He's too young,' Dev said, and she realised that her paler skin, upturned, must make her far easier to read than he was.

'So were they,' she said. 'And yet it is Christopher Wiley who deserves vengeance? How can you live with that?'

He held her gaze for a long time before looking away, not to the house but to the mountains lying dense and black against the shining sky.

'So you will take vengeance for those children? You have the training, after all.'

She didn't. She did not have any training in vengeance, only in subterfuge and silence and secrets, in holding your breath behind a closed door, parameterising your expression as a guard read your papers, comforting a tired, crying child in the dark, lending a fighter courage knowing they might die.

'You believe that of me?' She wanted to hear him say it. To say, as a stranger, yes he thought her capable of killing, or no he did not. Perhaps it would help her to know.

'I think you would do anything to guarantee your father's safety.' He smiled, teeth flashing. 'And I think Thiago would do anything to guarantee yours. Which creates a bit of an impasse, no?'

'Who are you? What will you do?' she said. She heard movement beyond the courtyard's pool of light and although it was most likely Thiago, she pictured Kai out there, half-fox, half-dream, wholly lost.

Dev laughed quietly. 'Good question,' he said. 'You don't know anything about me, do you? No, don't answer that.' He shook his head and took a step away, still watching her. 'More importantly though, Lina Stephenson, who are *you*? And what is it you need most in the world? Because I'm not sure you know, and I think you might need to choose.'

She did not answer and he took another step away, laughing again, softer this time and sadly. 'Goodnight, Lina. Tomorrow the storm.'

Tomorrow the storm.

Lina slept badly. Woken once by Genni screaming, she sat for an hour in the dark as Genni clutched her fingers and whispered hoarsely about bones and pale faces, teeth in her skin, someone laughing. 'Hush,' Lina said, over and over, as Genni fell silent and drifted back towards sleep. But then Lina's own dreams were haunted by the martenitsa dancing on the end of its rope in a terrible parody of joy. A silver-blue box and her father's silence, the fractured wood of a broken door. Them all in endless variations and one single fear. Teeth and knives skittered through her dreams and a gold-eyed fox laughing, whispering, *The monster is coming*.

Her alarm was a relief. Even with the first tatter-banner storm clouds in the west driving smoke and the dawn ahead of them, she was glad to be up out of those dreams. Because the storm meant there would be no time to worry for her father or Genni, to turn Dev's words over in her mind in endless configurations that led to her father's safety, her own; orphaned children and revenge.

But then two messages arrived on her tablet and Lina leaped for it. The first was Kolya. Hope and relief and the dying wildfires made Lina's lungs resonate in her chest like bells.

Message undelivered. This account no longer exists.

She sank onto her bed and set the tablet down, closed her eyes, heard Thiago moving downstairs. So Kolya was gone then. It had seemed likely, Kolya had known it was likely, and both Kolya and Lina had known that it would be because he had guided Lina's father and Genni through a crowded train station in the dawn.

So, she thought. When she left, she would have no help but Thiago's friend. Not quite impossible but so much closer to being so than it had been yesterday.

There was a storm coming and work to be done, but she remembered the other message and opened that.

Dr Stephenson,

Your father attaches a message below. We are similarly likely to be offline from tonight or tomorrow, after which perhaps we should talk. Your father's physical health is improving well, but his mental wellbeing is of some concern, I believe. I have been advised by ESF Investigators that they would be willing to intervene if, or when, the unofficial pursuit of you comes to an end. It is unclear what the source of this activity is, but their stance at the present is that it is most likely covert action by London State and thus places your father as a risk to you.

We can perhaps discuss more after we are both back online.

Yours etc.

And then, finally:

My beautiful children,

I like to picture you both in the room I saw so many times on my screen, with the mountains behind you and the forest like a sea. I like to think you are there now, reading this together, and that later perhaps you will go out to watch some foxes play as the sun sets. I have so many things to be grateful for, but the greatest of all is that I was able to be a father to you two. And that I can picture you safe, so far away from the corruption and the hatred and fear. I wish I could see your faces.

I am told that it is better for you that I remain here for now. So of course I do so happily. I am your father and will do everything in my power to keep you both safe. We'll see. I am told I will hear more after the storm. After the storm; as if cataclysmic events can ever change those most fundamental of truths. Love and hate. Hate is changed by the small things, I think, not the large. And nothing at all can change love.

Look after yourselves through the storm, and always. Wherever you are, I am beside you.

Your father.

Lina went outside numbly, the low wind picking at the shutters waiting open against the wall. Shutting them slowly, blinkering the house into blindness, creating a small, still hollow to hide from the ruination of the world. A predawn thrush began to sing and Lina thought of those fragile lives singing oblivious, how little it took for them to die; how in their unknowing, they could sing until the storm came.

He would wait until the storm had passed. She reread his words and had to believe that. The storm would pass, the Wileys would leave and if Dev chose his old loyalties over his ambivalence then all it would take would be a name, then two, then three. Perhaps they would still use her father as a lure to bring her into their hold, or perhaps they would not bother with such finesse.

He had spoken of himself in the past tense.

She set the bar across the shutters, her fingers cold and stiff. Her reply to the lawyer had said only, *Please check that he has no hidden medicine. No silver-blue tin.*

We'll see, he had said. *We'll see.* And, *Look after yourselves through the storm, and always.*

Then Genni woke and they went up for a hurried breakfast of yesterday's bread with the dawning sky starless beyond the windows.

Lina watched Genni watching the mountains and decided that she could not show her the email. She thought of James, and how seldom you get to say goodbye, and how many times you missed that chance because you were too full of hope.

How could she possibly be placing her own morals above her father's life? And yet she had watched her mother die when she was eight years old, so how could she do anything else? The storm that was coming would be terrible enough to kill them all...

'We need to tape the windows,' she said to Genni, and to Xander who had just slid silently into the room. 'I'll go get the tape.'

'You seen my mum?'

Lina turned at the top of the stairs. Xander was staring at her with a belligerence that looked paper-thin. 'No,' she said. 'Is she not asleep?'

'No.' His fists were flexing at his sides. 'Dev's with Thiago. She's not in her room.'

Remembering Silene's grey form in a dawn that felt years ago. 'Perhaps she's gone for a walk.' Remembering Kai.

'She wouldn't, she was too...' he hit his fists leadenly against the back of a chair. 'She was too scared of something out there. She's just ... she's gone.' A break in his voice that seemed to infuriate him. 'What have you done?' he said. 'What have you done to her?'

Lina leaned back against the newel post and kept her face calm. 'We'll find her. I can send drones out before the storm comes. Thiago can check the cameras,' she paused. '*You* can check the cameras, right?'

'If you've–'

'Let Dev know, Xander. Then check the cameras.' She moved before he could choose between accusation or obedience. She would not comfort him. Nor contemplate his pain. She would set drones out and tell Thiago, and not think about Silene wandering into the forests after a silvery boy.

The coming storm would be terrible enough to kill.

Chapter Thirty-Five

Thiago was on the barn roof, grimly hammering storm frames over the centuries-old tiles when Lina went in search of him and her tag-seeking, heat-seeking drones. He climbed down and wiped the back of a hand across his brow, listened without expression when she told him about Silene.

'Bloody idiot,' he said when she had finished.

'She's not–'

'I meant Kapoor.'

Well, yes. Dev had been playing her drugs like a game and he'd misjudged, perhaps catastrophically. Perhaps, for Lina, fortuitously. It was a terrible thought but she could not quite silence it.

'Xander can check the cameras. I've got too much to do.'

Lina met his black gaze and realised that he too was weighing lives. Those of everyone here over that of one addled woman. It was an easier equation that Lina's own. 'Right,' she said. 'I'll get the drones up then help you.'

'We won't have the net for long.'

So she would not hear from her father again. Not till after the storm. 'I know.'

She watched the drones lift and tip into the uncertain wind. They would not survive the storm, of course, but might last longer than the net and the camera signals, and some would head for the plains because that after all was where the BB had taken Dev.

'Kai,' she called. The air smelled dense and dark, and the clouds tearing apart the sky were thickening. 'Kai.' Watching the track and the treeline but not expecting to see him. He had gone hunting monsters, and she turned back to the buildings because what else could she do? Go chasing shadows through a forest where night-time was blurring into the storm? Search for a boy who had already died? She shivered, looked up at the sky again, the horizon dark as mercury but the storm-front still hidden even though pressure changes were preceding it. The swifts had gone, climbed above the storm on their fragile sickle-wings. The birds were falling silent.

Up in the lounge again, she set Genni to taping the windows. Diagonals then crosswise, then quarter the squares; she knew how, of course, they all did. Lina did not lower the shutters yet because she wanted to watch the darkening world, and it also felt like abandonment to blind themselves to Silene.

'The net's gone,' Xander said, looking up and gasping at the falling light.

'Yes,' Lina said. 'I should get downloads from the drones for a while yet though.' Although the storm was coming upon them faster than she had believed possible. Her drones would be falling broken into the cinders of the plains.

'Lina,' Genni said from the balcony doors.

The storm was raising its voice behind the glass, bandwidths built of wind and the coming rain, of groaning trees and resonation in small spaces, a gathering static. Setting her tablet down she went to stand beside her sister. And finally, enormous in the west was the storm-front, black and curvilinear, sweeping away to the north like the skin of some incomprehensible edifice, a starship, a city wall. Trees were beginning to heave in the forest, the noise climbing to a roar.

They were out of time. Lina opened the door, shouted to Thiago where he was re-checking the shutters on the old house, then closed and locked them, taking the tape from Genni.

'Come help tape,' she said to Xander, and surprisingly, he came. Frowning and taut as a drum, and staring out of the windows as if into the jaws of a monster. He picked up a roll and set to the job beside Genni as if they were nothing like enemies at all, turning the storm into pixels, caging it out. Something, broken branches perhaps, scraped along the wall below the windows, and was gone.

Below them the front door opened and slammed shut heavily enough to reverberate the air, and Lina breathed out, realising that she had been waiting, counting the seconds.

'You're locking the doors?' Xander said, pulling his gaze from the windows.

The noise within the house was mounting and Lina did not notice Dev arrive until he spoke. 'Can we connect directly to the house cameras?'

'Yes,' Lina said to both their questions. 'The images won't be great but we'll be able to see if she comes back.' And yet she did not think anyone was expecting that. Even if Silene had been rational enough to make her own way back, the storm would now prevent her. 'Xander, can you do that?' He abandoned the tape, retreating from the false-night outside with palpable relief. Strange how no-one cared that Lina had referred to Xander's illegal skills and Xander had not even thought of denying them. It was as if the storm had suspended the outside world, reduced them to immediacy.

Dev took over taping the windows and Lina sat opposite Xander, checking her drone downloads. Despite their storm-forced truce, she would have preferred him shut away in his room or her in her lab. But instead she must sit close enough that she could lean forward to touch his knee, searching for a woman she would happily leave to the storm if it weren't for the angle of Xander's bent head.

'Nothing from the drones,' she said after a moment. 'And they are down now.'

'So what? We just sit here?' Xander stared at her, anger tightening his eyes.

Such convenient masks, Lina thought. Anger, and blame. She looked out to the occluded balcony and wished she knew what was happening to Kai, aware of how ridiculous her worry was but unable to quash it.

'Any luck with the cameras?' she said.

Xander turned his tablet screen towards her and as Lina reached to steady a corner, she remembered the USB micro-stick in her pocket. Now. It would be easy. Silene had made it easy. The camera images were amorphous blues and greys, debris skittering along the ground, rain blurring the details.

'Well done. We'll see her if she comes back.' She slipped a hand into her pocket, felt the slim edges of the USB stick. 'There are more around the back, let me just...'

Dev came over, patting Xander easily on the shoulder, his face and limbs utterly relaxed but his eyes on Lina intent. 'Any luck with the forest cameras? Or tracking her tag?'

Xander reached for his tablet. Lina held the USB stick in her palm, but the moment had gone.

Thiago reached the top of the stairs and scanned the taped windows.

'Downstairs,' he mouthed to Lina, then called to Genni where she had drifted back to the balcony doors, pressing her forehead against the glass, breath silver on the outer dark. Her face in the strange, underwater light was grey, her eyes wide so Lina rose, forgetting Silene and the USB stick and going to gather up more tape, reaching for her sister's hand.

'I can't find her.' Xander's voice was raised, but Lina did not look to see if he was talking to her. Let Dev handle him, she thought, the way he had failed to handle Silene. 'Dev, we have to find her. What if she's–'

Dead, Lina finished for him. What if his mother was dead.

'Come away downstairs,' she said to Genni. 'Let's do the bedrooms.' Distraction and occupation, for both of them.

'Lina,' Dev said over the wind, and she turned reluctantly. 'What's this?' He held up an elegant hand, letting the little red wool figure fall from his fingers to hang jerkily from its noose.

Lina put a hand on the banister, saw Thiago below her raise his eyebrows in a faint question. Something struck a window downstairs and Genni flinched. 'Go help Thiago, love,' Lina said, then went back towards Dev. 'Where did you find it?'

Xander looked up and recognised the martenitsa, his whole body stiffening.

'Downstairs,' Dev said.

Xander grabbed it from him, 'What the fuck?' Paling as he stared down at it. 'Where?'

Reaching over, Lina opened Xander's fingers and he let her more out of shock than willingness. She lifted the small thing and felt a stirring of idiotic pity for it; that something so symbolic of hope had become this. It was the one Kai had been holding yesterday, and she lifted her gaze from her hands to Dev, knowing what he was going to say and dreading it.

'On Silene's bed. What is it?'

'Fucking–' Xander stood so fast his tablet fell, landing screen side down. Lina touched her pocket again, then dropped her hand when Dev's eyes followed the movement. 'Fucking ... *no*. Oh god, *no*. Dev, *they've got her*.' His hands were wide white fists, his whole body leaning forward as if he were outside, fighting against the wind.

'This doesn't mean anything,' Lina said. 'There was one lying around here somewhere, so she must have found it. Maybe that's why she went out, but the BB haven't–'

'*Of course you'd say that*,' Xander snarled at her, 'Of course you'd fucking deny it. It was *you*. Jesus fucking Christ, it was *you*.' Lurching towards her, Dev grabbed the scruff of his shirt, pulling him back before Lina had even begun to move.

Xander fought Dev's grip, but he did not let go until Xander jerked the other way instead, away from both of them towards the windows.

'We have to get her back,' he said to Dev. 'Make *her* help us. She–' looking at Lina, 'I will fucking *destroy* you.' The storm yowled, something clattering against the window behind him making him duck reflexively, coming up angrier than ever.

Lina wondered whether the storm would be as bad when it spun over Slovakia. She wondered what her mother had thought of, at the very end. And James, and Kai, what had they been thinking? Autumn and Kolya and the helicopter pilots. She wanted to weep and scream and tear her nails down Xander's face.

'You already have,' she said, the words a roar inside her and so it was either a miracle or a curse that they emerged so calm, almost gentle. 'You have already destroyed my life many times over. And you have destroyed so many others as well, Xander Wiley. It is what you have been raised to do.'

Xander's face contorted, bewildered.

'Lina,' Dev said almost too quietly to be heard. Lightning flickered, still far away but approaching. The mountains would nurture it. It was startling how alike Dev sounded to Thiago, saying her name. She did not look at him.

'I have done nothing to your mother,' she said. Xander stepped closer, pulled by her unraised voice. 'Even though I have plenty of reasons, I have tried only to help. But that is never enough, is it? You will always want to destroy more. To tear anything down that is not yours. Where does it end, Xander? My god,' she broke off on a laugh that had no humour in it at all. 'You didn't blink an eye at your father murdering children. And now you will kill an innocent man, another child, me, to avenge a killer.' She shrugged. 'Will that be enough for you, Xander? How many deaths will make you happy?'

She was so cold. So terribly, painfully aware of every thread of noise from outside, the rain become hail, the low thunder distinct beneath the jet engine roar of the forest, the near-subliminal reverberation of the air as the whole house tested itself against the rising wind. It would not peak for hours yet, she thought. The brittle birds, the fox in her flooding den, the martens, the butterflies being drowned or torn asunder. She watched Xander but only because she could not move, too cold and too full heartbreak and the litany of deaths.

'Lina,' Dev said. Lina did not move, still watching Xander, his wide shoulders rising. 'Lina,' Dev said again and this time she turned, met eyes reflecting the lamplight darkly. 'Go help the others.'

She rose stiffly, unable to tell now whether the chill in her blood was coming from the room or herself.

'How dare you?' Xander said. Then louder, 'None of that's my fault. How fucking *dare* you?'

Dev laid a hand on the small of her back, turning her away, and for a moment she let herself be pushed. But then, because the world she loved was being torn apart, she looked at Xander once more.

'So you never knew any of the things your parents did? You

never shrugged and told yourself that some lives are worth more than others?' She tilted her head, ignoring Dev. 'Who are you lying to, Xander? Me or yourself? What are you trying to prove with all this?' Waving a hand at him, his fallen tablet, Dev. 'Your parents' worth or your own?'

Dev gave a short laugh and pushed her again, less gently. 'Alright. Much as anger becomes you, can you go now?' She turned her gaze on him and his amusement faded. 'I told you I am not your enemy,' he said, too quietly for Xander to hear. 'Let me deal with him.'

Chapter Thirty-Six

Thiago met her on the middle landing, Genni not in sight and the fury of the storm echoing up the stairwell. He put a hand on her arm and stepped close enough that they could hear each other without shouting. Lina wanted to check on Genni, touch her, watch her breathing. But Thiago's expression halted her.

'Xander connect to the cameras?'

'He showed me the house cams,' she said, then realised he meant the ones in the forest. 'No,' she amended.

Thiago pulled her into the bedroom beside them, lifted his tablet from the bed and showed her the screen. 'Got these before the net went.'

They were frozen frames from videos, the first few greyscale in the predawn, then slipping with dawn and the storm into browns and purple-blues and greens that were nearly black. And in each of them, Silene. Lina studied her, silvery in the passing night and wavering in the dawn, her hand in one image reaching out in front as if beseeching.

Thiago reached around her to open another screen. A map of camera locations plotting the path Silene had followed, straight as a pointing finger and vanishing at the edge of a clearing that Lina knew. Wet meadow full of sedges and marsh orchids, a lightning-struck pine in the centre, sentinel and blackened. 'The EM-tech?' she asked. 'Xander thinks it was the BB.'

The very lack of expression on Thiago's face made her heart fall.

'They didn't lead her there. She's alone until the meadow.'

No, Lina thought. They had not led Silene out there, but Lina knew who had. She remembered the old woman, Baba Ruzha, talking of ghosts and monsters and the waking forest; she had known about Kai and had been warning Lina long before Lina was able to recognise it.

'Why would they take her though?' Light blazed through the taped and shuttered balcony doors, vanished again, rendering Thiago a scorched silhouette. Thunder beat the walls, syncopated with the wind, the branches hitting the windows. If the BB had Silene, she thought, then at least she was not out in the forest. Xander had not though of that.

'T? Why would they take her? They know we might call the taskforce again. They've got way too much to lose.'

Thiago shrugged. 'No idea. Look, I want to check the shutters are holding in the old house.' The rain hardened to something else, hail, stones. Lina looked at Thiago's half-lit face and realised how frightened she was of the storm. The slim brick and glass that stood between them and unimaginable hell, the overwhelming awareness of power and fragility. It was different to other fears, no secrecy or hate, cunning or fierce belief; only a pure physical terror fibrillating her bones even as she studied Thiago's face and frowned.

He moved as if about to leave and she reached out to hold his forearm. 'Wait, T. Why would they risk this?'

Lighting burst over them, thunder followed. Thiago was watching the windows, his face taut and still. 'The tech, I guess.'

'No,' Lina said, watching him. 'It didn't work before, so they'd not stake so much on it working this time. Something's–' His gaze shifted to her and away. No, she thought. 'T,' his muscles tightened beneath her hand and stayed tight. 'T, you ... you called them in anyway.' He blinked, met her eyes. 'Oh god,' she said. 'You never called the taskforce off.'

Genni appeared in the doorway and Lina stared at her blankly, looking at her because she could not look at Thiago. 'How could you?' she said. Genni frowned, a roll of tape hanging loosely from her hand, pressed against the doorframe as though its solidity were a comfort. Lina lifted her gaze to Thiago's, saw him wince. 'We promised. How *could* you? Does Iva know? Of course, that's why she came. They know, so they took Silene.' She let go of his arm and stepped back. Hail screeched against the window and Genni pressed herself back. 'They have nothing to lose, so they took her and now...' she stopped, the relentless noise pressing against her lungs until she thought she might choke.

'I said they would pay,' Thiago said. Unrepentant.

'Don't make this about me,' she realised she was whispering, fear of the storm and habit. 'Don't you dare make this about me. I won't have that on my conscience, Thiago.'

'Lina,' Genni said.

Lina could not hear her, but the shape of her name on Genni's lips made her open her arms, made her anger morph as her sister stepped into her embrace, press herself against Lina the way she had pressed herself against the bulwark of the house.

'Of course it's about you,' Thiago said fiercely. 'All of this is about you.' Gesturing around them; Genni, Xander; the missing.

It was the accusation Genni had made too. It still lay there, even if Genni had begun to forgive it. Lina tightened her hold on her sister and found her voice. '*All* of it, T? It's not about you giving them illegal tech, or about you keeping your own past hidden? Not about you needing to prove something to me, to yourself?' He lifted a hand but she spoke before he could. 'You'd kill people for that? You'd make children orphans for that, T? Because that's not...' her throat closing, her hands shaking and the storm raising its impossible roar again, again. How long could they bear this? she thought.

'You wouldn't?' Thiago said. 'You *wouldn't* do those things to protect Genni, your dad?'

She took a step back, pulling Genni with her. Thiago raised his voice but she still read his words more than heard them.

'You're glad she's gone, Lina. You're wishing Xander had gone with her.' He stepped closer, so close she could feel his heat and his breathing. 'You're the same as me, Lina. I just know myself better.'

She spun away from him, anger briefly overpowering the storm as she led Genni away. She would stop the taskforce once the storm was gone. She would get Silene back, even though they were enemies, because *that* was who she was. She saved people, she did not kill them. She found other ways to fight. She *would* find another way. Genni watched her sidelong as they climbed the stairs and Lina wanted to crawl into darkness, close the world and her sister's wary gaze away.

As soon as she reached the lounge, Xander pushed past her and downwards, his headphones on and neither the music nor his heavy footsteps audible at all. Dev was sitting watching the windows speculatively, turning a cup of coffee within his hands, the colours the same. Lina came to sit opposite him, pulling Genni onto her lap although she was really too big for it, wondrous all over again when Genni did not resist, curling to tuck her head against Lina's neck. *Oh child*, Lina thought, *oh my poor child*. Realised she was not thinking only of the one in her arms. Where was he? she wondered again. Where had he gone once he had wreaked his revenge and his twisted protection?

Dev pushed a mug into her free hand, amused that it surprised her. How much of the ironic humour was a mask though, and how much was real, and would he be as comfortable with murder as Thiago was? And had she ever truly understood what that meant until now?

'Xander?' she mouthed at him, not wasting herself on trying to be heard. The windows flexed and groaned. Dev had lowered the shutters, she realised belatedly; the tape and the surreal daytime dark had hidden them from view.

Dev shook his head. 'He'll keep,' he mouthed back. 'BB?'

So Xander had told him what the martenitsa meant. And she had denied it before. She grimaced, shrugged, seeing again Silene's silvery figure passing beneath dark trees. Dev nodded and lifted his coffee, steam wavering in front of his eyes. 'I owe Chris, you know,' he said.

Lina frowned, not sure she had heard him correctly, and then not sure what he meant by it. Apology? So that was his decision then. 'You owe us too,' she said futilely.

Lightning and thunder shaking the house, turning his face briefly into blackened bones. He looked at the windows, frowned, said loud enough to hear. 'The other house will be safer if the windows give.'

Lina remembered her promise to Iva, and realised that she agreed. Not because of the domovek, but because the old house had always felt more immutable than this one, more like home. The air in the room sucked away, her ears popping and Genni giving a small, sharp cry, then a bang and reverberation and the room again a false, cocooned stillness.

'That's Thiago,' she said. 'Gone to check if you're right.' She set Genni beside her to go to the balcony doors, pressing her hands to the shuddering glass and trying to piece the world together through the shutter's gaps. But there was only the deep purple storm-light made black by movement and the rain, reflections of lamplight. She should have gone with him, however angry, however desperately she wanted him to be wrong.

Genni came to stand next to her, pressing her own palms on the windows. Looking from the partitioned storm to Lina. 'Are we safe?' she said, muted by the wind.

Lina was not sure. It was impossible to rationalise engineering and probabilities as the storm pushed against the house like some monstrous, malevolent sentience. 'Yes,' she said. 'We might move to the old house to be sure. But yes.' She removed a hand from the cold glass and brushed her knuckles over Genni's cheek. 'It will pass,' she said. And then ... and then...

And then lightning. White chequerboarded blindingly, a shutter-image of the courtyard a whirlwind of debris, the forest and oceanic clouds. A face. Genni leaping backward and darkness again, her eyes burned blind, the rain driving through the shutters to paint the window in shadowy tears. She heard her own breathing, the window trembling, straining to see beyond the shutters to the balcony. Then movement and the lamplight behind her caught something pale against the metal screen, and Lina stared at it for a long minute before she realised what it was. A small, white hand flattened against the shutter.

Then lightning, and she was looking right at him as the world blazed, his eyes gold and black in his deathly pale face.

'Kai,' she whispered. Darkness and afterimages, the lamplight picking him out in fragments, fleeting. 'Kai.'

He had been smiling.

Something hit the windows on the next wall and Lina turned reflexively. Dev was already up, running a palm over the glass and she knew what he had found before he looked at her. 'Time to go,' he mouthed, no amusement, but no fear either, and her own fear faded a little, seeing that. The wonder and horror and sorrow persisting like a low beat beneath her heart.

She reached for Genni's hand. 'Grab those two torches there, love. We're going to head over the courtyard.' And when she straightened again, Thiago was standing at the top of the stairs.

He crossed quickly to where his coat lay on a chair. Dev and Lina and Genni did the same, Lina making Genni struggle into three jumpers, a padded jacket and one of Lina's thick coats. It was not about the rain, after all; it was about the branches, bits of tile, stones.

Something was wrong, she thought. Kai standing on the balcony smiling, her fight with Thiago, the ending of the world. Something else. The prospect of going outside made her legs leaden and shaking, but she fitted a bike helmet over Genni's thick hair and somehow made Genni laugh as she did so. Thiago checked all the bedrooms on their way down, closing each one.

At the front door, Thiago paused, his hand where the bar had been before he removed it to go out. Dev was watching him, and Lina watched them both and gasped. 'Xander,' she said. Loud enough that everyone looked at her. Thiago frowned, Dev shifted his intent gaze from the door to Lina and Lina stared at Thiago's hand where it held the empty bracket, his coat that he had only just put on. His dry skin. Dev leaned closer to be heard. 'Let's cross over first.'

They did, Thiago at the last minute swooping Genni up into his arms, Dev and Lina together having to wrestle the door closed, the wind trying to force it from their fingers, from its hinges. Then pressed against the walls, tracking blindly around the new house, the barn shadowy and creaking, lightning and between slitted eyes Lina saw it strike in the meadow, a geometric blaze behind her eyelids as rain made her vision swim. The wind shoved her but something solid held her up. Rain or leaves or hail struck her face and she might be bleeding but could not tell. Then the old house door came from nowhere, Thiago huddling Genni against it, his back to the courtyard and when he opened it the storm thrust them inside.

They shed clothes like skins, water and debris pooling at their feet, Thiago handed out towels and Lina wiped the rain from Genni's face, checking her skin, her limbs until Genni pulled away impatiently. Lina's ankle was singing and she remembered half-falling, Dev catching her, some of the wetness against her heel was warm so she left her shoes on rather than see what she had done.

'Xander's gone,' she said finally.

Thiago was studying the shuttered windows and frowning, but at least they were smaller here. The storm pierced through gaps and air pockets in the thick walls, but they were at least marginally in the lee of the big house down here, the noise not quieter but different, more tonal. Iva's bowl of milk caught the lamplight like the sallow face of the moon. Lina stared at Dev.

'You let him go.'

Chapter Thirty-Seven

Dev dropped his towel onto her workbench and folded his arms. 'Are there internal shutters for this place?' he said.

Lina opened her mouth but the door vibrated beneath a surge of wind so she said only, 'They're in the office.' It made a crazed, desperate sense that Xander had hurled himself out into the storm after his mother. Perhaps he *had* seen the images tracking her through the forest, or perhaps Dev had said something. Or Lina's words had meant something.

She had not thought him brave enough, physically, to do this. But bravery did not matter; she knew that. It was only how much you stood to lose and how certain you were that you could not bear to do so. Throwing yourself into the path of another's death was not so much about trading your own life for someone else's as about not wanting to live without them.

She understood.

Dev stepped around her to lift a stack of shutters and she looked up at him. 'Did you know?' she said.

There was no lamp in here yet, so they were both in shadow, the storm pressing close, a chink in the mortar around the window singing piercingly. Lina remembered Kai singing to her as she drowned and wished she knew where he was, and that he did not frighten her so much. Both his existence and his potential. He had seen Silene with tablets, but he had not mentioned the knife.

'No,' Dev said eventually. 'I told him it was madness.'

'But you didn't stop him.'

Thiago entered the room, making the small space crowded. He

was out there now, she thought. Searching for his mother.

'Tie him up? No.' Dev studied the shutters in his hands. 'Upstairs?' he said, reading the label. He would not act, she realised, because he wanted to watch. Watch Xander and study his choices. Test the son the way he had not perhaps tested the father. He had been right; she did not know anything about him.

'We're going to get him,' Lina said. Thiago raised his head.

'No, Lina.'

Dev glanced at Thiago and smiled. 'Finally we agree,' he said as lightning burned shadows in the room, thunder ricocheted off the walls. Then, to Lina, hefting the shutters again, 'You struck a nerve. This is him proving himself. Let him, he's not a child. Plus he's carrying a beacon.' He smiled very gently and then moved towards the stairs before she could reply.

Thiago lifted a board up to the first window, clipping it carefully into place. Outside's shutters, the old glass, and now these inside. A triple layer protecting them, and a boy who was still a child whatever Dev said, out there. You are always a child when you lose your mother, she thought. And if her own words had driven him to this then...

She moved without really choosing to do so, Genni watching her from where she had curled up on the bottom step of the staircase. Thiago started on the next shutter, Lina opened a map and scanned for local signals, watched the progress icon loop and loop and loop.

'Where is he?' Genni said, and Lina jumped. The wind rendering her senseless unnerved her. 'Where are they both?'

Lina watched the circling icon and shook her head. 'I'm trying to find out. Idiot boy. God, what was he thinking?'

'Are you going after him?'

Lina threw a quick glance over her shoulder, but Thiago would never hear them and his back was turned. 'Yes,' she said. 'I have to.'

Genni nodded slowly, then pressed her forehead against Lina's arm, closing her eyes. The icon stopped spinning and a pulsing dot appeared on her map. He had seen the camera images then because he was following them, but slowly, barely a quarter of the way along. Lina reloaded the page agonisingly slowly and the dot did not move.

'I have to,' she repeated. 'He might be hurt.' She rose, pulled a mini tablet from a drawer and set that to loading the same data, ignoring a sharp pain flaring in her ankle. She gathered torches, a beacon, a knife. Thiago had gone into his office and Dev was still upstairs, so she moved fast, pulling on her sodden waterproofs, her attention on those and on Genni's face fading to grey with fear. She paused, laid her palms on Genni's cheeks and bent to kiss her forehead. 'I'll be fine,' she whispered with her lips against her sister's skin. 'I know the forests, I'll be fine. And Thiago and Dev are here to protect you, so you'll be fine too. I promise.'

The wind threw itself against the house, forcing itself into the room, stirring Lina's hair. Genni shuddered.

'It's okay,' Lina whispered. 'It's just a storm, and this is the worst of it. Soon it will pass.'

'It's okay,' Genni repeated, her breath audible in the sheltered space between them. 'It's okay. It's okay.'

'I have to go now,' Lina said, still holding Genni's depthless gaze. 'I'll be back soon with Xander, then we can shout at him for leaving.'

The shadow of a smile, a deep breath. 'It's okay,' Genni whispered. And pulled away from Lina slowly.

'Lina,' Thiago said, audible across the room in a pause between the storm's raging pulse. He was holding a tablet and crossed the room so fast it seemed impossible that he could stop without barrelling into them both. 'What the fuck?' he said, making a sweeping gesture to encompass her clothes and the absurdity of what she was about to do. 'You can't go. Are you insane?'

Lina laughed a little, showed him her own tablet. 'He's not moving. He might be hurt. I have to go.'

'No, you—'

'I have to, T,' she repeated. His face was twisted with anger, frustration, fear, and she took his empty hand in hers. 'You know I do.'

'Have you got a death wish?'

Did she? Is that what she was doing, tearing out into the

maelstrom? Lina shook her head, not because he was wrong necessarily but because she did not think it mattered. She wanted to tell him that he had been right to say that this had begun with her, and so it had to end with her too. Tell him that she didn't know how to stop any of it, but if she didn't go after Xander then she would not be worth anything at all. But she could not say those things and still make him release her, so she stood with her hand in his, and waited.

He stared at her, something large struck the courtyard wall, struck it again further away. Lina thought of the birds again, their tiny hearts and sodden feathers, the dormice in their grassy nests, the fox kits and bear cubs and ancient trees dying. She held Thiago's furious gaze and his fingers tightened around hers spasmodically before they released her. 'Fuck,' he said, and then again, '*Fuck.*'

She stepped back, resting a hand on Genni's shoulder. 'Look after each other, you two,' she said. Lightning burned through the shutters again, thunder made the room tremble and Thiago flinched, swore again, his eyes on Lina.

'Wait,' he said, as she turned away. 'You need to see this.' He turned so that only he and Lina would see the screen of his tablet. Lina looked at the images he was showing her, recognised the house cams that Xander had connected to earlier, only half her mind on them because lightning struck again, close enough to taste ozone intermingled with rain and enormity. She would be going out into that chasing a boy who wanted to destroy her. It made no sense. Thunder and hail thrummed against the door and she listened helplessly.

'Lina,' Thiago said. 'Look.'

She fought her attention back to him, accumulating dread, but he clicked on one of the vids and Lina saw now. Ice ran along her spine like the lightning falling to earth, and this was why Thiago was looking at her like that. There were shadow figures creep-crawling along the far side of the new house, crouching, one held by another, others made monstrous by the packs on their backs and doing...

'What are–'

'Laying fuses.'

No. *No.*

'This house should be safe,' Thiago said. But he could not be sure and it was not like him to lie.

Lina met his gaze and realised that someone would be dying soon. And that she did not care so long as it was not Genni, and was not Thiago. She straightened, looked across to where Genni had put headphones over her ears to try to block out the world.

'You'll stop them,' she said to Thiago. 'You and Dev will stop them.'

Thiago nodded shortly, and she believed him. She would be no use at all, at this, and there was still Xander. Dev appeared at the base of the stairs as if summoned, immediately watchful. Lina pushed her shoulders back, looked again at the hunchbacked figures planting death just metres away, and there was no space in her now for anger, at Thiago for pushing those people to this, or even at *them* risking their own deaths for vengeance. They were only desperate, she thought, and only as desperate as her, and Thiago, and Xander.

It would be meant, she thought, to look like a lightning strike.

'Okay,' she said, more to herself than anyone, and went to the door, feeling Thiago's eyes on her unwavering. Genni looked up wide-eyed, hands in fists, but when Lina gave her a fierce, false smile, she managed to return it. Thiago took the door and as he pulled it open and the storm burst inwards, he gripped Lina's shoulder hard enough to press against her bones even through all her clothes.

'Stay low,' he shouted, 'And in the denser growth.' Then he gave her a push against the wind and she was out, the door was closing behind her, shuddering.

The meadow would be the worst, the wind unfettered and able to carry its gathered weaponry faster than within the forest. She reached the corner of the old house, breathing into her collar. Xander had already done this, she thought, and braced herself.

'Lina,' Kai said.

She realised she had been expecting him. The storm had changed him, made him more solid, his hair dark with rain and his wet skin reflecting the storm ivory and damson.

'Kai,' she said, rain running into her mouth. 'Kai, what are you doing?' *What have you done?*

'I took them away,' he said as clear as the aftertones of a bell. 'I took the monsters away.'

'Yes,' Lina whispered. Something struck her shoulder and she flinched. Thiago would now be loading guns, arming Dev. How long were the fuses the black figures were laying, how safe was the old house? She wanted to run out into the meadow, and back to Genni, and did neither.

'Are you going to kill him?'

'Oh god,' Lina said. 'No. No, Kai. I'm going to bring him back. I have to go now.' Lightning blazed, burning the world the colour of blood, rain on her cheeks thick and cold.

'We can beat the monsters though,' Kai said, his cold fingers slipping into her own, his face upturned, water falling into his feral eyes. 'It's okay, I'll help you.'

'No,' Lina said, but lightning came again and his whole body seemed to come alight, as if the storm were charging him with potency. She tasted metal in the air, scrambling for words that would keep him here. 'You have to stay, to protect Genni and Thiago. Can you do that for me, Kai?'

Please, she thought. Please let me go.

'Genni doesn't love you.' Kai dropped his hand from hers and frowned.

'But I love her. And I need you to keep her safe.' She searched his fox's eyes for the child he had been. 'Because you are brave and fierce, and we need you. And because,' taking his icy hand again, 'because if you are here, then I know you'll be safe too. And I want you to be safe, Kai. I want you to always be safe from the monsters.'

He watched her and beyond him the door to the old house opened. 'Please,' she said to the lost boy.

Kai nodded and smiled like the dawn.

Chapter Thirty-Eight

Lina slipped quickly around the house, took one great breath and threw herself out into the meadow half-blind, bent low and running, stumbling, her ankle buckling but holding, things hitting her in points of pain. And then the treeline, the immense purple darkness within it, the wind battling the trees louder than the end of the world. Somewhere something roared and fell and her heart constricted, but no, she thought, it was a tree and ahead, and Genni was guarded by Iva's domovek, by a fox-child and the strongest man she knew.

Still bent against the wind that bucked between the trees directionless, shoving her forward and then sideways, her muscles cold beyond pain which was a blessing. One step to this tree, another lurching to the next. Remembering to check the map because this place was nowhere she had ever travelled.

Another step. Lightning and thunder and still only darkness behind her. Another step away from Genni and towards Xander, which was so terribly wrong. So terrifyingly dangerous for her and her family, and yet another step, and another. The forest howled and roared, she searched for an unmoving boy while a small voice, quiet beneath the storm but clear as a bird, whispered that if she found only a body would it be so bad? Would it really be so bad?

Time became each fought-for metre, became two markers on a map converging, became cold and distant pain, thoughts like broken glass. Time passed. And then she found him.

He was not dead.

The voice in her head wept sibilantly. Lina wrapped her arm around a tree that flexed against her, looking at the hunched figure on the ground. He had his arms tight around his bent head, knees up, a shoe missing and a great tear in his coat pulling wide, baring a shoulder, part of an arm. He was rocking slowly.

He would not, she thought, last until the end of the storm. Unprotected and hypothermic, crushed by the galactic, relentless noise. The forest was full of monsters and this one was outmatched.

A tree nearby screamed, exploded, and Lina braced herself for the fall. But it did not come, and when she looked back to Xander he was staring at her. His mouth was open and moving but she did not think he was speaking. Blood was running down his face, black in the storm-light, and she thought he was crying or somewhere beyond crying.

'Lina?' he said.

Pushing away from the tree, Lina bent and moved to his side, crouching against a small boulder, moss covered and slick. 'Are you hurt?'

He was still staring at her, and was not shivering, she realised. Beyond shivering like he was beyond crying. He would not last the storm.

'Your boyfriend killed my dad,' he said eventually. The words misshapen and blurred. 'Your mum bombed parliament.'

No he did not, Lina thought automatically, and yes, she did, but the building was empty. Her hair whipped across her face, she fought it back with nerveless fingers and leaned close. 'Your dad killed children,' she said into his ear. 'He killed a boy called Kai. He killed James, he killed my mother.' Or his predecessor had, or his subordinate. It made no difference.

'Why did you come?'

The rain could not wash away the blood flowing down his face. 'I don't know,' she said. She didn't. She did not care for him. She cared for her father weighing his own life quietly, for Genni, who had surely lost enough. Every one of the ghosts whose deaths diminished her, who had not deserved death the way Christopher Wiley had deserved his.

'I'm going to destroy you.' Slurring again, his head tipping and straightening drowsily. 'I said that. I said that to you.'

He had. Lina rubbed rain and gritty dirt from her face. 'I know,' she said.

'They'll kill your dad. And you. And Genni'll go back to the camps.'

Lina closed her eyes. She felt the pressure of Genni's head resting against her as if she were here now, in the noise and the chaos. Her mother had screamed when they had taken her, and in Lina's memory, she had screamed Lina's name. Her old name, her first. What had she been thinking when they walked her out into daylight and that wide expanse of concrete, chains around her wrists and a blindfold waiting? Lina had never known before, but she did now.

Guilt and love and fierceness, tracking the choices that had led to abandonment.

How had Lina ever doubted it?

Her mother had died thinking of her child.

Lina rose to her feet. Xander tipped his drooping head sideways, eyes unfocused then finding her.

'No-one is taking Genni away from me,' she shouted over the roar. 'Not because of me. Not because of you.'

She stepped backward, the wind unbalancing her, and grasping for support her hand scraped broken wood. Heat on her palm and salt and earth in her mouth. This was for Genni. It was the choice her mother had not made. It was because love is the greatest thing we have. It was because nothing must ever matter more than the heart of a child.

Xander watched her, exposed skin white as bone, blood forming maps on his cheek. Lina turned away.

One step into the wind for Genni. Another for her father.

Hail tore through the canopy, leaves and ice lashing her blind. One step for her mother. Another because no-one deserved to die for someone else's sins. Or for someone else's hates.

Another. No-one should ever die for someone else's love.

Wind shoved her against a tree, branches moaning, her ankle a lightning rod of pain. Pressing her palms against the bark she laid her cheek between them, closing her eyes, the tree shuddering beneath her touch.

'Lina.'

How had she possibly heard him over the storm? Perhaps she hadn't, and it had been only her mind. Perhaps she would always hear him saying her name the way she always heard her mother screaming it.

The terrible thing was that he had not yet done anything wrong. If he had, then this would at least be vengeance.

Turning her head against the wood she blinked her eyes briefly clear, lightning blasting the forest a chiaroscuro then darkness again and Xander's slumped figure. One heartbeat, two, three, thunder growling.

It was possible that what she did next did not matter at all. If her father had chosen not to wait, if Iva had been wrong and Thiago too slow and he and Genni were dead then why would she care about anything at all, her life or her honour? Better to sink to her knees right here and wait five paces from a dying boy.

But if they were not dead then she might still lose them, and she would lose them because of that fallen figure impossibly fragile on the forest floor. She breathed rain and wet earth and endings, and pushed from the tree.

Turned away.

Stood watching the heaving canopy above, awaiting doom. Almost hoping for it. Beginning to cry.

Mum, she thought. *Oh god, Mum, I can't.* Leaning into the wind but unmoving.

Oh god, I can't. I can't. I can't.

She turned around.

Chapter Thirty-Nine

The journey back to the station was a nightmare of suspended death, furious noise, despair and despair and despair. Xander limp, slipping in and out of awareness, hanging on her heavy as shame. At the edge of the meadow, she let him fall and crouched into the flattened grass. *You have to look*, she told herself. You have to look, you have to know. It seemed impossible.

The meadow was oceanic and purple movement cut with rain, and beyond it was the station. The station whole, unshattered.

She lowered her face against her knees and shook and shook and shook.

Xander stirred and suddenly the open sea of the meadow did not seem daunting at all. 'Come on,' she said into his ear. 'Nearly there. Come on now.'

He moaned wordlessly and she pulled him upright, pain electric beneath a cold gone far beyond physical. 'Nearly there,' she repeated. 'It's okay. It's okay, Xander. You'll be okay.' Mindlessly repeating herself and hating herself, the wind trying to tear them apart, her clinging on. And was it that the station was whole or that she had chosen so terribly but the meadow felt less deathly than before, as if the storm was relenting, as if it had done all the damage it had sought.

It was only the wind and Xander's weight that made her open the door, but then Thiago was there, taking Xander and leaving her suddenly weightless, adrift. Someone closed the door and Genni was against her, pressing into Lina's icy coat, and Lina held her.

She held her and every single gram of her failure pressed down on her until she thought she might shatter there against the sister she had condemned.

No, she thought. *I can't bear it. I can't live with this.* She wouldn't have to, of course, but that made it worse. That she would escape penance.

It took an age before anything else reached her past Genni's arms and the cold occupying her bones. Silene was in the corner wrapped in blankets, her hair straggling around her face. How was she here? Dev and Thiago had taken Xander out of the room. They would undress him, Lina thought distantly, warm him up then feed him. Genni pulled away enough to look up at her.

'You're soaking,' she said, and Lina grimaced, lifted her hands to undo her coat and saw that she had left a bloody handprint on Genni's cheek.

Kai was standing beside Silene, his hand on her shoulder and his smile to Lina across the room was victorious and sad. 'She came back,' he said. 'But it doesn't matter.'

Her coat fell to the floor and Genni handed her a towel, pushed her onto a stool, crouched to undo her boots. Silene looked up, her gaze slipping over Lina and Genni without recognition but settling on Kai.

'No. It doesn't matter,' she said. 'My boy is gone so it was all for nothing. It was all for nothing.'

'Your boy is gone,' Kai repeated. Silene nodded, ragdoll-like.

'*You* know why I did it? It was only for Xander, because what Christof did ... they were going to tear us down and then they'd have taken him away...' she swayed and smiled up at Kai brokenly. 'It was so easy, wasn't it? You saw. It would have worked even without you but you helped. They were going to blame those people and Xander would be safe and I didn't hurt him. I didn't make him bleed.'

Lina stared, aware that Genni had paused after pulling one boot off. Kai's fiery gaze was on Silene.

'You made the monster sleep,' he said. 'And I made him bleed.'

'Yes,' Silene murmured. The storm was surely passing, Lina

thought, because even with it, she heard her. 'We killed the monster, didn't we? But it doesn't matter now because my boy is...' She stared at Kai, almost begging, 'Where's my boy?'

'He's upstairs.'

Silene and Genni and Lina all flinched. Dev and Thiago were standing at the base of the stairs and it was Dev who had spoken, his face drawn and exhausted, his wet hair unruly.

'He's safe, Silene,' coming to her side, crouching down and taking her hand. 'Lina found him. He's safe.'

Silene studied his face dazedly. 'That's good, Dev darling. That's good then.' Tears began to run down her sallow cheeks and Dev sat back on his heels, turning to look at Thiago, who met his gaze without expression.

Genni rose, looking from Silene to Lina uncertainly. 'Silene killed Xander's dad?'

'Yes,' Dev said before Lina could. 'I believe she did.'

'What?' Xander said. He was standing behind Thiago, in shadow and blankets, leaning against the wall as if it was the only thing holding him up. 'What?'

Thiago took hold of him with that shocking gentleness which he so rarely showed strangers and led him away again, and Lina said into the quiet and the storm, 'I need coffee.'

Dev bowed his head briefly, then rose to his feet. Kai had moved, standing against the door with the fox skull held in both hands. But as Lina opened her mouth to say something, anything, Genni pulled her other boot off and she cried out, her head spinning in darkness.

'Oh god sorry, oh god—'

'It's okay,' Lina said quickly, nausea rising, Genni's face fracturing then coalescing again. 'It's okay.' And when she looked again, Kai had gone.

It was Dev who made the coffee and Thiago who knelt at her feet cursing, stripping away her socks and wiping blood from her skin. 'This will need restitching,' he said, scowling up at her and the simple ferociousness of it made her smile. She did not know anymore where the balance of her world lay. It had been lost and now perhaps it was not. She did not know, too cold and hurting and shocked, too close still to the realisation that even to save her family, she could not make herself a monster. That by failing to become one monster, she was simply a different one. She had thought she was stronger than that and now she did not know. She did not know.

'Xander?' Dev said, setting mugs down on the bench. Coffee for herself and Thiago, a thick, aromatic hot chocolate for Genni. Lina smiled up at him unthinkingly as Thiago wrapped gauze firmly around her ankle.

'Resting,' he said, rising to his feet unusually awkward due to the blade and fatigue and likely a dozen other things. 'It's over, I think.' Looking at Dev who looked at Lina to reply.

'Agreed.'

Lina pulled Genni back into her arms and rested her bruised cheek against her sister's dense hair.

It was as she watched Genni drink the dregs of her chocolate with something like contentment that Lina remembered Kai. She rose, wincing, and went towards the door.

'It's passing,' Dev said just as Thiago said, 'Don't you dare.'

'What happened?' Lina asked. She ought to have asked before, but there had been Silene, and then Genni's small, brown hands wrapped around a mug that smelled of heaven.

Thiago and Dev shared a quick, hooded glance. Even if Genni had not been here, they would not have told her everything. But she had been out there too, differently, so she could imagine.

'There were three of them. They offered us Silene or the station.' Thiago lifted one shoulder, showing no inclination to add anything more.

Lina looked at Dev.

'We got two, the other one ran. The storm seemed to be on our side, plus Ferdinando here is pretty useful, it turns out.'

Thiago shifted his gaze from Lina, but Lina said to him quietly, 'I'm glad.' Her hand against the old wood of the door, feeling its tremors subsiding.

He had made the choice she had been unable to. Because it was more immediate perhaps, or because he was stronger.

Beyond the door came the sound of laughter. High as a bird and clear, and as Lina turned towards it she saw the other three do the same.

'What—' Dev said, but Lina was already moving.

'I'm just going to look,' she said, stepping out into wind that was terrible but not deadly, rain that was only runoff from the roof. The clouds were more than leaden darkness now; they had contours and shades. Lightning scattered laterally and Lina saw a pale figure at the edge of the courtyard, his face upturned, silvery hair lifting.

'Kai,' she said and he turned, laughing again. Genni was beside Lina; they put their arms around one another and even if Genni could not see what Lina saw, she watched.

'I did it,' Kai called. 'I stopped them, didn't I?'

'Yes,' Lina said. 'You did.'

'And I protected Genni, and I saved you from the monsters.'

'Yes,' Lina said again.

'I was fierce.'

'You have always been fierce.'

Kai laughed as the clouds above them roiled and shuddered. 'I killed the monsters,' he shouted and laughed again, spinning on one heel, running into the meadow with his arms stretched high.

'No,' Lina called. 'Kai, wait.' But Genni pulled on her hips like an anchor and Kai did not stop running.

The clouds stilled, light fractured the world and Lina screamed, static and blindness shaking her bones and when the light was gone, the meadow was a little brighter than it had been, the clouds turned silver. And Kai was gone.

Lina stared out at the storm-shattered meadow, but there was no pale child seeking monsters. Thunder pulsed around them and someone laughed.

'Lina,' Genni said, and Lina realised she was weeping again, her eyes scalding, Genni's hand pulling her back inside.

'What was that?' Dev asked. Lina took a breath, then another, wiped her face clear. Thiago leaned against the bench watching her steadily, without judgement or disbelief or surprise.

'Just the lightning,' she said.

Chapter Forty

Xander did not wake for two days, as the rains slowly stopped and sunlight turned the meadow into phantasmagoria of steam. As trees stopped falling and the first miraculous bees emerged, as frogs resumed singing in their overflowing pools. Two days to begin repairs and listen to Genni recounting the storm, her fear, Thiago's bravery with the words shaking her less and less each time. With Silene sleeping, crying, sleeping; and if some of Xander's sleep was healing then some of it, Lina thought, was also escape.

Two days. Thiago gently restitching Lina's wounds, them talking of all the things about each other that they had guessed, and learned, but not really shared. Realising that knowing each other's past selves and worst selves still changed nothing about who they were to each other now, here.

Two days without news. Lina did not know how she continued to breathe.

'Was there a right choice?' she asked Thiago eventually, watching Dev persuade Silene to eat, wondering whether he would still have come if he had known from the beginning, and thinking yes, he would have done.

Thiago narrowed his eyes thoughtfully. 'No,' he said. 'Sometimes there just isn't.'

Lina nodded. Genni was scrolling news sites, mapping the storm's destruction like it was a tally of their own survival.

'But given that choice,' Thiago added, 'you chose to do what would hurt you most. Many people wouldn't have done that.'

She smiled at him just a little, unconvinced. The net was back up but she had heard nothing.

'He'll wait,' Thiago said. Then repeated it. 'He'll wait for you.'

Then the ESF telemedic sent a message to Lina's tablet saying that Xander was awake, so she rose and went upstairs.

'Hey,' she said, coming to sit on the bed beside his knee. His eyes were drowsy but she knew he had remembered.

'I'm sorry,' he said as if he had been repeating it in his mind. As if he had been hearing it repeat itself.

'Just don't run off into any more storms for a while.'

He frowned, shook his head. 'I don't mean that.'

'Oh,' she had not let herself think about this, but realised she knew what to say. 'No, don't be. You were fighting for someone you love. There's nothing to be ashamed about in that.'

'But she wasn't–' he cut himself off abruptly and Lina wanted to say, no, you are right. She was not a good person, nor was she worth what you would have made us pay.

'She's your mother,' she said quietly. 'You will love her anyway, even though she betrayed you. And that's okay.'

Xander turned his head against the pillow, the light from the drawn curtains a shimmering gold. Lina did not speak, or even watch him, instead studying the cut across her palm that had left blood on Genni's skin.

'Where's Dev?' Xander said eventually, sounding no older than Genni.

'I'll get him,' she said, and rose.

'Weather window this afternoon for their airlift,' Thiago said the next day. There was a pearlescent fog lying in the meadow but the sun's soft halo was slowly strengthening. 'I really do need to clear that rockslide.'

Lina looked at him narrowly. 'Good idea.'

A half-smile. 'I'm not apologising.'

No, but she had forgiven him anyway. What might have been different if the others had left before the storm, if she had left too and tried to cross a weather-paralysed Europe without ESF help and without a plan? Xander might have carried out his threat, her father might be dead. She might be dead, and Genni lost yet again. Xander might not have done anything after all; she doubted even he knew whether his grief would have trumped his understanding of what his father had been.

When Xander came to find her and Thiago, he had something small in one hand, fingers moving it restlessly. Lina knew her job; it was a canine tooth from a small carnivore. 'You ready to leave?' she said.

Neither Thiago nor Lina had asked Xander what he was going to do. She had wanted to, but his terrible pallor, his silence, had stopped her. Dev must have done so, and she guessed at what he would have said. 'Are you going to Paris?'

'So my mum isn't arrested, you mean?' His voice both dull and angry.

Yes, that was what Lina meant. She looked at him helplessly. I know, she wanted to say. And I'm so sorry. It doesn't get easier but you survive it, you carry on. 'Dev will look after you.' Possibly. With luck.

Xander looked out at the shrouded, watercolour meadow. Somewhere, a thrush began to sing, its mere existence a miracle.

'This airlift,' Xander said to Thiago. 'ESF only, is it?'

A nod.

'People you know?'

Another nod, the tiniest, tiniest hint of a smile. Lina began to realise that there was a third option after London and Paris.

'Thing is,' Xander began, looking at the wall behind them, the fox's tooth roving between his fingers. 'If they could, like ... forget Mum and I were on board, we can ... I swear it's not to cause trouble, I just...'

'You have somewhere to go?' Thiago sounded unsurprised, but satisfied. Xander stilled.

'Tromsø.'

'Tromsø?' Lina said. 'But that's–' A malaria ridden border-town full of the exiled and the rebellion.

'I know,' Xander interrupted her. 'But I ... know some people there. And I can sort the IDs and stuff.'

'But she...' This time Lina cut herself off. She killed your father, she wanted to say. Don't throw your life away to keep her safe. You are worth more than that, more than both of them.

She thought fleetingly of a video she had watched long ago. The way Xander had not spoken to his mother, but had sat with her at night.

It was such a terrible weight for one young man to carry.

'You aren't responsible for her, you know,' she said eventually, inadequately. 'Or for anything they did. And you aren't to blame for...' lifting her hands in a gesture that made no sense and yet he still understood.

He looked at her with a sort of sad gratitude, then shrugged and surprised her by saying, 'I don't want Dev to have to risk it, for us I mean.'

Lina studied his restless hands and thought that he would not have worried about such a thing a few days ago.

'Anyway,' he added, 'I think I've run out of time. ESF were onto me, so London would have been soon. It's safer for me too.'

Thiago lifted his chin in agreement, but Lina said, 'ESF could use you though. Someone as good as you. They grant immunity.'

He had clearly not thought of that and took the time to consider it. The contours of his face were clearer now, some of the veneer burned away. 'Thanks,' he said eventually. 'Not yet though. I need to sort things out first. And ... and think.' Looking at Thiago again, waiting.

Thiago held his gaze, then nodded once. 'Good luck,' he said. 'Next time, don't tell us where you're going.'

Xander shifted, met Lina's gaze very steadily. 'I destroyed it, you know. No-one'll find any of it now. Not ever.' He lifted one shoulder then turned away as if he had not just changed the world.

Silene climbed into the helicopter unresisting, but when Xander sat beside her, she clutched at his hand and began again to cry. He did not try to comfort her, but only wrapped his fingers around hers and met Lina's gaze without blinking. She and Thiago were both reaching out, quietly, to people who could keep a kind of guard. She had not told Xander, because she thought it would hurt him to hear it, but it was something he could discover himself if he looked.

The sky was shorn of clouds finally, the fog sunk back into the wet earth and the swifts had returned to weave their tapestries above the meadow. Lina lifted a hand and Xander nodded to her.

'If you're ever in Paris,' Dev said, hefting a bag into the helicopter and reaching out a hand for hers. She gave it to him and said goodbye.

Once the helicopter had passed beyond view, the station seemed abandoned; grasses and nascent flower heads slowly righting themselves in the meadow. Thiago put his hand on her shoulder, just as she had done with Genni in the dying storm. 'I'm off to blow up some rocks,' he said. They shared a smile, no sound but a blackcap singing and a buzzard calling for its mate.

She sat at her desk, picked up her tablet, and there waiting for her as if time had never mattered at all, was a message from an account she did not recognise.

Please, she thought one last time.

I'm out and on my way. I love you both.

Time passed, another miraculous bird began to sing, and eventually Lina brushed her hands over her face then turned them up to the sun to let them dry. Then she rose to find her sister, making in her mind a list of all the things that she would do when she returned. Help Thiago make repairs, clear their tracks of fallen wood, check for lost tags and damaged base-stations, locate the mother bear and her cubs out to the east, pray that they had survived.

Wait to hear from Xander, surprised at how much she wanted to.

Persuade Iva to come back. Say goodbye to James once more.

Remember her mother more often.

But first, but first she would go to her father, and bring him home.

Acknowledgments

If you are reading these then thank you, reader, for getting to the end of my book. I cannot tell you how surreal it feels to think of strangers reading a story that once existed only in my head, and I so hope you enjoyed it.

To get the important thanks out of the way – the cats. Thank you for sitting on my keyboard at inopportune moments, for yowling at me, and for pretending to listen when I talk to you.

Thank you to Francesca Barbini and everyone at Luna Press Publishing for being so truly supportive of writers for whom the doors of publishing might otherwise remain firmly closed. I am so lucky. A huge thank you also to Francesca for seeing the soul of this book, and to Daniele Serra for cover artwork that captured it so beautifully.

I am incredibly fortunate in having writerly friends who have encouraged, critiqued, given proverbial kicks-up-arses, and generally never let me give up hope even when I've wanted to. The Randoms, and my SE group, I love you all. Fiona Erskine, Jane Jesmond, Knicky Laurelle, and Matt Willis all beta read an early version of this book, and their comments and belief were beyond price. Fiona, Jane and Shell Bromley in particular all managed to catch me mid-fall and set me back on my feet, thank you, you gorgeous things.

To the forests of Eastern Europe and Russia – may you long outlive us all. And thank you to the wolves for not eating me those two times, it was much appreciated.

Finally, my family. My mum and sister, Shelagh and Jennifer, have believed in my ability to do this whole writing thing from the absolute start. They courageously read the earliest and most terrible drafts of everything, and their unstinting love and support make me braver than I would otherwise be. My mum raised me on a strange and varied diet of books that shaped my entire world view (reading Solzhenitsyn at twelve is ... formative...), so if I don't write happy stories she only has herself to blame, but the fact that I write at all is also her doing. Thank you to Len and Stuart too, who have both unfailingly cheered me on from the sidelines. And Jared and Meghan, aside from the writing, you two have perforce shared the chronic illness 'journey' with me as well, which is not the easiest task in the world, but you are the centre of that world and I could not do any of this without you. Jared, you are my safe haven and you make the best cups of tea. Meghan, I'm really sorry about the skull in pond thing – I'll get it into another book, I promise.

Lightning Source UK Ltd.
Milton Keynes UK
UKHW010817070921
390173UK00003B/416